Ignite the Fire:

Inferno

KAREN CHANCE

Author's Note:

This is the second part of a two-part novel as the story was too large for a single book. For best results, *Ignite the Fire: Incendiary* should be read before this book.

Chapter One

I landed on a dark street with little tendrils of fog curling up everywhere and immediately dropped into a defensive crouch. I looked around wildly for a second, breathing hard and feeling very confused. Maybe because, a second ago, I'd been plummeting through the middle of a huge forest, headed toward my death.

The forest had been on Faerie and like nothing I'd ever seen. A cathedral of wood instead of stone, it had boasted trunks as big around as apartment buildings, as well as crazed fey, flying spells, and a dangerously flimsy path of forest gunk and prayer that had stretched between the branches and offered a fragile lifeline. One that I'd managed to miss.

But there was no forest here, or screaming allies, or murderous fey. Or much of anything else except for cold fog, mildewed bricks and mucky cobblestones. The latter had sent something squelching up through my toes that might have come from the back end of a horse, but I was too freaked out to worry about it.

I told myself to calm down, but my brain was stuck in fight or flight mode and ignored me. The only thing it suggested involved running down the street screaming, which showed what it was good for. So, I just stayed in my crouch, trying not to hyperventilate, and waited for an attack that didn't come.

After a while, I started to feel a little silly. And even more confused, because I wasn't dripping in blood or covered in ashes. I should have been both, considering that I'd just helped to rescue a master vampire and a war mage from an army of fey, while dual wielding sabers and dressed like a pirate.

It had been a strange day, even for me.

I was still dressed the part, in knee-length, frilly bloomers meant to be worn as underthings in the Edwardian era, which was where I'd picked them up. And a lace shirt that had seen better days since it used to be the top half of a dress. And a fey sword belt, only the swords were missing.

I must have dropped them in the fall, which left me with no weapons. And it wasn't like I could kick someone to death, since I was barefoot. Probably just as well since all the grime on my feet and legs kept me from seeing how bruised and scratched-up they were.

Otherwise, I seemed fine.

Yeah, sure.

Because that was how my life went, right?

My name is Cassie Palmer, and I have the dubious honor of being Pythia, AKA time's bitch. My official title is Chief Seer of the Supernatural World, but thanks to the current war, I do less Seeing and more running around the timeline like a crazed chicken, trying to keep it from making forays into unchartered territory thanks to our enemies. Only this time, I had been the one venturing through time, trying to help a friend.

It hadn't gone well.

It had started out simply enough: retrieve a little goat-like creature—some weird sort of fey—from a castle in Romania, where he was being held against his will. And considering that I'd been taking a master vampire and a next-level war mage, two powerhouses of the magical world, along with me, you'd think that would be fairly easy, right?

No.

No, it would not.

The castle was in the eighteenth century, a difficult time jump on its own, which meant that I couldn't take along additional back up. And the tumbled down structure had turned out to be stuffed to the rafters with time traveling fey, under the command of a king whose capitol we'd recently helped to destroy. And the king himself, a gigantic prick named Aeslinn, was currently possessed by the spirit of an elder god and looking for some payback.

So, yeah.

The usual, then.

What had followed was a whirlwind of activity: a desperate escape from the enemy-filled castle into the time stream, a mad flight back to modern day Las Vegas, and then something like a hand, reaching out of nothing, to snatch me right back in again. It hadn't snatched Mircea, the vampire in question, or the odd little fey that we'd somehow succeeded in rescuing. It also hadn't grabbed John Pritkin, my lover and the best war mage I knew. But it had gotten me, and had almost caused me to become unstuck in time.

Since that would have resulted in a perpetual free-fall through the centuries—essentially a death sentence—I had been a little concerned. Fortunately, I'd been caught by a member of my court before that happened. Being Pythia had its drawbacks, but the savvy women I worked with weren't among them.

This one's name was Hilde, and she'd forgotten more about this job than I'd ever known. That wasn't surprising since she was pushing two hundred, while I'd barely managed to survive twenty-four years and wasn't looking likely to see twenty-five. And she'd needed every bit of her knowledge and experience to wrestle me back from a vengeful god.

Even then, she couldn't hold onto me, but she could change my direction, sending me screaming through time at her sister, the Edwardian Pythia named Gertie. Who had caught and grounded me, because Gertie was awesome like that. And thus, she'd thwarted godly attack number one.

Attacks number two and three had quickly followed, but I'd survived those, too, thanks to Gertie and her court—and to Pritkin and Mircea. The latter two weren't there, or even in Vegas anymore, having followed the goat through the city to a hidden portal. Apparently, the crazed little thing had not viewed what we'd done as a rescue, but as just another kidnapping.

I guessed Mircea hadn't had time to explain that he didn't want to hurt him. He just wanted to ask some questions about his long-lost wife, who the goat guy had apparently been friends with. Mircea was trying to find out what had happened to her, and the little creature was his only lead.

So, when it ran, he and Pritkin followed—all the way to Faerie.

Yet, despite being a hundred years and a world away, they had managed to save me. Or we'd saved each other, I guessed, since we were currently in a spell together—called Lover's Knot—which allowed us to share power. But nothing in magic is free, and this spell came with a major caveat: if one of us died, we all did.

So, that had been a close one.

But shortly thereafter, I'd been on my way again, looking for answers. Not because I wanted to be, and not just because I had a vengeful god on my ass. But because he was three hundred years back in time with a damned army.

The god in question—crafty old Zeus—had been joy riding around the timeline, having hitchhiked on my shift to allow him abilities he shouldn't have had. But once our fight was over, he'd been pulled back to his starting point—AKA eighteenth century Romania. Which was where another time traveler had dropped him off before I'd stumbled across him.

I'd killed the bastard in question, a necromancer named Jonathan, a while ago, but now it looked like I had to clean up his mess. I didn't know how he'd managed to transport an army three hundred years back in time, but I needed to find out. And to decide what to do about it—and about Zeus, and about Aeslinn, and about whatever the hell they'd managed to screw up in the past.

Only that was proving to be a real bitch.

Pythias were the guardians of time, but that usually meant chasing down individual time jumpers—dark mages up to no good, cultists out to change the world, or reckless grifters trying to make a buck. That was bad enough, as you never knew what small change could send the timeline veering madly off course. Like a spark on dry tinder, it could quickly turn into a conflagration.

But a possessed fey king with hundreds of soldiers, three hundred years back in time?

That was already a five-alarm fire.

And it was my fire, whether I liked it or not. So, my first stop had been old Romania, for some sleuthing into what Zeus had been doing there. What I'd found had posed more questions than answers, but it had led me to stop number two: medieval Ireland. Where I'd discovered Aeslinn, the possessed fey king and Zeus's current best buddy, up to no good. And then . . .

Well, then it got weird.

Because I hadn't traveled through time to Ireland. I'd traveled through the mind. More specifically, I'd traveled through something called an imprint.

Imprints were someone's memories which had been carved into a physical item by trauma, like grooves being etched onto a record. And like a record, they could be replayed by someone with the talent. But my talent hadn't extended far enough to control all the imprints that had been left on the arrow that I'd picked up at that damned castle, so Gertie had brought in an expert, a part-fey named Guinn, to help me out.

Guinn and I had entered the imprint to view what had happened in the past as if we were watching a movie. Only imprints were usually less movie-quality and more like bad surveillance camera footage—a few seconds of lousy video and maybe a scratchy sound track. Often, it was hard to tell what was going on.

Not this time.

This time, I'd gotten full-color and Dolby surround sound. The memory had also been in 3-D, allowing Guinn and I to walk around as if we were really there. We hadn't been able to interact with anyone or to change anything, but it had seemed completely real.

Kind of like this place.

I glanced around again. A line of dark houses hedged the street on either side, with soot-stained bricks, crumbling steps, and cracked windows. One hazy, gas-type streetlamp was valiantly battling the gloom—and losing. As a result, I couldn't make out much else, even when the dark, low-lying clouds overhead parted a little, leaving things momentarily less murky. But I knew one thing: this wasn't Faerie.

A breeze came by, making me shiver, but I didn't move. I didn't understand what was going on, and I needed to. I needed to badly!

Because I hadn't stayed in Ireland.

I'd had some fairly pressing questions about what Guinn and I had witnessed, leading me to try to access Pritkin's mind to ask him about it. A younger version of the war mage I knew had featured prominently in the imprint, so I'd thought he might be able to help me out. And since he and I were currently able to use Mircea's gift for mind-to-mind communication, it hadn't seemed like that big of a deal.

But I'd forgotten something: Lover's Knot was a soul bond. Pritkin, Mircea and I were able to share abilities since, as far as our magic was concerned, we weren't three people anymore. We were one.

The spell essentially melded our spirits for as long as we were under its power, ensuring that, when I tried to visit Pritkin's mind, I didn't just contact him mentally. My soul reached out through the spell, maybe part of it, maybe all of it—the jury was still out. But some aspect of my spirit had entered Faerie—

And then so had the rest of me. Because Faerie doesn't *have* spirits. Their universe works under different rules than ours, and any souls who venture in, as my one-time ghostly companion Billy Joe once discovered, end up being clothed in flesh.

And so had I. My body had abruptly landed in the world of the fey, leaving me seriously confused since it was supposed to be snoozing in front of a fireplace at Gertie's. And because I didn't know the damned rules anymore!

I didn't know if I had two bodies now, or if Faerie had pulled in my old one along with my spirit. I didn't know if I had half a soul or a whole. And, more importantly, I didn't know if I could die like this, and if I did, whether it would doom Mircea and Pritkin as well.

So, yeah, I had some freaking questions!

The dark street, however, was not forthcoming. It was clammy and uncomfortable, with waves of fog that curled about my limbs like sodden silk. They felt entirely real, as did the cold stones under my feet. But then, so did everything in what was called the Common.

Which, unless I was very much mistaken, was where I was.

The Common, as Guinn had explained it, was the reason that fey imprints were so much more impressive than human ones—because it wasn't just one mind making them. The fey had some kind of collective consciousness that I didn't understand. Or maybe subconsciousness would be a better term, since even they were often unaware of it.

Guinn had said that fey souls were tied to their bodies in a way that human ones simply weren't, which was why they didn't leave ghosts. Their souls could not survive without a body, and were only freed from that union once their physical form melted back into the soil of their home world. Then they rejoined some kind of uber soul, that of Faerie itself, where they stayed until their world felt like putting them into another body and pushing them back out again.

It was very odd.

But the result was that, sometimes, living fey received brief flashes of past lives: from their own former selves, from ancestors, even from friends. They were all part of the same soul, and linked on some level. These flashes, however, were usually pretty minor—a snippet of a song they'd never heard, a taste of a food they'd never eaten, or the memory of what lay down a path they'd never walked. It was the sort of thing that brought a wistful smile to the face, or prompted a feeling of wonder and joy at how connected everything was.

Only I wasn't feeling so joyful.

I'd been getting flashes of this group consciousness ever since I landed in Faerie. And it hadn't been the usual quick snippets about a flower or something. I'd been going on panoramic adventures, which had started out fun and then gotten really scary, really fast. I wanted off this ride, particularly now, when I didn't know where my body was or what was happening to it while my mind was off in La-La Land, or maybe I'd finally had a psychotic break.

Let's face it, I was due.

So, I was fifty-fifty on what I was looking at here, particularly since my previous visions had mostly been of places and people inside of Faerie. Which was what you'd expect, since they were supposedly the memories of millions of dead fey. So, what was a street straight out of Charles Dickens doing in there?

I didn't know, and it was creeping me out.

I told myself to get a grip and strained my ears, hoping for a little extra information. But all I heard was what might have been a ship's horn sounding in the distance. There was no other noise, with the fog muffling any city clamor as if a fuzzy blanket had been draped over the world. And nothing moved except for the surface of a nearby puddle, shivering in the breeze.

Until a horse-drawn carriage came racing down the street, and almost ran me down.

I managed to stumble back at the last second, but it caused my already overloaded adrenal system to start screaming internally. Not one more thing! Not one more goddamned—

Wait.

Was that Pritkin?

I'd ended up on the sidewalk, where the streetlamp was shedding a hazy circle of light. It blinded me for a moment, dim though it was, and made me wonder if I was seeing things. But that sure looked like him, stumbling out of an alley at the end of the road.

I moved out of the light and there was just no doubt at all. I felt my heart leap in my chest as I started running toward him, almost dizzy with relief. Only to stop in confusion after barely a couple of steps.

Because there were two of him.

I hadn't noticed the second man until then, who had been hidden by the shadow of a building. Which he'd just been thrown into, I assumed, since he peeled himself off the sooty bricks, leaving a slightly paler outline behind. And launched himself . . . at himself.

The two Pritkins staggered back into the street, kicking, punching and spell throwing. Meanwhile, a cloud of magical weapons circled overhead, occasionally glinting in a spare beam of light. They weren't taking part in this, having been enchanted to never harm their owner.

And they didn't seem to know who that was, any more than I did.

Both men were blond, green-eyed and muscular, with fair skin that had a slight tan from the Vegas sun, and probably more than a slight flush from anger. I couldn't tell for sure about the latter, since the dim light leeched them of color, leaving them looking almost black and white. And their clothes didn't help me tell them apart, either.

They were both wearing dirty, sweat-stained, eighteenth-century shirts, gray breeches and worn vests. In other words, the same thing that Pritkin had had on at that castle, where this whole thing started. And where he'd been playing the part of my and Mircea's coachman.

And, sure enough, right on cue, I spotted a couple of old, blue coachman's coats flung over some nearby steps, probably to allow their owners to pummel each other more effectively.

So, what *was* this?

"Pritkin?" I said cautiously, and both men's heads jerked up.

One of them slammed an elbow savagely into the other's face, causing him to stagger back. And before he could recover, a coat went flying off the steps, and it didn't seem to have the same reservations about entering the fight that the weapons had. It wrapped around the wounded man like a strait jacket, including his head, and sent him stumbling about blindly.

Meanwhile, the victor came running—straight at me.

Considering everything that had happened lately, I decided that backing up was justified. I didn't know what I was dealing with; I didn't know *who* I was dealing with. And the Jack the Ripper ambiance wasn't helping!

But then the familiar face changed as the man came closer, and it was filled with such surprise, such relief, such *joy* . . . that I found myself stopping my retreat and even starting toward him instead.

That was stupid, but I didn't care. I'd been so worried, and he'd looked so lifeless, back at the fey camp. To see him up and moving around and happy—it was everything I'd dared to hope for.

He caught me and spun me around, like some ridiculous scene in a movie, and I didn't care about that, either. "We made it? We actually made it?" I asked, gripping his head with my hands.

And then I kissed him before he could answer.

It was Pritkin; I'd know that kiss anywhere. He had a two-day old beard that was rough and bristly against my palms, his breath wasn't the best, and he smelled like sweat and spent magic. And I'd never been happier to see anyone in my life!

We didn't break apart until a second coach came rumbling by, causing us to run further onto the sidewalk. And it was then that I caught sight of another familiar face, only this one wasn't quite so pretty. Nigel, the hulking part-fey I'd seen in one of the visions from the Common, was standing in front of a house down the street. I recognized him by his clothes, having never seen his face.

It wasn't a particularly attractive face, now that I did get a look at it, nor did it show any signs of his fey heritage. It was almost flat—nose, chin and forehead—as if he'd run into a wall a few times, and was attached to a tall, stoop shouldered body that looked like it was accustomed to having to bend to fit through doorways. It was topped off with dark, greasy-looking hair, which didn't appear to have been washed any more often than his clothes.

But him being there confirmed where I was, at least.

"We're in the Common?" I asked Pritkin. "Why? What happened?"

He took my face between his hands and kissed me again before answering. Which already told me that I wasn't going to like what I heard. Green eyes met mine when we broke apart, and there was grief in them, but also fire.

"We made it," he said, answering my previous question. "Mircea and I. You didn't. The vines caught you, but the Svarestri reached you before we could. You're with Aeslinn now."

Chapter Two

I took a moment to absorb that, but it didn't work. The pavement felt like it had just been jerked out from under me, like a rug. Pritkin caught me when I stumbled, and then summoned the other coat and put it around me.

"Why am I alive, then?" It came out harsh, but I couldn't help it. Going from relief and elation one second, to terror and dread the next had restricted my vocal cords, as if my throat had been caught in a mailed fist. I was just glad that my voice hadn't broken halfway through.

If Pritkin noticed, he didn't comment, and he also didn't sugarcoat his answer. Most people would have played for time, or struggled with what to say, or downplayed the danger to make me feel better. Pritkin was not one of those people.

He believed in having all possible information in order to deal with a crisis, even if it wasn't information you liked. Which is why he just told me. "He's offered a trade. Blasted it through the forest. You for me."

I stared at him for a second, unsure that I'd heard right. "What? *Why*? If he strips my soul, he can bring back the gods—right now. He can have everything he wants—*right now.*"

That was my prevailing theory: that Zeus wanted to get the old gods back to Earth and needed my power to help him. Or, to be more precise, he needed the Pythian power, a store of godly energy once gifted to the Pythias by the god Apollo, which had since become rather independent-minded. It allied with the Pythias; it didn't obey us. But I assumed that it would obey Zeus, that it would have to after he drained my soul, giving him my access to Apollo's power.

Why he needed it I didn't know, since he was a god himself. But since he hadn't yet torn down the barrier that my mother, better known as the goddess Artemis, had put up to cut off Earth and Faerie from the realm of the gods, I assumed that he did. It all made sense.

Except for his weird obsession with Pritkin. Aeslinn, Zeus's current ride, had been hunting him in Ireland long before meeting me or any other Pythia. And Aeslinn's people had just captured him in Faerie and put a crap ton of guards around him, ones who'd obviously had the fear of God—or *a* god, at least—put into them.

So, what did a fey king and the king of the gods want so badly with a war mage?

I had no idea, and Pritkin didn't look like it made any more sense to him.

He shook his head. "I don't know. It's obviously a trap of some kind, but I can't figure out Aeslinn's play. If the gods return, he doesn't need to worry about the rest of us. There won't be anything that I, or anyone else, can do to stop him. And he has you, meaning that he has the power he needs in his grip. Yet he's given us until dawn—"

"Dawn?"

"—so we have time."

"How much time?"

He did hesitate then. "Perhaps three hours." I stared at him. "We've worked with less," he said fiercely.

Yeah.

Yeah.

I felt sick again, and must have looked it, too. Because he led me over to the steps in front of a house. It was good to sit; my head felt swimmy and my stomach was making unhappy churning motions.

Maybe the gods were used to this kind of breakneck pace, but I wasn't one of them. I was a freaked out little demigoddess and I wanted a bath. And a meal. And a stiff drink, but I wasn't likely to get any of them.

I settled for dragging Pritkin's coat closer about me. "And Rhea?" I said, asking about my heir, who had gotten pulled into this along with me. "Guinn?"

"Safe. While you were freeing us, they encountered a dark fey refugee group. They have a hidden base not far away from the camp, which they've been using to raid the Svarestri. When they saw us attempting to escape, they pitched in to help."

"You're sure you can trust them?" I didn't trust anyone in Faerie right now.

"Guinn seems to think so, and they have a contingent of trolls with them."

I blinked at him. "Is that . . . good?"

"If you wish to know which side a group is on, yes. To the Svarestri, trolls are the most corrupted form of life. They don't even consider them sentient, merely beasts of burden. They would not be working with them."

I felt my spine unclench slightly. At least something had gone right tonight. "And Mircea?"

Pritkin hesitated again. "He's . . . unhappy."

"Meaning?" I asked, since that word didn't sound like Mircea. Master vampires didn't do unhappy—or any other tepid emotion. Especially that one, and especially after the last few days.

"When I left, there were six large trolls sitting on top of him," Pritkin admitted. "The pallet they put him on looked like a boat on the high seas—"

"A boat?"

"He would rage and buck and almost throw them off, and they would ride it out. Trolls are, for the most part, stoic creatures, but it looked like he was making an impression. I do not believe they had met a master vampire before."

I frowned. "What in the world was he trying to do?"

"Go back to the fey camp—"

"*What*?"

"He was . . . fairly insistent," Pritkin said dryly. "Which was obviously absurd. He has a

heart wound and is half exsanguinated. If they took his head or sliced through his jugular—"

"It would kill him." I felt a shiver go through me.

"As I pointed out. But he is stubborn—"

"Always was."

"—and I could travel faster on my own in any case."

"I—what?" It took me a second. "Wait. You weren't planning to give yourself *up*—"

"Oh, no. It was far dumber than that," someone said.

I looked up to find the other Pritkin, with a swelling jaw and a nose that looked slightly off-kilter, standing just out of reach. Which turned out to be a good thing, since my Pritkin immediately launched himself at him. But the second man had expected that and disappeared, only to rematerialize a second later on the steps beside me.

He reached down and pulled me up in front of him, while my Pritkin picked himself off the road.

"Don't you hurt her," my Pritkin seethed. "Don't you *dare*."

"Hurt her? I *saved* her—"

"You've never saved anyone in your life! You selfish, self-centered, narcissistic *prick*—"

"Narcissistic? Brother, that hurts."

The comment had been lightly mocking, perhaps intended to soften the mood. But if so, it was a serious miscalculation. My Pritkin gave what could only be described as a roar and hurled himself at us, at magically enhanced speed.

But the other man was even quicker, shifting us to the opposite side of the street as easily as if he'd had Pythian powers. Which, if he was who I suspected, maybe he did. Or maybe—

"This is all in our heads," he confirmed, before I could ask.

"So, we *are* in the Common."

"Mentally, yes. Physically, we don't know where you are."

"And you kidnapped her mind, dragging us in here, before we could find out!" my Pritkin said, appearing out of nowhere.

I had a sudden wash of sympathy for my vampire bodyguards, who tended to freak out whenever anyone shifted in beside them. The Pythian power allowed for spatial movements as well as ones through time, but they could be a little startling. Some of the guys had gotten used to it, at least enough not to shriek whenever it happened, but others never had, even after all these months.

Maybe because it wasn't just the visual shock of seeing someone appear out of thin air. It was also the air itself, which was displaced by abruptly having a body in it, and blew over you in a wave. And the fact that Pritkin didn't give proper space like Gertie and others I'd had flash in beside me, but appeared all of a few inches away.

It made me want to run screaming again, and I wasn't even the one he was threatening.

"You weren't going to find out," his doppelganger replied, dodging behind me. "You were going to get us both killed—"

"Typical!" It was biting. "With what we're facing, *that's* what has you worried—"

"Yes! Yes, it is. Excuse me for not wanting to die like a simpleton!" The doppelganger looked at me. "He was planning to sneak around the fey camp, to discover where they're holding you. Which would have resulted in them capturing us and keeping you to boot. We'd have lost our lives and gained nothing—"

"As opposed to sitting on the sidelines and also gaining nothing, whilst the gods return and slaughter us all!" My Pritkin said furiously.

"I am not sitting on the sidelines! I *have* a plan—"

"Yes, to keep yourself safe at her expense. You'd rather see her die than risk—"

"Careful brother." It was low that time, and menacing, with none of the Puckish good humor that this Pritkin had shown before.

"I am not your brother!"

"Wait!" I said, getting an arm on each man's chest and pushing them apart. "Wait."

To my surprise, they waited.

I had about a thousand questions, but went with the easiest first. "Who *are* you?" I asked the other Pritkin. I thought I knew, but wanted to be sure.

"You know who I am," he said impatiently. "Or did you forget all our times together? Almost dying in Wales, almost dying in London, almost dying in Faerie . . . all right, I can see your point—"

"Don't believe anything he says," my Pritkin cut in. "He's a lying bastard!"

"I have never lied to Cassie!" the other man said. I looked at him. "All right, I might have exaggerated a few things, in a good cause—"

"But who *are* you?"

"For pity's sake! I'm him! The incubus part of him, at any—"

"I know that!" I cut him off. "But how does this work?"

I looked back and forth between the two men, and just the visuals made my head hurt. Things were happening too fast, and I was feeling more and more like my brain might have had the right idea from the start. Running screaming was starting to look like a plan.

"Have you ever heard of someone being of two minds about something?" the incubus asked.

"I—yes," I said, trying to focus. "I guess so."

"Well, it's like that, only worse. Infinitely worse."

"I don't understand," I said, because I really, really didn't.

"We can discuss this later—" my Pritkin said. And then cut off when his coat, which was around my shoulders, suddenly flew up into the air like a wooly bat. He looked at the incubus with furious, narrowed eyes. "Don't even *think*—"

And then he was staggering into the street, the blue assailant wrapped around his head and pummeling him with its flat, empty arms.

That would have been fine, and even vaguely funny—if a horse drawn bus hadn't taken that moment to come thundering toward us.

"Pritkin!" I screamed, and tried to shift him. But the incubus knocked my hand aside and the spell went wild, carving a chunk out of a nearby building and sending it smashing against the sidewalk on the other side of the road. And Pritkin—my Pritkin—stared at me through a rent in the coat from the back window of the crowded bus, which had somehow picked him up.

And which was now taking him away.

"What—" I began, only to be cut off by the incubus.

"I shifted him on board, but none of this is real, remember? He'll be fine."

That had looked pretty real to me. "Bring him back!"

"He'll bring himself back soon enough. Look, we don't have much time, so I'll make this brief. I have a different point of view from my dear brother about how we should proceed—"

"No," I said flatly.

"What?"

"I said no. I'm not listening until you answer my question."

He looked confused. "What question?"

"Who *are* you? Why should I believe anything you have to say if I don't know anything about—"

"I'm *him*. I'm me. I saved your *life*—"

"You saved *your* life!" It was vicious, but I was past caring. "We're linked—as you reminded me yourself. If you hadn't saved me back in London, you'd have died, too. You're going to have to do better than—"

"All right, all right," he said quickly, casting a worried look down the street, in the direction taken by the bus. "It isn't all that difficult. You have two lungs, yes? Two eyes, two ears, two kidneys?"

"What does that have to do with—"

"Just answer the question!"

"Yes!"

"All right, would it be surprising, then, to learn that you have two brains, as well? The body tends to duplicate important organs whenever possible in case of injury. One kidney may not be optimal, but it will keep you alive. One eye might be vexing, at least for seeing three dimensionally, but you can still see."

"But we don't have two minds—or two hearts," I pointed out, struggling to see where he was going with this.

"I'll grant you the heart, although with the way the human venous system is set up, two hearts might do more harm than good. But you *do* have two minds—or two lobes which act quite independently—"

"I do not," I said, and crossed my arms, not buying any of this.

"Everyone does!" the incubus said, running a hand through his spikey hair cut. "Haven't you ever heard of Phineas Gage?"

"Who?"

"A construction foreman for the railroad in the nineteenth century. One day, his crew was blasting rock in Vermont to clear a path for a new line. Unfortunately for Gage, rock wasn't the only thing that ended up being blasted. An iron rod was sent hurtling through his skull, obliterating much of his left frontal lobe in the process. He afterward became famous for having a complete change of personality."

I waited, but the incubus just looked at me. "And?" I finally said.

"Do you not see? Destroying much of one side of his brain allowed the other to take over. And they had very different natures."

"That's absurd. The poor man probably just had brain damage—"

"Well, yes, he had a metal rod through his head, but that's not the point."

"And do you have a—"

"Yes! I have a point!"

I waited.

"All right," he said, licking his lips nervously. Which was so weird to see from Pritkin that I almost did a double take. "What about this? When the corpus collosum—the bundle of nerves connecting the two halves of your brain—is severed, whether by an accident or on purpose—"

"Why would anyone—"

"To help with epileptic fits, and don't interrupt me!" he said, a little shrilly.

"Fine."

"When it is severed, the two brains—which is what your two lobes essentially are; we know this thanks to Gage and others who lived quite well with one or most of one destroyed—can no longer talk to each other directly. As a result, in experiments where a split-brain patient was asked to choose a colored block, the hand controlled by the left brain would often make a different choice than the hand controlled by the right. They had their own opinions, their own preferences, their own personalities, you see?"

I frowned.

"The two sides also can and often do argue with each other," he continued. "One split-brain patient grabbed his wife in an argument and shook her aggressively with one hand, only to be fought off, not by his wife herself, but *by his other hand*. And even in people with the corpus collosum attached, research has suggested that hesitancy when making decisions may come from the two sides of the brain having different opinions—literally being of two minds."

"So, you're saying that you and Pritkin . . . are two sides of the same mind?"

"Yes! Yes, good girl!" He grabbed my shoulders and squeezed. "You have it now. Which is why you can trust me!"

I just looked at him.

He made an exasperated noise which, I had to admit, sounded a lot like Pritkin.

"What else do you need to believe me?" he demanded.

"I don't know. More than that."

He looked around the street as if searching for inspiration—or for his other half. "All right, you know that the man you call Pritkin has had trouble with his magic, yes?"

"No. He's one of the most powerful mages I've ever—"

"But not what he could be—not even what he used to be. He's told you that himself; I know he has!"

"Okay."

"Well, this is why. Separating the two parts of his nature caused problems, just as it does in split-brain patients. For example, the right lobe of the brain is important for understanding object and facial recognition, whereas the left specializes in math and logic. They can each do both of these things, of course, as they must when one lobe is damaged and the other has to compensate. But that part of the brain will struggle with what it isn't good at, and the whole person will therefore be weakened."

"Like Pritkin is without you," I said, since that was obviously what he was getting at.

"Exactly! It isn't a perfect analogy—we aren't human, after all—and the two halves of the mind in our case is really more like two halves of a soul, but you get the idea. 'Pritkin' severed the connection between us after that unfortunate incident with his wife—"

"*His* wife?"

"Yes," the incubus frowned. "I never liked her. But as with humans, one side predominates, and between the two of us—"

"It's me," Pritkin said, reappearing with the shredded coat in hand, and breathing heavily. And then slugged his counterpart in the mouth, so hard that I flinched just from the echo off the buildings.

Chapter Three

Before I could blink, Pritkin—my Pritkin—grabbed my hand and—

"What are you *doing*?" I said, as the street went swimmy.

I stared around blankly for a second, caught between two worlds, and unable to get a visual on either of them. Then I pulled back, and the dingy street snapped into focus again. Leaving me breathing hard and Pritkin looking angry and frustrated.

"Were you trying to take me out?" I demanded.

"Yes!"

"Why? My body is a *prisoner*. If I go back—"

"You'll have a chance to see something, hear something. Perhaps enough to tell us where you are!"

"And can I get back here with that information if I do?"

"Why wouldn't you? You've been in and out of the Common all day—"

"How do you know that?"

"I've been following you!"

I'd been about to say something else, but that brought me up short. "What?"

He ran a hand through his hair and down to his neck, looking pained. "Each time you entered the Common, I could see what you saw. Not reach you, not contact you, not interfere. But I could see. We're linked, remember?"

"You saw Arsen, the hidden capitol, everything?" I asked, referencing a fey lord that I had inadvertently been following around.

He nodded.

"But . . . but I couldn't contact you. I tried and tried!"

"I know." Pritkin swallowed, looking a little calmer now. As if his brain was finally taking over from his feelings. But the mere fact that he'd been emotionally compromised enough to try to push me out of here, without even talking to me about it, demonstrated how much trouble we were in. "Mircea almost managed to throw off the effects of that potion yesterday—the one the portal was rigged with?"

I nodded. Mircea and Pritkin had followed the little fey through a hidden portal into Faerie, and been hit with some kind of potion bomb as soon as they emerged on the other side. It had stolen their abilities, leaving them almost helpless.

"But we were caught and he was staked before he could get completely free," Pritkin added. "After that, we lost the ability to communicate with you, or anyone else."

"But if our mental connection was cut off, then how—"

"I don't think this is a mental connection."

"Then what is it?"

He glanced around, and a shiver went up my spine at the expression that crossed his face. It was gone almost immediately, but for a second there, he'd almost looked . . . afraid. And if something frightened Pritkin, then it creeped the hell out of me.

"The fey have a belief," he said. "That interacting with the Common is talking to Faerie itself. Not telepathically, as even those with no mental gifts can sometimes manage it. But rather, as if you're engaging with its very soul."

The creepy feeling intensified. Guinn had said something similar, but it had been easy to shrug off coming from a stranger. It was harder with Pritkin.

"And you believe that?" I asked. "That Faerie has a soul? That it's like a person?"

"I don't know what I believe. I just know that, when you entered the Common, so did we. As if the soul bond we share dragged us in along with you."

"You have to admit, it fits," the incubus said groggily from the pavement, and got a boot to the face for his trouble.

Pritkin grabbed my hand again and shifted us back across the street. "Cassie, listen to me," he said urgently. "I have tried to send you power, so that you can shift away from wherever Aeslinn has you. But it doesn't work—"

"Why not? If we're linked—"

"I don't know. Arsen said you fed from him, that you took enough of his strength to get to us—"

I nodded. Arsen, the fey I'd been mentally following around, was one of Aeslinn's nobles, yet he'd ended up joining us. First physically, when I somehow pulled him to me across half the length of Faerie, and then in common cause, since he seemed to hate his king almost as much as we did.

"—but when I tried to shift to you or to give you the power to come to me, nothing happened. Possibly because I'm drugged—or because you are."

"Me?" I looked down at my bedraggled form. "Why would anyone bother with me? I'm tapped out—"

"But the fey don't know that. And you've developed quite a reputation in Faerie. The daughter of Artemis, the victor at Issengeir, the killer of two gods—I heard some of the guards gossiping about you. They talked as if you were halfway between a monster and a god yourself."

"Same thing," I muttered, and clasped my arms around myself.

"My point is, they would not have left you sober. And that drug of theirs cuts you off from your magic—and from mine. You can't shift away, and I can't help you, unless I know *where you are*. Do you understand?"

"But you already know where I am. You said Aeslinn has me—"

"Yes, but *where*? It's been hours since you were taken. And the king has a portal and camps all over Faerie. You could be anywhere by now."

Okay, he had a point.

And then he had a trip into a wall, courtesy of a pissed off incubus. Who threw him so hard that there were impressions of the bricks on his face when he staggered away. Including the manufacturer's name, incised into his forehead.

"I have a counter argument," the incubus said fiercely, and shifted us to the top of a building, just above where we'd been standing.

I glared at him, before looking over the edge of the roof to see Pritkin down below, searching for me frantically. I almost called out to him, then I hesitated. I needed to make something clear to the incubus, and this might be my only chance.

"Can you influence him?" I asked, turning back to the creature. "Control him at all?"

"What? Who?"

"Pritkin! I don't want him surrendering himself for me, you understand?"

"I don't think he's planning—"

"Maybe not now. But when the minutes tick down and the chance of rescue fades? What about then?"

He didn't answer, but his eyes grew shifty. As if he knew Pritkin, too. Which . . . yeah.

"Aeslinn wouldn't offer to make that trade if he planned to deliver," I pointed out. "And he's wanted Pritkin for years."

"He's wanted us?" The incubus's eyes narrowed. "Why?"

"I don't know. But he was after you in Ireland, sometime back in the Middle Ages. He'd captured a lot of part-fey, but considered you the prize—"

But he was already shaking his head. "You must be mistaken. We weren't even on Earth then."

"I know that! He hired some demons to go into the hells and drag you out."

"What? Who did?"

"Aeslinn!"

The incubus just blinked at me for a moment. "A king of the fey hired a squad of demons to—no." He shook his head again, this time smiling slightly. "Cassie, you have to understand—"

He broke off when I grabbed him by the front of his crappy shirt. "And you have to understand that I'm not some charlatan with a neon hand in my window and some cheap tricks to impress the masses! I'm Pythia, I'm a powerful touch telepath, and I Saw it in an imprint. And another, even more powerful telepath, Saw it with me!"

"That's where Guinevere comes in," he guessed, using Guinn's full name.

I released him. "Yes, so you can get her to vouch for me, if you doubt my word—"

"I don't doubt you, and I'm sorry that I gave that impression."

"—but whatever you think, we have to—" I broke off. That apology had actually sounded sincere. "Then . . . you believe me?"

"I have no choice," he said, running a hand over the back of his neck, as if it hurt. It was the same gesture the other Pritkin had made, probably because they'd been out of it all day, and the fey had allowed their captives' necks to loll with no support. I had a sudden urge to massage it, to soothe the pain away, and had to tell myself sternly to cut it out.

"Then why don't you sound like it?" I asked.

"It's just . . . that isn't the way things are done in Faerie, and certainly not by the Svarestri. If dark fey are scum in their eyes, and humans barely sentient barbarians, what are demons?"

"Employees." He rolled his eyes. "And maybe that reaction is why they got away with it."

He had been about to say something, but at that, he paused. And a slightly different expression came into his eyes. As if he was actually starting to listen.

"All right," he said slowly. "But then why don't I remember this?"

"Because your memory was erased."

"That's not an easy thing, to erase the mind of a powerful demon lord. Which, whether my other half likes it or not, is what we are."

"I don't know about that; I just know he did it—"

"Who? Not Aeslinn, surely?"

"No," I shook my head, trying to keep from going off on a tangent. There were a thousand things I wanted to know, to talk about, but some were more important than others. And one was paramount. "It was somebody else, somebody with him; it doesn't matter! What matters is that you have to keep Pritkin away from the king—"

"How?" the incubus spread his hands. "I'm not in control; he is."

"It doesn't look like he can control you right now," I pointed out.

"Not at the moment, no. The potion rendered both of us virtually powerless—"

"So, you can stop him!"

He gave me a look. "How many times have you succeeded in stopping John Pritkin from doing anything?"

Damn it!

"Then what about help? Caedmon has an army invading Aeslinn's lands," I said, talking about the king's chief rival. "If you can get word—"

"Yes, he would likely intervene. Except that we are on the opposite end of Faerie, somewhere in the Shivering Wood, between Golden Hall and Burning Swamp—" he broke off. "Those names mean nothing to you, do they?"

I shook my head.

"It's an area where few ever go," he summed up. "The swamp has eruptions of noxious gasses, which can be set alight by the slightest flame, causing a conflagration that can spread like wild fire and burn for days. There are plenty of blackened skeletons below the waterline attesting to how easy it is to die there. The dark fey move through it when they must, but everyone else steers clear."

"So Aeslinn thought it would make a good hideout."

He nodded. "And Golden Hall is a ruin, long believed to be cursed, while the forest—"

"Yeah. I got that one," I said dryly, remembering the army of mobile trees that Guinn had briefly commanded.

"How did you find us?" he asked incredulously. "There are no portals anywhere near there, other than the one the Svarestri must have cut for themselves—"

"It's a long story," I said, not wanting to get into that now. "And there must be another portal somewhere—"

"Yes, if you don't mind traveling three hundred miles."

"Three *hundred?*"

"Which is why Mircea and I didn't make for it. Well, that and the fleet—"

"What fleet?"

"The missing airships you wondered about, from Aeslinn's capitol? They were there, in the camp, coming and going all morning. The Svarestri were bringing back fey of all types, hundreds of them, packed into those little vessels. They took them to—" he broke off abruptly, and held up a hand.

"What is it?" I said, glancing around, but I didn't see anything.

"One moment," he said, and shifted us into an alley. Where we huddled back against the damp wall in darkness, while a colorful spell lit up the air overhead. "Good one," he muttered, staring up.

We stayed in place for a moment, listening to what happens when a powerful mage loses his cool. There was no shouting involved, which was more frightening than the reverse. Pritkin loud was just blowing off steam. Pritkin completely silent while he wrecked the hell out of a roof?

Yeah.

Not so good.

The incubus apparently didn't think so, either. His eyes had gotten big, and the rest of him had gotten small as he shrank back against the bricks, looking like he'd really prefer to be somewhere else. I got the feeling that he was the lover, not the fighter, part of this equation.

Which was too damned bad, because I actually was somewhere else, and I needed information!

"What happened?" I repeated, poking him.

"Keep your voice down!"

"If I do, you won't be able to hear me," I said dryly, as what sounded like a chimney exploded overhead.

"And neither will he," he pointed out, before I fisted a hand in his shirt, since that had worked last time.

"Talk!"

To my surprise, he did. "I am going to take a moment to catch you up, all right? It is difficult to converse otherwise."

I nodded.

"Very well. After you left us in the tunnels, I used a *pedisequus* charm—a tracking spell that highlighted only our footprints—to allow us to find our way back to the portal. But we found it closed and locked and we didn't have the password to reopen it. There were dark mages everywhere, I was almost out of physical magic—potion bombs and the like—and the drug the damned fey had exploded in my face was preventing me from accessing my own. We couldn't risk staying."

"So, you left to find another portal."

He nodded. "But by the time we finally made it out of those tunnels, it was morning, and we were in unfamiliar territory—and right in the middle of three Svarestri encampments."

"Shit."

"Very much so. We didn't have a way to do a glamourie and stealing a couple of hooded cloaks didn't help, as even the vampire is a foot shorter than the average Svarestri. The camp was also set up as a processing center, with the guards constantly on the lookout for runaways."

"Processing what?"

"The prisoners. The fey were separating them, putting some into cages within the camp, while others were being taken into the tunnels. Afterwards, I didn't see those again. I don't know what happened to them."

I scowled. Aeslinn was still hunting, then, but not because he needed new abilities. He already had plenty of those, and as he'd proven on the Thames, they didn't ensure victory. So, what was he likely to get from random fey that would help him win the war?

"When they separated them out, was there any reason you could see?"

He shook his head. "One of their priests came forward to check them. He looked into their faces, waved a hand over them, and indicated right or left. Right, they went into the tunnels; left, they landed in the cages. But what he was looking for, I couldn't say."

God blood was the obvious answer, given what I'd learned in Ireland, but how much were random fey likely to have? Even taken en masse? I bit my lip, feeling like I had a puzzle with the outline filled in, but not enough pieces for the middle. Aeslinn was ignoring the rest of the war, allowing one of his capitols to fall and another to be besieged, while he rounded up random fey?

It had to be for a reason.

"As I said, it's hundreds of miles to any portal I know of," the incubus continued. "And there were too many troops, both on the ground and in the air, for us to have any hope of making it out unseen. Not without our abilities and not whilst wrangling another who did not want to go."

"The goat," I guessed.

The incubus scowled. "He has been . . . annoying. Although he did tell us that the drug would take days to fully wear off. He's dealt with it before. And with that information, and looking at our situation, we decided to find a place to hide—"

"Good." That's what I'd have done.

"—wait for nightfall, and sneak back in—"

"Wait. Sneak back in where?"

"To the only place we knew to find a portal—"

"You have got to be kidding!" I stared at him. "You said those tunnels were crawling!"

"And so was the camp outside. The difference was that, inside, they weren't expecting us, allowing us to possibly make it—"

"To a portal that was shut down!"

"And which couldn't stay that way," he argued, with Pritkin's usual stubbornness. "The army had to be fed and information had to be conveyed. It seemed reasonable that they would open it up again, once they assumed that we had fled."

"And did they?" I asked grimly, already knowing the answer.

"I have no idea." He scowled. "The Svarestri are lords of earth. They can reshape it with no more difficulty than we would rearrange furniture. In our absence, they had restructured the tunnel system. Everything looked the same at the entrance, but before we'd gone very far, we realized that it had all changed."

"And they caught you." I crossed my arms and glared at him.

He looked offended. "Not immediately. We managed to get out again, with a squad of dark mages on our tail, along with half a dozen fey guards. We overcame them, but one got away and summoned the army, leaving us faced with hundreds of fey, converging on us from all sides."

Of course, they were! I wanted to scream, but managed not to. It wouldn't do any good, and he was still talking.

"They staked the vampire and drugged me again, knocking me out. I didn't fully wake up until around an hour ago, and my power remains compromised."

"That's why you're . . ." I waved a hand, indicating the general weirdness of two Pritkins.

He nodded. "Not that it has done me any good. He can't do much right now, but neither can I—except get curious."

"About what?"

"About you. About *this*," he waved a hand around, I suppose indicating the Common. "About what you're doing here."

"What *am* I doing here?"

The green eyes gleamed, catching a beam of spell light from above. "That's a very good question, and the more you think about it, the more interesting it gets. You've never encountered the Common before, and I—well, there were flashes, brief ones, when I was exploring as a child. But nothing like this. I've never heard stories of anyone being able to access it like this. Yet you, a complete novice, are hopping about all over the place, getting the full cinematic tour. Doesn't that strike you as odd?"

"It didn't until right now."

"Well, it is. Even more suspiciously, you haven't been hitting random points, have you? Watching someone repair his boots or fish in a river. But you should have been. That's the sort of thing that the vast majority of fey experience as the Common. And that is all.

"You, on the other hand, spent hours following an extremely important fey, who you later turned to our cause—using the very information you were given. And now, just after being captured by your worst enemy, you're here again. It's almost as if someone wants to show you something."

"Show me . . . what?" I asked, taken aback, but he just steamrollered on.

"Meanwhile, we—Mircea and I—were allowed to tag along mentally, to see what you saw. Yet neither of us could manifest physically, to talk and interact with you, until we were freed. And

Mircea remains absent. Why do you think that is? What is the difference—the one big difference—between us at the moment?"

"He's wounded," I whispered, glancing around. And thinking that I might finally know where the incubus was going with this.

"Yes. And someone wants warriors, Cassie. Or, more accurately, some*thing*."

"You aren't actually suggesting—"

I broke off, but not because he'd interrupted me. But because what I was thinking sounded so ridiculous. So completely impossible that I didn't have words.

Like the rest of this week?

I realized that I still had my hand in his shirt, and released him in order to hug my arms around myself. And tried to ignore the goosebumps that had just broken out on my skin. But the incubus was smiling slightly, having finally gotten a chance to make his case.

"That's exactly what I'm suggesting," he said gently. "Think about it, Cassie. You're smarter than people give you credit for, when you stop to think."

So, I did. I thought about Faerie, not as an inanimate thing, the way I usually did, or even as some kind of strange, sentient being. But as what it was: a mother.

A mother whose children were being scattered, far beyond her reach, by senseless wars. A mother who had lost pieces of herself, over and over, when they failed to come home. A mother who was now confronted by the possible return of the gods, the very beings who had experimented on and warped her creatures, those they hadn't killed outright.

A mother who was mourning, and hurting, and furious, and vengeful.

A completely new kind of ally that I had never even thought to look for.

But who had somehow looked for me.

"There are older powers than the pantheon we are fighting," the incubus said softly, echoing my thoughts. "Ones the fey used to worship, before the coming of these new gods.

"Ones who may have now awoken."

I licked my lips, feeling even more off-kilter than I usually did. I'd started to learn a bit more about my mother's people, started to understand them. But a sentient world? That just made my head hurt.

But I didn't have to understand it. I just had to understand this, whatever this was. I looked up and met the incubus' eyes, so familiar and yet so different from the ones I knew.

"I think . . . I want to see what she has to show me," I whispered.

He quirked an eyebrow. "She?"

"Yes, I think it's a she. And that she brought me here—brought all of us—for a reason. I want to know what that reason is."

"As do I," came a rasp from behind us.

I turned to see Pritkin standing there with a scowl on his face. The clanging and banging from above—a spell I assumed—continued, cast as a diversion while he searched for us. But now that he'd found us, although he was staring down his counterpart, he wasn't slugging him.

I decided that I'd take what I could get.

"Then let's go."

Chapter Four

You'll be needing the password, love," a woman said, as Nigel pulled back his hand with a curse.

She came out of the shadows of a hall and sat near the bottom of a set of stairs, facing the doorway. The one where a ward was spitting and hissing—and occasionally biting—Nigel. He sucked on his latest burn and glared at her.

She grinned saucily back, clearly half drunk.

She looked about thirty, with dyed red hair that had gone to frizz and her skirts hiked up enough that baggy gray stockings could be seen. The stockings needed a wash and some mending, but if she'd done that, they wouldn't have matched the rest of the outfit. The fact that she was here at all should have made Nigel rethink his evening's plans, which had relied on stealth, cunning and his former burglar's training.

Not that he'd ever burgled a house with the people in it watching him before, but there was a first time for everything. Like that, he *thought, as a man stepped out of the shadows to join the woman. A purple man.*

Nigel blinked at him, wondering if he belonged to a circus and hadn't bothered to remove his makeup yet. But he doubted it. The only thing around his loosened collar was a sweat stain.

And yet, he was very definitely purple.

Nigel paused to reassess things.

The pretty brunette that he'd followed here was a honeypot—an assassin who used her good looks and apparent vulnerability to lure men to her house and then dispose of them. And she was a good one, or she wouldn't have been given this assignment. Which meant that she was rich, and right now, she was also distracted.

He'd expected to make a quick smash and grab whilst she was busy 'entertaining' her mark, but there were already three things wrong with that plan. Thing one was the quality of the ward that he'd encountered just past the flimsy front door. Not only was it one he'd never seen before, but in ten minutes of standing on the stoop like a chump, he had yet to be able to get past it. This was not a thing that had ever happened to Nigel.

Thing two was the smell of this place. The ward didn't keep in scents, and despite the prevailing air of coal dust, piss and garbage from the street, Nigel's nose could pick up other smells from inside the house. Strange smells. Ones he could not identify despite the fact that he relied on scent as much as sight, his fey heritage giving him a nose far keener than any human's.

And now there was thing three: the purple man.

Nigel sized him up as the man wobbled slightly, clearly as drunk as the woman. He listed against the side of the stairs, although Nigel wasn't sure that he knew it. He had the expression of someone wondering why the world was suddenly tilted, but not caring enough to ask.

But other than for his very odd color, there was nothing particularly remarkable about him. He was tall, skinny, and dressed in a pair of tweed trousers, with dirty cuffs to match the shirt, and an old pair of suspenders so stretched out that they weren't really suspending anything. Which was why the trousers had become baggy about the knees.

But if he had used a glamour on his skin tone, Nigel could have passed him in the street any day of the week and not looked twice. Until a third arm detached from his side, to palm a bottle from the woman. Probably because his other two were busy holding him up.

"Try abracadabra," he suggested, and upended the drink.

"I'm interested in acquiring lodging," Nigel said, attempting to sound both respectable and unruffled.

"Was that why you was tryin' to break in, then?" the woman asked, and she and the purple man laughed.

"I've a right to stay here. Same as anyone else!"

"Said the rabbit to the hound," the purple man muttered, and took another drink.

"You can get a kip two streets over," the woman said, nodding at the road behind him. "For fourpence, or thruppence if you just want a bit o' floor—"

Nigel felt his face flush. "What d'you take me for?"

The purple man opened his mouth, then shut it again and shook his head. "Too easy," he muttered.

"Let me in or I'll gut the lot o' yer!" Nigel yelled, grabbing the bars of the ward without thinking. Only to find that they dissipated under his touch, without so much as a final shock, causing him to fall onto his face.

"If you knew the password, why didn't you say?" the purple man asked, as Nigel scrambled back up.

"Yer wasting yer time," the woman said, leaning back on her elbows and grinning at him sloppily. "This place ain't for yer kind."

"I'll decide that," Nigel snarled.

The woman wafted a negligent hand at the hallway beside the stairs. "Then be my guest, sillean."

"What's *sillean*?" I asked Pritkin, as we followed the bruiser down the narrow hall.

"It means boy in Gaelic. She's being rude, but is also warning him that he's as prepared for what he'll find ahead as a child would be."

"What . . . does lie ahead?"

"This is a boarding house for demon kind, usually part demon, part human. They don't really belong anywhere, but on Earth, they can at least exist. In the demon realms, their lives would be short."

I nodded. And then something occurred to me. "We just got here. How do you know so much about this place?"

"I know who runs it."

"And who is that?"

"My wife."

I stopped walking for a second in surprise, then had to hurry to catch up.

Suddenly, a number of things about my previous visit to this part of the Common made sense. Like the woman's name—Ruth—which had gone over my head, since I didn't think about Pritkin's late wife a lot. Except to wonder why a half demon had been named after a Biblical character.

But then, many names in this period had been religious, and I guessed that she and her family had wanted to fit in. Only that didn't appear to be what had happened. Because the boarding house wasn't just a boarding house, I realized a moment later.

It was an entrance.

A rainbow of shifting colors spilled into the hallway from a frosted glass panel in a door at the very end. Given its location, the door should have led onto a back garden, assuming that this place had one. But Nigel wasn't placing any bets on it, as it didn't even have a kitchen, the space for which had been partitioned into small rooms to let. He assumed that the nicer sort were upstairs, including the owner's, but he didn't go up there.

Because she hadn't.

Amid traces of unwashed bodies, coal dust dragged in from the street, sex, garbage, someone's recent pork pie, someone else's spilled gin, and rat droppings, he caught it: the thread of her perfume. She'd gone through the door with the moving colors, and taken her mark with her. They'd passed this way not fifteen minutes ago, which should have left a brilliant trail for him to follow.

It hadn't. Instead, it was shredded, faded, barely discernable under the other smells drifting in from that same door—a mountain of them. One that confused his mind and made his nose twitch. Like in the foyer, these weren't smells he knew.

Nigel thought about just turning around and going back. Nothing about this evening had worked out the way he'd planned, and his hopes of making a quick score were getting dimmer all the time. Not to mention that two people had seen him already, and it sounded like there were more beyond the door, possibly many more.

He'd do better to go have a drink at his local, and forget all about it.

But before he could move, the door was flung open from the other side, and a wash of sound swept over him, as well as light, colors and—

"Stand aside, gov. Yer blocking the whole passage, and it's none too big as it is."

Nigel stood aside, plastering his bulk against the corridor wall, and a man came in. And then came in again and again and again, because there were numerous copies of him, all in a row, as if his body was an accordion stretching out. Or the first in a line of paper dolls, all cut from a single sheet.

Nigel blinked, and the many men became one, but one who blurred when he moved, as if threatening to come apart again. He passed down the hall with a strange, fluttering motion, and Nigel watched him go while blinking excessively, his eyes certain that they could sort things out.

They couldn't, and it became worse when he turned back the other way, and stuck his head out of the open door.

And found himself in a pub, all right, but nothing like the one he'd had in mind.

Some things were familiar: a long, wooden bar, scarred with moisture rings and lacking polish, except where some old, yellowed shine remained in the corners; dingy, red brick walls, some patched with plaster, and a wooden ceiling with massive old oak beams; a scarred wooden floor, almost covered with small, round, close packed tables and a few booths along the walls, which seemed insufficient for the crowd; and a tiny stage shoved into a corner, where a lone performer—all that could fit on that thing—was fiddling out a tune that Nigel couldn't hear over the din.

But that was where the similarities with the world he knew ended.

Instead of pert barmaids or beefy barmen, drinks were being delivered by trays that seemed to zip about all by themselves. That wouldn't have surprised Nigel, who had visited a few mage bars in his day, but these trays were not magical. These trays—

"Get in or get out," one of them said, pausing in front of his face. Only it wasn't the tray talking, he realized. It was the tiny, angry creature below it that Nigel could just glimpse in flashes as the heavy wooden platter bobbed about in front of him.

He bent down slightly, and—

His brain broke a little.

What the devil was that?

It had a small, pixie-like body, if pixies were naked and glowing and iridescent blue. It had furiously whirring wings, clawed hands and feet, and a demonic-looking pointed tail. And a terrible little scrunched up face with oversized, yellow eyes, a fleshy beak for a mouth, and an annoyed expression.

"Are you deaf, you great lummox?" the creature asked. "Buy a drink or get out, and either way, move!"

Nigel moved—over by the bar, as it was nearest. Where he managed to snag a spot at the end, whilst also managing to avoid the flying trays zipping about everywhere. The creatures underneath came in many colors, all of which glowed faintly, explaining the moving lights he'd seen outside. And although they would have been the main attraction anywhere else, here they barely scratched the surface on the strange.

Nigel didn't even try not to stare at a nearby table, where several bluish creatures with eyes on stalks were talking, whilst one had his drink set alight by a tiny orange waiter. Or at a booth, where a searingly yellow woman with purple hair and long, dagger-like fingernails was chatting up a bloke with transparent skin. Those fingernails could put his eyes out, although Nigel supposed there were worst things.

Like at the next booth, where another woman sat flirting with a couple of men, and flashing fangs longer than any vampire's, along with a black, forked tongue whenever she laughed. Behind her was a man with red skin and two heads; cattycornered to him, at a small table with three normal looking blokes, was a blue-green feathered creature with elaborate plumage; and across from them, near the stage, was a shadowy being that Nigel had to catch out of the corner of his eyes, as he couldn't see it when he looked directly at it. He wasn't the only one; somebody tried to sit on it a moment later, apparently thinking the table free, and caused a mild altercation.

And then a bartender with six arms asked him what he wanted to drink.

Nigel stared at him blankly, despite the fact that he looked fairly normal compared to the rest of the room. "Whisky," he said hoarsely.

The man filled his request, while serving several other patrons and wiping down the bar at the same time. Nigel slid a coin to him when his drink arrived, hoping it was enough, and he supposed so. But he didn't get any change back.

For once, he decided not to ask.

Then he caught the honeypot's scent again, a barely-there hint on the air, and remembered what he was supposed to be doing. He belted back his drink and made his way through the pub and out a door on the other side. Where he found a street, which if possible was even more closely packed than the premises behind him.

Nigel's eyes took in a long rectangle of open night sky arcing over a dirt road that was sandwiched between two long stretches of buildings. He'd stumbled across a hidden street, he realized, maybe more than one, as he could see a bit of a crossroad up ahead. A hidden enclave then, with vividly colored lights that smeared the darkness wherever he looked.

That should have resulted in a brilliant haze, one visible above the nearby buildings. But there'd been nothing to see from the street outside, so somebody was paying to hide this place. And they were paying plenty.

Glamours that big were expensive, both to buy and to maintain, which probably explained why the street was so crowded. Whoever *was in charge didn't want to stretch the protection any further than necessary. But that left a throng of what looked like thousands jam packed together, almost shoulder to shoulder.*

Nigel stared about as he was jostled on all sides, and didn't even think to retaliate. He was used to being the biggest and strongest in any room, the one hired for brawn rather than brains. But he wasn't sure that he could best some of the women here.

He wasn't even sure he could tell which ones were the women, as only perhaps a third of the crowd looked human. And even those that did . . . had issues. Like the mostly ordinary looking man sitting atop a cart full of barrels parked nearby. He had on a shabby, but colorful, outfit of green checked wool with a red vest, topped off by a ridiculously small stove pipe hat, which was the only thing that could fit between his large, ram-like, curled horns.

And he was telling jokes.

"A judge asked a man, are you aware of the penalty for bigamy, sir? Indeed, I am, the man replied. Two mothers-in-law.

"Sir, you are prevaricating, the judge insisted. Now did you or did you not sleep with this woman? Sleep? The man says. Why, not a wink, your honor.

"The man's wife had had enough, and leapt to her feet. I do believe, sir, that should I die tomorrow, you would marry the devil's own daughter, if you could get anything by it! Oh, no, the man replied. You can't marry two sisters."

The comedian's patter formed a surreal backdrop to a scene of creeping horror for Nigel. As his shock wore off, his concern grew, helped by a sea of creatures that he didn't even have names for. Some were covered in fur; some had scales and huge, gelatinous eyes, like fish risen out of the sea; and others had masses of pointed horns sticking out, not only from their heads, but from their bodies, too.

One of the latter, a mottled green and yellow creature with a reptilian head topped with long, black spikes, bumped into him. And the slender end of a horn-covered tail wrapped around his wrist. It wasn't slimy, any more than a snake's body would have been, and the tiny spikes at the end were on the outside, not ripping into his skin.

But he could feel the creature's pulse against his own, a terrible, sluggish beat, and when he tried to pull back, he went nowhere.

"I'd like to buy some talcum powder," the comedian continued, from above him. "Well, walk right this way sir, the tradesman said. But if I walked that way, I told him, I wouldn't need the talcum powder."

"Pardon," Nigel muttered, whilst trying to free himself from the tail's iron-like grip.

It didn't work, which caused him to have an unaccustomed feeling that he slowly identified as panic. Nigel did not panic. It was one of his big selling points, that he was Gibraltar when everyone else lost their nerve, helping to keep a crew together and focused. But for the first time, he began to understand what those other, punier men felt, when confronted with a crisis. For the first time, he felt puny.

He didn't like it.

The comedian, on the other hand, was riding high on a swell of laughter from his audience. "Can you support my daughter, sir? the fond father asked. Indeed, sir, I have two strong arms, the suitor replied. But can they support her? the father insisted. Well, they often have, sir."

"Let go," Nigel growled, but nothing happened. Except for the tail twining another time around his wrist, and climbing up his arm. He wanted to pull out his knife, but was afraid of what would happen if he did. Even discounting the tail, the creature's arms were bigger around than Nigel's thighs.

It pulled him in close, with no discernable effort despite the fact that he was now leaning back as hard as he could. It bent down to say something in a language he didn't know and didn't want to know, a terrible, sibilant whisper. Followed by a thin, dark blue snake of a tongue pushing out at him, as if scenting the air.

Only, that wasn't all it was doing.

"She was only a photographer's daughter but she was very well developed.

"She was only the fireman's daughter, but she was guaranteed to put out.

"She was only an optician's daughter but she sure made a spectacle of herself."

Nigel had a panicked second to feel a gritty, almost sandpapery, sensation on his cheek, sliding wetly upward; to smell the creature's breath in his face, hot and fetid; to see the terrible, lashless, reptilian eyes narrow. And then he screamed, a high-pitched sound completely unlike him, which was lost in a bellow of laughter from the crowd. He tore away from the creature's grip, panic lending him strength, spied a hole in the throng and dove for it.

He tried to make his way back to the pub, but a mass of people going in the other way swept him into the street, where a flurry of impressions hit him from all sides: two men, balancing on a tightrope overhead, sword fighting so ferociously that sparks rained down onto the mob below; several open fires burning in barrels which they did not consume, but when the crowd ran him into one, more sparks flew hotly into his face; a red devil of a man on top of another barrel, putting him well above the masses, sucking in flames from a torch before spewing a huge, golden plume over everyone's heads.

For a moment, all that Nigel's dazzled eyes could see was fire. "I'm in hell," he thought, while monstrous faces leered at him from all sides.

And then a short, squat, man-like creature with huge gray eyes, a too-wide face, and a grip like an entire battalion, darted out from a shop to feel of Nigel's arm.

He must have liked what he found, as he immediately began trying to drag him inside. Nigel stared from the man to his shop, where haunches of unfamiliar meat hung from hooks, where a butcher with a red stained apron was cutting up something with an enormous cleaver, and where a third man was feeding the bloody pieces into a grinder. Nigel saw the raw flesh coming out the other side, what looked like an endless river of it, a river that could have been anything, anything at all. And he screamed again.

And, this time, he didn't stop.

Chapter Five

T his is useless!" Pritkin said, as a tide of remembered emotion threw us out of deep immersion. And almost threw us out of everything else, too, when the street abruptly came to a halt.

"He's following Ruth," the incubus argued, as I tried to keep my footing while reality trembled around us. "We need to stay with him."

"We need to stop wasting time!"

"We're in the mind. All this takes but a moment—"

"You don't know that—"

"I do know that, and so do you. We've been following Cassie's adventures for half the day!"

"Then why were you in such a rush before?" I asked.

"I was afraid of him," the incubus nodded at Pritkin. "Dragging you off somewhere before we understand what is happening. And he's afraid—"

"Of nothing," Pritkin snapped, cutting him off. He was standing under a red light, which ironically made him look more devilish than his counterpart, who was bathed in blue. "I want to make a plan! Not wander aimlessly about London's demonic underbelly!"

"Is that where we are?" I asked, and then wondered why I'd bothered. Because obviously.

The incubus nodded, but kept his eyes on Pritkin. "It's one of the few places locally where part-demons can shop, drink and have a meal out, without having to use an expensive glamourie."

"It looks like a meal out is what he's worried about," I said, watching Nigel. Who had been frozen in the middle of fighting with the butcher, as frantically as if his life depended on it. And maybe it did.

But the incubus just rolled his eyes. "He's being ridiculous. If he doesn't stop, they're going to ask him to leave."

I thought Nigel might be really grateful for that, right about now. "Or barbeque him."

"He isn't in any danger," Pritkin and his incubus said at the same time. And then scowled at each other.

"We used to take recruits to the Corps here, to help them learn to spot the different sorts of demons who frequent Earth," the incubus said. "I can assure you; we never lost anyone."

"Okay, but Nigel isn't a war mage," I pointed out. "And he's been assaulted twice, and he just got here."

The incubus frowned. "Assaulted? When?"

I gestured at the butcher. "*Right now?*"

"If you think that, you're looking at it wrong. Here, look again." He took me by the shoulders and pointed at the battling duo. "Ask yourself how you'd interpret this if it was happening on another street—a human one."

I looked again. The fact that the two men weren't moving helped, although not at first. At first, all I saw was a scary-looking guy who, despite being little more than half Nigel's height, seemed to be holding his own. And then it dawned on me to wonder why he was only using one arm, when his species had the usual two.

One hand had a grip on Nigel's coat, despite ducking to avoid a haymaker. But the other was pointing at a nearby folding chalkboard, with some writing I couldn't decipher on top. And on the bottom . . .

"He's trying to show him the day's specials," I said, as light dawned. "Not make him into one."

The incubus nodded. "This isn't the Shadowland, Cassie. The people who live here are under the jurisdiction of the Silver Circle, and have to abide by its rules. Not that most of them wouldn't, in any case."

Pritkin snorted.

"Oh, yes," the incubus said. "Let's just tar everyone with the same brush, why don't we?"

"When it comes to demons? Yes, why don't we?" Pritkin agreed. But then he looked at me. "However, assaulting someone in full view of hundreds of witnesses would be foolish. It could result in the whole place being shut down."

"But . . . what about the other guy?" I asked.

"What other guy?"

"The lizard-looking one, back there." I turned to see if I could find him in the crowd, and caught sight of the spiky head protruding at least a foot above everybody else. Luckily, it didn't look like he was following poor Nigel; he'd probably found easier prey by now.

I turned back around, to meet identical looks of disbelief.

"That . . . wasn't a man," Pritkin said, after a moment.

"She wasn't trying to eat him, Cassie," the incubus added. "Well, not that way—"

"She was propositioning him," Pritkin said, shooting his counterpart a look. "She's one of the local working girls."

I took a moment to absorb that, and then looked up. Where a rain of suspended sparks was lighting the air around the two ferocious sword fighters. "And those two?"

"Buskers. They put on a good show, then pass the hat."

The incubus nodded. "The district is always crowded. The performers have to get up off the street in order to be seen."

I looked around again, this time with new eyes, and saw, not a crowd of hellish monsters, but a sort of carnival. Barrels dotted the street haphazardly, with some pushed to either side in front of bars and dancehalls, and others parked in the middle of the road, so that the crowd had to move around them. And almost every one had a performer on top.

Many of them seemed to be previewing the live shows inside various venues, with the entertainers dressed like those decorating the colorful posters on the walls behind them. Others were doing their own thing, while their assistants worked the crowd for tips. And they were getting them, since the acts were pretty fantastic.

Just from here I could see an exotic female dancer with deeply orange skin and a tiny, spangled costume contorting her body in impossible ways; a man with four arms, each of which was keeping a fiery baton twirling; a tower of five acrobats in bright gold costumes that had a few dozen plates spinning despite sharing a single barrel; and a couple of jugglers atop overhanging roofs on opposite sides of the street that were sending glowing clubs back and forth above the heads of the crowd.

"Nigel is afraid because his prejudices blind him," the incubus said. "Not due to any real threat." He shot a glance at Pritkin. "Like someone else I know."

"Wait until a cutthroat gets him in an alley," Pritkin said. "Then let's see how real the threat is."

"Which could happen just as easily on any of the streets outside—"

"Not just as easily, as you know damned well—"

"—because there's good and bad out there, in the human world, just as there is in here, just as there is in the hells, but you won't see it—"

"We're not doing this again," Pritkin said, and turned away, raising a hand.

The frozen street slowly started up again, but it didn't reach full speed, since the incubus knocked Pritkin's arm aside halfway through the motion. "And who gets to decide that?" he demanded.

"I do. I'm in charge, remember?"

The incubus flushed. "Not now. Not this time. You can't silence me—"

"Is that a challenge?"

"—or keep me locked down, as you have for a century, while you revile me and my kind—*your* kind—"

"They are not my kind."

"We are half of you! We *are* your kind! You're more demon than anything else, yet you never gave us a chance, just blamed us for every single—"

"I blamed you for *what you did*!"

Pritkin's own skin was getting flushed now, or perhaps that was the slowly moving light shadows from the busker's batons, which had started to rotate again. But the incubus didn't seem to notice. He had a lot of pent-up emotion, along with a century's worth of unsaid words.

And he was saying them.

"You have it all laid out in your mind the way you want to remember it. The way that leaves me at fault, allowing you to continue hating demonkind. But you know—you've always known—that there was nothing I could have done about what happened to Ruth—"

"And you wouldn't have, even if you could. You wanted her power—"

"She didn't have any power!" the incubus said furiously. "That was the point! She started that damned spell to try to leech ours—"

"You didn't want her power for itself," Pritkin snapped. "You wanted it to enslave me, to get me used to the taste of it, the lure of it, just like Rosier—"

"That old lie again. You trot it out like clockwork to avoid facing the truth—"

"The truth is that you were born *weak*—"

"—that this isn't about us. It's about *you*; it was always about you—"

"—as all demons are, always craving more and more!"

"And look at us now," the incubus said, flinging out his arms. "In a position where we could use a little more!" He turned to me. "It's true that demons crave power, because we know we need it. There was only one group in this entire realm who opposed the gods, Cassie. The fey didn't do it; the humans didn't do it, didn't rise up until Artemis herself led them. Just another godly army, slaves to a different name.

"But the demon lords—they stood firm. They refused to pay tribute, to send their people to be consumed by an ever-growing horde, to lie down and accept the boot on their necks. They decided that they would die before they became slaves, and they did—in multitudes beyond imagining. Yet they fought back, and continued fighting as their worlds fell apart, as their people were slaughtered, as their children—"

"Stop this!" Pritkin snapped. "Of course, the old order didn't want to give way to the new. That doesn't make them heroes!"

"Nor does it make them villains. Power doesn't make you a monster, and lack of it doesn't make you good."

"But love of it makes you dangerous."

"As does fear!"

"Fear of what?" I asked, a little confused by the break neck speed of their conversation.

"Of himself," the incubus said. "My dear brother is afraid of what he—of what we—might become. He felt himself growing, changing, in those years in the hells. Felt the awesome power of his demon blood, felt its potential—and turned his back on it. Looked for reasons to hate it. Went back to puttering about Earth or studying fey magic, thinking that he'd never grow too powerful there. And cut me off, at the first opportunity—"

"And will again," Pritkin said bitingly. "Enjoy your lies. You won't have the chance to spew them soon."

"Then I'd best take this one, hadn't I?" The incubus turned back to me. "The hells are everything he has told you, and more. I won't deny that. You're seeing them broken, shattered, and in recovery from the colossal destruction the gods wrought. But there is beauty there, too, and knowledge beyond human understanding, and courage and nobility—"

Pritkin laughed scornfully.

The incubus shot him a purely vicious look. "But you haven't seen that, having only heard part of the story." He took my hands. "You have half the picture. You need—you deserve—all of it—"

"She needs nothing from you!" Pritkin said, and knocked his hands away.

"I think she needs a great deal from both of us. Tell me, *brother*, if she dies tonight, if we are not strong enough to save her, who are you going to blame? What story are you going to invent to ease your bloody conscience then?"

Pritkin's face abruptly changed, causing me to suck in a breath, having never seen that particular expression before. His skin flushed, his hands fisted, and a vein stood out on his neck. And his eyes—his eyes were terrifying. Slitted and, in the low light, as dark as his counterpart's when his power was up, only without any stars. There was murder on that face, writ so clearly that a blind person could have read it, or at least could have felt the rage coming off him in waves.

If that was how he looked on a hunt, I thought dizzily, I was surprised his prey didn't have a heart attack before he could kill them.

I thought he was going to jump his other half again, but instead, he turned on his heel and pushed off through the crowd. It took me a moment to notice that he was wasn't moving randomly, but was tracking Nigel again. The part-fey had thrown aside the confused looking butcher and was on the move.

And he was moving fast, despite the fact that we were at quarter speed. And I guessed that Pritkin was too angry to notice and rectify it, since it stayed that way. Or maybe the slower pace just made it easier to catch up to Nigel.

After a brief pause, the incubus and I followed in their wake, with me pushing past a cascade of sparks like a beaded curtain, feeling their heat on my hands, and seeing their light spangle my fingers. Then slipping between the crowd around another dancer, this one a pretty, blue skinned boy, the firelight gleaming off his bright red costume. And, finally, squeezing past a baked potato seller that Nigel had shoved aside, causing him to overturn his shiny metal roasting can.

"I'm sorry, Cassie," the incubus said, dodging a slowly flying potato. "I shouldn't have dragged you into this."

"Circumstances seem to have dragged me into it."

"Perhaps. But mentioning his current lover's peril whilst he's grappling with the last one's betrayal . . ." he shook his head. "Incubi are supposed to be more diplomatic than that."

I shot him a look. "I've never known Pritkin to care much about diplomacy."

"You've never known him at all," he was suddenly fierce.

"That's a big statement."

"But true. How could you, when he doesn't know himself? Although that isn't entirely his fault."

"Then whose fault is it?"

He sighed, and stared up a male and female acrobatic duo, dressed in silver spangles and not much else, who were posing prettily on a platform above us. The platform extended out of a second story window, using the protruding roofline as a support, giving them more room to work with than most of the performers. And they were using it. The act probably looked impressive at full speed, being full of lifts and twirls and spine cracking, backward bends.

But slowed down to a sensual gyration, it was just this side of public sex.

The incubus looked somewhat wistful. "Many people," he said, after a moment. "Rosier, primarily, but bad luck and bad timing played a part. Bad everything, really. It almost couldn't have gone worse."

"Tell me." It wasn't exactly my business, but I'd never had the chance to hear this story from Pritkin's other half. And, if my suspicions were right, I never would again. Pritkin had not looked like a man who intended to repeat this conversation.

"You know most of it," the incubus shrugged. "Rosier wanted a son to help him hold onto power, and after centuries of trying, he finally found a woman who could give him one. She was part fey, but he thought that only to the good. Perhaps it would give her the strength to carry the child to term, unlike his former lovers. He never went beyond that; never for a moment stopped to ask himself how a child might feel, born suspended betwixt heaven and hell."

"Faerie seems pretty hellish to me," I said.

"And so it can be. Just as the hells have their redeeming side, although Pritkin never saw it. Rosier compounded his error, leaving him to grow up on Earth, completely alienated from his native world."

"Earth is his native world, too," I pointed out. "And Rosier told me once that he thought he was doing him a favor. That if Pritkin didn't turn out to have demon magic, he'd be better off on Earth than in the hells."

"Perhaps," the incubus said. "Or perhaps it was easier than constantly defending a child—one who might turn out to be useless. We'll never know, will we? But the point is that Pritkin did have magic—entirely too much of it. It hadn't fully manifested then, but it was there, a tangled mass of conflicting abilities, leaving him unsure of what, or who, he was. And Rosier's decision to leave him on Earth, where he interacted with humans and—especially—fey, those beautiful, powerful, seductive creatures that his mother had so adored—"

"Confused him even more," I finished. I'd seen that much with my own eyes, when I'd traveled back in time to find him. I'd ended up in sixth century Wales, following Pritkin's soul as it flashed back through the eras of his life, after the demon council cursed it to unravel all the way to the moment of his conception. And then to wink out.

They had wanted a way to kill him that even a time traveler couldn't counter, and they'd nearly found one. But their decision had given me a unique window onto Pritkin's early life. And it had been eye-opening.

I'd discovered that his father hadn't been the only one looking for power. His mother had been, too, in a different way. Morgaine was the granddaughter of Nimue, leader of the Green or Water Fey. But she hadn't been treated like it.

Her mother had been half human—Nimue's mixed blood daughter, Igraine. Nimue had used Igraine to round up other humans to be sent back to Faerie to serve as brood mares for the Green Fey, who needed human fertility to provide them with soldiers for their never-ending wars. Nimue had promised to take her daughter to Faerie one day as a reward for her service, but that day never came, and it never would have.

Human blood was useful in the fey understanding, but tainted. Nimue's part human descendants would never see Faerie, never sit the throne, never be anything but useful slaves on Earth. The hope of anything else was merely a carrot to be dangled forever in front of them that they would never be allowed to catch.

It was something that Morgaine had eventually figured out. And had refused to be a slaver like her mother, instead being determined to force the fey to accept her, and give her what she viewed as her rightful place. She had slept with Rosier, not out of love or even lust, but because of his gift, which allowed him to greatly magnify power during sex for both parties involved. And which, on occasion, could also pass abilities from one partner to the other.

She'd known that he had been with many women, some of them part fey, and she wanted their magic. And she got it, adding to her natural ability with water, talents with earth, air and fire as well. She'd claimed all four elements in the end, something that no other fey had ever done, and had thought it would be enough. That they must love her then!

But they hadn't loved her. They had rejected her as polluted, horrific, cursed. She hadn't received the power naturally; she had stolen it from a demon lord, and they wanted nothing to do with her.

Or her equally tainted child.

"I'm glad that mother had an epiphany at the end," the incubus said, as if following my thoughts. "And realized what a hash she and father had made out of everything, but that doesn't change it, does it? She abandoned us, father stuck us with a pig farmer and his shrew of a wife, and no one gave us any mentoring, any care, any instruction at all."

"Rosier said he sent the bard Taliesin—"

"The sot, you mean?" the incubus said dryly. "He was in his cups by noon, if he lasted that long. He was primarily there to see that we didn't get ourselves killed. We learned some things from him, yes—reading, writing, how to play a lute—but nothing about who we were, or who we could be. What we learned there, we learned on our own, and despite my brother's supposed hatred of power, we were drawn to it.

"And, tell me, Cassie, who were the strongest people around?"

I didn't have to think about that one.

"The fey."

Chapter Six

T he incubus nodded, and pulled me away from a group of drunken sailors who were spilling out of a pub, and who I would have assumed were human except for the gills in their necks. A rousing drinking song followed them into the night; at least, it would have been one at normal speed. At whatever speed we were currently experiencing the music had a strangely mournful tone, coming to my ears in somber, stretched out notes.

> I'll leave all my people, both my friends and my foes;
> From the prettiest girls in this world I will go;
> But from you, my darling, oh, never, oh no!
> Till I lie in my coffin stretched cold and low.
>
> For you are my delight, my delight, my delight,
> You are my delight and my darling,
> You are my delight, my comfort all night,
> And I'll cherish you until the morning.

It sounded like a Greek chorus, I thought, shivers creeping up my spine. And you knew things were bad when one of those showed up. I hurried past, but if the incubus noticed, he didn't comment.

He just continued his story, which wasn't much more cheerful.

"My other half fell in love with the fey," he said. "Just as mother had. Or with the idea of them, which bore little resemblance to the truth. But it was hard to see that then. They were the ones who first trained us in magic, after one of their religious orders took pity on us following Nimue's rejection. She was disgusted by our demon blood, appalled by the anger that an abandoned child would obviously carry, and worried about our strength.

"But Pritkin didn't see her prejudices, her blindness, or her outrage. He only saw his own inadequacy. Once again, no one wanted him. And why?"

"Because they were stupid," I said, which won me a small smile.

"Because of this," the incubus shoved out his forearm. "Because of the blood he didn't want, but could not deny."

"But Rosier didn't reject his demon blood," I said. "He wanted it, and the magic that went with it—"

"But a lonely little boy didn't know that, Cassie. Only that his father had left, that they all had, because he wasn't good enough. It spurred him to study, to learn, to grow his skills. To prove his worth. And, for a while, it felt like we had." His eyes grew distant. "We were happy for a time; we had friends; we knew who we were—or we thought we did. Surrounded by other part-fey children, the ones who didn't have enough magic to be useful and who had been dumped back on Earth . . . well, we didn't seem all that different. For once, we were just . . . ourselves."

"Until Rosier came back," I said grimly.

"Until Rosier came back," he agreed. "To see how his little experiment was going. And he—oh, he was thrilled with our power, wasn't he? So proud of the strong son he'd made! And then it was all gone in an instant, as we were dragged off to the hells without a moment's notice. Without even a chance to say goodbye.

"For what was the human world, that we should miss it?"

He gazed around, and the colors of the night shown in his eyes. It made them look otherworldly for a moment, strange, fire-lit, and boiling with sparks. Beautiful—

Until he shook his head, and smiled at me once more.

"And yet, even then, it could have worked, had he approached it the right way. But that wasn't likely, was it?"

"Wasn't it?" I asked, feeling strangely off-kilter.

"No. Father's own upbringing had been lacking, to say the least. Grandfather had been disgusted with his too-soft son, who reminded him more of his wife than the manly warrior he had wanted. And thus, he didn't train him much at all, didn't teach him, didn't prepare him for rule that he was never meant to have. It caused father to struggle terribly, just to keep his throne, after grandfather died.

"He was trying to do better by us, to give us all the training that had been denied to him. But he rushed it. It was too much, too fast, too everything. He didn't bother to think that we'd just been stripped away from the only home we'd ever known, our friends, our lovers, our entire world. Even the cool greenness was gone, the soft summer rains, the rushing gray rivers and crashing seas. It was an arid, dry, desert world we woke up to, lovely, yes, in its own way, but foreign. Everything was."

"And people were trying to kill you," I said, remembering what Pritkin had told me once. He'd had to flee his father's world for Rosier's secondary court on another world, in order to save his life. And it had been a close thing, even there.

The incubus shrugged. "They were trying to test us, although some were certainly jealous. Father hadn't expected that, as it hadn't happened to him. But then, he was a known quantity and fully demon. We weren't, and needed to be vetted. But the constant attacks, plus father's idea of training, which exposed my other half to some of the less . . . salubrious . . . parts of the hells too soon . . . it was too much.

"Pritkin went from shocked and confused, yet cautiously excited—to have a father, to feel wanted, to see a vast universe opening up before him—to the opposite, very quickly. All those old fears and doubts came rushing back. He was horrified by some of the things he saw, frightened of the changes he felt happening in him, dismayed by thoughts of what he might become. Father took him to a High Council meeting to show him off, to introduce his heir to the other lords, but all Pritkin saw were monsters.

"It all fell apart very quickly, after that."

"He freed a slave girl," I said, remembering something I'd been told. "And killed a demon lord in the process . . ."

"And was promptly exiled for it. The other lords didn't know what to think of him, this strange hybrid that Rosier had created, who was too alien and too powerful and looked at them as if they were dung under his bootheel. And, worse, who had the blood of their old enemies in his veins, the ones they feared and hated above all others.

"Nimue carried the blood of the ancient gods, and thus, so did we. And thin though it was, the demon lords feared it and wanted us gone, and Pritkin was more than glad to oblige them. But when he returned to Earth . . ."

"Everything had changed," I whispered. I'd known much of this before, but I'd never put it all together, never thought about the effects of blow after blow on a young man with little life experience, and little time to absorb each one before the next one fell.

And then to finally escape, to return to the place he must have dreamed of, only to find that he didn't recognize it anymore. Time ran differently on Earth than in the hells. And while it hadn't felt like

Pritkin had been away all that long to him, hundreds of years had passed here.

His world had been swept away, and replaced by one he didn't know at all.

And where, once again, he didn't fit in.

"And then dear Ruth came along," the incubus finished. "Just when we finally—once again—had begun to build a life. She shattered it to pieces, tried to steal our power and ended up forfeiting hers—as well as her life. And thus gave Pritkin a perfect excuse to lock away the last of his demon blood for good."

"But you can't really blame him," I began, only to be savagely cut off.

"Can't I?" Green eyes blazed. "I who bore the brunt of his pain, his fear? Yes, I bloody well can! I understand him—of course, I do. What else have I had to do all these years, but think? But understanding doesn't excuse. We need him—demonkind, humankind, every kind—to be what he was meant to be. To put aside the fear and explore his power—and we need him now. It's been a hard road, yes, but its going to be a harder one if—"

"If we miss this while you're busy whining," Pritkin said sharply, suddenly appearing in the road in front of us. And pulling me into an alley, where I saw Nigel splayed against a wall, just up ahead.

The big part-fey looked completely freaked out, with his barrel chest moving quickly up and down, his eyes huge, and his grubby fingers gripping the bricks behind him as if he was trying to dig into them. Possibly because he'd ended up in exactly the type of place that Pritkin had said he should avoid. Only this alley didn't look so bad.

It wasn't all that dark, for one thing, being splashed with light from the street and from a string of paper lanterns overhead, made to look like gaping fish. I guessed they belonged to the food vendor who had set up shop at the alley's mouth, where he was frying up what looked like a whole boatload of fillets on a griddle. The lanterns swung in the breeze over his head, advertising his wares regardless of what language someone spoke, and shedding soft blue, green and white light down onto his stall.

The lanterns didn't highlight Nigel, however, who was farther back in the shadows. Until he tore himself away from the wall and took off again, heading for an outdoor staircase on the side of a building, where colorful graffiti glowed against the bricks. The words weren't in any language I knew, but Pritkin must have been familiar with this one, because they rearranged themselves into readable phrases as I approached.

Some were ads for local businesses, with somewhat scathing reviews of the same scribbled underneath them. A few looked like something kids had done, with a big-eyed doll with trailing ringlets, and two stick fighters fighting with swords. While others touted the charms of somebody named Fat Bottomed Bessie, with two round globes sketched alongside the words that I assumed was meant to be the body part in question, and which was twerking at me suggestively.

I stared at it as we mounted the sagging wooden steps. I didn't think the movement was due to the flowing light from the street; I was pretty sure that Bessie's assets were actually jiggling. But before I could ask, the street winked out again, when Nigel disappeared through the door at the top of the stairs.

"—antidote, damn you!"

The angry voice was a man's, causing Nigel to pause halfway down a narrow hall. He'd just dropped the silence spell he'd used to get in the door, which had popped his ears and left him slightly disoriented. And that wasn't what he'd hoped to hear.

He'd expected womanly giggles, soft male replies, maybe even the sounds of them already going at it, depending on how impatient the woman was to get her mark into a vulnerable state.

Instead, what was this?

"I have a commission," the woman said fiercely, her formerly dulcet tones nowhere to be found.

"Which I'll double if he lives," the man's voice snapped. "If he doesn't, you can pay me—in blood. Now get it!"

Nigel heard the woman's soft footsteps hurrying away, while he remained where he was, caught in indecision. He didn't want to stay, but he didn't want to go back to that awful street, either. He wanted to get paid, and he wanted a safe way out of here, and the woman could provide both.

He just needed to get her alone.

He slowly edged down the hall, to where he could just see the pretty, dark-haired assassin through a crack in a doorway, coming back into a small sitting room. She did not look happy. She had a bottle in her hand, which she handed over to someone Nigel couldn't see from this angle.

Until he adjusted his position a bit, and managed to bring an enormously tall, fat man into view. He was so large that Nigel briefly considered giant's blood, but giant's blood didn't make one's stomach do that. Nigel felt a chill go up his spine at the way the man's enormous belly churned under his smart gray suit, like a pregnant woman's after the baby has started to kick.

The street outside was looking better all the time.

The fat man took the bottle and bent over another man who was sprawled, unconscious, on a settee. Nigel recognized the subject of his evening's surveillance, now boneless and with his eyes closed. His blond hair was still damp from the night's fog, despite the cheery fire in the nearby fireplace, and Nigel had to give the woman credit.

That had been quick work.

But the fat man—the fat demon, he supposed—did not seem impressed. He pulled up the blond man's head and forced the entire contents of the bottle down his throat, massaging the muscles so that he would swallow it. Then they waited, the demon keeping an eye on the man's face and the woman pacing agitatedly.

"I didn't know he was of interest to you," she said. "I would never have involved myself if—"

"Who commissioned you?"

That brought her up short. "I—I'm not supposed to say. One can acquire a reputation—"

"Then let me tell you," the demon said, without taking his eyes off the blond man's face. "An intermediary contacted you, old Silas, one of your usual touts—"

"How did you know that?" it was sharp.

"He was rather forthcoming, after some persuasion. I assume it was a different sort than the kind you used."

"I don't know what you mean." That time, her voice was icy.

"Ah, forgive me," the demon's voice was vaguely mocking. "I simply meant that the fee was outrageous, far higher than normal, so of course you would want the name of the originator. You're too professional to risk getting drawn into a vendetta." He finally shot her a look. "You must have been surprised to get such a lofty commission. Or do you usually work for a king of the light fey?"

She didn't bother to deny it. "No. First time—and the last."

"Yet it was a lucrative contract, and the Svarestri do not often frequent Earth. You must have hoped that this would be the start of a profitable arrangement."

The woman didn't answer, but she bit her lip.

"What, precisely, were your instructions, may I ask?"

It was put politely, but even Nigel could tell it was an order.

The woman must have thought so, too, because she didn't hesitate this time. "To kill him. Immediately."

"Nothing else?"

She shook her head. "No, disposal of the body was left up to me."

"That wasn't what I meant."

She frowned.

The fat demon was silent for a moment, before moving to a chair by the settee and lowering his large, oddly shaped body into it. "Port," he said. "And something for yourself."

The woman moved out of frame to comply, and Nigel thought about taking the opportunity to slip away. But there was always a chance that the demon would leave first. He seemed interested in keeping the blond man alive, and if he survived, he might just take him and go.

Leaving Nigel alone with a woman who killed by poison, since she wasn't strong enough to manage it another way.

He stayed where he was.

She was back in a moment, with two glasses and an entire decanter of ruby liquid. She poured the drinks, then awkwardly sat on the only other surface available, a tufted pouf near the man's feet. She looked uncomfortable, but she was clearly treating him with kid gloves.

They sipped in silence for a moment, or at least, the demon did. The woman didn't look like she had a taste for it. Nigel would have made her drink first, all things considered, but the demon didn't look worried.

She did, though. She kept glancing at the blond man while trying not to look like it. Must have been strong, whatever she'd given him.

She didn't look like she was sure that the antidote would work.

"You weren't hired to kill him," the demon said suddenly.

The woman started, enough to send a bit of wine sloshing over the lip of her glass and onto her pretty blue skirts.

"My lord?"

"You were hired to capture him. Others—powerful mages and fey operatives—had tried and failed. It was decided to use a different strategy."

"But . . . that's not possible," her voice went noticeably higher. "I was given strict instructions. I could not have misunderstood!"

"You didn't. And Silas didn't make a mistake. The change in the order came from the source, a fey functionary named Dahlman."

"He defied the king's orders?" It sounded like she found that hard to believe, but the demon nodded.

"Easy to forget about functionaries," he said, with a sigh. "They're always there, to the point that they become like furniture. But they have eyes and ears, and a select few know how to use them."

"I don't understand."

The demon glanced around the well-appointed room. It was a cheerful burgundy, with furnishings and accessories that screamed comfortably middle class. Unlike the boarding house, which had had her scent all over it, but which was far less respectable.

Nigel didn't know if she preferred to live here, in more comfortable surroundings, or if she merely took her marks here, to dispose of them with no witnesses around. With the ruckus outside, nobody would notice a little extra screaming, assuming a hit went awry. She thought of everything, she did.

"You've set yourself up nicely," the demon said, in apparent agreement. "But this can't be all you want out of life, surely?"

"I—I don't intend to do this forever. I bought an investment property recently, down the road. A boarding house—"

"A boarding house." The amused pity in his eyes made even Nigel flinch. "On Earth. In a slum."

The woman's back had already been ramrod straight, thanks to her corset. But now her shoulders joined it. Nigel couldn't see her face unless she was looking at the blond, as she was turned away from him. But he didn't need her expression to see that the blow had landed.

"It's a stepping stone," she said tightly.

"To what? A slightly better boarding house? You're never getting out of here—"

"I am!"

"—without help."

The woman, who was nobody's fool, suddenly froze. "I . . . would very much appreciate . . . help," she said carefully.

The demon toyed with his wine glass, which she hurriedly refilled.

"Then let me tell you a story," he said. "One that I think you might find . . . of personal interest."

Chapter Seven

The demon settled back into his chair, which groaned alarmingly under his weight, with the sound of nearly splintering wood. Although that wasn't nearly as alarming as the way the giant belly moved. It adjusted to his new stance independently of the rest of the body, as if there was something in there that was listening, and wanted to be comfortable, too.

Nigel licked his lips, tasting whisky and fear, and thought again about leaving. He was a small time operative; this was well beyond his reach. But the demon was speaking again and, sometimes, information was more valuable than gold.

"Long ago, in the age of the gods, war was brewing," the demon said. "They were ungovernable creatures, the so-called gods, greedy, grasping, vicious, never at peace for long and always wanting more. I think they thought that coming here, that finding a way into an entirely new universe, one where they were so much more powerful than any native force . . . well. That it would be enough.

"But nothing ever was; nothing ever could be. Contentment was not in their nature. Not when so few of them had the ability to make their way into the hells, where powerful demon lords waited, full of *millennia of stored power and ripe for the plucking. They were much tastier than anything to be found in the realm of men, but they couldn't be plucked if they couldn't be reached, and most of the gods failed to get past the enchantments that guard our worlds. They had to wait for their prey to come to them.*

"And while they waited, they fumed, they seethed, and they fought, each jealous of the other, each plotting to bring down their rivals. But as soon as they did so, the moment that one fell, the remainder turned on their former allies and savaged them instead. The demon lords saw, and we realized: we could not overcome them on our own, but we could perhaps help them to destroy themselves.

"It didn't appear to be an impossible task. Rumors abounded that war was coming. There had been one already, when two rival camps of gods fought for dominance, and another could not be far off. Everyone knew it; everyone felt it, and we demons did all that we could to encourage it. Whispers in this ear; warnings in that; messages deliberately designed to be intercepted, and to ramp up the gods' suspicious and jealous natures.

"Having them kill themselves off seemed like our best chance for survival, and we worked tirelessly toward it. All without knowing: one of their own was plotting, too, and far better than we. But not so well that someone else didn't notice."

"Someone else?" the woman said, a little breathless. She sounded like Nigel felt, like all this was beyond her. But she leaned in nonetheless.

"Oh, yes," the demon sipped wine, with ridiculous daintiness for one so huge. *"Their king approached me during one of my trips to Earth. I had been tasked as a spy by the Demon High Council, to keep them informed as to what the gods were planning to do next."* He made a moue of distaste. *"As if most of them ever planned anything.*

"That was why we found them so difficult to predict. They were capricious, like overpowered children, and all the deadlier for it. Although I must say, Zeus schemed better than most. You can imagine how surprised I was to find that some of those schemes involved me."

"He approached you?" the woman sounded puzzled. "You mean to say, he attacked you?"

The demon glanced at her. "No, although I can understand your confusion. I, too, expected to be a light supper. But instead, he wanted my help."

"Your help?" Now she sounded astonished. "What could one of us do for one of them, except to die?"

"Help him not to," the demon said dryly. "He was worried about one of his fellow gods. She whose memory will be reviled forevermore—"

"Artemis?"

He scowled. "I would prefer that you not use that name. But yes, word of her depredations in the hells had reached his ears, reached and worried him. He did not care that she left our realms in blazing ruins, but he did care—very much—about what she did with the power she obtained thereby. She had already been strong, long before she invaded us; what was she becoming? He didn't know, but he feared, and he chafed at the fact that one of her gifts was to pass so easily through our defenses, whereas he . . . could not.

"Or, rather, he could not unassisted."

The woman made a surprised sound. "You mean—"

"Yes," the demon shrugged. "He often did that sort of thing. Broke off a bit of his soul and put it into others, riding them around without their knowledge, whilst gaining much for himself. Yet he wasn't sure that he could manage it with a demon lord, since it was only a small part of his power, which might end up feeding one of us instead of controlling us. Yet a weaker being could not take him

everywhere he wished to go. He therefore offered me an arrangement: help him, and he would spare me and my world in the coming conflict."

"But . . . your world wasn't spared, if I remember my history correctly—"

"You remember it." The words were clipped. "But my story isn't over yet."

He leaned his head back against the chair and stared moodily at the fire. It gleamed on his wine, on the woman's dark hair, on the fine ormolu clock on the mantel that was busily ticking away the seconds. But the demon was in no hurry.

The woman finally drank her wine, giving Nigel the impression that she merely wished for something to do. He couldn't see her face, but he knew it was being kept carefully blank. She was cautious, this one, not even her mannerisms gave anything away.

But he didn't need them. He could read her like a book, because she was just like him. Growing up on these unforgiving streets, constantly angry that others with lesser skills got ahead and she stayed in the gutter, where society had decided she belonged. And where it felt like they were determined to keep her, come what may.

But she had different plans. He could almost see the wheels turning in that pretty head; why was the demon telling her this? What did he want from someone like her, and how could she use it to her advantage? How could she make sure that this night was the first of a new and better life?

Nigel felt the same, determined to get a piece of whatever she was being offered—for his silence, for his help, for something. He'd work it out. Instead of enemies, they could be partners, two half breeds against the world.

He liked the sound of that.

"It was an interesting sensation," the demon finally said. "I who had invaded so many others' bodies, to find my own being used as transport. But I carried him where he wanted to go, nonetheless, for what choice did I have? And once Zeus was in place, I had no way to alert my people, no way to resist, no way to do anything but follow his commands. And shadow the great defiler of worlds on her latest conquest, despite the risk."

"If she'd seen you—" the woman began, her hand on her breast.

"I would have been dead like all the rest. And Zeus would have found another cat's paw. But my years as a spy stood me in good stead, and I was not discovered. We tracked her across the hells, past worlds beyond memory, and what do you think we found?"

The woman, who had been leaning in as the story continued, almost toppled over as he let the pause draw out. "What?" she asked. "What did you find?"

The demon lord nodded at the blond. "That one's grandfather. She who's name will be cursed throughout the ages had entered his realm to assault him."

"His . . . grandfather? But I was told that he was weak, merely a part-demon. I was told that he wasn't a threat. I was told—"

"Calm yourself," the fat demon said, as her voice had gotten a bit shrill. "You were told correctly. He is half incubus—not what one would normally consider the staunchest of opponents."

"Incubus? But aren't they—"

"Spirits, without bodies of their own?" He nodded. "Normally, yes. But the royal house has many gifts that the lesser sort do not. Another of which is to magnify power, many times over, during sexual congress. To take a small amount and make it large; to take a large amount and make it huge; and to take an already colossal amount, the kind derived from assaulting a thousand worlds, and make it . . . god destroying."

"She intended to take him on," the woman said, her voice soft and amazed. "She intended to take on the king of the gods."

The fat demon looked at her mockingly. "Now you have forgotten your history. She intended to take them all on. To rule this universe alone, yet there wasn't enough demon blood in all of the hells for that. Her raids had taught her that much, and she despaired, until learning of one famously weak race which could make her . . . invincible."

"And it did," the woman said, her voice awestruck. "She used his power, made herself stronger than the entire pantheon, and took this space, all of it, for herself. Determined to be ruled by no one!"

"You almost sound as if you admire her," the demon said, his voice deceptively gentle.

The woman didn't miss the threat. "No," she said, without missing a beat. "No, not at all. That's . . . merely the story everyone knows."

"Yes, that's the story," he said dryly. "What the story doesn't recount is that she missed one. She fought the other gods, killing or banishing them from her realm, but one remained—or part of one."

"You mean . . . the piece you carried?"

The woman was quick, Nigel thought. He hadn't understood what the demon was getting at. But now . . .

His eyes grew wide.

The demon nodded, and drank more wine.

"But shouldn't it have been banished with all the rest?" she asked.

Her companion shrugged. "I can only tell you what I know. Once that one's grandfather was killed, his realm closed down. The portals around their world slammed shut as soon as the great defiler left, and stayed that way for some time. And no amount of bribing, cajoling or threats would open them up again.

"By the time we finally managed to return, it was all over. Earth and the demon realms were engulfed in war, with everyone trying to take advantage of the new order. My world was scorched, as were many others, practically to ruins. And the council was in disarray, scarcely managing to hold anything together. Whereas the gods . . ."

"Were gone," she whispered.

"Except for one. Perhaps being in a far-flung demon realm instead of on Earth had protected that bit of soul, or perhaps being inside my body had done the trick. But the piece of himself that Zeus had broken off remained and was leeching my power, as it no longer had a source of its own.

"It forced me back into the hells, afraid of she who will be reviled forevermore. She had been wounded in the battle, severely from what I heard, and had gone to ground. Many thought that she had died, but we knew better. He could sense her, and for the first time in his life, great Zeus trembled.

"For while she was wounded, he was a shadow of his former self. Merely a tiny scrap of his once vast power, now cut off from the rest, and caught among hostile enemies. I was his only ally, and I was unwilling."

"You couldn't break away?" she sounded surprised. Nigel wondered how powerful this being was supposed to be.

"No," the demon said. "Although I did not tell him that. I pretended to sympathize with his plight, to hate his enemies— including those who had destroyed my world—and to want both revenge and reward, once the gods returned.

"He therefore decided to tarry in the hells, where time runs faster than on Earth. To see what she would do, to wait for her to die, and to build up his strength. He even wanted me to go back to my world, to gather up what few of us remained, and to feed him their power— what little they had left."

"And . . . did you?" she asked tentatively.

Nigel wouldn't have asked at all.

His instincts were better than hers, it seemed, because the demon's eyes flashed dangerously. "No," he said flatly. "I did not. I told him that it might alert others to his presence, as it would be out of character. That seemed to surprise him, as if he had assumed that we were no better than them, feeding wherever we can, on whatever we can, like a pack of wild dogs, like carrion eaters. The gods are savages; they understand nothing but power!"

"Power is important," the woman said diffidently, playing with the fringe on her pouf. "Particularly for those who have none."

The demon eyed her narrowly for a moment, before slowly reclining back against the chair again. "So it is," he agreed. "And mine was waning. Centuries of accumulated energy had been siphoned from me, almost all that I had. Yet Zeus knew if he let me die, he would be left with no protection, and with enemies on all sides.

"He finally decided to risk a return to Earth, where he hoped that the centuries would have destroyed his great foe. But alas. He felt her presence and fled once again, this time into Faerie."

The woman shuddered, and the demon agreed. "Pernicious place, full of fell creatures. But some of them remained loyal. I pawned him off on King Aeslinn—a true believer in those days. He was actually happy to take the vicious leech."

"In those days?" the woman repeated.

The fat demon smiled. "One should never meet one's idols. Particularly not when the meeting is so . . . prolonged."

"And now?" she asked. "Where is it now, this remnant?"

He shrugged. "With Aeslinn. Who has discovered that feeding a god is not so easy, or so rewarding, as he had hoped. Which is where you come in."

"Me?" The woman sounded surprised, as if she had almost forgotten why she was being told all this.

"I have certain long-term plans in the works," the demon said. "Having a light shone on Earth would interfere with them. A light such as the death of Rosier's son."

"Which is why you wish to save him."

The demon inclined his head. "However, I cannot allow Zeus to use him to multiply his strength, as the world defiler once did to his grandfather. Nor can I watch the boy night and day, or have my people do so, without attracting attention. I need someone at his side. Someone no one will notice. Someone who can alert me if there are signs of further interest."

The woman looked at the blond again, and Nigel saw her frown. "But if I fail in my task, the king will merely send another. Likely within a week. That was all the time I was given."

"Leave that to me. I have ways of making things slip Aeslinn's mind. And Zeus, in his current state, relies on his host's abilities. Erase the king's mind, and it will fog the remnant's—for a time."

"How long of a time?"

"Long enough." The demon didn't look like he was used to being questioned.

"And what do you wish me to see to? Exactly." Her voice was suddenly harder than before. But then, they were negotiating, and Nigel knew that dance as well as anyone. Look weak now and it would cost her.

But the demon did not look interested in haggling. "Your usual fee times ten," he said casually. "Per week. That should buy any number of boarding houses soon enough."

"For doing what?" the woman insisted. Her voice hadn't changed, but her hand had clenched on the side of the pouf—the side away from the demon. She wanted this; wanted it badly. But she also *wanted to know what she was getting into. "Merely alerting you to any signs of danger? What if I miss them?"*

"Make sure that you don't," the demon said dryly. "Stick to his side; make him fond of you. I know you know how to do that."

"And what else?" Her voice remained hard. She didn't like being reminded of what she was.

"Nothing more than you were planning to do in any case. If I send word, it means they have remembered or been reminded, and my efforts to prevent them from coming for him have failed. In that case, you are to kill him immediately."

"But . . . I thought you said that would interrupt your plans."

"Less so than the return of the gods," he said dryly. "I prefer him alive, but I need insurance. Now, do we have—" He broke off abruptly, and cocked his head. "Ah. It seems that we have a visitor."

"What?" the woman said, and spun, surprisingly fast, toward the door.

Chapter Eight

"What happened?" I asked, as the scene froze, leaving us crowding the narrow hall behind a startled looking Nigel. "Why did it stop?"

"He died," Pritkin said hoarsely, and broke away, heading for the stairs.

A hand caught my wrist as I started to follow. "Don't," the incubus said. "Give him a moment."

I jerked my arm free and pushed past him.

"Or not," he said. "I'll just, er, I'll just stay up here, shall I?"

I didn't answer. The brief pause had cost me time, and Pritkin was already out of the door. And while I could hear his footsteps hitting the sagging steps outside, he'd cleared them by the time my own feet touched the ground. I glanced at the fish seller, whose silly looking lanterns were flapping in the breeze, like the day's catch twisting on a line. He was doing a bang-up business, and it didn't look like any war mages had shoved their way through the thick crowd around him recently.

So, I looked the other way, and spotted Pritkin at the far end of the alley, facing an old brick wall with some fading advertising posters on it and a wooden door set into it. But he wasn't headed through the door. He was just standing there, staring at it.

I walked that way.

It was darker down here, and quieter, away from the busy street. There was a little ambient light from above—not starlight, which couldn't penetrate the city's smoggy haze, or the moon, which was absent tonight. Just a thin yellow sheen slicked the darkness, from distant streetlamps and house windows on the other side of the wall. It clashed with a bluish blush from the street behind us, which limned the side of Pritkin's face as I approached.

He turned slightly, and for a moment, was bisected by the two shades. Pale gold leaking through a gap in the door gilded one cheek, and bleached the eyelashes on that side of his face nearly to invisibility. While pale blue silvered the other half, making it look gaunt, almost alien, and colored his fair hair.

It reminded me of the disguise I'd seen him wear once in medieval Wales, when he'd taken on the persona of another part fey, part human. He'd looked like someone had cut one of each down the middle and sewn them together, with ebony hair on one side and silver on the other, and different skin and eye colors. It had been a completely over the top look, which was probably why he'd gotten away with it.

Nobody had thought that someone in hiding would dare to draw so much attention to themselves. Or take on an identity so easy to remember. But Pritkin had been hiding all his life, one way or the other, and he was good at it.

Except for now.

Now, his face was naked, with his emotions laid bare, and more vulnerable than I'd ever seen it.

I didn't say anything. I'd intended to, but the words stuck in my throat and wouldn't come. I was off balance, with my head buzzing and my body cold. I wanted a moment, as well, but I also wanted to be with him.

In the end, I just held him, my arms going around him automatically from behind. It felt good, the solidity of him, the warmth despite the loss of his coat, because Pritkin was always warm. The way his body fit mine, as if we'd been designed to go together, like two puzzle pieces that only made sense when joined together.

I hugged him hard and held on, and despite the fact that I'd meant to comfort him, I felt my own breathing even out after a few moments.

The air was colder here, away from the street, where the press of bodies and the fire barrels had driven away much of the chill. The fog was back, too, although not as much as when I'd come in. Instead of a waist high haze, it had formed itself into smoky tendrils slithering across the ground like ghostly snakes.

I watched them for a while, my cheek against the warmth of Pritkin's back, and eventually, he spoke.

"Did you understand all that?"

His voice was a rasp, and barely recognizable. But mine was clear when I answered. I wasn't calm, but somewhere along the line my brain had decided to remain functional.

"More or less," I whispered. "I'm sorry."

"For what?"

I started to answer, but then I paused, because where to start? My mother slaughtering his grandfather to get the energy for her war? Her actions thrusting an unprepared Rosier into a position that intimidated the hell out of him, and for which he'd never been adequately prepared? And which had resulted in him looking for a powerful son to back him up?

It turned out that my mother was the reason Pritkin existed at all, as well as being the source of most of his problems.

It was kind of dizzying.

Or maybe we could start with the fact that his hatred of demonkind hadn't saved him from being hunted for his father's blood. I didn't know why Zeus hadn't gone after Rosier instead; maybe he thought the half breed son would be an easier target. Or maybe it was because Rosier was paranoid, not even trusting his own court, and was rarely anywhere that he was supposed to be.

It seemed that, for once, that the old man had been right about something.

And if that wasn't enough, maybe we could chat about Pritkin's wife being an assassin who had been paid to be with him—and to kill him, if it came to that. That would be a fun conversation. He'd known about my mother, at least in part, but he hadn't known about Ruth.

And how hard must that have been, even after all these years? To hear that someone you'd held in your arms, and promised to love and cherish, had never been remotely who you'd thought? He'd known that she had deceived him, that she'd tried to steal power from him, but this?

I guessed she must have decided that even the king's ransom she was being paid wasn't enough, when she could have the wealth of a whole world and power besides. Instead of being a flunky, she'd be another Artemis, a conqueror who took what she wanted. And, of course, she'd never bothered to think about what that would do to the man she betrayed.

After all, why should she?

She'd never loved him anyway.

I felt my fist clench against Pritkin's stomach, as it had back in that cramped hallway. Where I'd had to listen to a couple of bastards haggling over price while he fought for his life on the damned settee. For the first time, I had an emotion about Ruth, and it was violent.

His hand covered mine, as if he understood.

"Everything," I said harshly, and he nodded. But he said nothing.

It didn't look like he knew where to start, either.

After another moment, I let him go and sat on the bottom of a second set of steps, trying to order my thoughts. It wasn't easy. The demon's conversation had been short, but it had packed a punch.

"At least I know what Zeus meant now," I finally said. "In that vision he sent me."

"What vision?"

I moved over, to make room, but Pritkin didn't join me. He didn't look like he could have sat down if his life depended on it. Energy practically thrummed off him, but I didn't know what kind and I couldn't read his expression.

It was strange, I thought, looking up at him. I knew the mask he wore so well, could have explained every nuance, every gesture, the meaning behind every clipped word. But this strangely open face . . . I didn't know at all.

He was in pain, but I wasn't sure why. There was so much to choose from. Like the big thing we had to talk about, the one that the demon hadn't spelled out. The one that had made me let go of Pritkin sooner than I'd wanted to, since I was afraid that he'd feel me trembling.

I searched his face, but couldn't tell if he'd figured it out yet.

Stupid; he was Pritkin.

Of course, he had.

"During the battle at Gertie's," I said, answering the question he'd asked, instead of the one shivering in the air between us. "When we were fighting him off. He said that he wins no matter what we do."

"Classic intimidation tactic, meant to demoralize you."

"Maybe. Or maybe he meant that he wins because he's already back. We kept focusing on keeping him out, when a part of him never left."

Pritkin didn't reply, but his jaw clenched. I started to speak again, but he slashed a hand through the air violently, stopping me. "How do we know that any of this is real?" he demanded suddenly. "How do we know it isn't another trick, another lie? That is all the gods do—they lie."

"Pritkin—"

He'd started to turn away, as if intending to pace, but now he spun back and went down on one knee to take my hands. "This could all be an illusion," he said fervently. "Not run by some spirit of Faerie, or whatever we're meant to believe, but just another trick—"

"For what?"

"I don't know! To confuse us, make us focus on the wrong things, waste time—"

"Pritkin—"

"—it could be anything! I've never seen the Common like this—nobody has. Not to mention that this memory or vision or whatever it is, is from Earth. We shouldn't be seeing it at all—"

"We're seeing it because Nigel saw it," I reminded him. "And he is part fey—"

"Who died *here*. If his body never went back, his soul was never reabsorbed. And none of this would be in the Common at all!"

"He might have transmitted it back while he lived," I said, even knowing that I was a coward. We had something to discuss, and it wasn't Nigel. It wasn't even my mother or Pritkin's wife, either of which would have been an easier subject. But I postponed that conversation for another moment.

Suddenly, every second seemed precious, like a jewel I clutched with both hands, not wanting to let go.

"Some of the fey seem to have that skill," I added roughly.

"Not a half fey!"

"And we don't know that he died here. He could have had his memories erased. That big demon was the same one who blanked your memory once—and Aeslinn's, making him forget about you for centuries. If he could do that—"

Pritkin shook his head. And didn't ask what I'd meant about his memory, although that would have been the first thing out of his mouth normally. But nothing was normal tonight.

"They would have killed him," he insisted. "They wouldn't have taken that chance—"

"Perhaps they were worried that somebody would remember him. That a witness might have seen him enter that building—"

"That's not how demons think!"

"—and that erasing his memory was easier than answering questions. Or maybe he did die here, but his body somehow made it back to Faerie. Perhaps that's how Ruth disposed of her victims, sending them to another world—"

"Stop it!" Pritkin exploded.

He let go of my hands and abruptly rose to his feet, then started the pacing that he'd aborted before, striding back and forth in front of me. His movements were unaccustomedly jerky and he kept rubbing unconsciously at his neck. But it was his eyes that told me that what I'd suspected was true: they were jerky, too, never lighting on anything for more than a second, as if trying to outrun his thoughts.

"People die here all the time," he finally said. "In this area, they sometimes molder in an alley for days, along with bloated horse carcasses, until somebody gets tired enough of the stink to report them. If they're not someone important, nobody cares!"

"Okay—"

"Or perhaps he had a worse fate," Pritkin continued, not letting me speak. "The Asakku might have jumped at the chance for a new suit, and one that was part fey as well—"

"The what?"

"The demon." He waved a hand back at the building we'd just left. "Asakku are small and frail, and thus form a bond with one of the larger, more dimwitted varieties of demonkind. The Asakku acts as the brains, giving his 'ride' a much better life than it would have had on its own. Meanwhile the Asakku gets a stronger, more mobile body. Or, in this case, one that could carry him into Faerie as easily as Earth."

"Maybe that's how the body got back there, then," I said—and immediately wished I hadn't.

"It didn't get back there! It didn't merge with Faerie! This is a *lie*—"

"And yet another, similar vision showed me the truth about Arsen, which brought him to our side," I pointed out. "Why give me that information—the only thing that allowed us to get out of that camp alive—if someone wasn't trying to help?"

"I don't know—and neither do you. Neither of us understands anything about this!"

"We understand one thing," I said, and then didn't say any more. I'd kept my voice steady, but there was a lump in my throat. Probably from the same reason that had Pritkin arguing about whether a part fey's body had ended up back in Faerie or not. He didn't care about that, any more than I did. He cared about something else. But he didn't want to face it, didn't want to talk about it, didn't even want to edge up onto the subject.

But he had to. We both did. Which was why I got back to my feet and walked up behind him again. He had been about to turn around, but feeling me, he stiffened and stayed where he was.

Yes; he knew.

I slowly circled in front of him, put a hand on his cheek, and turned his face toward mine. The bristles were rough and prickly, but I didn't mind that. Or the sweat that had broken out on his brow, despite the cold. Or the way that his bottom lip trembled slightly under my thumb, and then under my lips when I kissed him.

I did mind the expression in his eyes, when we broke apart, and would have given anything to change it. But there was nothing I could do. Nothing but this.

"You have to let me go," I told him softly. "You have to end Lover's Knot."

Pritkin didn't even try to pretend that he didn't understand. "No."

It was as flat as any word I'd ever heard in my life.

I caught his sleeve with a hand. "Pritkin—"

He shrugged off my hold, almost violently. "I said no!"

"You have to lift the spell!"

"Why?" It was belligerent, almost like the man when I first met him, when he'd had every hackle raised against me. I'd torn them down, one by one, over these long months, as he had mine. But you couldn't tell it now.

Now, they were back up with a vengeance, and the green eyes were as hard as glass. "He has you. Nothing has changed—"

"*Everything* has changed. You know that. You heard—"

"I know nothing of the kind."

And there it was, I thought, staring up at him. The only thing that could successfully war with that powerful intellect: the vast line of stubbornness running through his nature. Not like a single mule, but more like a whole herd.

And, right now, they were galloping.

"Zeus isn't after me," I said, emphasizing each word, making him hear them. "He doesn't want me. Aeslinn did, when he saw me at that castle, the little human who had dared to defy him. But Zeus only became interested after I took in some of his power, when he felt the bond between you and me, and remembered you. And realized that he could get to you through me.

"He wasn't trying to kill me at Gertie's. He was trying to absorb you through our link. But he wouldn't admit it in case it didn't work, in case a piece of a piece of a god couldn't overwhelm us. He was attacking me, but he was trying to get to you."

Pritkin's jaw clenched. "Your power will allow him to bring back the gods—"

"But he won't. Not until he can be sure that he can control them. Your incubus told me once that Zeus would come back with an army, not having to worry about being controlled like Ares or Apollo. But what we just heard showed that he *does* fear revolt—"

"I'm not listening to this."

I grabbed his arm before he could turn away. "Zeus needs your power, or else it'll be just like last time. Constantly having to worry that someone like Artemis is plotting to overthrow him. But with your power, he doesn't have to worry about that—ever again. He knows what mother did, how she cast him down; that's why he's waiting on you, why he hasn't killed me yet. He doesn't want me—"

"But he *has* you! He'll use you as leverage, and if I don't come forward—"

"When you don't."

"—he'll kill you." The voice was suddenly hard, almost cruel. Trying to scare me, trying anything that might work. "He'll strip your soul, add your power to his, and come looking for me anyway. And that time, he'll have time travel on his side. I can't outrun him—"

"You won't have to."

"—so I'll stand and fight him now, before—" he broke off abruptly.

Pritkin was smarter than me; he always had been. He'd gotten this, probably at once, he just wouldn't allow himself to think it. But there simply wasn't any other choice.

"She doesn't expect us to fight," I said gently. "Faerie or whatever her name is. That wasn't why she brought us here."

"Don't."

"She expects me to die. She just wanted to show me why I had to."

Chapter Nine

I'm not listening to this," Pritkin said again, but he was. It was all over his face. I could read it now, and God, I wished I couldn't. But I pressed on anyway, since I didn't have a choice.

"If Zeus uses me to get to you, then it's all over. And it always will be. Nobody will be able to overpower him. Not one of the other gods, not us, not anyone, ever again. Mother used your grandfather's abilities, then killed him, probably so that no one could pull the same trick on her. Or maybe the strain killed him—I don't know. But Zeus doesn't operate like that—"

"Damn it, Cassie!"

"—he thinks long term. Not for one battle, but for all of them, every potential battle to come. He won't use your power, he'll strip your soul and add your gift to his, like Jonathan did to Jo, or Aeslinn did with that giant—"

He tore away, but I followed him, got in front of him.

"—and it will all be over. Your ability ensures that he can make himself more power, as much as he needs, whenever he likes. He felt

it when we battled him, when we won. He knows what you can do—
"

"No!"

"—and I'm going to die anyway! Better that it's by my hand—"

"Why should you?" Pritkin yelled. "*I'm* the one he wants—"

"And I'm the one he has. You said it yourself. And you have to—
"

"No!" he said again, and shook me, hard enough to hurt.

"Pritkin," I said, trying to keep my voice from breaking and not entirely succeeding. "I was dead when he caught me, we just didn't know it yet. We do now."

He released me, abruptly enough that I staggered, then turned around and slammed his fist into the door. The blow must have had a spell behind it, as it disintegrated the entire thing—the door and half of the wall besides. But that still wasn't good enough, because he continued wrecking things, in an out-of-control rampage that had me stumbling back a few yards, while the entire street outside the enclave was systematically demolished.

I felt a hand on my arm, pulling me even farther back, into a hug from behind as wood and bricks flew, as buildings crumbled, and as the road I'd come in on flew up and then apart, exploding into a thousand flying cobblestones.

The incubus and I took shelter behind the staircase, not that much debris was making it this far. Just a few scattered cobbles and a lot of dust. And unearthly howls that weren't rage, that weren't even pain, but which transcended both.

He sounds like a demon, I thought. A powerful demon lord, as the incubus had called him, howling his fury at the night. Because he didn't know how to deal with this any more than I did.

All that power had never helped him, had it? It had only hurt. Ensuring that he lost one world, Faerie, when Nimue turned her back on him; that he lost another, Earth, when Rosier came to claim him;

and that he'd rejected a third, the hells, when he discovered that his power was all that anyone cared about.

But it wasn't what I cared about. I'd loved him when he was nothing but a renegade war mage, on the run from the Silver Circle for refusing to kill me. I hadn't known anything about his background then; hadn't cared.

I still didn't.

"And that is why he loves you," the incubus murmured.

"Can you break it?" I asked him softly.

He didn't reply. But I knew he'd heard me, and that he'd understood. His arms had just reflexively tightened.

"Can you?"

"Perhaps." His voice was a gravelly rasp in my ear.

"Wait until I'm gone," I said, pressing him. "And do it carefully, so that he doesn't know, and doesn't reapply it."

"Cassie—"

"Save him and Mircea. There's no reason they have to die with me—"

"Isn't that their choice to make?"

"No. Not this time."

I turned around, and up close, it was impossible to tell them apart. There were the same pale eyelashes, barely visible in the shadow from the stairs; the same thin mouth, stretched into an unhappy line, until it almost disappeared, too; and the same expression. It was the one Pritkin had worn right before he went ballistic.

Only this one was worse, because it wasn't angry. It was heartbroken. So much that it hurt to look at him, and made me wish that I hadn't turned around.

"If we're linked, Zeus might be able to reach you through me," I said roughly.

"Then why hasn't he?"

"It didn't work last time; he wasn't strong enough—"

"That was merely a piece of a piece of him," the incubus reminded me. "A piece of a piece; just whatever you managed to absorb during the fight."

"—and he's cautious. He probably will try it, but not while there's another way, an easier way. He'll let Pritkin come to him. He knows how we feel about each other, and that you risked your life to save me in London. Why wouldn't you again, especially if you don't know why he wants you? If you think it's an even exchange."

The incubus didn't answer for a moment that time, and when he did, he sounded strangled. "Smarter than they give you credit for," he repeated.

"Then you'll do it?"

No answer.

I clutched his arms. "He'll strip Pritkin's soul without him even being there. And use his power—*your* power—to destroy everything. To wreck Earth, Faerie and the hells, all over again!"

And then I died for nothing.

I didn't say the last part out loud, and neither did the incubus, but it hung in the air between us. I saw something cross his face, some emotion I couldn't read, before he blinked it away. But it was back again almost immediately, as if he couldn't fully control himself.

"I don't think removing the spell will save him," he said hoarsely. "I don't think he can come back from this."

"He can. He did after Ruth—"

"He didn't love Ruth! He wanted to love her, wanted to love someone, wanted someone to love him. But it was a lie. I don't think he really loved anyone until you. And I don't think he can come back. Not this time."

"He can!" I said savagely. I had to have this; had to *know* this. Or I couldn't do what I had to do. "You can help him—yes, you can. You can do this!"

"And what if I love you, too?"

I gazed into clear green eyes, so familiar, so beautiful. And for the first time, I believed him. I believed that he was the same man.

"Then do this for me. Not only the spell but . . . help him. As you've always helped him—haven't you?"

"I've tried, but—" he shook his head. "He won't listen to me, Cassie. He never listens."

"Then make him. He'll need you after . . . make him listen, all right?"

He swallowed. It was silent, but I could see his Adam's apple, bobbing up and down. I had a flash of memory, more sensual than mental—of sucking on it, of feeling it move under my tongue, of biting down and feeling it give, just slightly. Of hearing him moan, in pleasure that time.

Because there had been pleasure, and joy, and happiness, in the middle of all this. In the middle of war and pain and terror, there had been love. And there still was. And I *would have this*.

"He has to live; he has to *remember*. Or what has any of it been for?"

"What has it been *for*?" He blinked at me, and then his face went slack with shock. "What has it been for?"

"I just meant—"

"No, you've talked. Now I do," he said, finally looking angry. The green eyes flashed in the darkness, as if they contained their own light, and maybe they did. I realized suddenly that I knew so little about this side of him, about this version of the man I loved.

And now I never would.

I don't know if something of my thoughts leaked over, but it was his turn to grab me. "You gave us a *life*, do you understand? For the first time—"

He stopped abruptly and turned away, leaving me with throbbing shoulders from how hard he'd gripped me. Then he turned back, and there was some of his counterpart's savagery on his face. For some reason, it startled me.

"We were lost in darkness for so long, that I began to think that was where we were destined to live. That it was all life would ever be. That any last shreds of hope had died with Ruth, and they had not been very bright, in any case.

"Then you came along. Naïve to the point of disbelief, almost completely ignorant of the magical world, much less of the office to which you'd been called. He couldn't understand why the power would pick you, of all people. You seemed so wrong for it: you argued over everything, you ran headlong into danger without a thought, you needlessly risked yourself for others—"

"I didn't—"

"Do you remember the day that MAGIC collapsed?" he demanded, talking about the supernatural version of a United Nations. "Apollo tore open the skies and almost killed himself, getting past your mother's spell. And we were left with a prison full of trapped people, under a glass slick in the desert—one that was about to crush them all, if they didn't drown first.

"We ordered you out of there, thought you had that much sense, at least. Yet you stayed. Stayed when you couldn't help, when you could only die along with us, stayed so that we had to get out, had to find a way—"

"But not this time," I said. "He can't help me this time—"

"That isn't the point I'm making!" the incubus glared at me. "I looked into his heart that day, and saw something I hadn't seen in a very long time, and hadn't expected to see again. A tiny shred of hope, shining in the darkness. A purpose, reignited. A chance to do some good in this world, to help someone he had already grown to admire, although he wouldn't admit it. To protect someone he had already started to love.

"You did that. You reminded us that life was more than the blood pulsing in our veins or a meal in our stomach. It was purpose, meaning, love—a *reason*. You became our reason, and now . . . Cassie, what in the nine hells is he going to do now?"

"Live! Fight. He still has a reason—"

"If you think this has been about the war, then you are a fool, Cassie Palmer. He came back from the brink for you. He risked his life, time and again, for *you*. And now you expect him to stand aside, and let you die?"

"Yes."

He just stared at me. "You *are* mad."

"*Promise me.*"

He looked away again, and when he looked back, his face was bleak. "I promise I will try. Do you want me to send you back now?"

"No, not yet." I could already feel the tug of that other place, wherever it was. This show was over, and another was beginning. But I wasn't ready to go. "Give me a minute."

The destruction in the street had stopped, maybe because there wasn't much left to come down. The alley let out onto the same foggy road I'd come in on, through the now destroyed door. I walked past piles of rubble, past whole buildings that were missing large pieces of what should have been required to hold them up—walls, stairs, foundations. But, since this wasn't real, they didn't fall.

They just stayed there, like a photo with pieces ripped out of it, improbably balanced on whatever was left, and showing nothing whatsoever on the inside, because Nigel hadn't seen that.

Except for one family, which he must have glimpsed through a window, and who were quietly eating dinner around a small table as if nothing had happened. An entire wall of their flat was missing, opening them up to the street, and fog was curling around their table legs. But they didn't notice.

I passed on.

It took me a while to find Pritkin, since the sounds of carnage had quieted. All I could hear were distant, tinny notes of music from the demon enclave, which was also spilling light into the ruined street. Pink, green, yellow and blue, it reminded me of the colored lights on a sandwich seller's cart, in the demon world known as the Shadowland, where I'd first realized that Pritkin might love me, too. Or of the stained glass at Dante's, the colors of which had fallen over his bed in the tiny room that he'd briefly occupied, what felt like a lifetime ago, while on the run from the Silver Circle.

The first time I'd kissed him had been in that room. It felt fitting that the last would be here, in a ruined street like a tumbled down cathedral, that was nonetheless splashed with beauty. And where I finally found him, kneeling in the rubble.

He didn't say anything, although I knew he'd heard me approach. Pritkin had the best spatial awareness of anybody I'd ever seen. He didn't get surprised, and certainly not by me. I'd never learned how to walk quietly even when I wasn't picking my way over a shard-strewn street.

But he didn't speak, so I didn't, either. Just found a piece of flat stone and sat down. With the fog swirling around us, the mountains of debris, and the tinny, almost hurdy gurdy music playing in the background, it felt like a place out of time.

The silence stretched on, but I didn't mind. This hadn't been about that; I'd already said everything. I just wanted another moment, that was all.

But Pritkin did have something left to say.

"I can't do this," he told me, without looking up.

He looked more defeated than I'd ever seen him, with his shoulders slumped, his hair covered with plaster dust, and his shirt torn. I wanted to hold him, but I didn't know if that would make this better or worse. Didn't know anything.

"Pritkin . . ."

"I can't." I got green eyes then, hot and lost and bewildered. "I can fight for you. I can even die for you, as I promised Lady Phemonoe, as I promised you. But I can't do this. You ask too much."

"I'm not asking you to do anything—"

"And that is what I can't do! Sit on the sidelines, while you go off to—no. You cannot ask that of me."

I didn't say anything.

"You *can't*; I *can't*. Do you understand?"

"I understand," I said, and then I did move. To take his face in my hands, and repeat what he'd once said to me. He'd been the first to say anything like that in my life, and the first to mean it. "I understand that you're the strongest person I know."

He stared at me for a moment, and then his face crumpled. He pulled me into a hug so hard that I couldn't breathe, but he didn't say anything else. It was what I'd thought before; there wasn't anything left to say.

We stayed there for the longest time, with me listening to him breathe and feeling the warmth of his body, and his fingers digging into my back. It felt like he wanted to meld our bodies together the way that our souls currently were. And I didn't know how to do this, any more than he did.

I didn't know how to let him go.

In the end, I didn't have to. He pulled back and gripped my shoulders the way his incubus had done. "Listen to me. You will find a way. You always do—"

"Pritkin—"

"No! Listen! You go back there, you find a clue, any clue, to where you are, and you come back and tell me. It doesn't matter what it is—a sight, a sound, a smell—I will figure it out, and I will come for you—"

"Damn it, Pritkin, what did I just say?"

"Then I'll send our forces, all right? The dark fey—they're used to raiding Aeslinn's camp; they've been doing it for weeks, getting their people out. I'll tell them where you are and they'll find you. They'll get you out. *All right?*"

"Pritkin . . ."

"And if you can't come back, then do something to alert us. Knock over a lantern and set a tent on fire, scream and startle some horses, set off a weapon, any weapon. Some of those spell bombs of theirs can be seen for miles—"

He kept talking, in a feverish, almost frantic way, and this time, I let him. But not because I thought that any of it would work. Even if Aeslinn was foolish enough to leave his prize in a tent somewhere under minimal guards, Zeus wouldn't be. I was probably in a cell at Aeslinn's capitol, buried under a platoon. And without access to my power, I was likely to stay that way.

But I didn't point that out, because Pritkin needed this. The same way that I'd needed to know that his incubus could remove Lover's Knot. People facing the end cling to hope, and I couldn't deny him that.

So, I let him talk, as much as he wanted. And when he finally wound down, I let him pull me back to my feet, where we unconsciously moved together, in a slow dance amid the rubble.

While the same drinking song I'd heard in the enclave sifted out onto the street.

"Promise me," he whispered, his forehead pressed to mine, when the last notes had faded away. "Promise that you'll come back."

I didn't answer for a moment. I didn't want to lie to him, even now. But the truth wasn't anything he wanted to hear. "I promise I'll try."

His hands tightened, like he didn't believe me. Or maybe he just didn't want to let go. I didn't either, but it wasn't a choice anymore. That other place was pulling at me, harder and harder, as the time Faerie had allotted me ran out.

He hugged me tightly again, but this time, I could barely feel it. I was slipping away, and try as I might, I couldn't hold on. But as the street faded around me, I heard it, for the first time: Pritkin was singing. It was a low, broken sound, but beautiful nonetheless, a perfect tenor.

> For you are my delight, my delight, my delight,
> You are my delight and my darling,
> You are my delight, my comfort all night,
> And I'll cherish you until the morning.

Chapter Ten

"What's wrong? Why aren't we moving with the rest?" The voice was a man's. It sounded young and slightly nervous.

"Don't have the word yet." The terse reply was also male, and sounded bored.

"Yes, I noticed. My question was *why*."

"*That's* why. The king is . . . busy."

I opened my eyes to see two silver-haired fey, maybe five yards off, standing in front of the opening to a tent. I'd been dumped on the ground inside, toward the back, and could hardly see anything. It was dark in here, and my lids were crusty with what was possibly dried blood. I wasn't sure, as I couldn't seem to move my hands, even to wipe my face. But the little I could see . . .

Was not encouraging.

Through the gap between the two fey, I saw Aeslinn, wearing a plain, black, caftan-style garment and striding back and forth in front of a campfire. His agitated movements made the small amount of firelight leaking in flicker each time he passed between us and the flames. The strobe-like effect was what had woken me, although it didn't get me very far.

I slowly realized that I was trussed up like a rodeo calf, with my wrists and feet bound behind me and a rope stretched tautly in between them. It was really uncomfortable, to the point that it made it hard to breathe, and left me practically immobile. But that wasn't what had me gasping.

No, that was the realization that Aeslinn was foolish enough to leave his prize in a tent, under minimal guards. And that Zeus had let him. It made no sense, but I wasn't in the mood to question it right now.

I just wanted out!

But despite my struggles, and the fact that the cords binding me were just rope, I went nowhere. Mircea's strength, which I'd unconsciously started to rely on, was completely absent. Without it, all I was doing was giving myself rope burns.

I stopped before I started to hyperventilate, and instead concentrated on what Pritkin had said. *Find a clue, any clue. It doesn't matter what it is—a sight, a sound, a smell—I will figure it out.*

I went with sight first, but there wasn't much help there. I was in a hide tent, or maybe it was some kind of material. I couldn't see a weave, though, and it was tannish brown, except for where golden fingers of flame lit it up. Some were coming from the campfire out front, distant though it was, being maybe twelve yards away. And others resulted from the torches that hurrying people were carrying past that occasionally flickered on the tent's sides, throwing grotesque shadows onto the material, like hell's puppet show.

There was no way to see anything else, as it was pitch dark beyond the splashes of firelight. Leaving me with only what was in here to work with, but that wasn't looking so good, either. Because the Svarestri were nothing if not Spartan.

There were only a couple of thin bedrolls as furniture, neither of which they'd bothered to put me on; a few blankets; a dirt floor; the breastplate of a suit of armor shining in the firelight, and propped against a tent pole with a hook on it that also held a small backpack; and a bucket by the door.

There was nothing else, not even the lantern that Pritkin had said I should try to knock over.

Damn it, Cassie!

Think.

Sound. There was some of that—more than I'd expected. Horses were neighing unhappily, as if they'd been rousted out of their night's sleep too soon. Tackle was jangling, light fey footsteps were running, and a creaky wagon was trundling by. There seemed to be a lot of activity.

But no one conveniently called out our location or anything useful. The only thing I did pick up on was that the noise seemed to be coming primarily from in front of us and to one side. It almost sounded as if the tent had been parked on the edge of the camp, backing up to the forest, which . . . no. That would be ridiculous.

Sound wasn't helping at all.

Smell, then. But that was a bust, too, something I already knew without trying. There was the reek of blood in my nose—mine, presumably, as neither of the fey seemed injured. And . . . well, shit. Literally. It was almost all I could smell, and it was also coming from me. I seemed to be covered in it, which I didn't understand unless they'd dragged me through a sewer on the way here.

Touch and taste were the only two senses left, and I couldn't touch anything trussed up like a turkey. And all I could taste was the coppery tang of more blood. I didn't know what Pritkin could make out of all this, and I wasn't going to find out.

Because try as I might, I couldn't get back there.

I couldn't return to the Common.

I tried again and again, but the same thing happened. Or the same lack of thing, since it wouldn't let me in. I couldn't see so much as a flicker, or hear a whisper, of that other place.

Faerie was closed to me.

No. No! I had been fairly calm until then, but at that realization, I started to panic. I could almost see Pritkin, standing in that road, waiting for me to return. To tell him where to find me.

But I couldn't reach him.

I began struggling harder against the ropes, until I felt blood start to trickle down my arms as I rubbed off skin and grated flesh, but nothing happened. Except that I had to bite my bottom lip to keep from screaming, and not just because of the pain, or the fact that I couldn't get back. But because I couldn't do anything else, either.

Bound up like this, I couldn't even take the other way out. I couldn't kill myself. Leaving my power as a banquet for Zeus whenever he decided he was hungry.

And the gods were always hungry.

I struggled some more, but it only pulled back my arms and flattened my lungs. I didn't know if that was on purpose or not, but it was a really good way of making sure that your captive could only struggle part of the time. For the rest, they had to take a break and breathe.

So, after a few frantic moments, I did, and tried to do it quietly, while the two fey had a conversation outside.

"How long has he been like that?" one of them whispered. His hair was neatly confined by a leather thong, and he was wearing a shiny breastplate over a padded jerkin.

The other was sloppier, with his hair loose and windblown, and wearing only a plain gray tunic and leggings that might once have been black like his companion's, but were now faded with wear. He also appeared to be the older of the two, although I couldn't have said how I knew. Maybe it was the air of world weariness he carried, which the other fey lacked. He wore no armor, just a knife in a belt around his waist.

"Ever since he returned," the older one said. "Looks like he's arguing with himself."

"I know what it looks like!" The younger fey said. "And keep your voice down!"

"Why? Do you really think he's going to notice?"

"I don't know, and that's not the point—"

"I think it is." The older fey glanced back at me, and then ducked inside the tent.

"What are you doing?" his companion demanded as I watched through my lashes.

"What do you think?" The older fey came over and looked down at me, before making a face. "Gods, she stinks!"

He went back to the tent door and fetched the bucket and a rag. "What are you *doing*?" his companion repeated.

"Cleaning her up. She's filthy."

"Why?"

The older fey set the bucket down on the ground beside me. "You know why."

"Are you *mad*?"

"No, just desperate. We've been out here how long? And we're not allowed to touch the prisoners—"

"Of course not! They're unclean—"

"Such the devotee. Fortunately, I'm not that pious."

"—and so is she!" his companion finished furiously.

"Yes, hence the wash." The younger fey looked like he was going to say something else, but the older one put up a hand. "Do you know who this is?"

"Human scum!"

"Not entirely. She's a demigoddess, or so they say."

"So she has god blood. So do plenty of others. That doesn't change—"

"She was the one who took down our shield at the capitol, leading to our defeat."

The younger fey paused. "That was her?"

"Didn't you pay attention at the briefing?" The older fey started washing blood out of my hair and off my face.

"What briefing?"

"Oh, that's right. You're new. We were told to keep an eye out."

"For what?"

"For the daughter of Artemis, or so they say—"

"They lie! Artemis was a virgin, everyone knows that. She didn't have any children!"

"Virgin merely meant unmarried to the ancient humans who called her that, 'one ruled by no man'." He huffed out a laugh. "And in any case, her daughter certainly isn't—"

"Isn't what?"

"A virgin. They say she's in an alliance with a master vampire and a mage of terrible power: part fey, part human . . . and part demon."

"Part demon?" The younger fey looked horrified.

The older one looked up from his work, clearly enjoying freaking out his counterpart. "And she takes them both, in unholy congress, melding her power with theirs. That's how she was able to defeat us at Issengeir."

The younger fey regarded me as if I'd grown horns. "I had comrades who died at Issengeir. People I grew up with."

"And yet you defend her."

"I'm not defending *her*! I'm defending—oh, what would you know? There's not a pious bone in your body!"

"Oh, I used to believe, some years ago—and still do, of course." The mockery was clear, even to the younger fey, who scowled.

"You believe in nothing!"

The older sat back on his heels. "I believe I need some soap."

"You need to get your head clear! If she's what you say—"

"She is. King confirmed it. I heard him talking to one of the captains."

The younger fey's eyes grew wide. "Then . . . then what is she doing *here*? With only two of us to guard her? And in *rope*?"

"Don't know; don't care."

"But if she wakes *up*—"

"What if she does? I dosed her good. She won't be using any powers on us."

"You're sure?"

"If I'd given her any more, it would have killed her."

The younger fey didn't look convinced, but his companion just grinned. "Relax. She'll be helpless for hours."

"If you gave her the right vial. Are you sure you didn't give her the antidote instead?"

The older fey frowned. "Do you take me for a fool?"

"Well, someone did it, just today. Got so nervous dealing with that vampire that they gave him the wrong thing. He killed ten of us before they realized their mistake!"

The older fey laughed. "Yes. I heard they had to stake him."

"Should have taken his head, too, and been done with it!" The younger fey snapped.

"Can't. The king said not to."

"Why, by all the gods?"

"Probably wanted to do it himself. They have to be alive, if you want to strip their souls."

The younger fey frowned down at me. "You think that's what he plans to do with her?"

"What else? What are we doing out here?"

"Cleansing the world," the younger fey said, suddenly sounding surer of himself. "Removing divine power from the undeserving—"

"—before they use it to destroy civilization. Yes, that's the speech they give recruits. But who decides who's undeserving?"

"The king does!"

The older fey shot his younger counterpart a sly look. "Ah. Not so pious, after all."

"What do you mean?"

"Just that you're trusting the word of a king over that of the priests who say this sort of thing is an abomination. That it diminishes the soul of all Faerie when its children's spirits do not return."

"They're not its children! They're polluted!"

"If you say so." The older fey suddenly seemed to lose interest in the conversation, possibly because the younger kept fingering his sword. "Hand me that towel."

The younger ignored him. "You ought to check."

"Check what?"

"That you gave her the right dose. She took a fall, before those vines caught her. Might have hit her head on the way down—"

"Or might have gotten hit, after our lot had to slash their way through a murderous jungle to get to her," his companion said dryly.

"—and be out for that reason, instead of the dose."

The older fey rolled his eyes, but tossed the younger a pouch off his belt. "See for yourself."

The younger fey pulled out two small vials, one black and the other a bilious yellow. The black one was half empty, and the younger fey's shoulders relaxed. "You're lucky you're right," he said, and tossed the pouch back.

"I'm always right when it comes to my neck. Now fetch me more towels."

The younger fey didn't budge. "You don't need them. She's clean enough—"

"For you, maybe. I'm more fastidious with my whores."

"She isn't—you can't—you're mad!"

"Perhaps. But don't you think we should get something for sitting out here for months? Besides, I never fucked a goddess before. Wonder if they feel different?"

The older fey reached down and tore open my shirt.

"Doesn't look like you're going to find out," the younger said. Because I was wearing a corset cover.

It looked like a modern-day camisole, with strips of delicate lace that the fey soon ripped through as well. Only to find the corset itself below, a rigid barrier that covered me from breast to well below my belly button and laced up the back. I would have taken it off when I arrived in Faerie, but I'd almost gotten used to it. And the upper layers took forever to remove without a maid's help.

As the older fey was discovering.

He couldn't reach the lacing that ran up the back with my arms tied behind me, and pulling on the thing did no good at all. After a moment, he scowled and pulled out a knife. Only to discover that the

Edwardians boned their corsets with thin strips of flexible steel. They caused him to nick his hand and blunt his knife, and made him curse repeatedly. He finally started hacking through the spaces between the sections, but the tough rows of stitching made him work for it.

"Is that armor?" the younger fey asked, looking intrigued.

"May as well be! How many layers do these bitches wear?"

"More than that," the younger fey said, as the final piece of fabric parted . . . to reveal a bra underneath. Because Edwardian corsets provided less than perfect support.

The older fey gave a muffled roar and sliced it to pieces, too.

"At last! I was beginning to believe she was made out of cloth!"

The younger fey laughed. "How many layers was that? Five? Six? I'll have to tell my sister when—" he stopped when the older fey grabbed my breast. "What are you doing?"

"What did I tell you? Or did you think I went through all that for nothing?"

"I thought you were joking!"

"Not likely." He grinned, running a rough thumb over a nipple, watching it peak. "Not looking so much like a goddess now, are you?" he asked me.

"Would you get away from her?" the younger fey hissed. "She's evil!"

"Looking forward to finding out."

"She's also the king's prize. Get your hands off!"

"No, I don't think I will."

"You *are* mad."

"Must take after my liege, then."

"That's enough!" A sword was suddenly at the older fey's throat. "You have no respect for anyone!"

"All right, all right!" the older fey looked up, keeping his neck well away from the gleaming edge that was maybe an inch from his jugular. "I shouldn't have said that. But look at him."

The younger fey glanced over his shoulder. "The king has reasons for what he does," he said staunchly.

"I'm sure." The older fey kept his voice neutral that time, but his eyes darkened as they followed Aeslinn's pacing form.

With the two guards out of the doorway, I could see a little more now, including the king, gesticulating wildly and yelling at what appeared to be thin air. He looked deranged, but I couldn't hear what he was saying over the sounds of a busy camp. It looked like the army was in the process of moving out.

The younger fey turned back and his eyes swept over me. "She doesn't look like a goddess," he said, sheathing his sword.

"You think it's a glamour?"

"I think she'd look better if it was a glamour," was the dry response.

The older fey sopped some water onto my chest with the sodden rag, and scrubbed the dried blood off my neck and shoulders. "She'll look better cleaned up. It's like she took a bath in shit."

"She did," the younger fey said, his voice cold. "Those vines she was controlling ripped Sigge apart. His intestines spilled all over her, along with his blood."

"That's . . . off-putting."

"Don't fuck her, then!"

The older fey shot him a look. "It's not that off-putting. Here, hand me my pack."

"Get it yourself."

"All right, but then you don't get a turn."

The younger fey laughed harshly. "As if I'd want one!"

"I'd think you would."

"Why, by all the gods?"

"Well, you'll never get a chance at one of her kind again, will you?"

The younger fey frowned. "Once the king brings back the gods—"

"If—" the older fey began, and then stopped, probably remembering the sword. "As if they'd want anything to do with you," he amended. "Even the half breed ones."

"Some might." But the younger fey sounded less sure.

The older tossed away another dirty rag in favor of a clean one. "I'll tell you what's going to happen. You're going to spend the rest of your life wishing you'd taken your chance, and wondering what it feels like. But I'm not going to tell you."

The younger fey licked his lips nervously, his eyes flickering to the tent door and back again. "It's forbidden," he repeated.

"Lots of things are—like what we've been doing all this time. You think any of the virtuous bastards back at the capitol would understand *that*?"

"Once the gods return, they'll thank us!"

"Yes, so people keep telling me. But so far, I've gotten nothing out of this—and neither have you. Don't you want a little something for your service?"

A series of pornographic images suddenly passed across my mind, flashing from fey to fey in what I guessed was the Common, since I didn't have my abilities right now. They were almost immediately shut down, probably by the younger fey, who looked shaken. "What are you doing?" he hissed. "Someone might see—"

"Everyone else is busy. And I aimed it just at you." The older fey grinned. "Like this."

Another vision, even more graphic than the last, flashed across my mind, and I thought about screaming.

The younger fey gripped the older one's shoulder, his fingers white.

"Still feeling so pious?" his comrade asked.

"All right," the younger fey whispered, staring at me. "What do you want?"

"Some soap and towels. And watch the door."

Chapter Eleven

A block of brown, homemade soap was tossed to the older fey out of a pack, and the younger took up position in the center of the door, blocking anyone's view inside. He blocked most of mine, too, with the only outlook I had left being the triangle of firelight between his legs. It allowed me to see Aeslinn continuing to pace back and forth, like a caged lion. He was obviously agitated, although not as much as I was.

The sounds from the camp were getting louder. People were yelling, tackle was jingling, a wagon had slipped off a path and gotten stuck in a ditch, and the horses were bucking and whinnying as multiple fey tried to pull them out. And I was grateful for all of it.

I'd started making little noises of my own.

They weren't words, or even syllables. Just glottal, animalistic sounds deep in my throat as the soapy rag was run over my neck, shoulders, breasts, and stomach. Which turned into high-pitched wheezes when the fey suddenly jerked my bloomers down to my knees.

He heard, and gave me a sly grin. "Beg me, little goddess. And perhaps I'll be gentle."

"Fuck off!"

"But that's what I'm doing, is it not?" His motions slowed down, into a parody of sensuality.

He held my gaze as he toyed with my breasts, and when that didn't get a reaction, started walking his fingers down my stomach. I refused to be the first to look away, even knowing what was coming. But the expression on his face as those probing fingers reached my groin, as they explored, fondled, *penetrated*, made me wish I'd swallowed my pride.

This wasn't happening, this wasn't happening, this wasn't—

"Scream for me, little Pythia. Just a small scream?"

"Go to hell!"

"Isn't that where you're from? Are you so in love with me already?"

"Faerie's the worst hell I know."

His lips twisted. "If we're talking about this part of it, I agree."

A second finger joined the first, and it was too much. I cried out as he began to core me open with quick, crude motions, causing the younger fey to look over his shoulder. His eyes widened.

"She's awake?"

"Obviously."

"You should gag her. She's a witch. She could cast a spell!"

"She's a drugged witch, and I like her voice." The older fey looked down at me and quirked his fingers again. "Let's hear that pretty scream."

I didn't scream. I did try, very hard, to access Pritkin's abilities. With them on board, I was basically a succubus, and the fey had left himself vulnerable. I should have been able to pull power off him— off both of them.

But nothing happened, no matter how hard I tried. Whatever dose they'd given me had done exactly as advertised. I couldn't use my own power right now, much less anyone else's. And using a weapon, even assuming I could get my hands on one, would require getting free.

Otherwise, I was helpless.

The realization settled into my stomach like a stone.

"Hurry up!" the second fey said. "I want my turn."

"And I want to enjoy this."

But the older fey did speed up. He upended the rest of the bucket of water over me, signaling an end to the bath and the start of something else. But there he met with an obstacle.

He'd already pulled my bloomers down, but he couldn't get them off, since I was tied up. He made a sound of irritation and cut them away, and pushed my knees further apart. But the ropes around my ankles extended most of the way up my calves, and I could only spread so far.

"What are you doing?" the second fey said, when the knife reappeared and dropped to the bonds around my legs.

"Cutting her loose. I can't take her like this."

"Well, you'd better make do—"

"Why?"

"—we don't have any more rope!"

The older fey cursed and put the knife away, before trying to untie the bonds. But they were tight and, thanks to my hasty bath, wet as well. He got back to his feet after a moment of struggle, leaving me trussed up in a patch of damp soil.

"I'll go find some more, then."

"Just take her like that—"

"I'm not taking her like that! I'm only going to fuck a goddess once. I'm doing it right!"

"Then I will—"

The older fey grabbed the younger by the tunic. "You do, and I'll make a gelding out of you. *I* cleaned her up; *I* get first go."

"Then you'd better hurry. If they decide they want her—"

"They'll be grateful that she doesn't smell like shit, won't they?"

The younger fey said something that didn't translate and the older let him go and hurried off through the camp. The younger guard took up his stance in the door again, I guessed planning to abide by his comrade's orders. I couldn't be sure, because I couldn't see his face anymore.

Which meant that he couldn't see me. I started working frantically on the ropes, hoping that the first fey had loosened them some. I was probably breathing loudly enough to have alerted the guard to what I was doing, but he was preoccupied with something else.

Something big.

I looked up after a moment to see the younger fey standing stock still, his back rigid, his stance wide, and his hand clenched on his sword hilt. I didn't understand it; he looked like he'd just seen a threat. But the only person out there—

Had just become two.

Despite everything, I paused for a second, my breath catching. My brain tried to explain what I was seeing, but my adrenal glands had just finished flooding my system, and I couldn't think. I couldn't hear, either, except for the pounding of my heart and the staticky white noise that had taken over my mind.

Because standing on the sandy soil near the campfire was a shimmering, nine-foot tall, golden god.

A head of wavy hair flowed down his back to just below shoulder length, the color of sunlight on polished metal. His face and body also shone, as the fey did on Earth, as if making their own light. Only he was far brighter than any fey I'd ever seen.

The brilliance washed out his features, cloaking them in a light shadow so bright that I couldn't make much of anything out, except for the eyes. They blazed through everything, so startlingly blue that they looked like an entirely different color than our paltry human shade. He was also clad in a full suit of gleaming, golden armor, which added to the shine.

I wondered why he'd bothered to manifest like that, and then I remembered: Zeus was the chameleon of the pantheon. He'd appeared to people as all sorts of things, even animals and inanimate objects at times, whatever he thought would help him. So, I guessed it shouldn't have been a surprise that, in a camp full of soldiers, he would choose to look like one of the boys.

No, *that* didn't surprise me.

The fact that he was semi-transparent, on the other hand, had my brain bending in all kinds of strange ways, trying to make sense of it. And failing, because there were no spirits in Faerie. I knew that beyond question; I was currently living proof.

So, what *was* he?

I could see the dark outlines of trees dimly through all that shining light, as well as the fey that were moving about, breaking up the camp. They didn't seem to see him, though. Not one so much as faltered as they passed, even those running through the circle of light that he was shedding.

It lit up their long, silver hair, glinted off of the hilts of their knives, and limned the edges of their strange, curved swords. But it didn't gleam in their eyes, which never turned his way. And even if you were used to having a deity hanging around the tents, a nine-foot tall, shimmering, half transparent god should have won a glance, at least.

But he didn't, so they didn't see him. But I did, and not just as a ghost. The sand under the great armored feet moved when he did, pushing up slightly as if under some kind of weight, and the wind tossed strands of that golden hair around.

He *did* have a body, then, just not one like ours.

I'd heard that the gods were energy beings, able to form themselves flesh whenever they chose, but not having to. They could exist in human form, as mother had after her campaign, blending into the regular population unnoticed. But this must be their natural state: not a ghost, but a being of pure energy, enough to rewrite the rules of anywhere they went.

Including those of a hostile world.

Perhaps that was why Faerie couldn't touch him, I thought. She didn't know this strange way of existing, so different from anything she had ever created. Unless I was reading this wrong. Unless this was some sort of mirage dreamed up by a panicked mind, only I didn't think so.

Mirages didn't grab fey kings by the front of their robes and jerk them up to their faces.

I strained my ears, hoping for some information, anything that might help. And discovered that I could just hear what they were saying. Maybe because the horse accident had finally been resolved and the loud cavalcade had passed on, leaving this corner of the camp dark and quiet.

Or maybe because the decibel level had abruptly gone up.

"You would challenge me?" Zeus thundered.

"I meant no disrespect," Aeslinn said, cowering slightly. It was strange to see the more than seven-foot-tall fey king looking small. But maybe that was why Zeus had materialized so huge.

He liked looking down on people.

But to my surprise, although he looked intimidated, Aeslinn didn't shut up or beg forgiveness. He shrank back into himself, with his eyes fixed somewhere on Zeus's massive chest, but he kept talking. And he talked a lot.

"But your pets are growing restless. Despite our best efforts, we are running out of food for them. Even great Nimue's power didn't satisfy them for long. What happens when there is no more? When they turn on us, instead of—"

"You assured me that wouldn't happen."

"That was before the witches' creatures destroyed my facility! I don't even know how they found it, but they left it a smoking ruin. Now, I can't promise anything—"

"You have others—"

"But not enough!" Aeslinn met the blazing blue eyes again, and his expression, while pale, was resolute. Whatever else he lacked, he did have courage. "We're out of time. We must act now, while we have the upper hand. You can end this tonight—"

"And do what?"

Aeslinn gaped at him, as if caught off guard. "Rule! Tear down that infernal barrier and restore the old order. We can have everything we've worked for, sacrificed for, all these years! Take her power and look for the boy later—"

"And risk someone else finding him first? No." It was implacable.

But Aeslinn wasn't hearing that. "This is madness," he raged. "You must see that! We've never been so close—"

"And, once again, you prove that you know everything about politics, and nothing about people," Zeus said flatly. "You don't rule merely through might unless you wish to fight all the time. You rule through *fear*. People must believe that they cannot win, that opposing you is ruin, swift and sure, and that the only path forward is obedience. *That* is how you keep them in line, particularly across multiple worlds. *That* is how you ensure loyalty."

Aeslinn didn't look like he was buying that. "It didn't last time—" he began.

And was backhanded so hard and so fast that he almost landed in the fire. He hit right next to it, and one edge of his robe did start to smoke, but he stamped it out. And looked up at Zeus with a less than worshipful eyes.

"Have a care, fey king," Zeus said, so quietly that I had to strain to hear it.

"My apologies," Aeslinn hissed, although it was less than convincing considering that it was through gritted teeth. His long hair had tumbled into his face, half hiding his expression, but his voice was just this side of vicious. "But none of that changes the fact that our position grows more precarious with each passing day. The drain on our power is becoming intolerable; we cannot support it forever. Your rebellious son is at my borders in force, feasting on my reserves, and waiting for my power to falter. And now that that wretch Arsen has turned on us—"

"Something that would not have happened had you killed him years ago, as I advised."

"He is beloved of the old order, the ancient houses," Aeslinn spat. "His family ruled before mine, and many of them consider his line— tainted though it is—to be the legitimate one."

"All the more reason, then."

"I couldn't move against him! Not without cause! It might well have resulted in rebellion. The other noble houses would have taken it as a sign that their blood isn't the shield they think it to be—"

"You overestimate them," Zeus said, sounding bored, and sitting on a log by the fire with his back to the tent. The proximity to the flames and his semi-transparent state left me looking at a creature that seemed to be made out of light. It boiled through his limbs, sparkled off his hair, and magnified the haze around the small blaze to the point that it looked like a spotlight had been turned on that part of the camp.

Yet no one noticed. No one except my guard, the young fey who either had the talent to see through glamouries or—more likely, since I could see the same thing, and I didn't have any talents right now—he didn't have to. Zeus simply hadn't bothered to shield from this side.

As a result, the guard had remained frozen in place, stunned or awestruck or frightened out of his mind, I wasn't sure which. But he wasn't paying any attention to me. Which was lucky, since all that light was gleaming off of something I hadn't noticed before: the older fey's sword, left half buried in the blanket covering his bedroll.

He hadn't taken it when he left; hadn't even had the scabbard strapped on. I should have noticed that, and been looking for it already. But now would have to do.

I started rocking my body over it, as quietly as possible.

"Do you know nothing of your own history?" Zeus was saying. "They are cautious to the point of immobility, those vaunted nobles of yours. Even the traitorous ones didn't rise until after dear Artemis made her play, and sent all of us packing. One would think you would remember that, considering that you fought in the war that followed."

"I remember," Aeslinn said, his face darkening. "I remember how many of them turned on me, my own *loyal* nobles, as soon as they saw an opportunity. I had to execute Arsen's father, the one they intended to lead them, although he had made no move against me. It forever soured his son, made him my enemy when he was in short clothes—"

"Enough!" Zeus bellowed, loud enough to make me flinch. "Cease this constant prattling!"

"I merely wished to point out—"

"You've made your case—long ago. And yet you go on and on. You sound like a woman!"

"Yes, father."

"Be careful there, too." It was dry. "You haven't earned that yet."

Aeslinn said nothing at all that time.

"Worry less about your cowardly people and more about the demon's spawn," Zeus added. "Once I have him, your wait is over. There is every chance you will have your victory—tonight—even without all your politics."

"And if he doesn't come?" Aeslinn said, glancing at the tent and causing me to pause and lie still.

"He will. He and the witch are bound together, along with the vampire. He has no choice."

"Unless they simply remove the spell, and leave her to her fate!"

"Ah, but there goes their power. They'd prefer to risk coming after her, particularly in a disordered camp, than lose the war with no Pythia."

"Like you're willing to risk losing everything to gain this boy?" Aeslinn asked pointedly.

I held my breath, expecting an explosion, but the look Zeus shot his ally this time was amused. "The bait is set and you have thousands of fey, concealed and on high alert. As soon as he steps foot anywhere near here, he's mine."

"You discount the girl. She's as bad as her mother, and the demon has abilities we know not. And the nobles, should they hear of this—"

"The nobles again." Zeus sighed. "As soon as my people return, you won't have to worry about them, ever again."

"But I do now, which is why I want this over with!"

"Patience. It is one lesson you have yet to learn." Zeus poked the fire with a stick. "Oh, and kill the guard. He overheard our conversation."

The god abruptly disappeared, the stick falling into flames, and the king cursed. The young fey just stood there, as rigid as if he'd been turned to stone. For a long moment, he and the king stared at each other, perfectly silently.

Then Aeslinn cursed again. "Keep your tongue behind your teeth," he snarled, and strode off.

Chapter Twelve

The young guard collapsed into a lump of black wool, breathing hard and looking like he was about to be sick. And I guessed that was an accurate read, as he got up after a moment and ran around the side of the tent. Where I heard him proving that humans and fey have one thing in common, at least, into some bushes.

That left me alone for the first time, and I took full advantage, finally reaching the sword that his partner had left behind.

It was obviously a much-loved weapon, well-oiled and wickedly sharp. But my hands were trapped behind me and I couldn't see them, resulting in me cutting myself more than the ropes. I kept at it anyway, and managed to cut the cord running between my bound hands and feet, which allowed me to finally stretch out my pretzel-shaped body.

And, oh, God!

Mistake!

Big mistake!

I had to bite my lip to keep from crying out, because it hurt like a son of a bitch. And by "it", I mean everything. I must have been contorted like that for hours, as half a dozen charley horses hit me all at once. For a moment, all I could do was writhe in the dirt and fight not to scream.

But, finally, a few of the cramps released, and the rest quieted enough that I could maneuver. My wrists and forearms felt like half of the rope in the world had been tied around them, with knots every few inches, impeding me even more. So, I started working on the bonds around my calves and ankles instead.

Being able to run was the priority right now.

And it looked like the fey had gotten careless. Instead of trussing me properly, as they had on my arms, there was only one knot here, with the rest of the rope just wound around my legs. Once I cut through the main problem, the rest fell away, and I surged to my feet—

And immediately collapsed, thanks to the blood flowing back into almost flattened veins.

I tried a couple more times, failed a couple more times, and started to panic. The fey would be back any minute, and I was as weak as a kitten and couldn't even stand. How was I supposed to get out of the tent, much less the camp? How was I supposed to do any—

My thoughts cut out as my eyes fell on a small, black vial, glinting in the dirt. It was the same one that the fey had been talking about, shortly after I woke up. The one that had been used to cut me off from my power.

I looked around frantically, trying to find its twin, the yellow one that might give me at least a fighting chance, but it wasn't there. And with its color, I couldn't have missed it. It seemed that only the black had fallen out of the pack.

The one that the fey had said would kill me.

I stared at it for a moment, my brain whiting out again, with that strange, buzzing sound. It was probably just the blood surging though my veins, but it sounded like a swarm of bees. It drove me mad.

After a second, I started working frantically on the ropes around my hands, hoping to be able to free them and massage some feeling back into my legs. But my eyes never left that vial. I could pick it up with my mouth; I didn't need to be completely free for that. Just pick it up with my lips, push out the cork with my tongue, and drink it down.

I could do that right now.

And I should, since I didn't see another way out of this. I couldn't run, I couldn't fight, and I couldn't let Zeus steal my connection to the Pythian power. So, what other choice was there?

None, so just do it, I thought savagely. Or cut your wrists on the damned sword a little more, and bleed out. Either way, get it done!

I sawed faster instead, still staring at the vial. It was as if everything else had faded away, and there was just that. Like it encapsulated my whole world.

I suddenly, vividly remembered Jo, the rogue acolyte that Aeslinn's pet necromancer, a man named Jonathan, had butchered. He'd grafted a piece of her soul onto his body, like an extra limb, to give him access to her power. It had given him something else, too.

That bit of soul had manifested a small, human-like face, just under the skin of his side, right beneath the rib cage. It had looked like a doll's face or a strange body modification, with pale skin stretched over top of it, yet the features perfectly visible and pushing upward. And this body mod *moved*.

The eyes had been sightless lumps that nonetheless turned in continuous motion, desperately trying to see. And the tiny mouth had stayed open and working, in a perpetual, silent scream. It had frozen me with horror then, and it did the same thing now.

Do you want to be like that? I asked myself harshly. Do you want to live like *that*?

Some part of me recoiled in terror, yet I didn't act.

I remembered Agnes' death next, as it was burned just as vividly into my memory. Her body had already died, but her spirit lived on, and had managed to possess another rogue named Myra. The girl had been turned by the god's lies against everything she had been taught, and Agnes's heir, she was Agnes's responsibility.

And Gertie's girl had done her job fearlessly to the last.

I could still see the spill of blood, so much as so red, after she slit her throat, thereby killing Myra and freeing her own soul. She had pursued her heir into the next world, to make sure that she didn't try to double back and possess someone, as the Pythias had the ability to do. And despite the fact that she must have felt the same pain that Myra did, I couldn't remember her hand shaking or her hesitating, even for an instant.

And yet here I lay, sprawled in the dirt, completely terrified!

I knew what I had to do, but I shrank from it, and not just for my own sake. But because Mircea and Pritkin were bound to me. I knew that, if I didn't know anything else, since I'd been able to understand the feys' conversation. And they hadn't been speaking English.

I didn't know why that ability worked when Mircea's strength didn't, but maybe because it was passive. The potion seemed to target anything useful in battle—magic or physical prowess—and I guessed that didn't qualify. But it was enough to tell me that, if I died, they went with me.

Why hadn't the incubus done his goddamned *job*?

And yet some part of me, some slightly more honest part, knew that his failure was only part of the problem. Knew that I'd be here, wasting time, even if he'd done as promised. I wanted to *live*, to see them again, to hug my court, to finish wrapping Christmas presents with my initiates, to—

You're not going to do any of that! I hold myself harshly. You're going to die, here, now! You have to!

And yet, I hesitated, despite knowing what the price could be, what it would be, when Zeus finished with me.

And then it was too late.

"What's this?" My shoulder was grabbed and I was jerked around by the older fey, who was carrying a coil of rope over his shoulder and looking furious.

He hadn't been quiet, and the other fey came running. And then stood in the doorway, taking in the sight of me, desperately sawing my last bonds on one of their own weapons. He came at me, his face furious, and before I could blink, he had me in one hand and the sword in the other, and looked like he was about to end my captivity permanently.

Until the older fey knocked his weapon aside. "And you call *me* mad?"

"I—" the younger fey stopped, realization coming over his features.

"Deprive the king of his prize, and neither one of us will see the dawn! By the gods, you're a fool!"

The younger fey sat down on a bedroll, his face white, probably from almost dying twice in a few minutes. He swallowed and tried to speak, decided better of it, and grabbed a flask out of his pack. He downed it in a couple of gulps, wiped a sleeve over his mouth and stared at me.

"We need to get moving," he said, his voice a rasp.

"You get moving," his companion said, dropping the rope. "I didn't go to this much trouble for nothing."

The younger fey put a hand on his arm. "We can't. The camp is tearing down as we speak and . . . and things are happening. Strange things—"

"Then watch the door. This won't take long."

"I'm not watching the door!" the younger fey said, his voice high and half hysterical. "I'm done with this! She goes to the king. They need to put her somewhere more secure!"

"The king can have her as soon as I'm finished."

The older fey grabbed for me, but the younger one leapt to his feet and knocked his hand away. "No! No more short cuts, no more rule breaking, no more anything. She goes to the king—"

"All right, perhaps you have a point," the older fey said.

And then gave his companion a vicious elbow to the face, as soon as he dropped his guard. The younger fey went staggering backward out of the tent, blood spurting from his face. And I found myself on my back, with the older fey between my legs.

I suddenly couldn't move, couldn't think, couldn't breathe. Everything seemed to slow down as I watched him rip apart the lacings on his leggings and pull me into position. I couldn't seem to speak, but the noises I'd been making suddenly got louder and higher pitched, until—

"Damn you!" the younger fey reappeared, with his sword in his hand.

But the older one wasn't caught off guard, this time. He threw dirt in the younger one's face, and when he cried out, knocked the sword away. They wrestled around on the floor for it, and I scrabbled for the nearest wall of the tent, with my wrists bound and my legs only half working.

Even worse, I couldn't see the vial anymore. I should have grabbed it and held it in my mouth, in case I couldn't get away. Put it under my tongue, like a suicide pill. But I hadn't and now I couldn't locate it in the gloom, not with two fey fighting on top of it.

Until, suddenly, they weren't.

The younger pushed the older off with a savage blow, but instead of following up on his advantage, he grabbed for me instead. And shoved a dirty rag between my lips, I didn't know why. Until the strange, high-pitched wheezes I'd been hearing suddenly cut out.

The younger fey looked furious. But instead of continuing the fight, he was simply glaring at the elder. Who was sitting on the ground, holding his jaw.

"I said you should have gagged her!" the younger whispered furiously.

"But I want to hear her scream."

"And do you want *them* to hear?" the young fey gestured outside the tent. Where a couple of soldiers with a heavily laden cart had stopped to look curiously in our direction.

The older fey looked back at them, and got a strange look on his face. "Now, there's an idea."

"What are you talking about?"

He didn't answer. He just kept staring at the soldiers, even after somebody shouted at them and they moved on. I watched them go and it was a dizzying experience, almost like falling off a cliff. I hadn't realized until just then, but I had subconsciously been expecting something to intervene: some interruption to take place; someone to call the guards away; some white knight to come charging in and save me.

But none of that was going to happen, was it?

As if he'd heard me, the older fey turned to look at me. He crawled over and jerked out the makeshift gag, leaving me tasting blood and worse as my chin was grabbed in a cruel grip. But instead of an assault, something else happened.

Something strange.

The tent abruptly skewed, and in place of his face, I suddenly saw my own reflected back at me: blue eyes wide and shaken, cheeks pale and clammy, a smear of dirt on my forehead that he'd somehow missed earlier, mouth slack with shock.

The image held for a moment, then slowly panned out, the view widening to show my body, also from the fey's perspective. I lay on my back in the dirt, in a partial recline since my wrists weren't free and I couldn't lie flat. My chest was bowed out from my arms being pulled tightly back, and my breasts were thrust comically forward with nipples tightly furled against the cold. And rapidly rising and falling, in panic and confusion.

For a moment, I didn't understand what was going on. Too much had happened too quickly, and I couldn't take it in. And then I did, and saw my face change, as horror and realization took over.

No. No! He'd be caught, punished, possibly executed. He couldn't intend—

But he was.

And the view was expanding. My ribcage came into the picture, a bit too prominent from rarely being able to finish a meal, then my stomach, currently hollowing out from too-quick, panted breaths, and then—

No, I thought, and started thrashing, I didn't—he couldn't—make it stop! But the view kept on widening, showing the dip under my naval, the mound of my sex, my thighs rising sharply on either side. And then pushed up and spread wide.

I lay there, panting, disbelieving, trying to close my legs, but not being allowed to. And that one thought drove me wild. Stop looking at me! I thought frantically. You don't get to look—

But he was, and so were dozens of other fey. He was blasting this through the Common, letting his friends in on the mental feed. And more and more were tuning in every moment, as news of my humiliation ran like wildfire through the camp.

And the watchers were receiving more than visuals. They felt the texture of my skin as the fey slowly ran his hands up and down my inner thighs. They heard my labored breathing; tasted the soap on my skin when he bent down to lick a nipple, felt my shudder of revulsion and then my panicked "No!" when one of his hands reversed course and slid between my legs again, letting them explore along with him.

I felt my head go swimmy.

"Do you see them, little goddess?" he asked, looking up at me. "All those eyes? They see you. Feel you, too. Lovers adept with the Common sometimes use it thus, to enjoy each other's bodies when far away. Just as they are going to enjoy yours."

I stared at him, panting in disbelief. "Why are you doing this? You'll get caught. They'll *kill you*—"

"I doubt it. We were told to keep you alive. Nothing more."

"But they'll punish you—"

"There are worse things. Such as losing those you've known all your life, your capitol, your *pride*. Our leaders seem to have forgotten that. Fortunately, some of us remember."

But not all of them. He was picking and choosing who he let in, probably trying to avoid discovery and the punishment that would follow, no matter what he said. But he wasn't being all *that* picky.

Through the Common, I saw four fey seated around a campfire, their tent broken down behind them, their belongings already loaded onto a cart. They were roasting some small animal over the coals while they waited for the call to move out. They were also sharing around a flask, which one of them abruptly dropped as the images slammed into him: a wave of red shame staining my cheeks and running down my neck in real time; my eyes shaded with disbelief as

I stared at him while he stared back at me; my body pale against the dark soil.

And then he was looking at the fire again, and at the bottle he'd been holding, which was leaking precious spirits onto the dirt. That earned him a cuff upside the head from a fellow soldier, and yells of outrage from others, all of which he ignored. He was too busy hurrying into the trees.

He wasn't alone.

My view expanded to show me fey after fey across what appeared to be three large camps, suddenly making excuses and disappearing into the night. Others, who were loading carts or driving wagons, couldn't leave, but found themselves distracted, dropping boxes and running off the road. And even more were about to, because the older fey suddenly decided that he had waited long enough.

He had given them time to adjust, wanting them to partake in the punishment of their enemy, to revel in my humiliation and his inevitable triumph. And they were. I suddenly felt hands on my butt cheeks, clenching, more on my breasts, fondling, one in my hair, fisting. There was no one there, no one else in the tent as I looked around frantically. Yet I could feel them, just the same.

They crowded close, as if I was being assaulted by a thousand ghosts, and I writhed and twisted, trying to get away from an attack I couldn't even see. The older fey's eyes gleamed as he watched me, and then he laughed and spread his arms.

"Remember, Villi, son of Kotti, gives you this! He gives you justice!"

And, suddenly, I was out of time.

Chapter Thirteen

The strange paralysis that had gripped me abruptly shattered, and I kicked out at my attacker as hard as I could. It was clumsy and ineffective, with one of my legs numb and the other only halfway answering my commands. But it seemed to surprise him.

I'd been almost passive before, too stunned to react. But I was reacting now, with strange sounds coming out of me that I didn't have a name for. They were primitive, almost animal-like, and I fought him like an animal, too, somehow managing to push him off me. And when he came at me again, I went for his jugular with my teeth like a vamp.

But I wasn't one, and he dodged with liquid speed, causing me to clamp down onto thin air.

So, I butted him with my head instead, since I didn't have anything else.

It connected hard enough to leave me feeling like my brains had just been bashed out, and caused my vision to go swimmy. But I'd thrashed hard enough to tear the final knot loose from my wrists, freeing my arms, and that seemed more important. I clawed for his eyes and missed, but cut several jagged lines down his cheek with my fingernails.

He drew back instinctively, blood dripping from the wounds, and I scrambled to my feet—

For about a second, until he snarled, caught my arm, and jerked me back down.

I went for his eyes again, but he'd expected it that time, and it didn't work. He belted me across the face, more of a contemptuous slap than a punch, but I don't think he'd dealt with many humans before. Because it rocked my head back almost hard enough to break my neck. It also stunned me, allowing him to grab my wrists.

They were raw from the ropes and hurt more than his fist, causing me to cry out, but I kept on fighting.

It was useless, even stupid. There were two of them, and both were far stronger than me. And while I knew some self-defense, I didn't know enough. And pissing him off was going to result in a much crueler experience, since Zeus didn't care what kind of condition I was in, just that I was alive.

But I couldn't seem to stop.

I caught a glimpse of myself in the Common, a skewed, shaky cam version as we struggled in near darkness. The distant, flickering firelight cast a strobe-like effect over the scene, highlighting pieces for the watchers: the fey's worn out tunic, now soiled from wrestling in the dirt; my equally filthy hair, greasy strands falling into my face; a drop of blood from the wounds on his cheek, shimmering on his jawline for an instant; more flecks of blood flying from my half-slit wrists. But my eyes were the truly terrifying part.

My eyes were crazy.

The fey must have thought so, too, because he snapped at his companion. "Help me with this hell cat!"

The younger fey stared at me blankly for a second, as if he hadn't expected my response, either, before moving to assist. He reached for my shoulders, but jerked away when I twisted and got my teeth into him. "She bit me!"

"Of course, she bit you! What did you expect? Grab her!"

But, this time, the younger fey didn't comply. I thought for a moment that he might intervene again, as he had once before, panicked at the thought of displeasing his god. But then his eyes moved down my body and his gaze hardened.

It seemed his piety had a limit, after all.

He wouldn't help his companion, but he wouldn't save me, either. Not the victor of Issengeir. The older fey swore, but it didn't matter, because the rest of the camp had already answered the call.

The firelight on the walls of the tent showed only two moving shadows, only two combatants locked in a desperate struggle. Even the young fey wasn't reflected there, having melted with the darkness behind me. But we weren't alone. Because little changes had started to show up on my body, as those especially gifted with the Common made their presence known.

Indentations appeared on my hips and breasts, as if invisible fingers were gripping me; my nipples distended, as if unseen mouths were sucking them upward; livid marks emerged on my stomach, thighs and sex, like love bites, only there was no love there.

Even worse, I could see flashes of them as they crowded around us, like explosions of hate across my vision: faces bending over me, with fierce satisfaction in their eyes; hands holding me down, with grips hard enough to bruise; the less gifted leaning forward with fists clenched, eager to witness my humiliation.

I stared back in shock. There were so many now, what must have been hundreds as word ran like wildfire through the camp. Far too many to contain news of what was happening.

But then, Villi didn't want it contained, did he?

He'd put it out there on purpose, and not just for the reason stated. But because he had never done anything of importance in his life. I saw that clearly through the Common, saw his whole existence flash across my vision in an instant: no money, no powerful allies, no talents of note. No reason for anyone to remember him.

Until now.

Now, his actions were being immortalized in a record that couldn't die, couldn't decay, and couldn't be erased. I could see glimpses of it being recorded in real time, including my terrified face as he jerked me under him again. And shoved my thighs apart.

My full-body shudder rippled through the watchers; my broken cry was echoed in a hundred throats. Or maybe that was something else. Because the next moment, a different sound drifted through the forest.

It was sporadic at first, distant and faint. But it quickly built to a crescendo. Until the whole camp echoed with the sounds of the fey screaming themselves hoarse, a collective roar, a great clamor like at a football game or on a battlefield.

It echoed in my brain until I thought I would go crazy. It echoed in my heart along with jeering, taunting, hate-filled voices. It echoed in my body in the strange, unseen assault that held me down even as I struggled, slamming me back against the dirt when I tried to run, while the triumphant cheers went on and on.

"What's that?" the younger fey asked, looking around. "What's going on?"

"They're cheering for us!" Villi said viciously. "They know what's about to happen." He bent over me, his gleeful face in mine. "Do you know it yet, little goddess? Do you *feel* it?"

He deliberately slid full-length against me, and I couldn't repress a choked cry. He laughed and did it again, more slowly. Allowing my alarm at what was coming to build for long seconds, knowing myself defenseless.

"That dread you're experiencing?" he hissed. "That's how we felt at Issengeir, when you took down our shield and unleashed your monsters on us. Helpless. Horrified. Exposed. Wide open to an attack we couldn't hope to win, and a fate we couldn't avoid.

"Let us see how well you like it."

I stared up at him, my skin icing over, my heart threatening to beat out of my chest.

This wasn't happening, this wasn't happening, this wasn't—

Until it was.

The fey pushed forward, only a small motion, hardly anything at all. Except that he was suddenly inside me, his flesh parting mine. He was thick and hot and eager, and I was unprepared, but that wasn't the worst part.

The worst part was that he wasn't alone.

He pushed and they pushed with him, what seemed like half the camp. And their link with the Common ensured that they experienced everything that he did. They all felt the warmth of my body as it opened before them; they all knew the grip of my flesh as it engulfed them; they all witnessed the stretch of my flushed skin around them, where our bodies met and merged.

They all stared back at me from the fey's eyes when he crowed in triumph, the heat of his groin flat against me like a brand.

I felt my world skew, heard my pulse beating hard in my ears, tasted panic bright and acrid on my tongue. I saw spots dancing before my eyes and thought I might pass out, and couldn't decide if that would be a blessing or not. I tried to tell myself to calm down, to remember my training, to *think*.

But the only thing that happened was my body frantically tightening around him, desperate to force him out.

"She does feel different," the younger fey said. And his tone, so calm, so matter of fact, so exactly as it had been a moment ago, was the most obscene thing I'd ever heard.

Until the storm of voices outside abruptly became a hurricane. I thought they'd been at a fever pitch before, but now they erupted in wild elation, screaming Villi's name across the camp. But there was something else, something underneath, something . . . I didn't know. But the younger fey heard it, too.

It was a haunting sound that suddenly had him looking spooked. He put a hand on his companion's arm. "Wait. Something's wrong—"

"Yes, you're in my way," Villi said, shaking him off and bending over me again.

And finally got the scream he'd demanded, although probably not for the reason he'd expected.

But because something that looked like a black hole had just opened inside of his face.

For a moment, I just stared; it didn't look real. Even this close, it didn't. Whatever was happening to him had distorted the features and stretched the skin, drawing it inward in deeply etched lines. As if someone had reached through the back of his skull, grasped his nose, and jerked. And at the same time, the skin itself was withering and shrinking, and flooding an old, brownish yellow.

His hands, too, were desiccating, shriveling up as I watched. In seconds, the fingers gripping me looked like lacquered leather and felt like bone. And little pieces of his hair, now dead white, were breaking off and blowing away on the wind whipping through the tent flap.

The same thing was happening to the younger fey now, too. He was writhing on the floor, and what had been a youthful body with long, fair hair and unwrinkled skin, had aged in the space of a few seconds to . . . something else. Something horrible.

I screamed again, and scrambled back from what suddenly looked like a couple of ancient Egyptian mummies. The fey were disintegrating in front of my eyes, but Villi, at least, didn't seem to know it. He gave one of those unearthly rattles, which I now recognized as a scream through shriveled up vocal cords, and lunged for me.

The grizzled hair was falling out in clumps; the eyes were huge and staring, and the skeletal hands were reaching out, the nails long and clawed from the flesh having pulled away from them. I grabbed a sword, I wasn't sure whose, and swung it wildly, just trying to keep the creature away from me. But it did more than that.

The blade slashed through him as if he was made out of paper mâché, and he fell, shattering against the hard-packed dirt, into a handful of cracked bones and an explosion of brown dust.

I didn't scream that time; I was all out, and it felt like a hand had closed around my throat in any case. I just crouched there, stunned and disbelieving, as events from the Common flashed across my vision. I could see three camps in close proximity, could see thousands of fey. And while many of them were fine, many of them oblivious, others . . .

Were bursting apart like brown fireworks.

It was like a dust cloud had descended on the camp, boiling up through the canopy of trees and sifting into the sky.

For a moment, I understood exactly nothing. And then I heard a voice in my head, a distant echo of something Pritkin's incubus had said to me once. *He won't do it for anyone else, but he would do it for you.*

It had been at Gertie's, after he had used his power to save us. He had been lamenting that he was weakened by Pritkin's refusal to become who he was meant to be. To reunify with his other half and make peace with who and what he was.

Pritkin, I thought desperately, and for an instant, I saw him: standing on a distant platform, high in a gigantic tree, with one arm outstretched. He was surrounded by strange looking fey I didn't recognize, including a bunch of the trolls he had mentioned. They were huge, powerfully built creatures, with arms as big around as most human bodies, but they were backing up, with worry and confusion on their faces.

Because that didn't look like Pritkin anymore.

Or, rather, it did, but Pritkin as he should have been, all along: eyes glowing like dark stars, ratty old coachman's coat billowing out behind him as if on its own wind, skin glowing with stolen power. Dozens, possibly hundreds, of fey were writhing, were dying, were dropping to their knees—

And then Pritkin thrust out his hand, grabbed something in mid-air, and *jerked*.

And the cloud became a storm.

I heard the sound of it, howling through the camp outside. Heard voices, suddenly raised in terror, and as quickly silenced. Only they weren't really silenced, were they? They screamed through the night like tortured shades.

Or maybe that was the wind. Because nature seemed to be reflecting my emotions, with what sounded like a full-on storm blowing up outside. The unsecured tent door was flapping like a laughing mouth, the walls were shaking, and that strange, unearthly cry was increasing as I stumbled back, hitting a wall and dropping the sword I no longer needed, since there was nobody left to use it on.

And I suddenly remembered what Pritkin had said to me, about the night his wife died.

Ruth had talked to Rosier, Pritkin's estranged father, about the ability of the incubus royal house to magnify magical energy. She'd wanted to know if it would work for her; and that, assuming she could persuade her fiancé to participate in incubus sex with her, it would increase her power and thus her status in the demon world. Because money hadn't been all that she was after.

She'd longed for rank, position, to *be* someone. And the demon lord she'd made a bargain with couldn't give her that. But the prince of the incubi could.

Rosier hadn't stopped to wonder what it might do to his son if his new wife died in his arms. Hadn't even bothered to warn him. Instead, he'd encouraged her, believing that a powerful demon lover might do what he couldn't, and lure his son back to the hells.

But Ruth must have known Pritkin well enough to realize that empowering his demon side was the last thing he wanted. So, she hadn't asked. She'd waited until their wedding night, then initiated the feedback loop herself, the way that Rosier had taught her.

And had gotten far more than she'd bargained for.

Pritkin hadn't had the demon version of sex before, and took a moment to figure out how to shut it down. And before he could manage, his much greater abilities had sucked Ruth dry. He'd described her as feeling brittle in his arms and looking like a dried-out husk.

I wondered now, if he hadn't managed to stop when he did, would she have dusted away, too?

Would she have looked like this?

Why did I think that the answer might be yes?

And, finally, I understood. Pritkin had a link with me through Lover's Knot, allowing him to see what was happening whenever I interacted with the Common. He must have seen what was going on, just as all those fey had, and realized that he had a way to stop it.

Lust is to an incubus what blood is to a vampire—a conduit into someone's life force. Or into many someone's, since the fey had linked themselves through the Common to Villi, which wasn't just a hive mind. It was a *soul bond*.

They were joined to him the same way that Pritkin was to me. That had allowed them to participate in the assault right along with him, just as if they were doing it themselves. And to experience everything that he did: anger, injured pride, vicious satisfaction—and lust.

They had offered up their power to the Prince of the Incubi on a silver platter.

And he was feasting.

The tent was shaking violently now, and the two fey had started to sift off into the air, the remains of their bodies sparkling in the firelight like gold dust. The fey out in the open, meanwhile, were straight up disappearing, their flesh streaming into the night, their skeletons collapsing at the feet of their horrified comrades. Or in the case of the more powerful ones, detonating like a fleshy bomb had gone off, and sending their fellow fey running through billowing gales of choking, ash-like remains.

And through it all, Pritkin only glowed brighter in my mind's eye. He looked like what he was, what he'd always been, no matter how much he'd tried to deny it: a demon lord of terrible power, now reunited for the first time in centuries, with all his abilities fully online. And with enough strength to burst through the potion's effects and unleash himself on Aeslinn's army.

And the king noticed.

I felt rather than saw the silver head turn, in a stuttering motion because we hadn't just gotten one person's attention. We'd gotten two. And they were coming, fighting their way through a storm of their own army's corpses, but not for Pritkin, who wasn't here.

They were coming for me.

"*Run*," I heard the single word reverberate in my mind, and wasn't sure if it had come from me or Pritkin or Faerie itself.

I also didn't care.

I ran.

Chapter Fourteen

Somehow, I thought to snatch up a blanket on the way out of the door. I left the sword behind, because it was huge and unwieldy, being longer than any human variety to match its master's height, and because I was too weak to wield it. My limbs felt like rubber, my knees were threatening to give way any second, and my hands were shaking.

But I remembered the blanket and threw it over myself, including my very non-Svarestri-looking hair. It was a terrible disguise, even without the fact that no fey would be five-foot-four, except for a child. But no one noticed.

The formerly quiet forest was quiet no longer.

Ducking into the night, I found fey puffing away into powder on all sides. It left brown, ghost-like apparitions in their place from the ash hanging in the air, until the next breath of wind came by and ripped them apart. I tried not to breathe them in, but it was impossible; they were everywhere.

We'd been almost alone in our isolated corner of the camp not so long ago, but it looked like some of the audience had wanted an in-person view. Or maybe they'd planned to be next. I didn't know why they were there, just that I stumbled through a ghostly crowd, choking on their remains, which the wind was fast turning into a brown cyclone.

Through the swirling bands, I noticed strange, indistinct colors flitting behind the trees. They were bigger than the fey, and oddly shaped. But I couldn't see them well and didn't know the cause.

And didn't care, not with Aeslinn coming at me like a boiling tide. His great power swept before him, or maybe Zeus's power—I didn't know. I just knew that I had to move and move now, only I didn't know where!

My heart was beating so hard that it felt like it would tear itself out of my body as I paused, looking frantically around, caught in indecision. And then a fey ran at me with his sword brandished, his mouth screaming and his eyes wild. And burst into a million fluttering fragments right before he struck, filling my nose and throat with brown confetti.

And causing me to flee in terror, but not into the forest behind the tent.

I couldn't think very well, could barely think at all, but I knew there was no safety there. Aeslinn had said that he'd stationed an army around the camp, to catch Pritkin if he came for me. There was no way I'd get through all that, and even if I did, I didn't know where my friends were and couldn't ask.

Pritkin had been able to get a short, one-word sentence to me, but the same wasn't true in reverse. I tried and tried, but the potion was blocking me, and the golden vial that might have restored my power was back in the tent, likely turned to ash along with the fey. And even if it wasn't, I couldn't go back for it now.

A glance behind me showed a dozen soldiers stampeding through the swirling ash storm and into the tent. Their torches caused it to shine like a beacon as they tore it apart, looking for someone who was no longer there. Instead, I was surrounded by disintegrating fey and darkness, with only a few campfires illuminating the darkness.

But they were enough for me to see how much trouble I was in.

I paused, halfway across an abandoned campsite, as a group of fey burst out of the forest on the other side. They ran straight at me, swords out and gleaming in reflected firelight. I froze; there was nowhere to go, and I would vastly prefer to be killed than captured again.

Only I was neither.

They parted around me, not even pausing, like people who had more to worry about than a freaked-out clairvoyant.

Probably because of that, I thought, staring ahead, at where some of that swift moving color had just burst through the trees.

It wasn't indistinct anymore. Instead, I found myself looking at a herd of huge, blue-gray oxen, if oxen had horns twice as long as my spread arms and stood twelve feet tall. And I was right in their path.

I did run that time, not that it helped. They stampeded right over me, dozens of them, when even one should have been enough to kill me. Yet they passed through me and kept on going, without raising so much as a breath of air in their wake. I didn't feel them, not even as I would have a ghost. It was more like a movie, playing across my body for an instant, and then suddenly gone.

Or, no, I slowly realized.

Not a movie.

An *imprint*.

I spun around and stared after them, and realized that Faerie must be helping me, using her abilities to terrorize the fey through the Common and keep them distracted. The creatures she was projecting into everyone's brains weren't real. But they looked real, and in a camp where random fey were dusting away to ash, that was good enough.

At least for a moment, until they figured out the deception, but I didn't waste any time. I took off, ignoring the sharp undergrowth biting into my feet, the cries of fey all around me, and an arrow that just grazed my thigh, opening up a line of dripping pain. Guessed somebody hadn't gotten the memo about keeping me alive.

Or maybe Aeslinn had rescinded it.

I could feel his anger, boiling through the forest, could hear shouted commands that might have been his, magically enhanced and reverberating off the trees. He was calling in the army, was telling them to tighten the circle, to make sure that nobody got through. He was going to trap me.

I ran anyway, although I wasn't sure where I was going. I wasn't sure of anything anymore, just wanted to get under cover. I grabbed a tree trunk after a moment, at the edge of a small copse, and held on while creatures out of legend—fey legend, I assumed—prowled through the forest. There was a huge white stag, its body and antlers boiling with pale fire, its eyes bright as starlight; there were massive, shaggy things with no faces, just mounds of trailing moss, like giants wearing Gilly suits; and there were tentacled horrors, because everybody's legends seem to include tentacled horrors, and watching them, I understood why.

They scared the hell out of me, even though I knew they weren't really there.

But they fey didn't know that. And more and more of the army was dusting away on the wind, causing others to flee in terror. Some of those even managed to attack their own people, slinging spells at apparitions only to hit real fey behind them.

But there were also pockets of soldiers crowding under masses of torches, grim-faced and determined. And spreading out, starting a systematic search while I stayed where I was, lost in shadows that wouldn't hide me for long. I had to get out of here; I had to *think*.

"Pritkin," I whispered, hoping that he could hear me even if the opposite wasn't true. "Shift me. Just concentrate and shift me to where you are."

I waited, biting my lip almost in two, but nothing happened. I tried again, and had the same result. My throat was raw but I felt like screaming, in frustration and fear and increasing panic. And confusion: why couldn't he *do* this?

Even if he wasn't able to hear my plea, Pritkin was smart enough to figure it out for himself, and he'd shifted us before. He'd taken us out of a burning building once, so I knew he knew how. And even if not, Mircea certainly did.

He had been jackrabbiting all over the timeline at one point, looking for his wife and evading me. And yes, this was Faerie, where the Pythian power didn't work, but we didn't need it. Pritkin had just pulled enough energy off those fey to get us all out of here!

"Pritkin," I whispered, my fingers digging into the tree bark. "Please *try*."

But if he was, it wasn't working. And, finally, I realized that that might be my fault. He wasn't Pythia and had to borrow the ability from me in order to shift.

And right now, all of my abilities were off-line.

He couldn't save me, I thought, blackness clawing at the edges of my vision. And I couldn't do it, couldn't do anything. That bastard of a fey had said that the drug he'd given me would keep me helpless for at least a day.

And I didn't have a day.

I went to my knees in the dirt, wishing to God that I had that black vial, because I would have taken it then. All of it, without hesitation. I'd have drunk it down and been grateful for it, not out of bravery, but out of fear, the most I'd ever known, clawing and tearing at me like the wind had done to those fey.

And like it was doing to the ground in front of me, pulling away a layer of loose soil and leaves, and revealing . . .

Something else.

For a moment, I just knelt there, staring at what looked like a glowing blue footprint. But not one made by the soft soled boots the fey wore, or even by the heavy combat footwear of a dark mage. But something that had imprinted *Salvatore Ferragamo* into the soil, with *Tramezza* just underneath. The Italian designer's bespoke, handmade line . . .

Mircea, I thought, my heart clenching. And then I was brushing away the leaves frenziedly, until I found another print, smudged and half erased but visible. And then another, but not an Italian loafer this time. But a steel toed boot of the kind that Pritkin favored.

I caught sight of a gleam of blue up ahead, scrambled forward, and found another print, and then another and another. Until I was looking at a trail of footprints shining with pale luminescence in the dark, following the tree line separating several camps. I stared at them for a second, unsure of exactly what was going on.

And then I remembered something Pritkin had said: *I used a* pediseequus *charm, a tracking spell that highlighted only our footprints, to allow us to find our way back to the portal.*

And he was using it again now, for me.

I lurched to my feet, my heart thudding again, hard enough to make me dizzy. Only, this time, it was with hope. And then I hurried off, following a pathway that it seemed only I could see.

Or part of one. The footprints had been there for more than a day, and were really faint. They were also missing in areas, where the fey had scattered them in their haste to leave or they had been covered up by dirt and leaf fall. And even when I could make them out, there was often no available cover, forcing me out into the open, through half packed camps and cleared spaces.

I didn't know how Mircea and Pritkin had made it across some of those when the fey were here. But I had it a little easier, since many of the campsites were now deserted. I passed a hastily abandoned dinner that was scorching the bottom of a pan; a couple of abandoned horses, seizing the opportunity to graze after their masters ran off; and someone's hose flapping on a clothes line, forgotten in the chaos.

But other areas were hives of activity. Commands were being shouted; torches were being swung around; and in some cases, were being thrust through the foliage almost on top of me. In those instances, I hugged a tree, pulling the dark blanket over my pale face and hair, and tried to sink into the bark.

I guessed it worked, as no one grabbed me.

Of course, they were distracted.

Giants were stalking the camp now, huge things swinging clubs the size of tree trunks at terrified fey. Screams, curses and shouted commands flowed over me like water as I used the distraction provided and doggedly stayed on the trail. And almost landed in a mess as a result.

The footprints had led me back to the portal all right, or to a rocky edifice that I guessed served as the entrance to the tunnels that housed it. But the whole area was packed with fey. Of course, it was, Cassie! I thought. How did you think they were getting out?

Pritkin had said that this was the only portal for hundreds of miles. The fey must have been using it to bring in food and supplies, as well as to allow them to bug out, should their enemies find them. It fit with something he and I had seen months ago, when we'd stumbled across a fey portal somewhere that it had no business being.

It had been in medieval Wales, which made sense to me now, as that was where the Green Fey had recruited a lot of the women they used to produce half fey children for cannon fodder in their wars with Aeslinn. The kids who hadn't turned out to have enough magic to be useful had been dumped back on Earth, the majority in their mother's homeland. Making it a windfall for Aeslinn, who didn't care about their abilities as much as the god-blood flowing in some of their veins.

He'd probably been using his portal network to help him hunt, and was now using it to stay ahead of our forces. But that meant that it was the only way out of here for three large camps. I was standing in the fey equivalent of Grand Central.

I pulled back behind a tree, panting in fear and exertion but trying to do it quietly. Not that it mattered. Chaos had broken out at the entrance to the tunnels, with everyone trying to push through at once.

No way was I getting through there.

I shouldn't even be here, I thought, panic threatening to swamp me. The large number of torches and lanterns being carried by the crowd was splashing the area around the entrance with light, turning it almost as bright as day. Every instinct I had was telling me to get somewhere darker and do it fast. But Pritkin wouldn't have brought me here if he didn't have a plan; I knew he wouldn't!

And then someone spotted me.

"The witch! The witch!"

"Kill her—now!"

"The king wants her alive—"

"And I want her dead! She killed my *brother*—"

A fey lunged for me out of the crowd, murder on his face. And was tackled by several more, who brought him down and held him back, I had no idea why. And then I realized: I'd instinctively raised a hand to ward him off, at the exact moment that another fey had dusted into powder.

Pritkin, I thought. Or maybe a coincidence. There was only one way to find out.

I walked forward a step, and another fey disappeared, except for some fragments of bone that rattled down onto the rocky ground with little plinks.

I stared at them, as most of the crowd was doing, then took another step, out into the firelight of a wavering torch—

And a fey puffed away from the back of a horse, causing it to buck and rear in fright, and the crowd to take a collective step backward.

That allowed me to see Pritkin's footprints again, smudged and indistinct, like blue confetti scattered over the dirt. But they stubbornly led the way into the tunnel, nonetheless, which looked like the gateway to hell. Torchlight on ochre soil gave everything a red tinge, and the leaping flames reflecting off the walls made it look like the whole place was burning.

But I took another step forward anyway. I trusted him, and there was no longer any choice. I'd been found; it wouldn't take long for word to reach Aeslinn. If I was getting out of here, it had to be now.

"I just want to leave!" I said loudly, my own voice startling me.

It didn't sound like normal; my screams had left their mark. But hoarseness made it lower, more resonant, and more commanding. Several members of the crowd jumped, and others stared at me as if they'd just heard the voice of doom.

"I just want to leave," I repeated harshly. "Let me go, unmolested, and I will not harm you. Otherwise, I swear that all of your bones will dust the earth this night!"

It was over the top, theatrical, and a complete bluff. I didn't know if Pritkin could dust them all. I didn't think so, as I doubted that everyone had been plugged into Villi's little show. And likely most of those who had were already dead. But I started forward anyway, trying to look confident.

And the crowd parted in front of me in an almost liquid motion.

"You can't!" the fey on the ground yelled, fighting and clawing to reach me. "What are you doing? She killed my brother!"

"And she'll kill us if you don't shut up!" someone else said.

"And what do you think the king is going to do?" the first fey asked viciously. "At least she'll kill you fast. Don't expect him to be so kind!"

Shit, I thought, and seriously considered breaking into a run. But I'd just passed into the tunnel system, and it was packed. People must have been following what was happening outside, because they were drawing back, were hugging the walls, were making sure not to touch me. But some were glaring with as much hate as the vengeful fey outside.

Showing weakness was not the way to get through this.

I kept walking, as fast as possible without looking panicked. It wasn't easy. I was tiny compared to them, and dirty and bloody and probably terrified-looking. I made a sorry excuse for a goddess, and I could almost see the wheels turning in some of their minds: how much the king would give to get his prize back; how easy it would be, in such close corners, to lash out and knock me unconscious; how life changing the result—

And the further I went in, the worse it got, because the fey down here hadn't seen what had happened outside. They might have heard, through the whispers running ahead of me. But they hadn't seen.

And that made all the difference.

But nobody wanted to be the first to chance it, and I didn't have much farther to go. The fey had reconfigured the tunnels again, to make the evacuation go smoother, and the portal was just ahead. I couldn't see it yet, but I could see the color that it splashed on the walls and floor.

Almost there, I thought, speeding up.

Almost there—

And then somebody broke.

Out of nowhere, a fist connected with my jaw, hard enough to throw me to the ground. And before I could even see who it was, someone else kicked me in the side. The pain was blinding and immediate, and when I tried to take a breath, one of my own ribs stabbed me like a dagger, cutting it off. Then a group of them were beating me, and they weren't merely trying to wound. I felt bones break, skin split, and something collapse in my chest.

I could see the swirl of light up ahead, but I couldn't reach it. I'd almost gotten to the point where the light would have splashed me, and where maybe I could have lurched to freedom even with what felt like a broken leg. But no way was I making it to that portal now.

And I didn't. Instead, it came to me, or rather, its light did, suddenly expanding and flooding over the ugly stones and uglier faces, extending outward like a divine hand. And it didn't come alone.

The light abruptly shifted, from a faint green to a hellish red, and out of the maw muscled a band of very strange creatures.

A small, horned man in a dapper green suit—the joke teller from the demon enclave—hit down onto the dirt. He had brown, button-up boots; I could see them from here, the leather shining in all that light. And they were soon joined by dozens of others.

I knew them all: the towering lizard woman who had accidentally terrorized Nigel; the strange, accordion-like man I'd encountered at Ruth's boarding house, who fluttered when he walked; a dozen of the bar's patrons, including the six-armed barman, the duo of blue creatures with eyes on stalks, the searingly yellow woman with fingernails like daggers, and the red skinned, two-headed man. Even the broad-faced butcher from the street was there, brandishing a bloody cleaver. And, finally, a flurry of the tiny, beak-faced waiters arrived, glowing in every color of the rainbow.

The beating had stopped, as the fey paused to stare at creatures that must have seemed as alien to them as they did to me. But when the waitstaff suddenly charged, all at once, chaos broke out, perhaps because the rest of the bar's patrons were right behind them. Or because they reminded everyone of pixies, and they're nobody's idea of fun.

But whatever the cause, I was suddenly being trampled as fey fought with fey, in a mad scramble to retreat.

I wondered how long it would take for them to figure out that my rescuers didn't actually exist, that they were echoes of people long dead, stored up in the Common's great memory. I decided not to wait and find out. And discovered that I'd been right: I couldn't walk, or even hobble.

So, I crawled instead. I could feel the light tugging on me, the portal trying to suck me in, even from here. But it couldn't quite manage it, and I guessed it was already at its maximum, since I didn't get any more help.

And I needed it.

Someone was coming.

I crawled as fast as I could, but I could barely breathe, with what felt like a collapsed lung, and even my "good" leg wasn't working right. I didn't know how long I could keep going with agony stabbing me in the side and my head whirling and darkness encroaching on my vision. But I had to try, because what sounded like a whole platoon of boots was pounding down the corridor after me.

It looked like Aeslinn had figured out where I'd gone.

And these must have been his elite troops, who were smart enough to realize that the creatures they were seeing were imaginary. Because they didn't even slow down. But they did get confused, when even more unearthly horrors vomited forth from the portal, far too many to fit into that small of a corridor.

But they did add to the chaos.

Suddenly, all I could see was flowing color and shuffling feet, some of which were real, along with the weapons that stabbed down at me. But the weapons didn't connect, since the fey couldn't see a damned thing, either. The portal was dazzling and the newcomers were everywhere as Faerie bought me one last chance to escape. And I took it, ignoring the swords, shouted commands, everything except the light shining from the swirling heart of the portal, just ahead.

And then all around me, when I threw myself forward, under a dozen reaching hands, and was through.

Chapter Fifteen

Something woke me, and for a moment, I didn't know who I was or where I was. The space around me was a boiling darkness, with only a little slightly-less-dark leaking through what might have been a window. I lay there, tense and jittery and not knowing why.

And then I remembered why and hit the floor, trying to scramble away from enemies that were no longer there. But I did it quietly, with my bottom lip clamped tightly between my teeth, as it had been in front of the portal. Any sound might have given away my location and resulted in immediate death.

So, the only noise was a vague thump when I landed on smooth old floorboards, which I vaguely identified as belonging to my bedroom at Gertie's. But I guessed that was enough. A moment later, Iris was through the door, with worry on her face and two war mages on her heels.

The blonde was a Grace Kelley clone and my self-appointed groupie at Gertie's court. So, I wasn't too surprised to see her up and about, even though it looked to be either really late or really early, judging by the view outside my bedroom window. But the war mages were a different story.

One was ebony dark, the other a pale-faced ginger. But both had stocky, powerful builds that made the small room feel even smaller, and neither looked like the old or infirm types that usually got shunted off to the Pythian Court. The Circle practically used it as a convalescent home, especially under a powerful Pythia like Gertie who didn't need much protection. But these two looked pretty healthy.

They also had shields up; I didn't know why. But I could see them, a faint blue-green sheen pulled in tightly around their bodies, almost like a second skin, the way Corpsmen wore them when they were trying to be discreet. Although that would have worked better in daylight, when the sun might have drowned out the glow, and if they hadn't just come in from the rain.

Droplets gleamed in the light of Iris's lantern, and ran down the surface of the shields in long lines, ruining the deception. Their armor's energy would evaporate the water pretty quickly, meaning that they'd just popped the shields and they'd just come in. So . . . were those for me?

I looked down at myself, a scrawny, barefoot figure in a rumpled nightgown, whose hands trembled slightly even though I had them tightly clasped in my lap. I assumed that I should feel proud that they thought I warranted precautions, but I didn't. Mostly, I just felt confused.

"Is there a problem?" I croaked, looking up. Iris sat down the lantern she'd been holding—and needed, since Gertie had never had electricity run up here—and snatched a blanket off the bed. She moved to wrap it around me, since the thin gown I had on didn't count as proper attire in the Edwardian period.

But that put her momentarily between me and the mages, which didn't seem to be allowed. The ginger one gripped her arm. "Don't touch her."

"She's cold—"

"She's also possibly possessed. You're not to be near her until she's been examined—"

"By whose orders?" Iris asked, looking indignant.

"The Circle's."

"The Circle doesn't have jurisdiction here—"

"It does in cases of danger to the court, and she's a potential threat."

"She is not!"

I wondered if the mages clumping up the stairs in their giant boots had been what woke me, and decided probably. I also decided that there wasn't much I could do about it. I was back in my own world, but my power was remained AWOL.

It looked like I was going to be asked some hard questions, which . . . good luck.

My brain felt like a sieve.

"Stand aside," the mage told Iris, looking grim, and then physically moved her out of the way before she could respond.

And promptly disappeared, the big, leather-clad figure vanishing out of sight between one blink and the next.

I hadn't done it; couldn't have if I'd wanted to. But the remaining mage focused on me anyway, and his hand dropped to his belt. I assumed that he was reaching for something to immobilize me with, which had me abruptly scrambling back, my heart pounding and my eyes blown wide. If he put restraints on me—

I would absolutely lose my shit.

"Don't move!" he warned, taking a step forward.

And I didn't.

Because the next moment, he vanished as well.

The droplets off his coat hit the ground in a miniature rain shower, but the half-evaporated water vapor hung in the air for a second, in a vague outline of his body. It reminded me of the fey and their dust doppelgangers, and suddenly, I was back in that fire-lit camp, trying to follow a mostly missing trail before I was savagely murdered. Which was why I scrambled back some more, until I hit the wall hard enough to rattle me.

I also succeeded in nearly turning over the bedside table, and the lantern along with it. Fortunately, Iris caught it and then she caught me. "Are you alright?" she asked, looking concerned.

Which wasn't helped when I burst out laughing.

I got myself under control pretty quickly, hearing the not-so-faint edge of hysteria in my voice. Iris had, too, judging by her expression, but she didn't comment. She helped me up instead, but even so, it took a couple of tries to get back on my feet, although not because I was clumsy.

But because my brain kept insisting that one of my legs was broken, and that the other was suspect. It was adamant that they couldn't support my weight. Like it kept telling me that my ribs were smashed on the left-hand side, and was convincing enough that I actually put a hand there.

Only to feel nothing but hard, strong bones curving under my fingertips.

I cleared my throat and hoped she hadn't noticed. "You, uh, you going to get in trouble for that?"

"For shifting the mages?"

I nodded.

She shook her head, causing her pearl earrings to gleam in the lantern light. "If anything, it's the other way around. The lady gave orders for me to see to it that you rested, and to bring you to her in the morning. Not to let you to be dragged away in the middle of the night for some sort of interrogation. The very idea!"

"What did they want to interrogate me about?" I wasn't aware of any rules I'd broken in Edwardian England.

"About what happened yesterday. Or so they say."

"I'm . . . having a problem remembering yesterday," I admitted.

"You and Miss Lacey went into the imprint," she reminded me, while sitting me on the bed and adjusting the blanket around me. "And awoke last evening after being unconscious for most of the day. We were starting to worry; I have never seen a dive take so long, and when you did return, you were . . . upset—"

Acting crazed, I mentally translated.

"—and attracted the attention of the knights who protect the court. But I think their real interest is in what happened the other day. We tried to erase their memories after the incident on the Thames, but those sorts of spells rarely work on them. They're trained to throw them off—"

"So, they were already wary of me, then saw me yelling about weird shit and assumed I was possessed," I finished for her.

It was fair. The last time they'd seen me, I *had* been possessed, and with the power of an elder god. I'd sucked down some of Zeus's energy during the battle on the river, and he'd managed to turn it against me. Not taking me over so much as trying to incinerate me from the inside.

The ensuing fight had been long, sustained, and loud. The mages had reason to be concerned. But Iris didn't see it that way.

"It was ridiculous," she said, her pretty face flushing. "We tried to explain that you had interacted with a dangerous imprint and were simply confused. It often takes a while to throw off the effects of such things, as they should know."

Yeah, only that wasn't what had happened. But I didn't try to correct her. On the whole, telling them that was easier than explaining that I'd accidentally kidnapped two people's minds and taken all of us into Faerie, where we'd gotten new bodies and fought a god.

A lot easier.

"Where did you send them?" I asked.

"A very nice pub in Gloucester," she said, fluffing my pillows. "It's not near any ley lines, and it's too late to hire transport. But they can likely get a bed for the night."

"And contact the Circle, who'll just send more."

"Then the pub will become crowded," she said grimly, before catching my eye. "They do this, from time to time. Pushing to see what we will let them get away with. I think they'd like to put us all in a box and only let us out when they want something. But we are not their pet clairvoyants; we are the Pythian Court. If they wish to see you, they can make a request from the Lady in the morning—should she choose to see them."

I blinked up at Iris, who for some reason I'd been mistaking for a lightweight. So, that's how you do it, I thought. Firm, kind, even gracious, but implacable. Impressive.

"Are you hungry?" she asked. "The kitchen staff have gone for the night, but I can see if there's anything left from dinner—"

My stomach rumbled assent before she could even finish the sentence. And I was reminded that I hadn't eaten in over a day. I hadn't drunk much, either, which was probably why I was swaying on my feet while not even being on them.

Iris seemed to realize this, too, or maybe my croaky voice had given it away. She made a disturbed sound and bustled out. And sooner than I'd have expected, she was back with a glass and a carafe, probably from her own room. And something in a napkin that I didn't see until I'd gulped down two glasses of tepid, bedside-table water that tasted like ambrosia and had my whole body tingling.

And then my nose twitched.

"Is that . . . a *scone?*"

She handed it to me. "I'm sorry; it's all I had. I think it might be a bit stale—"

I didn't know. Didn't care. A moment ago, I'd been cold, anxious, shaky and confused. Now, I was still all of those things, but I had a scone. I felt so grateful I could have cried.

Iris watched me wolf it down with obvious distress. "You're starving, poor thing! I'll find you some supper—

I threw up all over Gertie's nice, clean floor.

"—somewhere."

We both stared at the mess in dismay, Iris for obvious reasons, and me because I'd just lost my scone. And at that moment, and in whatever fucked up state of mind I was in, that was the worst thing that had ever happened to me. I burst into tears.

The next few minutes were a jumble of acolytes, summoned by Iris, as no staff slept over thanks to the Circle's paranoia. I wasn't normally the acolytes' favorite person, but they made no comment or even shot me any nasty looks as they cleaned me, cleaned the floor, and fetched a new robe that Iris helped me into. It weirded me out more than the mages had.

Iris also tried to feed me some more, having made a trip down to the kitchen, but even the smell of the very nice plate of food that she'd come up with made me nauseous. She took it away again and I sat on the edge of the bed, feeling embarrassed and stupid and vaguely ill. And then more so as the previous day's events caught up with me.

My brain was fuzzy and confused, which was probably just as well considering what I could remember. But that didn't help me physically, with my body feeling like it had been pumping out adrenaline while I slept and needed something to do with it. Only there was nothing left.

So, I just sat there some more, cold and miserable, with my limbs shaking and my stomach roiling and my mouth tasting terrible and wanting to tremble.

"Try this," someone said gently, and I looked up to see Rhea, holding toast and tea. And then not holding it when I jumped up and grabbed her, hugging her fiercely, and she dropped it and the teacup shattered.

That resulted in the return of the longsuffering acolytes, and me sitting very quietly this time so that I didn't screw up anything else.

"Guinn?" I asked Rhea, as Iris took charge and bossed people about. "Is she—"

"Here," Rhea affirmed. "In London, I mean. They sent her home . . . I think . . ."

"Home?"

Rhea nodded. She appeared almost as confused as I was, with her pupils blown wide, her normally sleek, dark hair everywhere and circles under her eyes. She looked like she'd just fallen out of bed, too.

"You need sleep," I told her profoundly.

The messy head shook. "M'fine. And Guinn—she didn't want to go. Put up a fuss. Wanted to fight alongside us—"

"Can't. She's from another time—"

"That's what I said," Rhea agreed. "But she wasn't listening. Grabbed my wand and was holding everyone off. Wanted to talk to you, but they'd already knocked you out—"

"Do I want to know why?" I asked.

She shot me a bleary look. "You were yelling and thrashing about on the floor, and we thought your leg was broken. But you wouldn't let anybody near you, so Agnes knocked you out—with a spell," she added, because Agnes.

I was kind of glad I couldn't remember that.

"In the end, Lady Herophile did the mind wipe on Guinn herself and sent her home in one of the court's own carriages. She deserved no less; she was very brave—"

That was an understatement. Guinn, the touch telepath who had been hired merely to help me navigate an imprint, had gotten sucked into Faerie along with me and Rhea. She was part fey, but had never been there, and knew little more about it than I did. Yet she'd saved my life several times over, risking her own in the process. I owed her a debt that I'd likely never be able to repay, since we didn't even live in the same century.

Unless it was by helping her people, I thought, thinking of all those fey and part-fey who had fled to Earth to avoid the dangers in Faerie, only to discover a bigger one stalking them here. No wonder she hadn't wanted to leave. She'd probably been after some assurance that Aeslinn would pay for his crimes.

I'll do what I can, I promised her silently, and meant it.

"How did you and Guinn get back?" I asked. The last time I'd seen them, they'd been up a tree.

Rhea frowned and glanced down at the bed, as if she felt it rocking a little, too. Or maybe not so little, since she put out a hand to steady herself. And missed.

She finally located the mattress and hung on, with the grim air of someone clinging to an overturned lifeboat. "Don't know. Suddenly turned up here. Think we left when you did."

I took a moment to try to puzzle that out. And then took another since the first one didn't work. And a third, because the more I thought about it, the weirder this whole thing became.

It looked like our souls had been linked on some level, and when mine left, it had pulled theirs out as well. And since we'd ended up back here, I assumed that part of my soul hadn't gone into Faerie, after all, but had remained in the body snoozing in front of Gertie's fireplace, holding down the fort. That part made sense, as the same thing happened in Chimera, a Pythian spell that allowed for the creation of an extra body to house part of a Pythia's soul, and allow her to be in two places at once.

Only I hadn't cast Chimera. I hadn't cast anything. I had merely tried to use Mircea's mental gifts to contact Pritkin and ask him about what Guinn and I had seen in the imprint, and then—

Well, it felt like I'd been jerked inside Faerie and dumped on the ground. And then taken on a tour of the Common that had felt very directed. So had my arrival been, too? Was Faerie responsible for dragging me—and Rhea and Guinn—in there in the first place?

That would make more sense than me doing it on my own. I wasn't in a soul bond with Rhea, much less with a telepath I'd only just met. But Guinn had been in my head, taking me through the imprint when we ended up in Faerie. And Rhea was a member of my court and bound to me on a metaphysical level. So, with a little help from a desperate goddess . . . yeah.

That might have worked.

Faerie had wanted to me rescue Pritkin, so that Zeus couldn't absorb his abilities. And when I succeeded in that, but failed at getting away clean, she'd shown us what was at stake so I would kill myself. Making sure that Zeus couldn't use me as bait, or try to drain Pritkin through me.

Yet, when I failed at that, too, she'd saved me. Or, at least, she'd helped. Was that because I'd chickened out and refused to die on schedule? Had she simply not had a choice?

Because she could have just let the fey kill me on that desperate run through the camp; plenty of them had seemed more than happy to oblige. And I couldn't be a conduit to Pritkin's power if I was dead, right? So, did she want something else?

I didn't know, and my head hurt too much to figure it out. But not nearly as badly as it should have. Like my body failed to show evidence of that last, terrible fight.

A leg had slipped out of my robe, and it bore scars from the battle with Zeus, but it was whole enough. That confirmed the idea that I'd dropped the body Faerie had made me when I went through the portal, and reintegrated with my old one, which explained my brain's confusion. It expected me to be in pieces and didn't know why I wasn't.

And neither did I, since I shouldn't have made it out of there.

I pulled my legs up, clasped my arms around them, and rested my head on my knees. And tried not to think at all for a while. It worked pretty well.

Until Iris came back in from somewhere and eyed the two of us, floating on our life raft and rolling with the tide. "You should go back to bed," she told Rhea gently.

But Rhea got that mulish tilt to her chin that I knew so well. "Staying here," she said, speaking carefully so as not to slur her words. "My Pythia needs me."

"And you need to sleep off the rest of the drought the healer gave you."

"Shouldn't have done that. Put it in my tea," Rhea informed me darkly.

And then she fell backwards onto the bed, and was out like a light.

She was hauled back to bed by Ermengarde, the teenaged linebacker of the court, who rivalled the war mages in physique. I just sat there some more, drinking a new cup of tea that someone had brought me, and eating a new piece of toast. It didn't seem to help much, but at least my stomach shut up.

And then I must have done a Rhea, too, because that was all I remembered.

Chapter Sixteen

The next time I awoke, I took it slower, just lying there quietly and clutching the bed so that I stayed put as it continued to imitate a boat. But not as much as before, when what had felt like a wave had tipped me onto the floor. This was more of a gentle rocking motion that slowly ebbed and then subsided over time.

And was replaced by something else.

Phantom hands slid over me, phantom mouths moved along my skin, phantom bodies pushed against me, hard and eager—

I shrieked and thrashed and tried to shake them off, as if a bunch of ants were crawling all over me. But they weren't ants and it didn't work. Instead, it got worse: wet mouths licked and probed and tasted; hard teeth nipped at my lips and tongue and clit; hands like shackles held me down, the imprint of their fingers clearly visible on my skin. While what felt like a very real hardness thrust inside—

I came off the bed with a scream before burying my face in a pillow to stop the sounds I couldn't control, any more than I had been able to back in that tent.

There's no one here! I told myself furiously. No one is hurting you!

But I didn't believe it. My body didn't believe it. It was shaking and sobbing and flinching away from hateful touches that it swore it could still feel.

I didn't know why I was reliving that, when what had happened in that tunnel had been far more brutal. Villi hadn't been able to kill me, or even seriously injure me, without risking his life. The fey in front of that portal had had no such qualms.

And, yet, that was where my mind went, not to the savage beating, but to the far more intimate violation. Not to the escape, as terrifying as it had been, where at least I'd had some semblance of control. But to the place where I'd had none, or any way out.

But I'd gotten out, I reminded myself. I'd gotten free! So why did it feel like I remained back there, trapped and helpless?

I didn't have an answer, but, eventually, sheer exhaustion did what I couldn't and caused the hateful sensations to taper off. I just lay there for a while, panting slightly and staring at the wall, clutching my pillow in remembered panic. And hating myself.

Is this who you are? my inner voice demanded. *Cowering in a corner, too afraid to move? Like you were too afraid to kill yourself when you had the chance. Do you think Agnes would have hesitated? Gertie? Any of them? This was your fault—*

It wasn't! I thought fiercely. *I didn't know I was going to Faerie. I didn't plan this!*

No, you never plan anything do you? The pitiless little voice asked. *You go charging in where angels fear to tread, expecting providence to catch you. Only this time, someone else did. And now look at you. Too gutless even to get out of bed, too afraid of a dead man—*

"Shut up!"

I yelled it out loud, desperate to drown out the voice. And then almost immediately regretted it when the door cracked and a faint flood of light leaked in. "Cassie?"

I turned over to find Iris standing in the doorway, this time with a candle. She'd changed into nightwear, a frilly gown just peeking out the top of a quilted robe, but she didn't look like she'd been asleep. The fair hair was perfectly combed and secured in its usual smooth chignon, and her face was porcelain pale, not flushed with sleep.

She hurried over. "Are you unwell?"

The beautiful blue eyes were concerned, and a small crease had appeared on the youthful forehead. For a moment, I just looked at her and couldn't answer. And then I found myself gripping her hand, the one she'd placed on my shoulder.

"What are you doing here?"

She looked confused. "Didn't I say? The lady asked me to watch over—"

"No. Here, at court. What are your plans? You must be almost old enough to leave?"

She looked to be in her late teens, although her perpetual air of serenity made it hard to tell. But she couldn't have been much older than that, because the initiates didn't stay with the court forever. Not even those who became acolytes.

One was chosen as the heir, and a couple more were made into Failsafes—powerful acolytes who kept their access to the Pythian power, but who led normal lives unless an emergency called them back, such as the untimely death of a Pythia. That was how I'd met Hilde, who had returned to the court to find out what the hell was going on after Agnes's death and her heir's disappearance. But the majority of talented little seers grew up, completed their training, and went out into the big, wide world, never to think about the court again. Except occasionally as the "boarding school" they all grew up in.

"Oh." Iris looked nonplussed. "I'm not certain. That is, it's such an honor to be selected by the court, and I have such wonderful memories. As well as friends that I'm sure I'll have for a lifetime. But, well, there's a boy . . . a young man now." She blushed slightly, something easy to see on those pale cheeks. "He's from my village. A distant cousin—"

"You should leave," I told her harshly. "Go home, marry your cousin, have lots of babies. And forget that the damned court exists!"

She blinked at me for a moment, then sat down on the bed and took my hand. She could probably feel me trembling, but she didn't comment. Just held on until, after a few moments, the warmth in her touch and her eyes steadied me somewhat.

Not a lot. I still wanted to cry; wanted to scream; wanted to throw things. But Iris being there made me feel a little stronger.

"Rhea mentioned that you encountered Zeus again," she said. "That he somehow assaulted you?"

"Something like that."

"He is foolish, that one."

It took a moment for her words to register, and then I wasn't sure that I'd heard correctly. I turned my head to look at her, and found her glaring off into space. "What?"

Her eyes met mine, and there was anger in them. It was strange to see on that perfect face. Like a furious Barbie doll.

"He was lucky the other day. He escaped you. I'd have thought that he'd be too afraid to try again."

"He isn't afraid," I said, wondering what the hell she was talking about.

"Then he should be!"

"He's a *god*—"

"And you're a Pythia! The best I've ever seen. Even Agnes thinks so, although she won't admit it, and she doesn't think much of any of us. I'd say that was an even match up, wouldn't you?"

"Even?" The rasp was back in my voice, despite the fact that these vocal cords hadn't been shredded screaming my head off in the middle of an enemy camp. "I couldn't even protect myself from—"

I cut off abruptly. Iris didn't need to hear about that. But it was true. I'd been terrorized by a couple of idiots, who were just there to see that I didn't somehow slip my bonds. They weren't needed to guard me; the army was already doing that. They were glorified babysitters, probably chosen for their ineptitude, to give our side a false sense of security in case they had some way to see me from afar.

They were pathetic, and yet I'd only escaped because Pritkin had saved me. But at what cost to himself? Was he alright? Was Mircea? Because I didn't think that I'd brought them out, too.

Theirs weren't replacement bodies. I hadn't pulled them into Faerie through some weird metaphysical loophole, so I couldn't get them out. And Zeus had known that they were close.

Could the dark fey really hide them from him? Could anyone? I felt my hand clench.

"From . . . what?" Iris asked tentatively, after a moment.

"Nothing. I . . . I need to go back to sleep," I said, despite the fact that that was obviously a lie.

I didn't think I'd be sleeping again for a while.

But she didn't argue. She just rose elegantly from the bed and dropped into one of her perfect curtsies. And looked up before she rose, with a strange expression on her face.

"Zeus is a monster," she said softly. "Nothing more. And you're a hero. If I was making a wager, I know who I'd put my money on."

She left and I stared after her, feeling strangely off balance. I waited for my emotions to sort themselves out and tell me how to feel, but they didn't seem to want to. Everything was a blur, everything was jumbled.

Maybe because my inner voice had been wrong. It wasn't a dead man I feared, or even a dead fey. It was one who was very much alive.

I sat up and hugged my knees, wishing that I'd asked for a room change. This one wasn't exactly conductive to sweet dreams, or to clear thinking, being the place where Zeus had almost killed me two days ago. That was after he'd almost killed me during a time shift and then again on the Thames, and before he'd had me kidnapped and brutalized.

And he hadn't even been trying!

He'd been toying with me, indulging his curiosity, and later using me as bait. Yet I'd almost died four times in three days. Meanwhile, his puppet Aeslinn had taken some damage, and even lost a hand. But Zeus?

Didn't have a scratch on him.

The worst he'd suffered was a small energy loss, and even that may have been calculated. His alter ego, Odin, was said to have given up an eye for knowledge; what was a little power compared to that? Yet that bit of power had almost overwhelmed me, Mircea and Pritkin.

Zeus was unlike any opponent I'd ever faced, and he was still out there. And I had no idea, *no idea*, what to do about it. If I couldn't even defend myself against one rag-tag fey guard, what chance did I have against the king of the gods?

The same chance you've always had, my inner voice said impatiently. *Nothing's changed—*

And that was another lie, because everything had.

Or maybe I was just seeing it differently now, after having been the one to suffer for once.

The people around me had been dealing with the consequences of this war for a while. Mac, a retired war mage and a friend of Pritkin's, had died for me during my first trip into Faerie. Rafe, one of my only friends as a child, had suffered horrific burns while helping me, and had only recently recovered. And Billy Joe, my long-time ghostly companion, had perished before the Battle of Issengeir.

And what had happened to me, while all that was going on?

Not much.

Agnes had shot me in the butt, a flesh wound that Mircea had healed soon afterwards. And I'd been knocked about, stalked by some psycho ex-acolytes, and missed some meals. But, as far as physical damage was concerned, that had been about it.

Mentally, I'd been through the wringer, with the learning curve on this job being whiplash inducing. I'd felt fear, plenty of times, but those had been with a lowercase "f". Something that happened in the moment, but could be shrugged off once the danger was over. It hadn't changed me.

I thought that this might have.

I threw off the covers, not knowing where I was going but needing to move. But it was really cold, and I quickly pulled them back around me again. And then just sat there, huddled against the headboard, watching rain shadows stream across the elongated gray square on the floor.

Nothing else moved, and nothing came to get me. I was safe but I didn't feel like it, and wondered if I ever would again. None of the other opponents I'd faced had managed to do this, to have my heart pounding and my breath hitching and my stomach roiling long after the danger was over. But then, that made sense.

They'd all been way less powerful than me.

I hadn't realized that at the time, hadn't understood just how much stronger a Pythia was than most of the competition, such as the acolytes the gods had suborned or the demigod sons that Ares had left behind. I hadn't been trained when I faced them, and had had a very limited skill set. But looking back, those had been pretty lopsided fights.

Things had been considerably more even when I was running from Gertie, before she and I reached an understanding, or the time I went to retrieve Pritkin from his father's realm after the old bastard snatched him back to the hells. But Gertie hadn't been trying to kill me; she'd wanted to capture me and find out why I was dragging a demon lord all over medieval Wales. And Rosier's people . . . well, they might have been more afraid of me than I was of them.

Artemis's name still struck terror into demonic hearts, and when her daughter rolled up to Rosier's palace in a chariot, unarmed and with only a single human bodyguard beside her . . .

Well, they'd probably thought that I was way more of a badass than I was, since who the hell would do that?

An idiot would do that, someone too ignorant to know how much danger she was in. No wonder Pritkin had freaked out! He'd taken one look at me and lost his collective shit, because he knew that bravado only gets you so far, and ignorance can get you killed.

But that was just it—it hadn't gotten me killed, even when I battled the gods. Because I hadn't actually battled them, had I? I'd taken the credit, but the truth was that I'd provided an assist at opportune times to the real MVPs.

Like the Rakshasas who had taken down Apollo. He'd been trapped in a metaphysical vortex, one of the deep wells of power that resulted when two ley lines crossed, and that was after he'd already fought his way through mother's barrier, which had almost killed him. The Rakshasas had savaged him, all but draining him of what power he had left, and caused him to get sucked down the vortex.

The only thing that Pritkin and I had done was to lead him there.

Ares had been a more direct fight, as in, I'd actually been part of that battle. But I hadn't fought him, either. I'd unleashed Apollo's hungry ghost on him instead, releasing it from the Badlands, a place where spirits go when they fade too much to maintain their grip on Earth. And where what was left of Apollo had been preying on their remains while waiting for some payback.

But he'd been more hungry than vengeful, and once released, he'd gone after Ares instead of me. Ares made a better meal, and if he didn't steal enough energy to reinvigorate himself, he'd be killed as a rival once the god of war finished with us. So, Apollo had attacked Ares, giving it everything he had, and then they'd both died when one of Ares' own spells was reflected back at them.

And what had I been doing in the meantime? Sitting beside Pritkin and watching the show from a distance. All we'd needed was popcorn.

And then there was Issengeir.

I tried to push that thought away, since it made me think of Villi's vicious words, and the hate in the eyes of all those other fey. A shiver broke over me, and I clasped my arms even tighter. They blamed me for the loss of their great city and the people who had died defending it.

And they were right.

Pritkin had advised caution after we learned that Jonathan, Aeslinn's pet necromancer, had slipped back in time to warn the king of our attack before it happened. He'd given him our tactics, our allies, a play by play of exactly what happened. Everything needed to make sure that, instead of the great victory for our side that the battle had been, it was going to be a slaughter.

Having been a war mage once, Pritkin didn't want to see his fellow Corpsmen slaughtered. He also didn't want humanity's defenses weakened: lose too many war mages, and the vamps or demons might well take advantage once the war was over. He had voted to warn the Circle and call off the attack.

Mircea, on the other hand, had wanted to go ahead. He'd pointed out that it had been difficult enough to talk the Circle into allying with the vampires, their old enemies, in the first place. It might be impossible to do so again, and since neither group was capable of taking on Aeslinn alone, the war could easily turn into a political quagmire fought out in council sessions instead of on the battlefield, while the king did as he pleased.

He had argued that we three could combine our abilities and turn the tide, ensuring another victory. And possibly even kill Aeslinn in the process, and end the war right there. That had made it one to one, giving me the deciding vote.

And I had voted with Mircea.

In the end, we'd taken Aeslinn's capitol and dispersed his army, although the king had been nowhere to be found. But victory had come at a high price. Only that price had been paid by the Circle and their men, and by Mircea's vampire forces, hadn't it?

Not by me.

Before the last few days, the worst I'd suffered in this war was the loss of Billy, and that was qualified. Ghosts who stayed around too long rarely had happy endings. They were cannibalized by other spirits, eaten by hungry demons, or just faded away when their energy ran out. As much as I missed Billy—and I did, every single damned day—his transition had also been a relief.

He was safe.

But I was not, and now I didn't even have the comfort of ignorance to shield me. Maybe that was why I'd been able to keep going this long: I'd been complaining about how little I knew about this job ever since getting it, but that very ignorance had kept me functional, allowing me to believe that I could actually do this. That we could win.

But now . . .

I felt them again, those hateful, phantom hands. Not in reality this time—I'd shaken off the nightmare when I woke up—but in my memory, where they'd probably been seared forever. They were dead now, dusted to powder by Pritkin's abilities. But the one who had commanded them, and who must have known what was happening?

He was still out there.

And had finally taught me the meaning of Fear.

Chapter Seventeen

Gertie was awake when I went to see her the next morning, but she was dressing, so I took a chair in the parlor outside her bedroom. I actually didn't mind the wait. It was a relief just to sit quietly for a while.

Especially here, because I'd always loved this room.

Gertie's favorite color was a cheerful red, and it had been splashed around everywhere. From the old Kirman underfoot, glowing in crimson and gold, to the thick velvet drapes at the window with their foot-long fringe, to the leather of her armchair over by the fire. The dancing flames in the hearth burnished it all, while also glinting off the crystals in a sconce and flickering over the oak paneled walls and floor.

The result was a room that was warm and rich, yet comfortably shabby, too, with the edge of the table top a bit worn, the leather on her chair cracked in places, and the carpet a little threadbare. Not because the court lacked the funds to upgrade, but because Gertie liked it this way. And nobody got this far into the inner sanctum who was likely to complain.

This wasn't a place for business; it was for family. I felt honored to be allowed in here at all. Much less to be able to walk in as I had this morning, barefoot, in a robe, with my hair down around my shoulders and no makeup on.

I'd never been able to do that, growing up. My old governess had been from the Victorian era, too, but she was the opposite of Gertie. More the spit-polished, stiff upper lip type, who believed in rising early, going to bed early, and in between staying busy on self-improvement projects.

It had been a weird juxtaposition: a proper Victorian upbringing interspersed with moments of terror, whenever my presence was demanded at court. My vampire guardian had held audience in the same sprawling farmhouse that Eugenie used as a nursery, but the structure had been built onto so many times through the years, that the two parts were well separated. Until she came in with that look on her face: carefully blank and yet with warning eyes.

Then I knew that it was time to put on my best, to carefully comb my hair, and to go downstairs to the big main room where the monster who controlled the house held sway. And where I would be expected to See for him, in a no-win scenario for me. If I was successful, I would experience horrible crimes, natural disasters, plane crashes—anything that foreknowledge of might make Tony money. And if I failed . . .

Well, what use was a Seer who couldn't See?

He'd had people killed for less; people who had seemed far more important than me. So, I'd hidden behind the grand piano, which was tall enough to shield a child, and which was positioned near the daily line up of downtrodden vassals that took place on either side of the great hall. The piano had been a huge old thing, with thick, highly carved legs, which used to collect dust in their elegant scroll work as Tony's servants weren't the best.

There, in its great shadow, I had tried to block out the court's business, which frequently got bloody if anyone told Tony something he didn't want to hear. Occasionally, one of the disfavored would make a run for it, and I'd see them out of the corner of my eye, bolting for the door. They never made it.

They'd be dragged back, usually by Alphonse, Tony's right-hand bruiser, and then things would get loud for a while. On one memorable occasion, a head had bounced back down the hall, shedding droplets of dark blood onto the hardwood floor, *bounce, bounce, bounce.* It had been screaming, since decapitation alone doesn't kill a vamp, although getting pulverized by Alphonse's number fourteen jack boot likely did.

I didn't know for sure, as I'd been busy tracing the piano's carvings with my finger. The old instrument had gotten progressively cleaner and shinier the longer I kept at it, which wasn't long. Tony had decided that he liked me where he could see me, and soon had me pulled into a position near the dais, in an act that had pissed off a lot of his vamps. There was a strict hierarchy in vamp circles, and closer to the throne meant more favored.

At least, usually.

In my case, it had meant giving me line of sight on Tony's visitors, as they groveled before him. Because try as I might, I had never been able to explain the difference between a seer and a telepath in a way that the old bastard could understand. And, occasionally, I did get flashes from someone, albeit in a vision and not by mind reading.

Tony sometimes found what I glimpsed to be useful, but he'd have probably had me up there just the same. He liked the fact that my gaze seemed to make some of his suppliants nervous. His had certainly had that effect on me.

Was I earning him enough to justify my keep? Or was I about to be thrown out to fend for myself, a child alone in the world? Or, worse, did I know too much—about him, his business, the whole criminal organization? Would I end up as just another victim, drained of life and disposed of in the big pit in the farthest field out back, where they burned the garbage, among other things?

I'd never been sure, and so childhood for me had been a series of charming Victorian illustrations splattered with blood and laced with anxiety. Mostly, I tried not to think about it. I didn't know why I was thinking about it now, except . . . I looked around the cozy little room again.

This was the kind of place I'd dreamed about, whenever I saw the warning in Eugenie's eyes: a Victorian home with no monsters in residence.

And no Gertie; she was taking her time this morning.

I got up and walked to the window, and some movement on the street outside caught my eye. I pushed aside the heavy velvet curtains surrounding the window and saw a dog, wet and shivering, standing in a flood of golden light from an open doorway below. And a lot of rain.

London was currently experiencing one of those dark, blustery patches that could last for weeks, where noon was gray and evening came halfway through the afternoon. And that was when it wasn't bucketing down. As a result, the view outside was as dark as night, except where that golden glow pierced the gloom.

It lit up the shivering pup, which was brown and only about half grown, with a missing ear from a street fight and a lopsided grin. I watched as a shadow obscured the light, which soon resolved itself into a pretty brunette housemaid. She had a head full of curls under her mob cap, and an umbrella that she held over the pup, preparing to bring him inside.

But right on cue, a dark shape emerged from the shadows beside the house. It was a war mage in a waterproof greatcoat that shone under streetlights that had never gone out, since the day had never really come. He was younger than most at court, but was limping slightly. Easy duty then, until he finished healing, or threw off a particularly stubborn curse.

He looked to be well on his way, with shiny auburn hair, clear skin and an easy smile. He had too little chin and too much nose, but that smile made up for it. That smile was movie star quality.

He showed it off to the girl and went down on one knee to pat the dog, and one of Mircea's passive senses kicked in, allowing me to hear their conversation.

"Not a fit day for man nor beast," the mage said, searching for the collar that this mutt had probably never had.

"You won't find anythin'," the maid told him, before he could ask. "That one's been a stray since he was a pup—and we've been feeding him 'bout as long."

"Ah, that would explain why he's such a fine, strong boy." The mage patted the dog's flank in approval.

Did she notice the discreet spell that he sent over the mongrel's coat, a brief green sheen? I doubted it. She was looking up at a flash of lightning that was bright enough to briefly illuminate the street, and to make me shiver in memory.

It gave the mage a chance to subtly check the beast over, to ensure that he wasn't the vehicle for a curse on the entire house. Or something spelled to allow a robber to see though his eyes and check out the court's defenses. Or a dark mage under a glamourie, although the dog looked kind of small for that.

But war mages don't take chances, so he probably checked him for that, too. And the pup must have passed, because the girl looked down to find the mage giving him neck scritches. She dimpled.

"His name's Toby," she said. "Though he answers to Pit—"

The mage looked up, appearing surprised at her knowledge of British parliamentary history. "For the prime minister?"

The girl frowned. "No, fer bottomless. He eats like he's starved for it, every time, even though I fed him meself just yesterday. And I fed him a fair bit!"

"You like dogs, then?" he asked, grinning as he stood back up.

"Oh, aye. I've always been partial to big dumb beasts."

"And what about those of us who aren't so dumb?"

The dimples reappeared. "They're all right. Long as they aren't war mages."

An eyebrow rose. "And what's wrong with being a war mage?"

The girl's umbrella twirled coquettishly. "I heard that they're all but married to the Corps, and don't have time for the finer things in life."

"Such as?" he asked, with a knowing smile. As if he could tell where this was going.

That wasn't hard; the girl was as subtle as a brickbat.

"Like the shows at the Coliseum," she said, referencing a popular theater. "Did you know they have lifts? You don't even have to walk up to yer seat!"

"You don't say."

She nodded enthusiastically. "Although I think I'd quite like to. They have marble staircases where you can show off your frock, and a tea room on every floor! It's ever so posh."

"So it would seem."

"And next week is the last for Mr. Cyril Maud and Miss Elise Craven. They're puttin' on *Jellicoe and the Fairy*. I've heard it's quite good."

The dog had been looking back and forth between the two of them, as if he couldn't believe they were doing this here, in the rain. He barked once, loudly, as if to say: just get on with it. Ask her already! And the war mage laughed and did exactly that.

"Perhaps I could tear myself away from my duties for an evening, if you're free?"

The girl dimpled again, but then remembered her dignity and said that she'd have to consult her appointment calendar. But perhaps she could work him in Saturday next? Saturday was agreed to, and finally the poor dog was taken inside for breakfast, wagging its stumpy tail and looking relieved.

I watched them go, expecting to feel the pang of envy that often accompanied seeing normal people doing normal things. It had always seemed so idyllic, the idea of waking up in the morning with nobody gunning for me. To live without constantly looking over my shoulder. To have my whole day's agenda be about feeding a dog and going about my business, possibly humming a tune as I did so while looking forward to my date. That kind of life was all I'd ever wanted.

But something was different today.

That pang wasn't there.

I walked over to the fireplace and straightened the small items on the mantel to give myself something to do. I usually found them fascinating, because Gertie's mantelpiece photographs weren't photographs at all. They were imprints.

Photography hadn't existed when she was a girl, and she'd never really learned to like it. Instead, she'd collected a variety of small items, each imbued with a brief flash of a much-loved face. And unlike the nastier type of imprints that I'd been dealing with lately, these were the rarer kind created by positive emotions.

I'd made a game of it, shortly after I started training here, trying to guess the identities of the people shown. I only knew for certain who one of them was: an old, somewhat fierce looking woman who I recognized as Gertie's grandmother. She'd lived in a small cottage by the sea, where Gertie had been staying as a young girl when she received the summons to court.

It made sense, then, that her item was a seashell, with the interior soft and pink, even while the outside was gray and prickly. I thought that that might be a commentary on the woman herself, who had been kinder than she let on. And the emotion attached to it, a mix of familial affection, nostalgia and warmth, reinforced that.

The other faces were strangers to me, including a dashing young redcoat with windblown, dark brown hair, bright blue eyes and a wicked smile who was represented by a lone musket ball. His imprint reeked of girlish infatuation, while that of another man— sharp-faced, black-haired, and playing with a knife—had exasperated fondness emanating from it that reminded me of my relationship with Billy Joe. I thought it appropriate that his imprint was on a single die.

A pretty young woman with red hair and a saucy grin was next, memorialized in a set of mismatched, amber beads. She simply had to be Hilde, with the strand suffused with familial love. Like that of an old man with a fishing pole, his memory captured by a worn chess piece, who emanated joy, laughter and childish glee. A grandfather, perhaps?

I didn't know, and hadn't asked, as it would have ruined the game. But today, I found it hard to concentrate on them, or on the others I had yet to figure out. My attention kept going back to Tony's instead.

Specifically, it kept going back to Alphonse, the hulking brute who had confused the hell out of me as a child. Sometimes, he had seemed to enjoy terrorizing me; others, he'd protected me and acted almost like a friend. I wasn't sure which category this memory belonged to.

I'd walked into his room unannounced one day, with some contact sheets he'd wanted. Alphonse had had a darkroom down in the basement, where he developed his own photographs—or where a couple of his stooges did, since Tony's second-in-command didn't trouble himself with the boring stuff. His boys regularly sent up print-outs of his negatives so that he could decide which ones he wanted them to work on.

As usual, I'd been the courier, having gotten old enough to be useful as an errand girl. But I'd picked a bad moment. Alphonse had just come back from a job, and was covered in blood.

Or, at least, his clothes were. His skin had already absorbed anything that touched it. But his suit, his shirt, even his hair . . .

Were dripping.

He'd looked up, halfway through untying a shoe, and for a moment, we'd just stared at each other. The nine- or ten-year-old girl, clutching some paperwork to her chest, and the huge, blood-soaked, fanged monster. And then he'd run a hand towel over his head, which came back bright red, and showed it to me.

"See, kid," he'd said. "Nothing to worry about. Blood washes off."

But did it? I wondered now, my hands stilling.

Did it for the Svarestri, Aeslinn's people, who had turned themselves into little more than a war machine? Killing and enslaving their neighbors, making themselves hated throughout Faerie, and sacrificing thousands of their own people for a creature who didn't give a damn about them and never would?

Or the Alorestri, the so-called Green Fey, who had made the kidnapping of human women into a business, in order to have a continual stream of cannon fodder for their wars? And who had made long-term war on the dark fey, taking their lands in compensation for those that the Svarestri stole from them? They had the right to protect themselves, but the way they'd done it made them little better than the ones they fought.

Or people like Guinn's family, who had been forced to flee their homes for an entirely new world to avoid the carnage, only to find plenty of it here? They still died, some from a broken heart like her grandfather, others from old enemies who pursued them here. While their children forgot their native land, their heritage, everything.

Blood washes off, but could it after the gods finished with us, after they warped and twisted us into . . . whatever we'd be by the time all this was over. Even if we won, could we just wash it all away? Could I?

They talked as if you were halfway between a monster and a god yourself, I heard Pritkin say again.

I didn't want to be either. I didn't want any of this! But, I slowly realized, I didn't want to be normal anymore, either.

Something had changed between last night and today, something significant. I didn't entirely understand it, but I could feel it, deep in my gut. Just as I'd felt it when I looked at that servant girl, sweet and innocent and clueless.

I would have envied her once.

Now, I just feared for her.

That pretty girl's life could be ended, at any time, by a thousand dangers that even the war mage couldn't see. I knew because I'd been her; the only difference was that I'd been aware of the danger, having grown up with the shrieks in the basement, with the stakes slipped into socks and the guns shoved into armpits, and the human-shaped bags thrown over brawny shoulders, headed for the garbage pit. It had been normal, and I'd hated that it was normal, had wanted a new normal, somewhere I could find peace.

Or at least, that's what I'd told myself.

But if that had been the case, I'd have stayed away, the first time I ran away from Tony's. I'd have gone to ground, let the trail grow cold, let my looks change until even a vamp would have trouble recognizing me. And they would have.

Even a person's scent alters as they age. Babies don't smell like children, who don't smell like teens, who don't smell like adults.

The type of bacteria that live on our skin differs in various stages of life and in different locals. And the chemical composition of our bodies can alter with time, too.

I was only fourteen when I first fled from Tony. Had I stayed away, I could have changed my hair color, bought a different style of clothes, and grown up. And eventually walked by one of his boys on the street without him ever being the wiser.

I even had the advantage of living with a group of misfits just like me, magical runaways and their kindhearted caretaker—who remained one of my best friends. I could have had it all, the family I'd longed for, the peace I'd sought, the normal life I had said that I wanted. Except for one thing: I'd lied.

Not intentionally; I'd been lying to myself as much as to everyone else. But now, it seemed obvious. I hadn't wanted peace, because peace came at other people's sufferance. I'd had peace at Tony's as long as I did what he wanted. As long as I put my power under his command. As long as I stayed in my chains.

I hadn't wanted peace, because peace could be taken away. I'd wanted power. Why else go back, as a seventeen-year-old, to get the evidence to set him up with the feds? To hurt him as he'd hurt me, and my parents? To maybe even get him staked by his own master, if the stink got bad enough?

Because I'd wanted him gone. I'd wanted the power to protect myself and those I loved from people like Tony—or Aeslinn, or Zeus, or anyone else who might try to hurt them. And I still did.

I caught a glimpse of my face in the mirror over the mantel, and for a second, I saw a different woman. Someone fiercer, more dangerous, more . . . I wasn't sure. Just that she looked like she wanted a fight.

I didn't. I didn't want to face Zeus again—ever! I wanted a different solution, something like Pritkin and I had done with Apollo, where I could just flush the problem away. I wanted to spare us and the fey more death, more pain, more needless war. I wanted to avoid becoming the monster they believed me to be.

But I didn't always get what I wanted.

And blood washes off.

Chapter Eighteen

T here." I hadn't heard Gertie come in until she spoke behind me, making me jump. And then did it again when she dropped a huge book onto the little card table by the window, hard enough to rattle it. "I've been reading."

This early? I didn't say. She was dressed like a Christmas tree, all bright green velvet and gold buttons, but she had the gimlet-eyed, pursed lip look she got when she was being serious. And God help anybody who crossed her then.

The free-flowing hippie vibe gave out really damned quick.

"About what?" I amended, walking over to the table and sitting down.

"About you." A pair of pince-nez floated over from the mantlepiece and settled onto her nose. "Or, rather, that was the idea."

"About me?"

Gertie sat down in the opposite chair and tapped the book. I thought I recognized it from the case she had by the door, where she kept reference materials that she used often. She had an expansive library downstairs, but I guessed this was handier.

Or maybe she found the librarian as creepy as I did.

"This is a compendium of Greek mythology," she informed me. "I have similar ones on Norse, Roman, Indian—" she fluttered a hand. "But the interesting thing to me isn't so much what the legends say as what they do not. Specifically, they do not mention you. Not a single time."

I frowned. "Should they?"

That won me another look, this time over top of the pince-nez. It made her appear like a disgruntled, purple-haired Mrs. Claus, a fact that I did not mention because I am not stupid. A well-groomed nail tapped the page again ominously.

"This is the story of Theseus fighting the minotaur. An impressive feat, to be sure, but less than you accomplished on the Thames three days ago."

I looked at tiny Theseus, who had an alarmingly "oh shit" look for a hero, which made me like him more. It also made sense. The Minotaur, the huge, raging bull-man of legend, was roughly three times his size.

"Well, I had help."

"Or here," Gertie flipped over another few pages, to a depiction of a rocky desert and a large, ancient city shimmering under a blazing sun. Swords glinted, armor shone, and two people faced off in superhero poses under a vivid blue sky. One was a man, tall, well-built, sun-tanned and fierce. And the other, surprisingly, was a woman.

She was as tall as the man and similarly armored, with arms and legs as heavily muscled as a body builder's—a male one. Her face was weather beaten, and her hair was shaved on the sides, with any remainder shoved under an ancient Greek helmet. But the breastplate above her leather skirt made her sex clear.

Not that that seemed likely to help the man.

She looked positively savage.

"Achilles battling Penthesilea, the Amazon queen, before the gates of Troy," Gertie said. "The artist did a good job, don't you think?"

I nodded. The woman's skin looked as tough as old leather, with long healed scars crisscrossing it with pale lines, and deep crow's feet cut into the flesh beside her eyes, as if the sun had aged her prematurely. But the expression in those eyes was cool and calculating, despite the snarl on her lips.

This wasn't Wonder Woman, also supposedly Amazon royalty, yet usually depicted as a pretty girl in a skimpy outfit. This was a hardened warrior who had come to the battle specifically in order to die. She had inadvertently slayed her sister and could find no peace. For an Amazonian queen, however, suicide was unthinkable, and would have incurred great dishonor. So, she had sought out the only warrior on Earth strong enough to kill her.

But she wasn't going to make it easy on him.

She wasn't going to make it easy at all.

"I am sure it was a sight for the ages," Gertie mused, also regarding the picture. "I am equally sure that it paled in comparison to what I witnessed on the river."

"If it even happened," I pointed out. "We're talking about myths here."

Gertie ignored that.

"Or this one," she said, flipping over some more pages. "Heracles, the greatest of the Greek heroes, bringing back Cerberus, the hell hound, as one of his famous labors."

That wasn't a story I remembered, but sure enough, there he was, a tiny hero enshrined in another brilliantly colored illustration, wrestling a dog the size of a bus. It almost looked like the artist had seen a Hellhound at some point, because he'd gotten it pretty much right. They were big, they were black, and they slobbered all over everything, which probably explained why little Herc there was looking pissed.

Too bad he hadn't had a pig's foot, I thought, remembering my own adventures with the beasts, who could be quite sweet if you, uh, treated them, um, right . . .

Gertie was glaring at me again. "Okay?"

The book slammed shut. "And yet, of Cassie Palmer, we hear not a peep!"

I frowned at some her more. "Gertie. The Greek legends were written down thousands of years ago. I wasn't even born then."

The pursed mouth became even smaller. "Then let us speak of prophecy, shall we? Of the Norse predictions about the end of the world, of Ragnarok and the conflict you are facing now."

I repressed a sigh. "Can we not?"

Jonas Marsden, Rhea's father and the current head of the Silver Circle, never shut up about it. He had been the first to figure out that the return of the gods had been foretold in the Norse legends. And that those same legends might offer us clues as to what we should do about it—if we could decode them properly.

But prophecy was never straightforward, and while in hindsight it was possible to see where reality and myth overlapped, at the time it was never so obvious. Which was why he'd been sending me massive amounts of stuff to read, I guess trying to prompt a vision. So far, it had mostly prompted headaches, but Eugenie would have loved him.

Finally, somebody was making me do my homework.

But Gertie was clearly waiting for a better answer. "I already know all about Ragnarok," I said.

"Really. Then perhaps you can explain the puzzle to me."

"What puzzle?" I asked, slightly distracted by the heaping trays of food that two servants had just brought in.

I didn't know for certain that somebody had told the kitchen staff that I'd been eating pies of dubious cleanliness bought from a street vendor recently, but it sure looked that way. The spread they were putting on the coffee table had a definite in-your-face quality about it, with fine bone china, pure silver cutlery, and a matching silver tea pot that reflected the flames in the fireplace like a mirror. Best of all, Gertie wouldn't care how much I ate. She liked her girls to have a healthy appetite, and somehow, over the months, I'd become one of her girls.

"Cassie!"

Of course, there were down sides to that, too.

"I don't know what you want," I told her honestly, turning back.

"Neither do I," she said surprisingly, since Gertie always knew everything. "I've been working on it for the last two days, yet I know little more than when I started. But I can at least show you the problem."

She grabbed her pack of Tarot cards, gave them a loose shuffle, and threw them onto the table. Not in a spread or pattern, but almost as if she was tossing dice. Most of them landed face down, but a handful stayed upright, and Gertie gave an annoyed huff at the sight.

"What a surprise," she said dourly, and drew them over.

I didn't know how to read a "spread" like this, but Gertie apparently did. She threw down one of the cards and frowned at it. It was the Emperor, which in the Marseilles Tarot was a jolly looking fellow in a multicolored medieval outfit, leaning against a throne. He looked like he might be on his way to a party, or was already at one, and waving his scepter at a servant to bring him more ale.

It was a lot less ominous than the version in my deck back home, which showed an old man with a long white beard and a golden crown, sitting on a throne decorated with ram's heads. They stood for his sign, Aries, which could have symbolized a lot of things, but since he was wearing a full suit of armor under his blood red robes, probably stood for war. In his right hand he held a scepter, a sign of his position, and in his left a globe, showing his dominion over the world. Behind him, a barren and desolate landscape indicated the devastation that his conquest had wrought.

He had power, but it had come at a price.

"The Emperor," Gertie intoned. "In our case, a god desperate to return to Earth, along with the rest of his kind." She threw down another card. "He has a helper at his side, the King of Pentacles, Lord of Earth. Clearly our fey king. He wants to expand his reach, and believes his godly protector will allow him to do so. Yet, when they somehow find a conduit that permits a limited amount of the god's power back into this world, what do they do? Do they use it to bring down the barrier preventing his return? Do they attempt to shift him across, so that he might bring it down himself? Do they attempt to return to an era before he was defeated, and try to reverse it? No."

"I don't think they have the power for that yet," I said, remembering Aeslinn's comments in camp. He had wanted to strip my soul right then, take the Pythian power and end this. But Zeus had vetoed it.

He was playing for higher stakes than just a fraction of Apollo's energy, which wouldn't last him long in a struggle with the other gods. He wanted unlimited power and thought he'd figured out a way to get it. He wanted Pritkin.

"Yes, I am sure he does want your young man," Gertie said, surprising me. "I spoke to Rhea yesterday," she added. "Her account was a bit hysterical, but I believe I have the gist."

"Then you know why Zeus is waiting. He's searching for Pritkin, and if he finds him—"

"Yes, yes," Gertie said, cutting me off. "That would be disastrous. But so would ignoring what else he is planning."

"And . . . what that?" I asked, unsure that I wanted to know.

"I have no idea. But we can assume that he has more than one iron in the fire. Zeus was famous for his strategy, cunning and intelligence—when he wasn't too lazy to use it."

"Lazy?"

"Oh yes, and quick to anger and frequently cruel—he was hardly a paragon of virtue. But he wasn't stupid; you can't assume that he will be."

"Okay—"

"Or that he only has only one path to his goal. From what Lord Mircea told Rhea, I understand that there is some demon involved in all this? The creature who carried Zeus about for a while, before he possessed this fey king?"

I nodded.

"I was also given to understand that he has been erasing Aeslinn's memory of your young man," Gertie continued. "The half demon?"

I nodded again. "Yes, he—"

"Well, there you have it." She sat back and looked at me, as if all this made some kind of sense.

"Have what?" I asked, confused.

"What were we talking about?"

"I have no idea."

She gave me one of her looks, the kind that said she thought I was slacking. Which wasn't true, but I wasn't at my best this morning. Which she must have realized, because she spelled it out for me—a rare occurrence.

"Zeus only remembered Mage Pritkin occasionally, when the king's mind fought off the demon's spell. In the meantime, what was he doing? Twiddling his thumbs? He must have had some kind of scheme, some plan for his return to power. You have to find out what it is."

"All right."

"And then there's this."

She threw down a third card, which turned out to be *La Papesse*, the female pope. She wore a golden crown that looked like a pope's miter on her head and held an open book on her lap. She also had the keys of Saint Peter swinging from her waist and shepherd's crook in her hand, because she was an allegory of the Catholic Church.

It had been the only way that the patriarchy of the day had been able to fit a powerful, knowledgeable woman who did not owe her position to a man into the hierarchy. By essentially making her not a woman at all, but a symbol of a male dominated organization. A statue of just such a woman remains in Saint Peter's Basilica in Rome.

But times change, don't they? And my Tarot deck back home didn't have *La Papesse*. It had the High Priestess instead, with a crescent at her feet and the triple crown of Isis on her head, representing the three phases of the moon. She sat in front of a curtain embroidered with palms and pomegranates, indicating her origin in the East, and blocking the way into a sacred temple.

She was obviously an ancient seer or priestess, who held her position in her own right. That was her temple back there; and your audience was with her alone. There was nobody else in the picture, not even a servant. If you wanted access to the sacred knowledge, you had to go through her.

"Zeus may be after the mage, but he is focused on you," Gertie said. "Why do you think that is?"

"I . . . don't think that is," I said, tearing my eyes away from the picture. "He's been trying to get at Pritkin through me—"

"Yet he attacked you, even followed you into a time shift, before he realized that you had a link with the mage."

"That was probably Aeslinn's decision. It was his body, and he hates me—"

Gertie brushed that away. "A king does not rule a god, particularly when said king needs a favor."

I glanced at the servants, who had almost finished loading up the coffee table. My stomach rumbled, but Gertie ignored it. Guessed the lesson wasn't finished yet.

"And the outcome?" I asked, looking at the cards she still held.

She put another one down, over the rest, crosswise. It was the Wheel of Fortune, looking incongruously happy and optimistic with the Marseilles deck's bright, primary colors. Only the crossing position was usually one of challenge, although whether that meant that it was challenging me or the other cards, I wasn't sure.

"I will tell you what it looks like," Gertie said, frowning at the cards. "It looks like he's afraid of you."

"What?"

"Or that he's afraid of something," she amended, seeing my expression. "Perhaps of the unknown—"

"You mean Zeus?"

"Yes.

"Okay. You're not making sense now."

"I think I am." She settled back in her chair, slowly shuffling the remaining cards, her eyes going slightly unfocused. "Zeus presents like someone faced with an obstacle he did not expect. An obstacle, moreover, that he can find no information about, as none of the prophecies mention you. Almost as if you do not exist—"

"Gertie—"

"You are not in the stories," she repeated stubbornly. "Even those which speak of future events. Apollo, the god known as Thor in the Norse legends, was supposed to be killed by a giant snake—"

"He was. By Jörmungandr, the spell that encircles and guards the Earth. That's what the Norse called it—"

"He was *weakened* by Jörmungandr," she corrected. "You finished him off. Sending him into the regions beyond time, before calling him back to serve as a distraction for Ares."

I was starting to regret trading war stories.

"You found a way to kill Ares, too," she added. "The god known as Tyr to the Norse."

"I didn't actually—"

"Yes, you did. I was there. You may not have killed him directly, but he died, did he not? And a great deal of that was down to you. Yet the legends are completely silent about Cassie Palmer!"

She slapped the big book on which the Tarot cards now lay. I stared at it, more than a little taken aback that she'd actually expected me to be mentioned in ancient prophecy. That some old, blind seer, like the one I'd had a vision about in her library once, might have looked at me down the tunnel of the centuries.

Only she hadn't, had she?

I wasn't there.

A shiver made its way up my spine, and I decided that I wasn't enjoying this conversation. But Gertie was on a roll. She threw down a fifth card, followed by several more in quick succession.

"The Queen of Swords: a powerful woman, but disruptive. Someone who throws a spanner in the works—a game changer. The King of Swords: an intellectual man, bound to the queen. An advisor, with knowledge that the queen needs. And, finally, the Tower: pain, destruction, the breaking of the old order. Unforeseen and violent change."

"You're not even putting them in a spread—"

"I've put them in spreads," Gertie said, her eyes flashing. "I've plucked them at random out of the pack. I've thrown them on the floor and let them fall where they will. It doesn't matter. These cards, and these alone, keep coming up. They plague my thoughts, batter at my mind, disturb my sleep. Desperately trying to tell me . . . something. But I do not know what it is." She sat back in her chair, a look of defeat on her face. "I cannot See it."

I just stared at her. I'd never known Gertie to be defeated by anything—including me. She'd kicked my butt all over early medieval Wales, before we knew each other, after discovering that I was taking a demon lord back in time. It was just Rosier, and we were trying to help Pritkin, who'd been in danger from a demonic curse, but she hadn't known that.

And, damn, had I paid a price for crossing her!

Yet her face was bewildered now, almost tragic, such as I'd never seen it.

"It's okay," I said, reaching across the table, and covering her hand with mine.

But she didn't seem to find the gesture as comforting as I had, when Iris did it. "It is not 'okay'!" she said fiercely. "I wanted to do this for you, to help you, one last time. But I can't, any more than I could on the river."

I frowned in confusion. "But you did help me. You kept us in transition, and somehow backed up Agnes at the same—" I stopped, after what she'd just said sank in. "What do you mean, 'one last time'?"

Brown eyes met mine, and they were sad but resolute. "I mean it's over, Cassie. I can't train you anymore. This . . . was our last lesson."

Chapter Nineteen

I'm sorry Cassie," Gertie said again, seeing my shock. And then said nothing else, because the servants were there. She motioned for them to bring us tea, forcing me to sit quietly while they did so, as this wasn't the sort of conversation that you had with an audience.

They worked swiftly, putting a steaming cup of something in front of me that I couldn't focus on. And that I couldn't have gotten past the growing lump in my throat in any case. I left it on its saucer.

They finally closed the door behind them, and I all but lunged at her over the table. "What are you *talking* about? You can't be serious—"

"I can." Brown eyes met mine again, and they were steady.

I knew that look. It meant she'd already made up her mind and this was her informing me of her decision. This was not a conversation.

I felt my own eyes narrow, because I wasn't taking that.

"It's for the best, Cassie."

"How? How is it for the best? Zeus is still out there!"

"Yes, he is. That is rather the point. Tell me, what would have happened if one of those energy bolts had hit Agnes the other day?"

"They didn't—"

"But if they had."

I knew where she was going with this, and didn't want to answer. But conditioning died hard. "She . . . probably wouldn't have survived."

"No doubt." It was dry. "And then neither would you, as her intervention will save your life once, I believe?"

Rhea had spilled the beans on that, and I guessed word had gotten back. One of Agnes' last acts as Pythia had been to warn me of an attack by some of Tony's thugs, who had tracked me to the club I moonlighted at in Atlanta. It had been anonymous, and before I even knew what a Pythia was. But it had absolutely saved my life.

Agnes and I had had our problems, but I owed her a lot.

"Yes, that's normally how it works," I said, trying for calm. Emotional appeals didn't sway Gertie. "But now—"

"There are no 'buts' Cassie. The untimely death of a Pythia can have a catastrophic effect on the timeline, causing a cascade that can end in a Crucible—a complete reworking of time. That is why Pythias aren't even supposed to speak to each other, lest one accidentally influence another—"

"But that was before!" I said, breaking in. "Now that we know about the gods—"

"Nothing has changed." It was implacable. "I have to guard this era, so that you may live to guard yours. I broke the rules to train you, for I sympathized with your dilemma. No one should have this much responsibility imposed on them, much less with no one to turn to for help or guidance. But we have reached the end."

"But . . . you said we had *months*—"

It wasn't an argument, but I suddenly couldn't think straight enough to make one. I'd woken up this morning feeling stronger than yesterday, more centered, more myself. And now I was falling off a cliff again, with no one to catch me.

"Under normal circumstances," Gertie said, not unkindly. "Although I've taught you the more difficult techniques already."

"This isn't just about technique! It's about knowing when to use what. Not to mention all of the other stuff, the . . . the diplomacy and the history and how to organize everything—"

"My sister can teach you that."

"—and how to be Pythia!" I stared at her some more, uncomprehending. "Can she teach me *that*?"

Gertie drank tea. She took her time about it, adding the milk first, then the tea, then stirring to achieve the optimum level of heat. She didn't take sugar, unless it was with coffee, which she said was bitter and needed the help. She also didn't drink Earl Gray, despite it being a favorite at court, for the same reason.

I knew that, like I knew so much about her. I'd watched her, learned from her, idolized her, because I'd never been like Agnes. I'd never been able to see myself in her organized perfection. Agnes color coded her *lipsticks*; I'd seen them, in the dressing room she had used as Pythia, all neat and tidy and ruthlessly regimented, like the carefully selected wardrobe that had spanned hundreds of years' worth of time.

And since Agnes and her perfect court had been the only example I'd had of a Pythia when I first started this job, I'd developed a serious inferiority complex. I still had it sometimes. I was too messy, too impulsive, too crazy. But Gertie . . .

Gertie had given me hope.

She'd been famous for climbing out of her window as an acolyte, off to enjoy the nightlife of the city, without risking a shift that might have alerted her old mentor. As a young Pythia, she'd learned to drive a two-horse phaeton, a light, springy carriage in which she'd torn about London, scaring the hell out of the war mages assigned as her bodyguards, and often leaving them in the dust. She'd changed the acolytes' dress code, which had been fixed in place for thousands of years, to something that, while scratchy and uncomfortable by modern standards, at least let her girls look like normal people. She'd been an original who did exactly what she wanted, and had made the hidebound old office the better for it.

I'd started to think, if she can be Pythia, maybe I can, too.

And now what?

"Hilde was given the same training that I was," Gertie said stubbornly. "At one time, we did not know which of us would be selected for the position."

"But *you* were. And you've done it. She doesn't have your experience—and neither do I!"

"You will learn—"

"If you thought that, you wouldn't have offered to train me in the first place. Or you'd have unloaded me on Hilde as soon as you found out she was at my court!"

I abruptly got up, intended to pace, then just as abruptly sat back down again, because it wouldn't help.

Only I didn't know what would.

"I can't take him," I told her shakily. "You know I can't. You're sending me to die."

Gertie didn't say anything for a moment, just turned her head to watch the rain hiss outside the window. It was coming down harder now, obscuring what little light had been able to make it through the gloom. The darkened glass left me with a perfect mirror of the face she didn't want me to see, which was no happier than mine.

It showed me something else, too.

The firelight glowed on her lavender hair and gleamed off the luxuriousness of her dress. But it also highlighted lines I hadn't noticed before around her mouth, and crow's feet beside the sharp brown eyes. Gertie was older than the woman I'd first encountered back in the last gasp of the Victorian age, and tonight, she looked every year of it.

Then she spoke, and it was in her voice, too: years of experience, paired with one of the sharpest minds I knew. "Who were your parents, Cassie?"

It was my turn to sit quietly, as I had during so many lessons, when she'd wanted me to think for myself. To puzzle things out, since that was what I'd have to do as Pythia. But this time, it wasn't difficult.

Fucking Aeslinn, I thought savagely. I'd lost a lot in this war, including a dear friend just recently, and now I was about to lose another. And for what?

That son of a bitch had had to challenge me here, blowing up everything I'd so carefully built. Of course, Gertie couldn't risk having me around anymore. I was a magnet who brought gods and kings and trouble, always trouble, in my wake. She had a court to protect. And she couldn't do that if a child of the very beings we were fighting against was bringing the war to her doorstep.

It had been a danger to train me in the first place, but a manageable one. Keep me away from everyone as much as possible, give instructions for the acolytes to ask me and Rhea nothing and for us to keep our mouths shut, then blank memories as needed once we were gone. The Pythian Court dealt with time travel regularly; this wasn't something entirely new to them, and might even serve as a lesson on the value of discretion.

But now? Gertie had been faced with something she couldn't handle, possibly for the first time in her life. She'd almost had her timeline blown to pieces thanks to me. She was scared, but she was also right.

"I understand," I said, and despite my best efforts, I heard my voice break.

Damn it! I couldn't even do this, couldn't keep it together for five minutes, long enough to get out of here. I drank tea, but the room blurred nonetheless. And the cup shook as I put it back on its saucer, for the last time.

And had my hand captured in another, one with prominent veins, crepey skin, and a few age spots just beginning to show. Yes, Gertie was getting older, and her heir wasn't completely trained. Agnes was excellent at the physical aspects of being Pythia, the spells and shifts and whatnot, but the diplomatic stuff came harder for her, as it did for me. She needed time to mature, which she wouldn't have had if the battle on the river had gone a little differently.

"Who?" she insisted, with a strange urgency in her voice.

I didn't bother talking about dad. He wasn't who she was asking about. "Artemis. My mother . . . was the goddess Artemis."

"Ah." Gertie smiled slightly, and squeezed my hand, although she didn't let go. "I thought it might be something like that. The goddess famed for her virginity having a child; no, Zeus wouldn't have expected that. But . . ." her eyes grew unfocused, while her fingers on mine tightened. "There is something more, isn't there? More to the story . . ."

I waited, despite the fact that my hand was going numb. But after a moment, she sighed in frustration and let me go. "I can't See."

"I didn't mean to deceive you," I said. "It's just . . . people act differently, when they know."

"And you wanted to be trained like everyone else."

"Yes."

"And so you have been."

I shook my head. "There's so much—I've learned so much from you, more than I ever imagined, but this job . . ." I looked around the room, but there was no help there. Just surroundings that I'd come to love, but that I'd never see again, because this place didn't exist in my time. It was gone, a casualty of the war, like so much else. And yet, it had started to feel like home.

"Cassandra," Gertie said, bringing my eyes around.

There was compassion in hers, and something else. Maybe pity; I didn't know. Couldn't think.

"You are the greatest pupil I have ever had. I no sooner introduced you to a concept than you mastered it, and with an ease the rest of us can only envy. But you are right: being Pythia requires more than skill. It demands compassion, intelligence, dedication and courage. And it is much easier to find the former than the latter.

"You are the rare soul who combines both.

"You may not feel ready, but you are, never doubt that."

But I do doubt it, I thought miserably, meeting those warm brown eyes. I always had. And now, without Gertie, I felt so lost, so alone.

"I can never come back, can I?"

She shook her head. "I will blank Agnes's memory tonight. I wanted to give her and Rhea a day together first."

I nodded and couldn't speak for a moment, and then I blurted out the only thing I could think of. The only thing that seemed to matter. "But you—will you remember me?"

Gertie looked surprised for a second, before catching me off guard one last time when the sadness on her face turned into laughter. "My dear Cassie. You are a hard woman to forget."

*   *   *

I returned to my time without Rhea, only my shifting muscle seemed to be sprained. It was probably the potion, the dregs of which were clinging to me, but it was bad enough that I ended up off course. I appeared in the butler's pantry of my Vegas suite instead of in the bedroom as I'd planned, and then had to clutch the marble countertop to stay upright.

And even that didn't work for long. My butt hit the cold tile between the wine fridge and the prep island, and I just stayed there, feeling sick and weak and hollowed out. Should have taken Gertie's advice and had breakfast first, I thought, which was a bad move. The name alone made me tear up.

Get up, I told myself harshly. Get to your room, wash your face, and make yourself presentable before anyone sees you! I was in my robe, because I hadn't waited to change. I hadn't waited for anything. It hurt too much to be there, knowing that I'd been exiled.

Get up and stop this! I thought furiously. Which would have been great advice, if my body had been listening. But it appeared to be occupied with other things.

Like making my hands shake and my breath shudder and my feet slide out from under me when I tried to stand. I ended up back on my butt, tears splashing down my cheeks, and my robe twisted around my legs. I didn't know what to do now, and I no longer had anyone to ask.

Gertie and I may have started out as enemies, but we'd ended up closer than friends. She'd given me more than she'd ever know, not just the basics of this job, but a ready ear, a shoulder to cry on, and an example of what being Pythia on a day-to-day basis looked like. Not to mention the understanding of someone who knew how crazy this position could be through personal experience.

Nothing had ever ruffled her.

Nothing had ever beaten her.

And now she was gone.

I stared at the back of the island, but didn't see it. I wondered if this was what every Pythia felt when their mentor passed away, and they suddenly had all that crushing responsibility fall onto their shoulders. If it was what Agnes had felt, when Gertie . . .

The sobs returned, and again I swallowed them down. This was stupid, stupid! I was mourning a woman who had died decades ago, long before I was even born. I should feel grateful that I'd known her at all.

I didn't feel grateful.

I just felt pain, because I missed her already, and panic, because I couldn't do this, I couldn't be this! If even Agnes had failed in the face of this war, what chance did I have? She'd thanked me for saving her daughter, one of the last times we'd spoken, but had I? Or had I only postponed the inevitable, and dragged Rhea into a war I couldn't win?

Because it was all on me now.

Maybe that was why I just stayed there, huddled in the corner, instead of getting up, finding a phone, and calling Jonas. Or trying to get in touch with the Vampire Senate, to tell them what had happened, and what was coming. Because what could they do?

What could any of us?

I started to pull my knees up, and realized that something had stuck to the back of my leg. I peeled it off, and discovered the Wheel of Fortune card, which had somehow hitched a ride. Its cheerful colors seemed almost mocking to me now, and its stupid imagery a deliberate caricature.

Yeah, that was me, I thought, staring at one of the figures on the front: a monkey in a skirt. Jumping around like a nut half the time, with no idea what I was doing. Which I guessed left Mircea as the bat winged creature at the top of the wheel, and Pritkin as the uniformed . . . something . . . on the other side. All of us just trying to hold on, while the wheel of fate spun faster and faster.

How long until we fell off?

I found myself suddenly, irrationally angry. I ripped the pretty card to pieces, and then ripped it again, until it was colorful confetti on the stark, white tile and I was a panting wreck in the corner. It didn't help.

Now the Wheel was just scattered more widely, like us, I thought, picking up a tiny piece showing the bat-winged creature.

Mircea had metamorphosized recently, which was what the card stood for: people undergoing change, whether for good or for bad. In his case, he'd acquired a new master power from Pritkin, or from someone whose soul Pritkin had absorbed once, while on a trip into the hells. Only the beautiful Irin wings, which should have been white and luminescent, had ended up black and leathery on him, like a goth angel.

He'd nonetheless used them to rescue me from Aeslinn at the castle, and then had reabsorbed them, leaving only a couple of subtle ridges over his shoulder blades where they had once been. He'd taken it in stride, having seen masters manifest far stranger things through the years. His gifts had mostly been invisible, being primarily of the mind, but he appeared pleased enough with his new advantage.

Pritkin was probably considerably less so about his.

Rescuing me from that terrible camp had required recombining with his other half, and I doubted that that was reversable. His incubus hadn't seemed like someone who would voluntarily go back into his mental prison, after working so hard to escape it. But, like it or not, Pritkin needed the extra power the union offered him right now, and I was grateful for anything that got him out of Faerie alive.

Even if I had to deal with the fallout later.

And then there was me.

What had I gotten, over the course of all this? Nothing, unless you counted a hell of a lot more traumatized. Or a pair of golden whips that only ran on godly energy, which I didn't have any of! Or a definite sense of exactly how vulnerable I was.

And now I'd just lost one of my greatest allies.

The panic attack I'd been fighting off for days hit with a vengeance, all at once. But there were no adoring acolytes around to distract me this time, just cold, stark fear, and a rising wave of blind panic, and nothing I did seemed to change that. I sat there, alone and paralyzed, my fingers digging into my flesh, my body shaking and my teeth chattering, and try as I might I couldn't seem to make them stop.

Behold your great Pythia! I thought, and felt hysterical laughter bubble up in my throat.

And then the door to the kitchen blew open and a vampire ran in.

Chapter Twenty

He was a sad excuse for a vamp, being small and chubby and not very menacing, especially not right now. He was wearing a wife beater that showed off pale skin and wispy chest hair, and a pair of ripped pajama pants over Christmas themed boxers that were covered with pert reindeer. Said reindeer had red, glittery noses that seemed to brighten when they hit the light, as if a bulb had come on behind them.

But that wasn't the problem. The vamp was named Fred, and Fred always had wardrobe malfunctions, not to mention questionable taste. Frankly, I'd seen worse.

He was also looking fairly wild, with his light brown hair even messier than usual—what there was of it—and his big, gray eyes wide. He'd just slammed the door behind him, and was holding it shut with his body. But that wasn't the problem, either.

The problem was that he was fighting a cookie—

And losing.

My distress washed away on a tide of what the hell, because I'd seen a lot of strange things around here, but this was new.

It was a gingerbread cookie the size of my hand, which was why it had managed to slip through the door unnoticed. It looked homemade, with gumdrops all over it instead of in an orderly line down the front, and icing features that were misshapen and kind of scary. It also had a shiv in the form of a broken candy cane in one mittened hand, with which it attacked Fred's leg through the ripped jammies.

He screamed, a cut off little sound, and stomped at the cookie. But it was fast, and evaded his flailing limbs, giving me a flashback to that scene on the river. That's how I must have looked to Zeus, I thought, staring at it. That's how insignificant I must have seemed.

Which gave Fred the part of Aeslinn, the huge, powerful creature who was now ceding the field, and running from a cookie.

Or he was until the door to the outer hall swung inward and knocked him on his ass.

I watched as he backed toward me in terror, while a murderous cookie stalked him across the tiles. This is what I have to work with, I thought. This is who I'm supposed to use to defend Earth.

We were all going to die.

And, apparently, Fred thought so, too. The murder cookie had no sooner raised its tiny weapon, than my supernatural defender let out another shriek. But this time, he had help.

This time, there was a new sheriff in town, and she wasn't taking any crap.

The swinging door that had rejected Fred had done so because there was someone behind it. A tiny someone with stand-up blond ponytails, a stained pink onesie, and a cross expression. Like a pissed off Cindy Lou Who.

She stood there for a moment, surveying the sorry sight we made, then decided that intervention was required. She toddled over, grabbed the cookie from behind, and turned it around to shake her finger in its face. "No! Bad!"

And then she bit its head off.

Literally.

"S'okay," she told Fred indistinctly, around the howls of the vanquished. "Safe now."

He stared at her.

Little crumbs of gingerbread fell onto the onesie, which was already smeared with them, along with icing and a lone, solitary gummy, bearing witness of massacres past. This one wasn't quite done, however, since the body of the cookie was still thrashing about. But it couldn't do anything, as our stalwart defender had grabbed it by the arm, immobilizing its tiny weapon.

Its tiny, blood-stained weapon.

"Hey," I told her, blinking. "Don't eat that."

She looked at me curiously.

I motioned her over and she came, ignoring the now shame-faced vamp. She crawled across him and held her fist out, before dropping the small, headless thing onto my palm. I picked it up by one leg and examined it, while it slashed at me blindly with its bit of cane.

I looked at Fred.

"Um," he said, but didn't get any farther, because the door to the kitchen slammed open and a crazed-face witch burst in.

"Fred! Did you find any more in—"

She stopped dead at the sight of me, and for a second, we both just stared at each other. Then she slowly backed up, letting the door swing closed in front of her. But not before I'd seen what was going on in the kitchen.

I got to my feet, prisoner in hand, and rounded the island to open the door.

And was greeted by a scene of pure chaos.

The nice, expansive space, with its white subway tiles, gleaming countertops, black framed, old-fashioned prints, and huge farmer's sink . . . was a horror scene.

A splatter of something that looked like blood but which, on closer inspection, was a spilled jar of strawberry jam, oozed down a counter to puddle on the floor. Bits of murder cookies covered the tiles, with their severed limbs trying to stab or kick. Whole gingerbread men lined the counters, lobbing jellies and whatever else they could find from makeshift catapults made out of spoons. They appeared to be targeting a small group of miscreants in the center of the room.

That would have been funny if I'd been in the mood, and if some of the projectiles hadn't been shards of broken glass. They twinkled in the overhead lights as they flew through the air, before tearing small, bloody streaks in the crowd, or sticking out of the large amount of exposed skin on display because everyone was in their nightclothes. The little group also seemed to be immobilized for some reason that I didn't understand.

Until I noticed: a small bunch of kids stood in the middle of the group, peering out of the forest of naked legs and giggling.

But they wouldn't be laughing for long. A mass of flour obscured the scene, as dozens of spoons all launched at once. And since flour couldn't hurt anyone, there was only one reason I could think of for the barrage.

"This way!" I yelled, holding open the door.

The group didn't move. The kids might have, but the t-shirt and nightie clad circle around them were witches, on loan to my court from the local covens, and retreat wasn't in their nature. Instead, they started slinging spells at the tiny army that was jumping off countertops and slamming out of cabinets, heading through the flour-y fog in an all-out assault.

The spells mostly weren't connecting, the army being too small and speedy, although I did see a few tiny warriors go up in fragrant puffs. But more were coming, and some of the spells were bouncing off of various shiny surfaces and ricocheting around the room. I didn't know what they were supposed to do, but since the witches were suddenly shielding and shouting at each other, it wasn't anything good.

And then things got worse.

The door on the opposite side of the kitchen burst open, and a bunch of grim-faced war mages rushed in. I immediately tensed up, because I didn't know these guys, who weren't supposed to be here. And because they weren't dressed right.

Instead of the usual brown leather coats worn over regular street wear, they looked like Darth Vader wannabees on their way to a convention. They were clad all in black, with what appeared to be military fatigues under their shiny new outerwear. The almost floor length coats concealed a mass of weaponry and also served as an extra shield in battle, which was fortunate, since several ricochets hit them almost as soon as they came in the door.

And, all right, that was enough because I knew what was coming; I knew war mages. I gathered what strength I had and shifted the kids to me. It was a little dicey without shifting part of a witch, too, but Gertie had made me practice that particular maneuver hundreds of times. After going through boot camp with her, I finally understood why Agnes's shifts had been so damned accurate.

She'd been afraid for them not to be.

But boot camp had worked, and while I didn't have Agnes' level of precision, I didn't shift anything I didn't want to, either. Which was why three toddlers rematerialized in a crouched position beside me, and promptly toppled over onto their fat little asses. But not for long.

I grabbed them and shoved them at Fred. "Get them out!"

He got them out, along with Cindy Lou, in a burst of vampire speed.

The swinging door had just closed behind him when the shooting started, and then abruptly stopped, because I was *pissed*. All the anger, confusion, pain and terror of the last few days coalesced on a target, one that wasn't supposed to be here, one that had been specifically barred from being here, and who had nonetheless taken it upon themselves to *shoot up my kitchen*. Only they weren't doing it now, since I had just stopped time.

It hurt like a son of a bitch.

I gasped and dropped to one knee. That spell hit hard enough when I was in decent shape, and under the circumstances, it felt like I'd just ripped my guts out. Not smart, but then, neither was letting a bunch of goons destroy my suite.

And possibly more, because the witches could shield, but the kids couldn't. And at least one of them had escaped her minders and gone exploring. If Fred hadn't gotten her out, she might have ended up back in the kitchen and—

My blood ran cold. And then went boiling hot at the possibility that those careless sons of bitches could have killed one of my girls. It made me gasp again, but this time, it wasn't in pain.

"Hey, hey," a war mage said, sounding alarmed.

It wasn't one of the goon squad, nor was it Pritkin. He wasn't back yet, or he'd have come running at the first spell. Everybody else certainly had, I noticed, finding myself jostled by a crowd of vampires, an acolyte named Annabelle, and the aforementioned war mage, a skinny guy named Reggie.

He was an awkward, jug eared, sandy blond with a buzz cut, who looked perpetually surprised, like maybe his eyebrows were set a little high. But he'd nonetheless ended up as the sole authorized

Circle mage at my court, since the others were dicks. Reggie had slightly better manners, or slightly better sense.

As demonstrated when he caught sight of his counterparts, now frozen in time amid a glittery cloud of spell fire, flour and bullets, and stopped dead.

"Oh, *geez*."

"What are they doing here?" I demanded.

"And why are they armed?" That was Paolo, one of my vamp bodyguards. He was a little guy with a nose almost as big as he was, but he never bothered with a glamourie to cover it up. Paolo was all about keeping it real. Only in this case that looked like it meant draining Reggie and tossing the empty out of the nearest window.

"I—you checked them over, too," Reggie pointed out, although the size of his eyes said that he'd gotten the implication.

"But I don't know all that shit," Paolo said, waving his hand around, as if casting a spell. "That's your job—"

"I did my job—"

"Yeah, it really looks like it!"

"Where's Marco?" I asked Fred, who had just come back in, sans kids. Marco was my head bodyguard, and I couldn't believe that he had just left a squad of unauthorized war mages in my suite without having them in cuffs. And beaten to a pulp. And possibly chained to a wall.

But apparently so.

"Off wrestling some furniture."

"Do I want to know what that means?"

Fred considered it. "Probably not."

"They're experts on fey magic," Reggie said, arguing with Paolo. "They probably used a spell I don't know—"

"Then what good are you?"

And maybe there was more backbone behind Reggie's youthful looks than I'd thought. Because the perpetually nervous, frequently jumpy, kind of nerdy guy suddenly reminded us all that he was, indeed, a war mage. And in the typical way.

"What to step outside and find out?" he asked, nose to nose with Paolo, for which he had to bend down slightly.

I started to push between them, but somebody beat me to it.

"We were doing some Christmas baking, and Vi thought it would be fun to animate the cookies for the little ones," Annabelle said.

She was one of my new acolytes, all of whom were friends of Hilde, which meant that they were pushing two hundred, although you couldn't tell in Annabelle's case. The fluffy filled out the wrinkles nicely, giving her chubby cheeks a smooth, youthful glow. It matched the white curls and the big blue eyes and the earnest expression, which always made me twitch.

She was a Pythian acolyte.

She had no business looking like that.

But right now, I had bigger problems, so I turned toward the kitchen. And, sure enough, Vi could be seen in the middle of the action. She was in a pale blue tank top and matching capris, with a mage's head under one arm, and her fist on its way to his face.

I turned back to Annabelle and waited.

"But, well, she isn't exactly the domestic type—" Annabelle began, her sweet voice sounding somewhat breathless.

"No shit." Vi looked like a younger version of Penthesilea, only with hair. Short, dark hair, to be precise, which was paired with big brown eyes and super long, natural lashes. And a physique that said she could win an arm-wrestling challenge with her pinkie, and if it was against me, she probably could.

Of course, the mage wasn't doing so hot, either.

"—and might have gotten her spells mixed up," Annabelle finished breathlessly.

"With what? A howitzer?"

"Sort of." That was Saffy, Vi's better half and the witch who'd interrupted us earlier. She'd slipped back into the pantry, having somehow missed the time spell, maybe by being out of the line of fire behind the door.

And, compared to the rest of us, she was looking pretty pulled together.

Her usual shock of pink hair was in French braids tonight, which kept it tidy, and was almost the exact color of her cheeks. And of the background of the short nightie she wore, which was otherwise decorated with wreaths and Ho-Ho-Ho's. She looked about as dangerous as Cindy Lou, but it was deceptive. Vi was as subtle as a rattlesnake; she could kick your ass and she looked like it. Saffy had better camouflage, but of the two, I wasn't sure I wouldn't rather face off with Vi.

"Most war spells got their start as something simpler," Saffy explained. "They're often built off of the kind of stuff that people use every day. A simple animate spell to make a broom sweep your patio, for instance, can be transformed into a weapon with a slight modification."

"So, all this is down to Vi throwing the wrong spell?"

"Um. Not exactly—"

"It's the clouds," Annabelle said earnestly. "It really wasn't Vi's fault. That is, she may have gotten the spell wrong—they really are quite similar—but it shouldn't have caused all this fuss—"

"There wasn't much magic behind it," Saffy explained. "Under normal circumstances, it wouldn't have been powerful enough to cause any trouble. A counter curse would have fixed it right up."

"But these circumstances aren't normal?" I asked impatiently.

"It's the clouds," Annabelle said again. "They're all over the place, although we'd been given to understand that the mages had cleared them up—"

"*What* clouds?"

She waved a hand. "You can see them if you look, just floating about. That's why we had to move the children downstairs, you see, into the vampires' rooms. And, honestly, Lady, the state of them! Cigars everywhere and alcohol—not to mention the ladies' unmentionables I found beneath a bed—"

"What were you doing under my bed?" Fred demanded.

Annabelle arched an eyebrow at him. "I didn't say it was yours, dear."

"What. Clouds?" I asked again, wondering if I was going mad.

Annabelle blinked at me. "Magic clouds. Look, here comes one now."

I didn't know what the hell she was talking about; magic didn't just float around. But then I followed her pointing finger, and thought I saw a golden shimmer by the door to the kitchen. It looked vaguely like my power when it had formed the whip that had taken Aeslinn's hand, or rather, like Zeus's power, since I'd mugged him to get it. Only this was thinner, weaker, just a pale glimmer on the air, and it wasn't forming anything.

Yet.

"So, Vi's spell hit one of these clouds—" I said, watching it warily.

Annabelle nodded. "You've got it now."

"—and blew up into . . . what?"

"We're trying to figure that out," Saffy said, while Annabelle made shooing motions at the floating cloud of energy, which had started coming this way. From what little I knew of magic, that shouldn't have made a difference, but apparently, I didn't know enough. Because the indistinct glimmer wafted about for a moment indecisively, then veered off course.

Straight onto Reggie.

His eyes immediately went wide, his limbs started thrashing around, and his mouth, which had been trading insults with Paolo, started yelling. "The guns! The guns!"

"You were supposed to take the mages' guns," Paolo said viciously.

"Not theirs, idiot! Mine!"

And, suddenly, my vampire bodyguards had something to do for a change, when items from Reggie's personal armory leapt out of his coat and—

Damn it!

I hit the floor, with no fewer than five vampires on top of me, as bullets from the war mage's animated arsenal strafed the room. Other vamps covered Annabelle, although nobody bothered with Saffy, who didn't need it. She'd had shields up in a heartbeat, although she nonetheless ducked behind the island with the rest of us.

"Shit," she said succinctly.

"I can shield myself, young man," Annabelle told Paolo, who was finding it difficult to protect that much fluff.

Paolo said something extremely rude in Italian, only to get a surprise when Annabelle said something appropriate right back, in the same language. And then pushed him off her with a shield that had to be half an inch thick, judging by the distortion of the room through it. Which was fortunate, as it was strafed with bullets a second later. They pinged about everywhere, including into the vamps on top of me, who swore.

And then swore again when they saw what was coming around the island.

What the *hell*?

Chapter Twenty-One

A war mage coat wasn't exactly an unusual sight around here, with both Pritkin and Reggie wearing them regularly. But said coats didn't usually stand on their own, with the approximate height of a man. And yet not in the shape of one.

The coats Pritkin and his incubus had fought with on the street had just looked like coats. Animated ones, via some spell I didn't know, but coats nonetheless. This one didn't.

Instead, it was floating on unseen currents, with the trailing hem billowing out behind, and all the little pockets and flaps and shoulder straps loose and fluttering. It almost looked alive, like a leather anemone come from the ocean to wreak havoc. And guess where it wanted to start?

Saffy threw a shield in front of me, only to have the coat lash out with its belt and shatter it to pieces on the buckle. Annabelle was next, lobbing a slow-time wave which did, indeed, slow it down. But only enough that the vamps were able to grab it.

And quickly wished they hadn't.

One of the sleeves snapped like a towel in a locker room, and sent a vamp flying through the wall and into the kitchen. Since these were not flimsy Vegas hotel walls anymore, but rather solid concrete block, that . . . wasn't good. And it was even less so when the now free sleeve formed a hand from its cuff and dug a potion bomb out of its pocket.

Saffy had to imprison the subsequent explosion in a shield, or we'd have all been coughing up our lungs. But the coat didn't like that, and jumped for her, only to have Annabelle reinforce the first slow time spell with another. That cut the coat down to almost human speed, letting Saffy hit it with a half dozen spells in quick succession while backing toward the door to the hall.

She didn't miss even one, but none of them did more than knock it back a bit. Because that coat belonged to a war mage, damn it! And I was pretty sure I knew which one.

"Release, you bastard! Release! Release!" Reggie was yelling—in his shirt sleeves, so yeah, it was his coat. I assumed that the cloud of magic must have come in from the kitchen, where it had blended with part of Vi's war spell, and gone looking for something more deadly than a cookie to bond with.

And it had found one.

War mage coats were leather than had been laced with spells for, in some cases, generations. They were considered heirlooms in some families, passed down from parent to child, and were intensely powerful items on their own. I did not want to find out what one newly imbued with a floating pool of wild magic was capable of.

But it was happening anyway, unless Reggie managed to get it back under control.

"Call it . . . off," I wheezed from under the vamp mountain. "Call it off!"

Reggie looked at me wildly. "It's not working!"

"Then use . . . the password! Doesn't your coat . . . have a password?"

As I'd found out after Pritkin gifted me a duplicate of his own coat, war mage attire and weapons were spelled to the wearer, with a password to avoid having them turned on their owner. If they were stolen, the owner could deactivate them by using the selected word or phrase. Or, if he was really vindictive, sic 'em on the thief.

But Reg didn't seem to like that idea.

He stared at me. "If I do, it'll remove all the enchantments. I'll have to redo the whole thing!"

I stared back. "*And*?"

He cursed inventively. And then the flailing arm of the coat found the knife drawer, and started chucking blades at everyone. Including Reggie, who ended up with a bloody sleeve.

"Okay, okay!" he snarled, and uttered a guttural incantation. It sounded old—like ancient Egyptian old—but it got the coat's attention. It paused for a second and turned toward him, with almost human-like curiosity in its movements.

And then it sent its belt to wrap around Reggie's neck, trying to strangle him. Or maybe to shut him up; I didn't know. But I didn't think the password was working.

Meanwhile, the war mage's backup system—the levitating guns, knives and potion grenades that could turn one man into a platoon—stayed on the attack.

Saffy kept catching the explosions from the latter, which was why there were suddenly transparent shield balls everywhere, filled with colorful smoke. They made the small butler's pantry look like hell's bouncy house, which was bad enough as they kept getting in the way and tripping people up. But if some of the weapons' fire managed to shatter one—

The same thought must have occurred to Paolo, who jumped up, grabbed a gun out of the air, and crushed it to pieces with vampire strength.

And, okay, that stopped it from firing, but created a new problem when the broken pieces immediately started zipping around, crashing through glass cabinets and putting a dent in the wine fridge. And in several vampire's skulls, because reinforcements had just slammed in the door. Only to get slammed right back out again.

"Now what?" Paolo asked, ducking a flying knife.

"Help Reggie," I said breathlessly. The mage was turning red in the face, since the damned belt had just dragged him off the floor like a hangman's noose. And I couldn't do anything for him myself.

I was flat out of power, or at least, out of the stamina needed to channel it. I tried calling up some from Mircea, but received nothing back. I tried again, putting everything I had into it, to overcome the muffling effects of whatever remained of the fey potion. But not only was there no answer to the call, there was no feel of him being there at all.

He also didn't answer when I tried calling him mentally, and neither did Pritkin. That had fear clutching at my throat and my mind racing. Where were they? I'd used Mircea's power maybe an hour ago, when overhearing the flirty maid's conversation. And I wasn't dead, which I would be if Aeslinn had caught up with them.

So why couldn't I reach him?

I didn't know. And I didn't have time to think about it. The coat was coming, and despite having four vamps on it now, trying to hold it back, it was coming fast.

Shit!

I tried to crawl away, which was a little difficult since the vamps on top of me hadn't budged. But then the coat spun, sending all of its outriders flying. And two of my personal squad jumped up to engage in what should have been a hilarious boxing match.

It wasn't.

One empty leather sleeve balled its cuff into a fist and began pummeling the first vamp in the face, hard enough to crack teeth. Meanwhile, the other sleeve expanded and engulfed the second vamp's head. It immediately contracted again, sealing him inside what looked like a leather mask, which would have been a death sentence for a human since I doubted that any air was getting in there. But vamps didn't need it, something that the coat seemed to figure out when he kept on fighting.

So, it started slinging the sleeve back and forth, slamming him between the island and the cabinets behind us. The blows splintered the latter, scattering shards everywhere. And if there's one thing that vamps' hate, its flying wood.

The one still on top of me freaked out, grabbed me around the waist, and started for the door. He was moving faster than eyes could track, but not faster than a crazed coat could move. It slung out a hem and caught me, wrapping around my ankle like a fist.

"Get her out! Get her out!" Saffy was yelling, while slinging spells that the coat shrugged off.

It did the same for the half dozen vamps who had jumped for it, trying to overpower it by sheer numbers, only for them to shriek and abruptly back off. Because each of those little flaps and flanges and shoulder straps had grabbed a broken bit of cabinet. Turning the floating terror into a vampire's worst nightmare, armed with at least a dozen stakes.

And then somebody started screaming. Fair disclosure, it might have been me. It was hard to tell, with glass shattering, people churning, and arms reaching, grabbing and pulling at me. But it was a safe bet, considering that the coat was pulling now, too—in the other direction.

"Let me go!" I yelled. "Let me go! You're going to rip me in half!"

That wasn't an exaggeration considering vampire strength. But they didn't let go, maybe because they didn't hear me. The background noise was deafening.

And it suddenly became more so when a roar like an angry bull cut through the din, and the big gun joined the fray.

Marco, I thought in relief, as a two-hundred-and-sixty-pound streak of pure muscle shot overhead like a bullet, grabbed the coat and tore it off me. And then started the biggest, baddest fight I never saw, because they were moving too fast. And because I was jerked out of the kitchen a second later.

Me and at least eight bleeding vamps staggered through the swinging door, and into the main hub of the apartment.

I landed on the back of one, still screaming. I tried to stop, but I seemed to have a lot of screams backed up, all of which wanted out. But nobody said anything; half of the vamps were screaming, too.

I didn't blame them since several were riddled with bullets, others had makeshift stakes sticking out of their bodies at random places, and one had an animated knife buzzing around his head. Or, he did until another vamp caught it and crushed it, and then kept on crushing it, wadding it into a little ball before slamming it into the wall, where it stayed, buried in the concrete and softly buzzing. We all stared at it for a moment.

And then we stared at something else, because the hub of the apartment . . . was not as I remembered.

Everything in the suite branched off from the large, round, main hub like spokes off a wheel—including the halls leading to the bedrooms, classrooms, living areas, and the audience chamber—which was why it was kept open and free of clutter. As a result, the only furnishings were an octagonal, fabric-covered bench in the center and some potted plants along the walls. Or, at least, that used to be the case.

Only the plants were no longer potted.

Or recognizable.

They had outgrown their tubs, which lay in shards on the floor, having sent out branches to scrawl all over the walls and onto the ceiling. It left the place looking like a jungle with a tasteful beige poof sitting in the middle of it for some reason. Underfoot, roots as big as my arm had woven an uncomfortable carpet that threatened to trip us up; from above, hanging vines drooped down to try and strangle us.

I was only gone for a few days, I thought, looking around dizzily.

What the hell had happened?

I didn't know, and I couldn't see well enough to find out. The vines had all but obscured the overhead lights, leaving the jungle fairly dark, with illumination having to cascade in from the halls and living room. One of the wall ornaments could be seen, peeking palely through the foliage. It was a carving of a Maori head, made from whale bone, which Tami had found somewhere and decided she liked. It usually looked out of place amid the tasteful blandness, but right now, it gave the area the definite feel of an old tomb.

Indiana Jones would have been right at home.

But I wasn't and I didn't like it. I also didn't understand it. I dismounted the vamp and stood up, but before I could ask what the hell, a handkerchief-sized tendril of magic peeled off of a nearby vine and floated into the air.

It looked like the cloud in the kitchen, except for being much smaller. It twisted and turned, a diaphanous, barely-there glister on the gloom. But I didn't look away, since it was more bizarre than anything else in sight.

Magic didn't do this. Despite what I'd seen in the kitchen and what I was seeing now, it didn't just float around. Wild magic rode lightning sometimes, or showed up around lava spills or danced with the Aurora Borealis. But it did not simply decide to invade hotel suites and poke about, looking to cause mischief.

I wasn't even sure how it had gotten in here in the first place, since we had wards to prevent magical attacks. Although, despite what I'd just been through, this didn't feel like one. I wasn't sure what it felt like.

The little tendril wafted a bit closer. It was a good six yards off, but I could nonetheless smell it in my nose, a rich, heady aroma. I could taste it on my tongue, sweet, sweet, like divine nectar, like life distilled. I could almost hear it, a silken glissando too low to really make out, but soothing nonetheless, like the rain against Gertie's window.

My stomach suddenly rumbled in earnest, and my head felt dizzy. The hunger I'd felt back in her sitting room came roaring back, only magnified a hundred times over. I made a small sound and somebody grabbed my arm.

"You okay?"

It was Fred's voice, but I was having trouble concentrating on it. Like I was having trouble seeing anything but that glistening strand. It was so beautiful . . .

And then there were two.

"Cassie?"

"I'm fine," I said blankly, watching as another tiny, golden thread drifted into the hub on a ray of light from the direction of the bedrooms. And then another emerged from down the hall to the dining area. And, suddenly, they were coming from all directions.

Some were miniscule filaments, only possible to see when they twisted just right, as narrow as a thread or a single strand of hair.

Others were literal floating clouds. And there was every size in between.

"Okay, what is going on?" Fred said, sounding panicky from beside me.

I didn't answer, since I didn't know.

But big or small, the threads changed things as they came. The canopy overhead became thick and lush as they brushed by, with the leaves of the different species of plants crowding out the plaster. Vines flopped down from the ceiling in clusters, some bursting with flowers, the latter of which sent flurries of petals swirling through the air. And a flock of iridescent green butterflies, as big as my splayed hands, erupted from fist sized cocoons to flutter about, mixing with the storm of white and purple petals currently obscuring my vision.

But all of that paled into insignificance when one of the golden tendrils came out of nowhere and wrapped itself around my wrist.

The vamps didn't notice. Some had gone back into the kitchen to help with what sounded like a desperate fight; others were busy battling the ever-growing thatch of vines, which had started to scrawl over the doors, threatening to block the exits. I had been right there with them a moment ago, wondering what fresh hell our enemies had unleashed on us. But now . . .

Now I had a pretty new bracelet, one that glimmered and gleamed against my skin.

I stared at it, mesmerized. It was so weightless that I almost couldn't feel it. But there was a warmth to it, and a frisson, which sent an echoing shiver through me. One that it seemed to recognize. Instead of fighting or hurting me, as I'd half expected, it was . . . nuzzling me?

The little tendril wrapped itself around my arm like an overly affectionate cat, almost purring. I felt some of the tension in my spine release, the kind that I carried about with me everywhere these days, to the point that I hadn't noticed it until it was gone. My whole body sagged in relief for a second, then straightened back up again, feeling stronger and happier than I had in a while.

And then it got better.

A vamp thrust me behind him, while the others attacked a huge root that had just pushed up from the floor and barred the door to the living room. I barely noticed. Because the tendril that had been rubbing itself against me suddenly decided to get a bit more personal. And sank into my skin, causing me to start in shock.

I started again a second later, but for a very different reason. I whipped my head around, and suddenly, I wasn't looking at a bunch of random magic. I was staring at . . .

A *feast*.

Renewed strength was coursing through me, just from that one small hit of power. Power that I recognized, since I'd pulled some just like it off a god. Power that tasted like ambrosia and raised a sudden, clawing, desperate hunger for more.

I felt like I hadn't eaten in a week.

I felt like I hadn't eaten in *forever*.

Suddenly, everything paled next to those glowing strands, all coming this way, muscling in from every corner of the apartment, searching, seeking, wanting—

Me.

I'd been right: magic *couldn't* live like this, without a host or at least a proper environment. It would dissipate eventually, scattering its power on the wind. Lost forever.

And even the idea of that filled me with such horror, that it barely registered when Marco staggered through the kitchen door, the coat shredded and with both its arms torn off, but with the remnant wrapped around his neck, trying to choke him. It couldn't, of course, but it could sever his head, something that looked to be a real possibility until it paused, tore off of him, and came flying straight for me.

It didn't reach me.

I'd thrown out a hand, barely thinking, acting on instinct—

And the coat paused, like a giant leather bat in the air. As if an unseen hand had caught it and knocked it back a little. And, somehow, that mass of shredded leather managed to convey surprise, as if it didn't know what was happening.

Neither did I, but I pushed ahead anyway, increasing the hold I'd somehow acquired on the creature, and squeezing—but only with one hand. The other was flung out behind me, calling to all that power that shouldn't have been there, but was. And which was answering the call.

I felt them when they hit—small thrills from the tiny filaments, gravitating toward me like iron shavings to a magnet; larger bursts from the bigger pieces, like bright scarves in the dim light, curling about my arms and waist and hair, making me laugh. And, finally, explosions from the bigger pieces, the clouds that Annabelle had spoken of, suffusing the very air around me like pollen, so that I breathed it in with every breath, absorbing it through my skin until every part of my body felt happy, well fed, and full of power.

All of which I threw at the coat. It turned and twisted in the air, trying to evade my grip, trying to claw and tear and bite, the energy it had absorbed along with all the spells that Reggie had layered onto it, year after year, fighting with me, giving the battle everything that it had. But I had more, all the power that the mages had missed because it wasn't fey; it wasn't fey at all.

And while I couldn't absorb it, once it had bonded with another host like the coat, I could destroy it, ripping it apart with golden energy, flinging tiny pieces of leather far and wide until they dissipated on the air, like black smoke.

The bright clouds that had been lightening the gloom also disappeared, having found a home, but the room didn't darken. It couldn't, not with golden light spilling out all around me now, and more flowing under my skin in strange patterns. I admired them giddily, laughing and half drunk on power I didn't fully understand, and right then, didn't care to.

Until I looked up, and saw the expressions on the faces of my unintentional audience: the vamps, covered in blood that they hadn't yet bothered to reabsorb; the mages, including those from the kitchen, who must finally have been released from my time spell; and Annabelle, with her usual jovial expression carefully blank. The witches were there, too, not just Saffy but Vi and Lilli, the third a diminutive woman with a Jamaican accent and big brown eyes.

Very big, at the moment.

They didn't look happy. Some of the war mages even had their hands on their weapons for some reason. I looked at Marco for reassurance, but even his face was shocked and his mouth, usually clamped tight around a cigar, was open and empty.

No, they didn't look happy at all, I realized.

They looked . . .

Afraid.

Chapter Twenty-Two

I lost it with all of those eyes on me and shifted. If I'd stopped to think, I wouldn't have tried using my power so soon after a time stoppage. I would have assumed that I wouldn't have the strength.

But I hadn't been thinking; I'd just wanted to get away. But that didn't work out quite the way I'd planned. I'd no sooner successfully shifted into the hotel lobby, feeling off balance and freaked out and in an Edwardian bathrobe, when I was mobbed by at least a dozen people.

Some were reporters yelling questions about the war. Some were flunkies of various self-important senators who believed that they deserved an audience for every little thing. And some, heartbreakingly, were people, regular people, who had lost someone in the war and were desperate for information I didn't have.

"Lady, please Lady, can you tell me about my son? He was on the expedition to Faerie, and didn't return. But he wasn't listed among the dead. Can you see him? Do you know if he's alive? Lady—"

"I have called and called, but your appointment secretary won't see my master; won't even put his name on the list! She had the audacity to tell me that she didn't speak English, but when I switched to French, *she* switched to some odd sort of patois that I'm not even sure is a real language—"

"Lady Cassandra, Melvin Monroe from the *Inquisitor*. Can you give us any information on what the World Senate plans to do next? Are they and the Circle gearing up for another invasion of Faerie, to find the king who escaped them last time? Or are they planning to stand down? In effect, is the war over or—"

"The war isn't over," I said harshly, looking for a way out. But all I saw were more people, some of them headed this way at a run.

"His name was David, Lady—here is his picture. Can you just tell me if—"

I shifted out again, this time to the roof.

I landed between one of the fake towers and the big, crenellated outer wall, feeling dizzy and very strange. As if I'd had to exert far more energy for that little hop than usual, and yet like I had plenty in reserve. It felt as if I could have shifted forever, like a stone being skipped over a pond, *shift, shift, shift,* all in a long line, wherever and whenever I pleased.

Unless I fell on my face first, I thought, as another wave of vertigo hit.

I grabbed the faux stones behind me for balance, and then just stood there, staring out at the Strip. It glittered in front of me, its lights mirroring those of the Milky Way far above. Wind blew my hair in my face, because it was always windy up here, but I didn't mind. It felt good.

"If it's not over, then what is the next step?" someone said, causing me to almost jump out of my skin.

I looked around to find the reporter, a skinny older guy with a gray combover that was whipping in the wind, emerging from the darkness.

I gaped at him for a second. "How did you get up here?"

"You tell me. One moment, I'm in the lobby, trying to get a question answered for once, and the next, I'm about to fall off the building! Do you often do that? Just pick people up and—"

"I didn't pick you up. I . . . I don't shift random people."

"Shift? Is that what it's called?" he took out a notebook and scribbled something inside. I watched him blankly, the realization of just how little most people knew about what the Pythias did, or could do, hitting me in the face. Ours was a closed world, and most didn't even have a window on it, much less a door.

Lucky them.

"Then how would you say I got here?" the reporter demanded, looking up.

"I have no idea."

It was the truth, but it didn't look like he bought it. "In any event, as I *am* here, and considering that you haven't given an interview in some time—"

"The Senate gives regular press briefings," I said, wondering at the single mindedness of the man. In his position, I'd have been screaming and clinging to the concrete. Yet here he was, trying to get a story.

Too bad I didn't have one that he'd believe.

"Yes, where they waste half an hour on platitudes and tell us nothing!" he responded tartly. "A suspicious mind might think that they don't have anything *to* tell. That they don't have a plan for this war at all, but are simply winging it." Sharp gray eyes met mine. "I rather think you might know more, since you seem to be leading this fight—"

"I'm . . . not leading anything. Pythias aren't generals."

"And yet, there you are, at every council meeting and in the vanguard of every battle. The rumor is that you took down the shield over the alien capitol single handedly, during the recent assault. Is that true?"

"I—" I stopped myself before saying anything that would end up on the front page of a newspaper tomorrow, but the guy wasn't having it.

"Come, come, Lady Cassandra, can't you give us that much, at least? When a dozen eye-witnesses have already confirmed it?"

"A dozen?" I had a hard time believing that. The only men in sight at the time, other than for Mircea and Pritkin, had been dead and piled up in heaps. The flies hadn't gotten to them yet, as the slaughter had been recent when we arrived, enough that their blood made the soil damp and spongy as we floundered across it. Yet things had buzzed around the fleshy mountains, nonetheless.

The dead mages' weapons, enchanted to fight alongside them, had formed distressed clouds in the air. They'd endlessly circled their fallen masters, waiting for instructions that would never come. I guessed they must have fallen to the ground eventually, after their well of power was depleted. Dead, like the men who had used them to fight so valiantly against overwhelming odds.

The reporter was talking again, but I couldn't hear him. All I could see was the vast battlefield: the stark and barren tundra, the jagged mountain range in the distance, and the black, leather-coated piles of the dead. And all I could hear was the wind that had blown that day, whistling through my head in a horrible, unearthly howl. It kept getting louder and louder, but I couldn't seem to shut it out, couldn't *think*.

But I could See—more than I wanted. The battle field came zooming at me suddenly, at a hundred miles an hour, until I saw the man in the picture that the woman had waved at me. He had dark skin and blue eyes, and was wearing the leather coat of a war mage. And he was flying, hanging off the swinging arm of one of Aeslinn's huge stone sentinels, which the king had magicked up out of the surrounding rocks in order to destroy us.

Each was a walking mountain, a man-shaped colossus with forests for hair and whole, babbling brooks cutting across their bodies—or veins of precious ore, or deep crags filled with bats that could suddenly explode outward like a black cloud. Some had sparkling crystal formations spearing out of their backs like the fins on a dinosaur. Others were incongruously covered in flowers, draped in a spring meadow like a pelt, as if they had been called forth from somewhere far from this forbidding land.

They came in a huge variety of types and patterns, each drawn from the earth that had formed them. But each was big, each was deadly, and each was a walking army, all on its own. An army that David was determined to bring down.

He'd seen the carnage, seen his brothers lying limp and broken on the soil, like ants who had dared to tackle giants. And yet they *had* dared; how could he do less? He thought of his girlfriend back home. Thought of his mother, who had begged him not to go to war, but to stay with her. Thought of his father, a war mage who had spent his whole career busting shops that sold adulterated potions, or old ones marked as new, or ones with half of the magic infused into them that was promised.

His father had never seen battle. He'd complained about the three days a year he'd been forced to take off from work in order to show proficiency in basic skills. To throw spells he'd never need, or shoot guns he rarely carried, or raise battle shields far stronger than anything he'd ever use.

"Waste of time," he'd always mutter. "When there hasn't been a war in centuries."

David wondered what the old man would think now, as the spell he'd used to snag one of the beast's great fingers finally hauled him up even with its shoulder and he jumped off.

This one was especially fearsome looking, having lava, red-gold and burning, seeping out of a fissure near its neck. Some of it had hardened, blackening the head and torso, while the rest left boiling red veins running through the cracked landscape. Even worse, a mass of steam erupted from the fissure as the heat of the melted rock met the cold winter's air, almost occluding the huge face.

And forming the perfect cover for the fey who ran out of the mist and tackled David with a yell.

It was the creature's owner, or whatever they called the soldiers who drew these things forth and then manipulated them, driving them around like cars—or tanks. But a tank needs a driver, and is useless without one. Just a hunk of metal sitting on a battlefield, and nothing more.

Like this one was about to be.

David landed on his back and immediately felt his coat start to melt. He swore, got his legs up, and kicked the fey off, sending him staggering back and throwing a net spell over him at the same time. The silver haired bastard didn't seem to know that enchantment, and hadn't managed to throw it off when it constricted, slamming him against his mount's burning hide.

The fey cursed when his skin came into contact with the burning surface below him, but while he might look like a bug caught in a spider's net, his creature remained active. As indicated when the light around David dimmed, and he looked up. To see a giant stone hand about to clamp down on top of him.

Magically enhanced speed allowed him to avoid being crushed, but his only escape route took him past the fey, who wasn't as trapped as he'd appeared. He'd managed to get a hand free and threw a spell of his own, tripping David up and sending him crashing onto the creature's rock-hard shoulder. And the bastard was on him an instant later.

But while he was tall, at least seven feet, and powerful, David was no slouch. He was a foot shorter but twice as muscled, and there was magic behind every punch, every kick, every gouge. He gave as good as he got—better, in fact, using his rage as his instructors had taught him, not to cloud his vision but to enhance it.

And then he saw it—a muscle twitch in the fey's left arm, even as the right sent a fist at his face. He ducked the feint and caught the fey's opposite wrist. And sent the fireball that the fey was trying to throw at him back onto its owner.

The fey went up like a torch, screaming. But the scream must have included a spell, since the flames were almost immediately extinguished. But not before he was seriously burned, leaving him injured and woozy.

But not dead.

Not yet.

David knocked him out with a muttered word, but didn't deliver the coup de gras. The plan had been to kill him and thus immobilize his transport, taking at least one of the colossi out of the battle. But now . . .

He had a different idea.

David could feel the fey's magic, still hot, still vibrant, and still flowing into the giant body below them. He didn't understand how the connection between the two worked, or how the colossus could be spewing fiery rock when no longer connected to the ground. But there was a link there, not only from the fey to the creature, but from both to the earth. He could sense it with his own magic, although not connect to it. The fey system was too different.

But then, maybe he didn't need to connect directly.

Maybe he had an in.

He sent a tendril of magic to wrap around the unconscious fey, as well as the alien power that thrummed around him. He was careful not to attack, or do anything that might cause the creature's natural defenses to kick in. His touch wasn't a punch or a slap, but more like a hug.

And when the fey's magic had sufficiently colored his, masking it, hiding it, and intertwining with it, he thrust them both into the great body beneath him, which had gone motionless from the lack of commands.

Until he gave it one.

He held his breath as slowly, slowly, slowly, the mighty arm began to move. It pulled off of the shoulder it had been holding, with the grinding sound of stone on stone, sending a cloud of black dust into the air to join with the steam. David gave another command, as he would to one of his arsenal, which was bound to him as the colossus seemed to be to the fey. And again, he received a sluggish response.

Which turned into a faster one as he learned how this worked, as he reinforced the command, as he watched the great legs move forward, taking one step, two steps, three. Until the huge body was on the move, blocking the way of another colossus that had been passing by. And causing its great head to turn toward them inquisitively.

David didn't see its rider, who could have been anywhere. But he got the distinct impression that someone saw *him*, through a deep, dark crevasse where the creature's eyes should have been. But, instead, twin stars glittered at him out of the darkness, maybe crystalline structures trapped far back in there, but catching the light when the thing moved just right.

Or maybe not.

He felt himself swallow, felt the hair on the back of his neck start to rise, felt chills flood his skin as some ancient part of his brain started screaming about danger—before he shut it down hard. He was a *war mage*. He had been *trained for this*.

Well, maybe not exactly this, but since when did battle go according to plan?

Then he sent his creature's great fist slamming into the other colossus, hard enough to send it staggering.

It righted itself and hit back hard enough that David could feel it, and not just under his feet. But in his own solar plexus, where his borrowed body had taken the hit. And he suddenly understood one thing, at least.

These creatures weren't tanks, after all; they were extensions of their master's bodies—an exoskeleton formed out of the earth by some magic he didn't know. But he didn't know how a car worked, either, not in every detail, yet he could drive it. And he drove this one, ignoring the steadily increasing moans of the fey at his feet, as their substitute body absorbed blow after blow.

But the other mountain soon looked worse. The Circle wasn't picky about how an enemy ended up dead, just that they did. And David had studied everything from kickboxing to jujitsu, not to mention the street fighting he'd picked up from the kids in his old neighborhood, who hadn't liked his blue eyes or the fact that his skin was too bright.

He'd kicked their asses, like he kicked the creature's now, driving it back, forcing it to give ground. He finally had it down, had a giant hand on its throat, had lava running down his arm to seep onto its face and cause it to writhe as if in pain, which its driver probably was. David felt like a giant bruise himself.

And then someone clapped him on the shoulder from behind.

The touch was startling and completely unexpected, not least because it didn't grab onto his creature's body, but his own. It made his brain hurt by reminding him that he existed in two places at once, and started all kinds of alarm bells ringing. He barely retained control of his strange vehicle as he swiveled his neck around.

And saw four of his fellow mages standing there, looking at him like he'd just discovered flight.

"*How?*" the one in the lead said, gesturing at the insanity that he didn't even have a name for.

David told them how.

"Fuck me," the leader said. And then they were gone, using their shields like hang gliders to propel them over to four nearby colossi.

David grinned, but he didn't have time to see if they managed to duplicate his feat. His own ride had started going crazy, thrashing about, swinging its arms wildly and letting go of the injured giant, before staggering into another. Maybe because the fey at his feet was also going into some kind of convulsion.

It was clear that the fey didn't have long, and once he died, David doubted that his hold over the great creature would last.

Even worse, the giant he'd been fighting had recovered enough to pull itself off of the ground and to join the fight, making it two against one. But his own colossus was talking to him now, if only dimly, and in pictures. But sometimes, they really are worth a thousand words, David thought, and sent a spew of molten lava out of his neck fissure, straight across his enemies' faces.

The first colossus staggered back, and then stopped moving, as a screaming, fiery fey jumped off the body and into the dirt. David seized the moment and turned his attention to his second attacker, only to have his fist stop halfway through the motion. But not because it had encountered the creature's body.

But because the fey at his feet was dead.

And, just like that, so was his connection to his ride. His colossus froze up, halfway between one step and the next, and toppled over, and it was all that David could do not to fall along with it. He heard when it hit, shaking the battlefield like an earthquake, but didn't feel it. He'd already launched himself into the skies, borne aloft by his shields and looking for another target.

He didn't find one.

He never knew which giant had seen him, such a tiny speck against all that pale blue. Never knew if it was the one that he'd been fighting or another; never even knew if the blow was deliberate or not. He was focused on the next task, right up to the end.

So, there was only pain, bright, brief, and disorienting.

And then there was nothing at all.

Except for a heart wrenching cry, echoing in the night. *"David!"*

It was loud and almost on top of me, jolting me out of the vision. I looked around in confusion, seeing a night sky, a smear of neon colors, and my hair blowing across my face. And a woman—the same one from the lobby, I realized, with dark skin and a dress the color of David's eyes.

I just stared at her for a moment, caught between worlds, and then was wrenched off the concrete by frantic hands. It was the reporter, looking a lot less cool and collected than he had a moment ago. He appeared spooked: aghast and afraid and furious, all at once.

"What did you do?"

"I didn't—"

"Of course, you did!" His spittle hit my face. "Have Pythias always been able to do that? To project visions into other people's heads? Is that how you control us? Get us to agree to—to—"

"To what?"

"To whatever you want!" He shook me. "Is that how?"

"Let her go."

The voice was the woman's, and she was back on her feet, too, no longer half hunched over with grief as she'd been a moment ago. It was on her face, etched into every line. But so was something else.

She took my hand, and that was a big problem right now. In a flash, I saw her pushing her son in a swing as a little boy; saw him standing as a young teen at his father's graveside; saw her watching him graduate from the academy, pride radiating from his face. Saw her clipping his father's war mage pin on him for the first time—

I let go, gasping and sobbing, and staggering with borrowed grief—and my own. Because I'd helped to make the decision to go ahead with that battle. The deciding vote that had sent David and scores of others to their deaths had been mine, and mine alone.

"I'm sorry," she said. "I didn't realize . . . I'm sorry."

I shook my head. I wanted to tell her that I was the one who was sorry. That I'd had a chance to stop that fight, but hadn't taken it, because we had to end this and it had seemed like our best chance. But Aeslinn hadn't been there, and all we'd won was a battle, not a war.

Had the price been too high?

For her, it definitely had.

"There are no bloodless wars," she told me quietly, as if she could read my mind. "He knew that. I knew it, too. But it is hard not hearing what happened, when they go away and don't come back. It's so hard . . ."

"I understand," I whispered, knowing that I didn't. That I never, ever could.

Just the echo of her pain was debilitating.

And yet, she smiled at me, a tremulous thing. I stared back, uncomprehending. "You gave me a great gift," she whispered. "Thank you."

"You . . . shouldn't be thanking me. You don't understand—"

"I understand that his battle is over, and that he is at peace. But that your struggle goes on. My son once told me that battle is easy; you just have to follow orders. What comes after is harder, when there are no more orders, no one telling you what to do or how to think, or how to process it all. I think . . . you're caught in the after, aren't you?"

I just stared at her.

"What the hell just happened?" the reporter yelled again.

"Go," she told me. "You have a war to fight."

I went.

Chapter Twenty-Three

Ah, there she is."

The voice boomed at me out of the darkness of my bedroom, as soon as I shifted onto my landing pad inside.

It caused me to whip my head around, and to almost shift back out when I identified it: Hilde. It should have been old and thin and weedy, considering that Gertie's sister was pushing two hundred, if she wasn't already past it. But, instead, she sounded more like a Valkyrie announcing the summons to Valhalla.

I was so not in the mood.

"Not now," I told her brusquely. And brushed past the grandmotherly figure in the flowered robe, heading for my bathroom.

Only to find her posse standing between me and the door. There was an even dozen of them, huddled together as if they had been a little reluctant to brave the bear in her den. Hilde, of course, had felt no such emotion. I sometimes thought that Hilde didn't *have* emotions except for a determined geniality and a ruthlessness that would have done Genghis Khan proud.

The group of acolytes she'd gathered together, on the other hand, were a bit more deferential—not to mention unbearably cute in their new finery. Augustine, the court designer, had finally finished creating an outfit to replace the god-awful Victorian one that Gertie had dreamed up. Which, in turn, had taken the place of even worse garb from centuries before.

It seemed to be a rite of passage for Pythias to determine what their courts would wear, like a bride deciding how bad she was going to be to her bridesmaids. Which in my case was not very, since I liked wearing normal clothes, too. But every once in a while, everybody had to get dressed up, and Augustine had come through beautifully.

Only I didn't think he'd anticipated that his soft, white draperies, layer upon layer of whisper fine, silk chiffon falling from a simple halter top, would be worn with chunky sweaters and support hose. Or in one case, with a pair of fluffy pink house slippers, because Annabelle had fallen arches and the matching ankle pumps hurt her feet. I'd seen the great man's mouth open, and then close again with a pop as she wafted around in his design and her booties, obviously delighted with the result.

He'd slammed the door to his workroom, muttering, but had been otherwise silent.

Join the club, Augustine, I thought.

Join the club.

"Take your time," Hilde assured me pleasantly, as I surveyed the girls. I suspected that she'd brought them deliberately, knowing that I wouldn't want to throw out a bunch of sweet-faced grandmas. And she was right, damn it! "We'll just wait here."

"I don't want you to wait here."

"Oh, it's no bother at all."

"But I don't *want*—"

"No. Bother."

She found a chair that would fit her ample proportions and settled in, giving off a very Gibraltar-y vibe. And, God, I so didn't need this! I wanted to disappear inside my bathroom; I wanted some time to think, to stare at a wall, to not see anyone for a while.

I wanted to grieve for a man I'd never known, and for the woman who would never get him back.

But if I didn't deal with this, Hilde would damned well be sitting there when I emerged. I knew that as sure as I knew my own name. So, I crossed my arms, widened my stance, and braced myself.

"All right, what is it?"

"No, no. Go get your bath, or whatever it is you do in there for hours at a time." She smiled sweetly at me.

I didn't smile back.

"Tell me," I told her. "Now."

Hilde gave a longsuffering sigh. "You already know what I want. But perhaps some dinner first?"

"I could get you something," Annabelle offered eagerly. She loved to feed people—and anything else that held still long enough. Her two cats were complete chonkers and could barely waddle around.

"Maybe later."

"It's no trouble at all. There's apple pie for dessert," she wheedled.

"You should eat something," Hilde opined. "You look terrible."

Annabelle sent her a look that clearly said, "Let me handle this." To my surprise, Hilde made a face but settled back into her chair, yielding the field. I turned on Annabelle, feeling annoyed and ganged up on and manipulated—and then guilty, because she was all rosy cheeks and flyaway white curls and big, innocent eyes.

"We had chicken and dumplings for dinner, and they were so nice and fat," she told me earnestly. "The dumplings, I mean. Would you like a tray? A small one?"

Considering the size of her pets, I wondered what counted as small. Not that it mattered, as I wasn't hungry anymore despite skipping breakfast. But I knew how well telling her that was likely to go over. The girls had decided that I was on the brink of starvation, and constantly pushed food at me. It drove Pritkin mad, who was trying to keep me on a healthy training diet, to keep up my stamina and improve my health, and healthy food wasn't the grandmas' specialty.

Instead, I found pastries on my bedside table, along with a nightly cup of tea. I discovered candy left in the pockets of my clothes, and milkshakes served to me with breakfast. Meanwhile Tami, who had done most of the cooking around here once upon a time, had been edged out of the kitchen by various grandmas, who thereafter sent a river of bacon-laced veggies and fatty meats to the dinner table, not to mention pastas with enough butter to have given Paula Dean pause.

But they thought they were helping, and my recent weight loss hadn't gone unnoticed. Several were frowning at me now, several more were whispering behind their hands, and Annabelle was biting her lip, obviously afraid that I would say no. And thereafter be found sprawled on my bathroom floor, dead of starvation, and it would be all her fault.

"Very small," I finally said, and she padded off happily.

I turned back to Hilde, who was looking self-satisfied enough that it counted as smug.

"What?" I asked again, only to have her gesture at the seat next to her, with the air of a queen giving an audience. It was bad enough that she was inviting me to sit down in my own room, but on top of that, I had the definite impression that *I* was the one having an audience with *her*. One I didn't even want!

"Tea?" she asked, as another grandma bustled in. I narrowed my eyes at the pot, which must have been started before I flashed in or it couldn't possibly have been ready yet. Of course, maybe they'd just been thirsty, but I was suspicious.

This was starting to look like a set up.

"There now," Hilde said, accepting a cup. "Isn't this nice?"

"What. Do you. Want?"

"Are you sure you wouldn't like to eat first?"

"No! I would like to know what the hell!"

"Fiery," one of the grandmas nodded. I thought her name might be Tillie. "Just like Gertie."

"And Lydia," another of the group added, referring to Gertie's predecessor. The acolyte was called Chloris, a delightfully old-fashioned name, which was fair since she looked like she'd gone to school with Methuselah. She'd shown up a little after the others, in the second wave of former acolytes who Hilde had summoned to court after realizing the extent of the problem, and I'd almost sent her right back.

Not that she wasn't nice—they were all nice, damn them! But I was afraid for her. She was one of those little old ladies who, instead of getting pleasantly plump and pink cheeked like Annabelle, had shriveled up on the vine. At least, I assumed she hadn't been born looking like a wizened old oak, skeletally thin, with a huge, grizzled afro that only added to the tree effect.

I found the Entwives, Treebeard, I thought, and immediately felt bad. "Could you please—" I began, but the chatter was already on.

"You knew Lydia?" Tillie said excitedly. She'd gone the opposite way from Chloris, and was threatening to rival one of Annabelle's cats. The cascading chiffon gave her approximately the same shape as a Christmas tree, one with a star on top courtesy of her vivid, dyed-blonde tresses. "You never told me!"

"You never asked." Chloris bared crooked yellow teeth at her. "I glimpsed her once at court when I was a child, during a visit my mother made to see my older sister—"

"Your mother went to *court*?"

"She never did!" another grandma said. This one was named Cecily, and had a topknot and half-moon spectacles. She looked almost exactly like the grandma from the Tweety Bird cartoons, to the point that I'd done a double take on first meeting her.

"Oh, yes. My mother was what they kindly call an old battle-ax." Chloris cackled. "Or a young battle-ax then, I suppose. In any case, she was used to getting her way. I always expected to grow up like her, but never had the knack."

"So few do," Hilde murmured, without a trace of irony.

"But mother deserved every bit of the term, and was determined to visit Hyacinth—my sister—who'd been selected as an initiate. She took me along; I assume to play on Lydia's compassion."

Hilde snorted. "I'm sure that went well."

"Oh, it was glorious!" Chloris's dark eyes brightened. "I'd never seen anything like it. My mother had always been the most dynamic person I knew, the sun around whom everyone else merely orbited, the hurricane in whose mighty winds I grew up. I had no notion that anyone else could match her forcefulness, much less exceed it. Not until that fateful day."

"Fateful? Is someone talking about fate without me?" Annabelle asked, bustling back in with a tray almost as large as she was.

"Annabelle's our resident Atropos," yet another grandma informed me, as I rose to help with the burden.

"Atropos?" I asked.

"One of the Fates. You know, the Moirae."

"It's just a nickname," Annabelle said, looking for a place to put down the tray, which I had started to take from her. But it was bigger than the little side table between me and Hilde, and would have sent the thing toppling right over. It was also loaded with the silver food domes that Tami loved to put on everything, and which had been left behind by the penthouse's previous resident, who had believed in nothing but the best. So, they were literal silver and heavy as hell.

But Annabelle didn't need the help. I was about to be impressed with muscles that an MMA fighter would have envied, until I realized—the tray was levitating. Of course, it was.

I sat back down.

"You're named after one of the Fates?" I asked her.

"Nickname," Annabelle said again, and sent the floating tray speeding over to the dinner table, halfway down the room, with a little push. "It's silly."

"It's not silly. She can see everyone's deaths!" someone said dramatically.

"You see people's deaths?" I repeated, taken aback.

"Not precisely. I have a knack for seeing major turning points in others' lives, assuming that they do anything worthy of the term." She shrugged. "But some people, well, I hate to say it, but the most significant thing they do is to die."

"Carpe Diem," Chloris cackled, and tottered off to see what was under all those domes. Several of her friends went along with her, including one who veered off toward the bar cart. It was starting to look like a party in here, when all I wanted was to be alone!

"Read me!" Tillie said, her blond up-do bouncing excitedly.

"You know I won't," Annabelle said crossly. "Why do you keep asking?"

"Well, why not? Everybody wants to know when they're going to die, and no clairvoyant can read themselves."

"And no clairvoyant can call up a vision whenever she wishes, either," Annabelle reminded her. "They come when they come, or not at all."

She turned away to talk to someone else, leaving Tillie looking sulky.

"I don't know why you'd want to know when you're going to die," Cecily said. "I mean, at your age."

Tillie frowned. "What about my age?"

"Well, what if she said tomorrow?"

"You didn't finish telling us about Lydia," somebody said to Chloris, who was on her way back sans food but with a cocktail in her hand. "You can't just leave us hanging like that!"

"Oh, it's been so long now, I can't remember everything," she demurred. And then she grinned. "But it was magnificent. Nobody knew how to put people in their place like Lydia. She told my mother, then and there, that she wasn't welcome at court, that Hyacinth had to get used to her new home. And that, if she wanted to spend time with a daughter, she should do so with me while she still could!"

"*That's* how you found out you were going to be an initiate?"

Chloris nodded.

"That's awful," I said.

She laughed. "Not at all. I was *thrilled*. Didn't I say? Life at home was like living inside a hurricane."

"And life at court wasn't?"

She thought about it. "Yes, but a different sort of hurricane. One where I had some power for a change. Something I realized when mother was kicked out and immediately charged the front door again, absolutely livid. Only to be shifted all the way back home— into a muddy back garden that she fell into face-first, thinking she was pushing on the door! It was *glorious*."

"Thank you, dear, but I have my tea," Hilde said, as an acolyte named Devi offered a cocktail tray. She'd been in training to be a dancer before getting picked for the court. I wasn't sure what kind, but maybe ballet, since she wore her hair pulled back into a bun. And managed to make something as simple as serving cocktails look elegant.

"Gin and tonic?" she asked me. "Sidecar? Between the Sheets?"

"I—is that a drink?" I asked, confused.

"Cognac, triple sec, light rum and lemon juice," she confirmed. "Oh, and I forgot. It's supposed to have an orange peel flamed over the glass before serving."

The aforementioned flaming peel suddenly appeared, causing me to rear back. It plonked into the concoction a second later, and the glass was placed on the small table beside my chair. Where I left it, preferring a clear head.

Particularly considering the look on Hilde's face.

"Now," she said, having arranged things to her satisfaction. "Can we agree that what happened to you the other day amounted to an attack?"

"The other day?" I blinked at her. That didn't exactly narrow it down much.

"Yes, the other day! When you were displaced in *time*?"

"Oh. That."

"Yes, that. Can we talk about the fact that someone or something is prowling about the timeline, attempting to catch you at a vulnerable moment? And that the most likely candidate is—"

"Aeslinn," I said wearily. "Possessed by Zeus. Can we talk about this later?"

"Possessed by—who?" Tillie asked, clutching her ample bosom.

"We fought him, Gertie, Agnes and me," I explained reluctantly. I'd planned to tell them, of course, just not right now. But it was clear that I wasn't going to get what I wanted. "It was a close call, but we won. And now I'm barred from the court—"

"What?" someone else said, sounding shocked.

"Gertie decided that training me was too dangerous if I was going to bring gods in my wake."

"Zeus. You are sure?" Hilde asked sharply. She didn't seem surprised by her sister's decision, which . . . yeah. But she was looking a little rattled suddenly.

"But he isn't on this side of the barrier. He can't be!" That was Devi, her big brown eyes looking shocked.

"That's what we thought about Apollo and Ares," I reminded her. "But they managed, didn't they?"

"Zeus!" Tillie said, in a high-pitched voice. And then she kept on saying it, like a parrot who'd just learned a new word and wanted to show it off. But the look on her face wasn't pride.

I wondered how many acolytes I'd have left by morning.

There might be a silver lining to all this, after all.

And then, right on cue, I felt bad some more.

"Stop that," Hilde said, causing me to look at her guiltily, before I realized that she'd been talking to Tillie.

"But . . . but it can't be Zeus," Tillie said, ignoring her. "How could he possibly get in?"

"It's complicated—" I began.

"And time travel. He can't *time travel*! This is outrageous!"

She actually looked pissed off, as if we'd all been playing a board game, and somebody had cheated. It made me feel slightly better, as that was how I'd been feeling. I'd been so sure that, at Gertie's at least, I was safe.

But these days, nowhere was.

"We don't know what the All-Father is capable of," Hilde said, before she was cut off, too.

"Don't call him that," Chloris said grimly. "He's not *my* father, and if he comes here, I'll give him what for."

She brandished a stringy old-lady arm, which the dress's draperies did little to conceal. It should have been funny, since she looked like a good gust of wind could knock her over, but it wasn't. She could wield the Pythian power, making her a much more formidable adversary than she looked, and she obviously had the courage of her youth.

I suddenly felt ashamed of myself, and the vague resentment I'd been feeling, ever since my new acolytes arrived. These women didn't have to be here. They all had lives, and probably comfortable retirements, which they could have been enjoying instead of spending their golden years babysitting a brand-new Pythia.

And fighting gods.

But they'd chosen to come, nonetheless, and to put themselves at risk, so that their younger counterparts could stay with their families. And so that I could give more of my attention to the war, knowing that my court was safe and well-handled. I had no doubt that they would die for the young initiates they cared for, or for each other . . . or for me.

I looked around the group, and for once, I didn't see the gray or white hair, the wrinkles, the overly delicate or too chubby bodies. I saw warriors, as much in this fight as anyone, despite being of an age when the rest of the world counted them as worthless. So, yeah, I was ashamed.

Hilde seemed to notice something, and her eyes narrowed. But she didn't comment. Except to agree with Tillie.

"He can't be here. This war would be over by now, if that were the case."

I nodded. "He isn't, not entirely. But part of his power is. Like Ares when he possessed that suit of armor—"

"But there are no such legends about Zeus, at least not that I can recall," she said, her brow furrowing.

"Nor that I can. I need Pritkin to do some research, and then I have to—"

I'd been about to spill the beans about that damned castle, which was the only place I knew to spy on Aeslinn that didn't involve going back to Faerie. And Gertie was right: Zeus must have been working on a plan before he remembered about Pritkin, and must have gone back to that time for a reason. I had to find out what it was.

But I hesitated. Aeslinn had somehow transported a couple hundred fey with him, and Hilde had almost lost her shit once about a single rogue acolyte skipping about the timeline. What would she do about this?

I didn't want to say anything that might cause her to push me into a decision before I was ready. Not against Zeus. And not at that damned castle, where Gertie and I had already spied on him once and where he'd probably be expecting a repeat.

That gate of his was either a portal itself, leading directly into Faerie, or else to one of those weird bubbles suspended in a ley line halfway in between. Magic—including mine—often became muddled near one of those gates, and could give out entirely without warning in favor of the opposite system. Not to mention that he could retreat into Faerie if things got hinky, just by ringing that great portcullis down, leaving us staring at him impotently.

Attacking him was going to be a bitch.

I blinked again, this time at myself, because of *course* I wasn't planning on attacking him! I'd almost died just yesterday, simply trying to get away from him. What the hell?

I glanced around at the now agitatedly talking women, and saw that battleground again, at Issengeir, heaped with piles of the dead. Only this time, it wasn't war mages scattered all over it. It was grandmas.

And what could they do against Zeus?

"Have to what?" Hilde asked, watching me.

I don't know what I'd have said, especially on the spur of the moment. But I didn't have to say anything. Because somebody caught my arm and jerked me around.

At first, I didn't know who it was. I should have; the clues were all there: curly white hair, pink cheeks, fuzzy slippers. But the eyes were wrong.

The eyes were terrible.

Huge and white and glazed. Blind eyes. Seer's eyes. They nonetheless seemed to stare directly into mine, as if they could see past the flesh and straight into my soul.

"Fortune's Child, so young and fair,
A goddess's final gift.
But inside Faerie's frozen lair,
There comes a seismic shift.

Beware, beware, the elven court!
And he who there resides.
For once inside, all time grows short,
And Cassie, sweet Cassie . . . dies."

Chapter Twenty-Four

Y ou can't stay in here forever, you know," Marco said, sometime later.

I looked up to see the huge vamp reflected in the mirror of my dressing table. It was the one in the master bath of my suite, instead of the one in my actual dressing room, which had been built for a vamp with perfect eyesight. The last time I'd tried to put on makeup in there, I'd ended up looking like Bozo on a bender.

Not that I was making up my face right now. I probably needed to, but I didn't care. I didn't care about anything.

"Mind if I come in?"

"You're already in." Which was why my huge bathroom suddenly felt small. Marco tended to have that effect on rooms, as well as on people. I'd seen six-foot-tall muscle-bound types cringe when he walked by, wearing one of his favorite polo shirts in some wildly improbable color like persimmon or passion fruit, because when you're a two-thousand-year-old ex-gladiator built like a tank, you wear what you damned well like.

"I got rid of 'em," Marco said, sitting on the edge of my massive, built-in bathtub. It was going to break one of these days, if he kept that up. But not today, it seemed.

"Who?"

"The old broads."

That got a blink out of me, at least. "You got rid of Hilde?"

He nodded. "For the moment. She'll be back—she's something, that one—but not for a while. We had words."

I stared at him.

He took out a new cigar, since I guessed the old one had been a casualty of the fight. "You look surprised."

I was surprised that he wasn't lost in a jungle in Borneo. "What did you say?"

"That she don't understand how things work around here."

"She thinks she does."

"Yeah, that's the problem." He chewed tobacco aggressively. This wasn't unusual, as Marco mangled more cigars than he actually smoked. I had a theory that they were substitutes for the people he'd like to be chewing on instead, but had never asked. Somethings it's better not to know. "She told me to stay in my lane. I told her that you *are* my lane. She didn't like that."

I bet.

"I told her that we've been doing this longer than she has. Maybe not the Pythia stuff, but the rest, the war stuff. The you-surviving-some-next-level-shit-and-freaking-out stuff. And that my job is to see to it that you have time to recover, so the freak out don't become permanent. Not to let you get ambushed and make things worse!"

"They didn't ambush me."

He shot me a look.

"All right, they sort of ambushed me. But they meant well."

"I don't care what they meant. You know half of them are senile, right?"

I smiled slightly. "They're not senile."

"And weird. You shouldn't take anything that bunch tells you to heart."

I didn't ask how he knew what they'd said. My room was supposed to be soundproofed, but Marco always knew everything around here. I'd come to expect it.

"I'm not," I said, instead. It was his turn to look surprised. "Prophecy hasn't exactly panned out for me so far."

And if I was going to freak out, I had plenty of other reasons besides Annabelle's terrible poetry.

"Well, good."

He chewed on his cigar some more.

We sat in silence for a while. Marco wasn't the type who always needed to talk. Yet the room, which had been large, cold and sterile a moment ago, was now smaller, warmer, and homier.

Not to mention smelling like tobacco and cheap cologne, since he liked the dime store stuff. Apparently, in ancient Rome, when you bought a scent, you expected a scent, and he found the expensive kind too subtle for his tastes. You always knew which room he'd just been in, because it smelled like bourbon and leather, the main notes in the solid cologne balm that he used like it was going out of style.

It blended well with the tobacco, I thought, and felt my muscles relax without me telling them to. It seemed that my body felt safe with Marco around, even if my brain was on overdrive. "Where did it all come from?" I finally asked.

"What?"

"The magic." I floated a hand around to indicate the nebulous clouds from our most recent crisis.

Marco scowled. "That little bastard you brought back. The fucked-up goat looking thing?"

I blinked at him. "What?"

He nodded. "Surprised the hell out of me, too. Didn't look like much, but he could fight. Of course, so can the master, and when he and Mage Pritkin ganged up on him, the little thing panicked and started . . . shedding."

"Shedding?"

He shrugged. "There's probably a better word, but I don't know it. And, anyway, that's what he was doing: shedding magic everywhere, like a damned lawn sprinkler. Which caused the whole apartment to come to life, and start fighting on his side—"

"*What?*"

Marco grinned, and paused to light his new pacifier. "You think we don't have any fun when you're gone? We have fun."

"But . . . what do you mean, come alive?"

"You didn't notice on your way in here? But then, I guess you shifted in, and we cleared out most of the junk already—"

"Marco. What are you talking about?"

He paused to take some little puffs, to get the cigar going. "Fun. Like when a folding chair suddenly starts snapping like a croc and bites your ass."

I looked at him some more.

"You just saw what a coat can do, and you're surprised about the furniture?"

I rested my head on one of my hands. "Not really. How bad was it?"

"Bad enough that the goat got away—"

"Out of here?" I already knew that, having seen him in Faerie with Mircea and Pritkin, but I was having a hard time visualizing it. The penthouse looked like an upscale apartment, one of the high roller palaces that casinos keep for big spenders, but it was guarded like a fortress. It was stuffed with wards, vamps, witches and acolytes, not to mention the hotel's own considerable defenses, all here to keep my court safe. And they did a bang-up job.

And yet this creature just walked out?

"He didn't exactly walk," Marco said sardonically, when I asked. "He busted out a window and skipped down the side of the building like those goats you sometimes see on nature shows, high on the side of a dam. They go up there to lick the salt that accumulates on the stones, 'cause they can climb on virtually anything, even a ridge no wider than a fingernail. As turns out, so could this son of a bitch. By the time we realized what had happened, he was already hitting the ground."

"And Mircea and Pritkin took off after him," I guessed.

"Of course. Leaving us with the mess. Most of the bedrooms survived, thankfully, as it happened on the other side of the suite. But the rest of the place . . ." he shrugged.

"And the kids?"

"Downstairs. We made room."

I nodded, remembering what Fred had said.

The vamps used to be spread around the hotel in whatever spare rooms were available. But after I inherited the penthouse, they'd taken over my old digs and added some additional rooms to make a new bodyguard suite. It was better for security, since they now occupied the whole floor below the court, providing a fanged buffer zone to the rest of the hotel. It also allowed them to live as they pleased and to cuss as much as they liked, since there were no little ears around to hear.

"We got the kids out first thing," Marco added. "Then started cleaning the place up. But it was hard with everything going crazy, and attacking us any time we moved. And with more magic floating around, trying to find something to bond with. We even had to take down the wards for a while, 'cause that *would* have been a mess—"

I winced. The wards around the suite were of the battle variety. Had they teamed up with a bunch of wild magic . . .

I decided not to think about that.

"—but we couldn't figure out how to get rid of the rest," he continued. "The witches tried to help, 'cause from what I understand, their magic is based on the fey system. Which is what we guessed that little fucker was, since none of us had ever seen anything like it. But they're not the magical equivalent of a hazmat crew."

"Hence the mages," I guessed.

Marco scowled. "I don't like having them here, and will be tossing them out on their smug asses very shortly. But we didn't know who else to call. And after a couple days . . ."

He chewed aggressively on his cigar, probably in lieu of a mage's face.

"Who are they?" I asked. "They don't dress like normal mages, even war mages."

"They aren't. They're some new crew the Circle has come up with, 'cause the war is shifting to Faerie. And the last time they went in there, they got their butts kicked."

I felt myself go rigid, and tried to keep any expression off my face. I doubt I succeeded, not that it would have mattered. Marco could tell the difference in my heart rate, or in the fact that I was no longer breathing for a moment, because it felt like I'd been punched in the gut.

"I say something wrong?" he asked, pausing.

"No."

To my surprise, he didn't push it. "They're specialists— supposedly," he said instead. "But they told me not an hour before you returned that they'd finished sopping up all the excess magic, and we could move back in whenever we liked. Assholes," it was vicious. "Fortunately, some of the witches wanted to bake cookies, and said the kitchen downstairs wasn't clean enough—"

"So, they came up here to cook, and got a surprise."

"We all got a surprise. I knew better than to trust a mage."

Or a fey, only that hadn't been fey magic. It had been the same kind of energy that I'd pulled off of Zeus. I might have mistaken it, even a few days ago, but now? I'd never forget that taste, that feel, that *rush*.

The small creature's magic had been slightly different from what I'd absorbed on the Thames: thinner, weaker, and with a flavor that buzzed with alien energy. But there was no doubt about what it was. That had been the life blood of a god, not a fey. Which probably explained why I was suddenly having visions when I rarely did anymore, and shifting people without realizing it.

It did not explain what god blood had been doing in . . . whatever it was.

I didn't even know what to call it, and couldn't think well enough to figure it out. I was mentally exhausted but physically wired, and had been ever since the fight. I wanted to curl up in a ball and cry my eyes out; I wanted to run around the building laughing hysterically. And I wanted to do them both at the same time.

It left me feeling twitchy and overwhelmed and worried and strangely giddy, with all those emotions fighting for dominance. I was kind of glad that my brain was fried. I didn't want to deal with it now.

But I was going to have to.

Because Marco wasn't just here to fill me in. He wanted an explanation for how I'd hoovered up all the magic that the mages had missed, and probably for a lot of other things. I braced myself.

But what he said was not what I'd expected.

"The kids have been asking about you."

"I'm fine."

"Yeah, but that's not what they're asking." I looked up, and he quirked a caterpillar of an eyebrow at me. "Kids don't, you know?"

"Don't what?"

"Worry. Not about anything that isn't a clear and present danger. And when something like that does happen, they run to the adults who make it all better."

"And what happens when you're the adult?" I asked harshly. "What happens when you don't know what to do, either? When you don't . . . when you aren't . . . when you *can't*—"

I broke off, because I suddenly had a Marco shaped blanket draped around me. It was only one arm, but when it was one of Marco's, that was saying something. And then a catcher's-mitt-sized hand was gripping my face, and turning it gently toward dark brown eyes that didn't take any bullshit, but which were currently gentle.

Like he was with the tiny girls he guarded for me, who never saw big, bad Marco. Who never even dreamt that he existed. Instead, they ran to him fearlessly, this huge brute of a man, to show him their latest drawings, or to paw through his clothes for candy, or to grab him by the hand—what they could grasp of it—and drag him over to see some new thing they were excited about.

And I had no doubt about why.

He was safety. He was big and warm and solid and there. With Marco around, there was never any need to worry.

I wondered how long before I got him killed?

He frowned. "Stop that."

"What?"

"Whatever is putting that look back on your face."

I didn't say anything. Right then, I didn't trust myself. And then I noticed something that drove my own problems out of my head.

"Are you alright?"

"I'm always alright."

"You're not, though." His current polo—a bright, Christmas red—had dark splotches on the front. I hadn't immediately noticed, being I preoccupied with my own problems, and because he had a cardigan over it. It was a terrible holiday thing with "Sleigher" written on the back in glittery letters, along with a punked-out Santa flashing the rock and roll hand salute.

Marco noticed me noticing. "Tami; she gave all the guys a sweater."

"That was . . . kind of her."

He laughed. "No, it wasn't. It's for the thing."

"What thing?"

"You'll find out."

"That sounds vaguely ominous."

"Wait until you see what she got you."

"And that's more so." I pushed up the polo and sucked in a breath.

He grinned at me around his cigar. "You should see the other guy. Reg was gonna need a new coat, even before you got hold of it."

"Fuck his coat," I said, staring at a torso that had already healed, without so much as a single scar, but the matt of dark hair on his chest told the true story. Marco had what was basically a pelt, only the attack had left him with pale splotches among all the fuzz, where blows from a dozen stakes had left their mark. It made me think of my burnt gown from the fight on the Thames, covered in weird polka dots, only those had been made by fire . . .

"You okay?" Marco asked.

"Just . . . haven't eaten in a while."

He didn't say anything for a moment, and I braced again. But when I looked up, he didn't ask. "Well, we need to fix that, don't we?"

"We need to find Mircea and Pritkin." I clutched his arm. Everything that had happened in the short amount of time since I'd been back had distracted me, but the sight of Marco's wounds had reminded me that I wasn't the only one in trouble. "I can't feel them anymore. I tried to contact them during the fight, but—"

"It's okay—"

"It's *not* okay. Have you heard anything, from either of them?"

"No, but that doesn't mean—"

"Then how can you say they're okay?"

"'Cause I know the boss?"

I frowned. "Mircea is powerful, but he isn't indestructible."

Marco gave me a look. "He's pretty indestructible."

"He is not! Neither of them is! Not when we're facing—"

I cut off, but he still didn't ask.

It was starting to freak me out.

"People have underestimated the boss for centuries, and it never got them anywhere," he said instead. "And he's not in serious trouble or he'd call." He tapped the side of his head.

"If he could."

"The blood bond isn't some spell, Cassie. He'd call." It was implacable.

I started to tell him what Mircea had said, about not being able to communicate past the feys' potion. But I didn't want to scare him, too, and anyway, that should have worn off by now. Shouldn't it?

Unless he'd gotten hit again. Or recaptured. Or—

I felt my blood run cold. But no, no they couldn't be dead. If they were, I would be, too. We were *linked*—

A finger the size of a hot dog pressed against my lips, making me look up.

"Listen to me," Marco said. "You listening?"

I nodded.

"Good. 'Cause I don't want to know what's up with you, all right?"

I blinked, having expected the third degree. Not only about tonight, but about the last few days. Marco was in charge of security around here. He needed to know about any threats.

His expression turned rueful. "Yeah, I'm curious, but I'll live."

"But your job—"

"Is to see to it that my girls are all right. And right now, you're not all right. Are you?"

I shook my head.

"That's what I thought. So, no big conversations. I want you to comb your hair, splash some water on your face, and come downstairs. We're about to do the thing, and you need to be there."

"Is that the ominous thing or a new thing?"

A black eyebrow raised. "Come down and find out. Or I'll be back up to fetch you."

Chapter Twenty-Five

That last sentence could have sounded like a threat, but it
didn't. Maybe because it was accompanied by a smile and a
ruffling of my hair. I sometimes didn't think that Marco
viewed me any differently than the rest of the girls that he watched
over, except for being slightly more troublesome. I watched him go,
and found myself feeling better for no good reason.

Colder, without that great arm around me, but better.

I got up, took a quick shower, and washed the wind-tangled mass
on my head. And then went to the walk-in closet off of my dressing
room, even though I didn't want to go downstairs and face all of
those eyes. Even more, I didn't want to face all of those *questions*.

Not when I didn't have any answers.

But weirdly, I didn't want to stay up here, either. That antsy-ness
I'd been feeling was getting worse, buzzing at my fingertips, making
me want to *do* something. Unfortunately, I didn't know what and I
didn't have anybody to ask.

I also didn't know what to wear. Marco hadn't said what this big,
important thing was, so I had no idea what was appropriate. I finally

opted for comfort, settling on a pair of jeans and a long-sleeved T-shirt that said "I RUN embarrassingly short distances."

If I hadn't picked that one, I had plenty of others to choose from: "Y'all realize I'm gonna snap one day, right?"; "So, apparently, I have an 'attitude'"; "Hold on, and let me overthink this"; "Cute but spooky but Cute but spooky"; "That's a horrible idea . . . what time?"; and my personal favorite, although it was currently dirty, "I feel like 2007 Britney."

They were all gifts from Pritkin. He'd waltz in and casually drop a package onto my breakfast table, and I'd know that it was on. I'd gotten him a T-shirt that said "I like Coffee and Maybe Three People"—which was *true*—a month or so back, and it had started a war.

But once it was a thing, I'd been determined to win. And had sent people to scour the local shops while I went online in search of fitting Tees for a grumpy war mage. The standouts included: "I never argue, I just explain why I'm right"; "I'm not old, I'm legendary"; "Sorry I'm late, but I didn't want to come"; "Sarcasm is just one of the services I offer"; and "If you met my family, you'd understand."

It probably should have concerned me that I was in a relationship where our deepest conversations took place through slogans, but it didn't. I just wanted him back. I wanted them both back before they ran into trouble—and they *always* ran into trouble! But Earth trouble they could handle, while Faerie was on a completely different level and—

Stop it! I thought, my hands clenching on a dress.

And then releasing fast, because of some annoyed fluttering.

The dress was an Augustine creation in a pretty, sky-blue velvet. Like all of the great man's stuff, it was not only beautiful, but mind-bendingly strange. In this case, that translated to a "pattern" of little birds with bright, jeweled eyes and embroidered feathers, that hopped about on tiny branches.

There were a couple of bluebirds, with coral beads scattered among the rust-colored patches on their chests. There was a yellow finch with onyx eyes and more onyx in the stripes on its back. There was a robin, its scarlet coloring splattered with small moonstones, as if it had been caught in a downpour and had droplets of water on its wings. And there were a whole bunch of little brown wrens, with no jewels at all but with such subtle stitchwork that I thought they might be my favorites.

The flock I'd accidentally disturbed had found a new perch on the shoulders of the gown, like brilliantly colored epaulettes, and were flapping discontentedly. They were doing something else, too. They normally gave off a variety of twitters and trills, if you listened hard enough, but not today.

Today, they were singing a different tune.

What the—

I went up on tiptoe to get a little closer, just as one of the birds finished a tweet and segued into something else. Something that sounded a lot like a groan, and in my voice at that. Because the dress wasn't just a dress.

It had been designed as a listening device, to hear and record any conversations in the vicinity. It was part of a new line that Augustine had invented to help me in my role as Pythia, and was meant for crowded ballrooms, where you never knew what some off-hand comment might reveal. Only those sounds . . . hadn't come from a party.

It took me a minute, and then I remembered: Pritkin had caught me up here, when I was trying on the dress, and things had, uh, progressed.

"I have . . . a meeting . . ." I heard myself say breathlessly.

"About what?" The question was low, and accompanied by a thread of badly suppressed laughter. He knew damned well that I couldn't remember my name when he did . . . that.

"To discuss bringing the Pythian library here," I said roughly. I knew his tricks, and I wasn't falling for them. I was not going to face a bunch of grandmas with knowing smiles on their faces, damn it! "It went up in flames when the London court was destroyed, and they won't give me any peace about it."

"How difficult for you." It was a deliberately sensual murmur, and had made me scowl.

"I'm serious. They've been hinting for weeks, and now I have a delegation waiting for me and . . . oh."

"Oh?"

"That was . . . interesting. Do that again."

He did it again.

"Oh!"

"Is that a good 'oh' or a bad 'oh'?"

"I'm . . . not sure. Keep it up and I'll tell you in a minute."

"But what about the library?" The faux concern was palpable.

"Screw the library."

I stood there, clutching the tattletale dress, and listened to us trying to be quiet. Soft giggles, softer moans, and then not so soft ones filtered out, however, because that had been a very good 'oh'. And while the silence spell on my part of the suite was excellent, it only worked from outside of my bedroom door. And caught up in the moment, we hadn't thought to place one of our own.

I'd shifted Pritkin back to his room afterwards, and walked out to talk to the girls with my hair combed, my face arranged and my clothes perfectly pressed. And hadn't seen any knowing smiles. I had, however, caught several blushes staining wrinkled cheeks, because I wasn't fooling anybody.

Probably not even the maids, considering that the damned birds were singing like canaries!

I pulled the dress off its hanger and shoved it into a padded trunk, and then sat on the lid. I put my head in my hands and stared at the boring beige carpet, feeling like I was going out of my mind. I didn't want to be here, in my comfortable suite surrounded by beautiful clothes. I wanted to be with *him*. I wanted to find him, help him, fight alongside him if necessary—do *something*!

But I didn't even know where he was.

And if he didn't come back, maybe I never would.

Stop it! I told myself again. This wasn't helping.

I did not stop it. He and Mircea should have been back by now. My abilities were back online, and they *did* work in Faerie—I'd discovered that for myself, after pulling enough power off Arsen for a small spatial shift. I couldn't access the Pythian power while there, but with Arsen's help, I hadn't needed it. And Pritkin had absorbed a massive amount of energy from all those fey.

He didn't need the Pythian power, either; he had his own. He should have been able to shift he and Mircea to the nearest safe portal and been out hours ago. So, where were they?

"Goddamnit! They're *fine*," I said, like it might help if I heard it out loud. But all that happened was a bunch of distant twittering, and then "They're fine, THEY'RE FINE, they're fine," emanating from the trunk, as if mocking me. While a different dress—a mermaid tail, off the shoulder ballgown—abruptly shaded from iridescent pink to blood red.

It had been based off a pair of cufflinks that I'd bought for Mircea's Christmas gift but which Augustine had found and snapped up. The cufflinks worked on demon magic, which he didn't know, but which he'd tinkered with excitedly for days until finally presenting me with the gown. It was supposed to be able to tell when someone was being less than truthful and I'd been known to wear it to court. It was fun watching the color deepen as some petitioner gave me his very biased side of events, and wait for them to notice.

It was less fun when it was directed at me.

"I'm not lying!" I told it.

The color darkened to something approaching black, with just a few red swirls in the highlights, and I jerked it off the hanger and stuffed it inside the trunk along with the birds.

That seemed to quiet them down a bit, but it didn't do anything for my stomach, which was tying itself into knots. Damn it, they were fine. They would have contacted me if they weren't, or if I was asleep, Mircea would have contacted Marco.

So, why hadn't I been able to pull power from them in the fight? And why couldn't I hear them in my head? And why weren't they *back yet*?

I bit my lip and frowned at the carpet some more. Maybe the t-shirt was right, and I was overthinking this. Maybe I couldn't contact them simply because they'd removed Lover's Knot, not wanting to risk killing me if they ran into trouble.

And while I'd been assuming that Pritkin knew he could use my abilities inside Faerie, what if he didn't? He'd been unconscious when I'd shifted into the middle of a ring of fey to rescue him and Mircea, and hadn't seen it. And he might not have heard my thoughts during my own escape, since I was drugged and having trouble contacting him. Sending me those footprints might have been his plan all along.

But Mircea should know that they could shift; he was there and conscious when I popped in to rescue them. But he had been staked at the time, and pretty groggy. He might not remember it.

And if they *didn't* know, that would explain why they hadn't shifted out—they didn't know they could! It would also explain why they might have removed Lover's Knot. After all, what good would the Pythian power be in a world where it didn't work? They'd be endangering my life for nothing, and neither of them would do that.

My spine suddenly turned to water.

Yes, that must be it. Why hadn't I thought of it before? That was perfect!

Way to freak yourself out over nothing, Cassie!

I laughed in sheer relief, and picked up a bright yellow feathered number that had slid off its hanger, and which would have looked exactly like Big Bird except for a nude-illusion body covered in silver embroidery. The feathers were clustered around the shoulders and trailed off the hemline to create a crazy sort of train. Their use was a little crazy, too: they were supposed to work like quills and zoom off on command, to go scribble a message to a designated recipient.

It was one of Augustine's less-than-successful experiments, with quills that tended to zoom a little too fast and to stick into people who got in their way. One of my most vivid recent memories was of a particularly condescending consular servant running down a corridor with three bright yellow quills sticking out of his posterior. I'd apologized, but I was pretty sure that he thought I'd done it on purpose, because he'd been avoiding me ever since.

I dragged my fingers through the extravagant fluff, wondering why I felt antsy. I'd come up with a perfectly good explanation, maybe even the right one. It all fit . . .

Except that it didn't. The guys wouldn't have cut me off from their power with no warning unless there was a reason. A damned good reason considering what we'd just been through! And an immediate one, because how long does a mental phone call take?

I finally admitted that I had no idea what was going on.

But there was one way to find out.

I sat cross legged on the floor with my back to the central shoe island, because this was the sort of closet that had a shoe island, and tried to relax. It was easier than I'd expected, since the closet was almost completely quiet, with the soundproofing on my rooms cutting out even the usual ambient noise. All I could hear was the distant whoosh of the air conditioner and my own worried heartbeat.

The latter of which slowly began to calm down.

For the first time since I returned, I was alone. Nobody was pulling me this way or that, and no craziness was ensuing. It was nice.

After a few moments, I was centered enough to be able to focus. If the guys had severed the spell linking us, I wasn't going to get much, except through the family connection I had with Mircea. He'd bitten me, marking me as his, months ago, and while it wasn't as good as the bond he had with his vampires, it was something.

I focused on them, trying to will myself to see them or the area around them. Trying to force a vision rarely worked, but this wasn't one. This was vampire magic, a completely different thing that I knew very little about.

And which wasn't working.

Come on, I thought, recentering myself and trying again. I didn't need to speak to him; didn't even want to risk it. I just wanted to see them, that they were okay, that they were on their way back to me. That was all I wanted in the world!

But all I saw was the darkness on the inside of my eyelids.

Damn it! I was starting to get frustrated, and told myself to stay calm, stay centered, stay on target. Getting upset wouldn't solve anything and would trash my concentration.

I took a deep breath and tried again. And failed again. And then again, and again, and again, until my fragile calm was shattered and I was hammering savagely on the barrier, trying to force my way—

Wait.

What barrier?

I stopped and something moved under my mental hands, as if trying to slink away. Oh, no, you don't, I thought, and grabbed it. And then held on as it twisted and writhed and almost escaped me, but I dug my 'fingers' into the surface and refused to let go.

And whatever it was didn't like that—didn't like it at all.

Which was nothing to how I felt!

It almost slipped my grasp and I snarled and dug my fingers deeper, determinedly hanging on. It took several minutes, with me writhing around on the floor of my closet like a madwoman, not able to see who or what I was grappling with. But it finally seemed to realize that it wasn't getting away.

Whatever it was finally calmed down, leaving me with the impression that we were staring at each other. Only there were no eyes looking back at me. There was no anything, at least, not that I could see.

But I *could* feel, although what I was feeling wasn't something so much as the absence of it. Like that idea of a barrier that my mind had thrown up at me. It was solid under my hands, and hard, but not like glass. More like a thick membrane.

I pushed at it, and it pushed back. After a moment of surprise, I did it again, and got the same reaction, only harder. But not an elastic bounce, as if I'd punched a gym bag or stepped on a trampoline.

It was more like a reflex, or a flinch. And the membrane felt more like skin than rubber, now that I thought about it, warm and alive. If I hadn't known better, I'd have thought that I had just touched a body I couldn't see, one that didn't want to be touched.

Or one that didn't want to be touched by me.

And, suddenly, all those jumbled emotions on the merry-go-round in my head stopped whirling and settled on one.

It was fury.

So, let me get this straight, I thought at Faerie, venom boiling in every word. You'll hijack my soul, jerking me into your realm when you decide I'm needed, putting my life in danger along with two other innocent people. Then, when I solve your problem for you, you'll tell me to *kill myself*, to clean up the mess that *your creatures made*. And now, when I want to talk to my friends, you're keeping me out?

The *fuck*?

I received nothing back, which only infuriated me further.

You want something, I mentally hissed. Don't tell me you don't. We both know you'd have let me die in that camp otherwise. Tell me, how much cooperation do you think you're going to get if you keep this up? How much help do you think I'm going to give you? You took Mac—you think I don't remember that? You let your damned forest *eat him*—

I broke off, thinking about the tattoo-covered old man, who'd helped me when he didn't have to, and had paid for it with his life. And then about Mircea and I pelting through the middle of massive stone carvings that had suddenly come to life, and done their best to smear our bodies all over the ground. And about David, the war mage I'd never known except through a vision, and all those other, nameless men and women, their bodies piled up in heaps on that windswept plain, never to see home again.

And suddenly I was beating on the barrier, battering it with all my strength, throwing myself at it. Not caring if I hurt her any more than she had cared if she hurt us. She'd been callous, unfeeling, and heartless until something that mattered to her was on the line, until people she cared about were threatened. What about the people I cared about? Did they not matter?

Obviously not.

And that thought was enough to send me into a frenzy, to the point that I didn't care that I was somehow mentally in contact with a goddess, and an alien one at that. Didn't care that I was probably pissing her off. Didn't care about anything except—

That, I thought, finally breaking through the barrier.

And then falling from a height, because Faerie was a vindictive *bitch*.

Chapter Twenty-Six

I plunged into what felt like a swimming pool full of wet leaves—over the deep end. I completely submerged, then found myself trapped in a sodden darkness that clung to me like a half rotten shroud. For a moment, I just stayed there, stunned and disbelieving.

Then I cursed Faerie with everything I had. I'd said I wanted to *see* them, damn it, and know that they were okay! Not to be back here again! I never wanted to be back here again!

There was no response.

Unless you counted something small and long and hairy, with what felt like a thousand legs, scurrying across my body. And causing me to curse even more inventively and to thrash harder, trying to dig my way out of my leafy prison. But I couldn't see, could barely breathe, and the surface was considerably higher than my head.

It felt like I'd been dropped into the Mount Everest of leaves, which, judging from the smell, had been accumulating and rotting for years. But I could see the surface, at least. Although only because everything else was so dark that the dim moonlight filtering through the loose cover overhead looked bright by comparison.

I focused on it until one of my flailing hands encountered a vine that I was able to use to pull myself up, grunting and cursing. But I tried to do it quietly this time, since I didn't know what was up there. And I doubted that Faerie had done me any favors.

I finally burst out of the top, panting and furious and immensely grateful, all at the same time. Only to immediately have to duck back down as what looked like a small comet tore through the air overhead. I stared around, leaves sticking to my face, my heart thudding and my eyes trying to see past the orange streak that had just been carved into my retinas.

And accidentally did a little more than that.

My eyesight rocketed ahead in a disorienting zoom, following the speeding ball of fire. Until it crashed through something in the distance that I shouldn't have been able to see at all, not with the night and the closely packed trees and a half mask of leaves. And the fact that human eyes don't have a damned telephoto lens!

But vampire ones do.

At least, Mircea's did, as I'd learned the hard way once before. And now again as my gaze focused on a flimsy highway of black felted forest gunk, winding through the trees and connecting a network of lookout platforms and hidden bolt holes, which had just been set alight by the comet's flames. Well, at least that answered the question of whether the three of us were connected, I thought grimly, right before my thoughts skidded to a halt.

The now burning highway was serving as a fiery arrow, pointing straight at—

Okay, I may have misjudged you, I thought at Faerie. Because there they were—Mircea, Pritkin, a bunch of assorted dark fey, even the damned goat—running down the disintegrating highway. And then leaping to the safety of a platform built high in a tree the size of a skyscraper, right before their roadway collapsed behind them.

The tree didn't appear to be much sturdier despite its size, looking like it was half decayed, with moss and mushrooms coating its surface and bark that was no longer silver, like the other colossi around it. Instead, it was a riot of colors: red, green, orange and even a few patches of blue. The mold was bleached by the night and by a few, misty fingers of moonlight, although it was vivid enough that Mircea's eyesight could make out the colors.

It was probably stunning in daylight, assuming that daylight ever really penetrated here, making me wonder why anybody would select it as a refuge. Maybe a case of hiding in plain sight? If so, it wasn't working.

Really wasn't, I thought, as several more spells screamed through the night, heading that way.

They lit up the forest floor in long ribbons of color, but didn't connect with the platform, falling just short. The three fey that I saw when I looked in the other direction weren't close enough yet. But they were coming fast, and they weren't on foot.

Mircea's vision failed me when I tried to focus on their mounts. All I could tell was that they were incredibly fast and incredibly black, blending into the darkness except for large, round, fire-lit eyes. And that whatever they were, they weren't on the ground.

And then neither was I, when one of the fey swerved down and snatched me up on the way past.

And got more than he bargained for.

I wasn't a helpless captive trussed up in a tent anymore. I wasn't a plaything to be toyed with and traumatized and tortured. I was a Pythia, with god blood in my veins and a snarl on my lips, and I launched myself at him and saw him rear back in surprise.

And then keep going when I called up Mircea's strength, belted him across the face, elbowed him in the stomach, and knocked him into a leaf pile.

That left me in charge of his mount, which did not have a saddle. And which I still couldn't see too well, because the creature was so black that it seemed to absorb all light around it. It was like trying to ride a puddle of darkness—one that was very definitely not happy.

And neither was I, when it gave a screech and twisted upside down, spiraling even as we pelted forward, trying its best to throw me off.

Its best was pretty damned good. Yet I clung on, even as we made several more rotations, cleaving to a bumpy hide that I couldn't even see properly. The creature screeched again, a stuttering, bone shivering sound, and spun us right side up again, before pausing in the air and trying another tactic best known to rodeo riders.

It could clearly tell that there'd been a change of rider, but I wasn't sure that the fey could. They had paused in the air and whirled around. But then they just sat there, maybe unable to tell me apart from their friend with the creature's camouflage in the way.

It looked like they were waiting for me to get my shit together. If so, they were going be waiting a while. But not just because of my ride slinging me around like a bucking bronco.

But because I'd just gotten my first good look at theirs.

One of the riders passed slowly through a patch of moonlight, giving me a glimpse of something shaped like an elongated serpent. It had a row of tiny wings on either side of its body, compact and delicate, almost like fins, and sleek, flat scales that caught what little light there was like shards of ebony. But they didn't catch the closely packed tree limbs, with their shiny surfaces providing nothing for the foliage to snag on.

They were mesmerizing, perfectly suited to their environment, and strangely beautiful as Faerie often was when it wasn't trying to kill you—or even when it was. Because the fey had drifted close enough now to figure out that something was wrong. Or maybe it was their buddy in the leaf pile who had clued them in, surfacing to scream something that was mostly incoherent.

But he was pointing at me, and they must have gotten the gist. An orange flame, looking impossibly bright against the darkness, erupted from one of their ride's mouths a quickly become a stream of fireballs tearing through the night. One hit a drift of leaves below me, scattering it like burning confetti, and the rest would have done the same to me, only my mount had suddenly gotten with the program.

It tore skyward just before the flames hit us, apparently deciding that I was the lesser of two evils. Or make that four evils, since the fey had gotten some back up and were now trying to flank us. Or maybe there had always been a squad of five, and I just hadn't seen the others in the darkness.

I saw them now as one broke away from the pack and flew at me like a medieval knight in a joust, with one of the long, spear-like weapons the Svarestri liked to use levelled in front of him like a lance. And since experience had shown that those spears were the equivalent of getting hit by lightning, I panicked and started throwing everything I had at him.

And I had a lot.

My ride was loaded for bear, with a couple of saddlebags secured around the creature's thick neck that were packed with weapons. I didn't know what any of them were, but couldn't afford to be picky. I grabbed several round, grenade-like things and hurled them at the oncoming terror, which quickly became even more terrifying when he burst into bright green flames.

I was treated to the sight of the rider, now enveloped in fire, coming at me like some kind of hellish specter. I couldn't tell whether he had shielded and the blaze was running over the outside of his defenses, or whether his mount was simply carrying a dead man toward me. And, right then, I didn't care.

I threw everything I could get my hands on at the fiery knight, just wanting him to *stop already*. He didn't stop, and yeah, he was shielded. The plume of fire stretching impossibly far behind him hadn't affected his posture one bit, or the steadiness of that spear.

Nor had any of it bothered his ride, which it merely bounced off.

His ride.

I saw the head of his mount, which was shaped more like a seahorse than a snake, with prickly spines and strange protrusions that no Earthly steed would have. I saw its elongated snout, something halfway between a horse and a crocodile's, with a maw of gleaming yellow teeth. I saw its slitted, golden eyes—

And then I threw a potion bomb directly into them.

I guessed the rider hadn't bothered to shield his ride, and why would he? It was impervious to almost everything. Except that, I thought, as the bomb exploded in its face in a full-on acid attack.

And ate those beautiful eyes out of its skull.

It screamed, a skin-shuddering sound that penetrated all the way to my bones. And showed my own bucking bronco how to really take the prize. The fey yelled something and dropped his lance, needing both hands to hold on. And then he dropped something else, too, in the few wild seconds that followed.

I got a flashback to the mages at Gertie's and their closely held shields. And how they'd been visible all the same, from the rain beading on the surface. Just as this one was from the fire that vaguely limned it.

Until the fey released it in his confusion, and screamed as the flames rushed in.

I didn't do anything else to him; I didn't have to. The fire did it all, sweeping over the body and eating him alive, but not as Earthly blaze would have done. This was more like dropping a match onto a piece of paper soaked in kerosine. One second, he was whole and solid and perfect; the next—

He was falling into the darkness in fiery chunks.

I was in my closet a few minutes ago, I thought dizzily, watching the top half of the fey's body basically evaporate, while the lower half continued to ride toward me for one beat, two beats, three. Until it fell away, too, dropping off with a sound like sand blowing over pavement.

For a moment, the remaining riders and I just looked at each other. Then they figured out what Hollywood villains never do, and ignited their spears almost in unison, sending arcs of lightning jumping from fey to fey to fey. And then lowered them and charged, all at once.

I tried to shift, because I am not stupid. And aimed for the distant platform, hoping I could catch up to everyone else. And that I could hit it from here without materializing into thin air and plunging to my doom.

I never found out, since the shift didn't take, and I didn't have time to refocus and try again.

In desperation, I pulled out the only weapon I had left, a glowing golden whip that didn't come from the fey's pack, but unfurled directly from my hand. It was something Pritkin's incubus had shown me how to do, fighting as the gods once had with my own energy. Which cut off the tops of the fey spears when I slung it around and would have cut them, too, if they hadn't veered off at the last second.

That left me panting and wondering what to do now. That ability ran on god blood, and mine was thin. And cold, I thought, as a shiver tore thorough me at the sight of the rest of the squadron, streaming out of the forest like a black wave.

It looked like I'd intercepted the vanguard, whereas Aeslinn had sent a whole damned army. And I guessed my reputation had preceded me, because they weren't even looking at the party on the platform. They were coming straight at me.

Which would have meant something, had the rest of my group been using this time to escape. But they weren't. A brief glance showed me that they weren't doing anything except milling about, as if waiting on a damned food delivery. They weren't even looking this way!

And, excuse me, but you'd think that a mid-air joust on dragon back might warrant a glance!

But I didn't get one.

I did, however, get something else.

My ride was shot out from under me, as a dozen energy blasts from the nearest riders hit it all at once. They would have hit me, too, but I wasn't there anymore. Because, instead of falling, I was somehow going the other way.

I had a disorienting few seconds to see the ground getting farther away, to watch the black river of mounted fey flow after me, to feel the wind on my face and my limbs scrambling in the air, because my skill set did not involve flight!

But someone else's did.

I found myself hauled up to a hard chest and a pair of blazing green eyes and some towering white wings that were surging hard to take us higher. They shone, shedding silver dander on the air, and making the man in between them almost seem to glow. With that and the moonbeams washing out his fair hair, turning it from gold to silver, he looked positively angelic—except for his expression.

"What the hell are you doing here?" he snarled.

I stared upward at Pritkin for a moment, wondering about my sanity, but the scene didn't change. "I could ask you the same thing,"

I gasped, seriously confused. He was dragging me upward while simultaneously standing a quarter mile away on the platform.

And then I made the mistake of looking ahead and—

"*Holy shit!*"

"Do you have a body?" Pritkin bellowed as we surged forward, like that was the important thing here. The biggest tree I'd ever seen in my life was looming right in front of us, growing from a barely-there silver pinpoint to a wall of bark in what felt like a second, because we were *moving*. And then we were dodging, slicing through the air just to the left of it.

And I do mean just.

I could feel the rough wood catching on my hair for a second, and could see nothing but a river of silver literally inches away from my face. But I didn't have time to adjust, because here came another one. We were moving through a forest of them, which would have been bad enough since we were also moving like a bat out of hell.

But then a river of flame gushed past us and set a tree alight, rushing up the bark and leaping to the canopy.

And the tree got up and ran away.

A few days ago, that would have been enough to break my brain. But I had more experience with Faerie now and barely blinked. I could see the tree off to the side and moving fast, like I could see Pritkin above me, beating furiously at the air. And Mircea across from us, the goat in his arms and his dark hair flying, as the leathery wings sprouting from his shoulders did the same. While an army of silver haired fey fell in behind us, riding more of the slender, black, odd-looking creatures that I finally put a name to.

"*Dragon?*" I yelled, as Pritkin swerved.

"Dragon," he confirmed, just as a huge leaf pile exploded below us.

Shit.

But these things didn't spit a long, continuous line of flame like normal dragons, or if they could, they weren't doing it now. They were spitting balls of fire that tore through the night in numerous small, highly explosive bursts. Like a machine gun of flame instead of a flamethrower, which was a problem as the smaller gobs seemed to go faster and farther. Which didn't help when trying to dodge them!

But somebody wasn't interested in dodging. Somebody was interested in vengeance. Somebody with a canopy now engulfed in flames darted out of the woods and swung a huge, knot-covered branch into one of the small dragon's mouths, mid-spew.

And the furious elm must have put some force behind that punch. The dragon went spinning through the air and smacked into the side of a different tree, hard enough to cough up another fire-ball. And was thus immediately subject to a beat down from the latest enraged piece of flora.

The elm, for its part, plunged its flame-laced head into a huge pile of wet leaves, sending a billow of smoke and burning plant matter skyward. I didn't see if the maneuver worked, as we were already past it now and Pritkin was yelling something at Mircea. It was a mental shout, but was loud enough to practically deafen me.

You saw?

I saw! Get closer, if you can!

"Closer?" I said, looking between the two of them.

Pritkin's jaw set. *That could leave us caught in the middle—*

Where do you think we are now? Mircea demanded.

I think we have Cassie now!

We don't. I told you—

And I told you—I'm not taking that chance!

I grabbed Pritkin's arm. "What do you mean, closer?"

"To the trees!" he said, as another barrage of fireballs erupted around us. "They won't fight for us, but they'll retaliate if the fey injure one of them!"

A fireball burst against the trunk we were speeding past, strafing us with chunks of bark and almost following that up with decapitation when the tree retaliated with branches swinging.

"What the fuck do you mean closer?" I screamed, which did exactly no good at all.

And a second later, we were flinging ourselves into the heart of the forest.

Chapter Twenty-Seven

If I'd thought the ride was crazy before, it was nothing compared to this. The tree trunks speeding around us were blurs across my vision, to the point that I had no idea how Pritkin was navigating at all. I had the impression of a huge space populated by silvery trunks and even more dangerous dark ones that we couldn't see until almost on top of them, and slanting beams of moonlight that confused the eye more than they helped.

It was scary as hell.

Scary enough that I tried to shift us all away, not caring if it wrenched my guts out, since that looked like a probable end game here anyway. But, once again, nothing happened. I tried again and again, but my spells simply weren't connecting.

Which made no damned sense! Yes, this was Faerie and yes, the Pythian power didn't work here. But I had energy of my own, after vacuuming up what had remained in the suite. I'd just proved that with the whip!

But nothing was happening, and that was a problem.

I saw Mircea turn his body completely sideways, slicing through a tiny gap in between two leafy behemoths, with the goat guy clutched to his chest. The little creature had lost his vest, and looked likely to lose his trousers soon as well; that was the face of someone who'd just wet himself if I'd ever seen one. Probably because Mircea had missed the bark on either side by maybe half an inch.

But Pritkin and I weren't doing much better. We took a sudden dive, leaving us barely skimming over the top of huge leaf piles, even bigger than the one that had caught me. It looked like wind never penetrated this far into the forest, allowing great masses of slowly decaying tree matter to build up. They gave off a musty, earthy smell, thick in my nostrils, and were multiple stories high.

If we fell into one of those, we'd never get out before our pursuers were onto us.

Not that they needed to get that close, I thought, as a line of fiery clots tore through the air where we'd just been. And then hit the space in between two trees up ahead, which had a pale blue membrane stretched across it, almost too dim to see. Until the flames hit, lighting up the shield that I guessed Pritkin must have thrown ahead of us, stretching it paper thin as the energy pushed against it.

But the shield held, at least long enough to snap back. Pritkin abruptly veered upward, having known what was coming, although I could feel the heat as the now combined ball of fire passed by, just underneath. Hurtling back the same way it had come—straight at the senders.

The fey had to do some serious contortions to avoid getting incinerated, but they managed. And came after us with renewed fury, the tails of their rides snapping, they were burning through the air so fast. Faster than us.

Pritkin tried to throw another shield behind us, but couldn't manage it and fly at the same time. Which left me dangling there, feeling useless, until I remembered: we shared abilities, right? I twisted in his arms, causing him to curse when he almost dropped me.

But he didn't, and I monkey crawled up his body, looped my legs around his waist, and—

"What are you *doing*?"

"You're the pilot," I panted. "I'm the gunner."

"Fuck!"

But he didn't tell me not to, since I guessed he didn't have any better ideas. I didn't either, because I couldn't shift us out of there. I also couldn't see worth a damn, with the great wings shedding dander in my face!

But I could do that, I thought, as the shield spell appeared in my mind and then flowed outward from my hand.

Only . . . not exactly as I'd planned.

"Did it work?" Pritkin asked, not able to look behind him, because the trees were so tightly packed that a second of inattention could kill us.

He was already having to swivel abruptly this way and that, including turning sideways as Mircea had done to make it through ridiculously small gaps. And then try to gain back the altitude he'd lost in the few open spaces he found. It was a wild, high-speed game of chicken with the fey, and I wasn't sure whether I'd just helped matters or not.

Make that not, I thought, as the shield bubbles I'd accidentally created instead of a barrier started ping ponging between trunks, ricocheting in all directions. One of them took out a fey, knocking him off his mount and into a mountainous pile of leaves that swallowed him whole. But another—

Was about to do the same to us.

"Duck!" I screamed, and Pritkin ducked, low enough to drag his feet through the top of a leaf pile before surging upward again. But that wasn't going to work for long, because there were too many shield balls now. The initial large ones I'd made, trying to form a barrier behind us, had separated into a hundred smaller versions. To the point that the forest now resembled the kitchen when Saffy had been trapping all those spells. But she'd known what she was doing, and had created stable containment fields, whereas I—

Had not.

Some of the shields had become huge, thin, soap bubble looking things that floated around, not doing much of anything. A few were popped merely by a fey flying through them, or by snagging on a protruding limb. Others were sturdier and more dangerous, getting batted about like baseballs by angry trees, and causing the fey to yell at each other and have to do more contortions to stay on their strange rides.

But they seemed to be doing okay with that. They'd already adapted, placing outriders on either side of the main group to magic the shield balls away from them, while the center cluster started spitting fire again. So, I trapped that in shields, too, otherwise we'd have been toast, but I still didn't know how to stabilize the spell. So now we had fiery shield balls ping ponging everywhere, and while one of them did smash an outrider against a tree and then popped, engulfing him in flames, there were plenty more where he came from and I didn't know this magic!

But I knew mine.

"What the fuck?" Pritkin yelled, as I rolled out the golden whip again. It looked like he and his incubus had some integration to do where their memories were concerned, because he didn't seem to remember that one. But I couldn't worry about it now.

I grabbed a fiery bubble and tried to slash it at a fey, but he sent a spell to throw it off course and it burst against a tree right beside us, raining fire down everywhere and singeing Pritkin's wings.

He managed to put out the flames with a spell, but the second it had cost him almost slammed us face first into a tree, and screw this.

I couldn't manage these damned bubbles, but I could manage *that*, I thought. And grabbed a dragon this time.

And just like with their more substantial cousins, these didn't burn. The whip caught it around the neck, looping five or six times, but other than for spitting sparks everywhere as it reared back, nothing happened. But that was okay.

In fact, that was perfect, I thought. The whip was as light as a feather, and even with the added weight of the beast, it felt like I was holding nothing. Because I wasn't—the power was.

For a split second, I allowed myself a small grin.

This was going to be fun.

And it was. I started slinging the dragon back and forth into the fey, who spiraled off course and in one case, was knocked into a tree with his mount on top of him, landing with a satisfying splat. Others slammed into each other, with the sinuous tails of two dragons intertwining and causing them to turn on each other, snarling and spitting fire. Several more fey were knocked off their rides and onto the forest floor, sending up great swirls of leaves as they tried spells to soften their fall and ended up causing a leaf storm.

Make that a burning leaf storm, I thought, because everything was burning now.

"What the fuck?" Pritkin yelled again.

It was becoming his mantra.

"It's a new thing!" I gasped, caught halfway between a laugh and a scream, because I couldn't believe this was working!

At least, it was until a tree grabbed the end of my whip, jerked it out of my hand, and started lashing us with it instead.

It went out pretty fast, but not before several fey went up in smoke, a quarter of one of Pritkin's wings was sliced off, and we started to sling about wonkily in the air, now being unbalanced.

Pritkin swore, then sent a spell to slice off an equal amount of the other wing, gasping in pain as he did so. And causing me to hold onto him tighter to keep from falling off. And to wonder where I'd gotten the nerve to think that I was helping!

But maybe I had, slightly. Because the fiery whip and the crazed human and the even more crazed trees had freaked out the fey. Not in a get-me-out-of-here kind of way; more in a let's-murder-them-all kind of way, which wasn't much different than we'd had before. Except that they weren't being careful anymore.

Instead, they sent a combined fireball erupting out of the throats of a dozen of their rides that came boiling toward us. Pritkin saw it, because I jerked his head around, but he didn't react. Until the last second, when he shot upward, his newly rebalanced wings responding with lightning speed, and the fireball hit below us—and it hit hard.

And, of course, it hit a tree. Only no; it hit a tree. This one wasn't a sapling like the crazed elm, which had been huge but that was relative. Around here, if you didn't rival the biggest redwoods in height and girth, you qualified for the term.

This one didn't.

In fact, I didn't even know if it would be possible on Earth, or if its weight would have felled it long ago. But Faerie seemed to have different rules, and it towered above the already towering forest, a giant among giants, a full city block wide and so tall, that I couldn't see the top.

But I was about to.

Because there was no way to dodge something that big and that close. Pritkin didn't even try. He went skimming up the side instead, almost completely perpendicular, while clutching me tightly against his chest as a river of bark flowed by right in front of us.

I didn't scream; I couldn't have, even if I'd wanted to. I could barely breathe, with all that wind rushing into my face. I ducked my head down, trying to find some air, and instead saw something below us that caught what little I had in my throat.

Two fey hadn't been distracted by the firestorm, and were right on our tail. And they were gaining. I could feel the searing heat of their breath, could smell the strange, brimstone odor, could see the world suffused by flame as they fired—

And then a branch sliced through the air in between us, catching them with a crack like a thousand balls hitting a thousand bats.

The closest rider was obliterated on contact. I didn't see it, but I saw the burst of flesh and flying blood, a great haze of it on the air, highlighted by the scattered embers of his ride's flames. The other, however, who had been slightly farther back, I did see. He or his steed had amazing reflexes, getting hit but only by the outer branches on the larger limb.

That was enough to throw him off his mount, but he caught one of the branches, flipped back around, and grabbed his dark ribbon on the way up. He had finally had enough, however, and veered off, merging with the night. And I wouldn't have seen anymore anyway, because Pritkin and I burst through the canopy a moment later, into a star strewn sky, both of us gasping for breath, although for different reasons.

I clung to him as we circled around on the air currents. The forest below was mostly dark, but I didn't have to ask where Mircea was. A line of fire was zigzagging through the trees, as whatever fey remained zeroed in on our third.

And then all the lights went out.

"Mircea!" I whispered, but he was okay. The next moment, a black bullet flew at us out of the treetops and paused in the air, right in front of us. It was an insane visual in a place known for them: a huge, silvered moon backlighting two angels, one dark and one light. With me sandwiched in between and wondering if I was going mad.

"What happened?" I gasped.

"Ambush," Mircea said, not struggling for breath but looking like he'd like to. "I noticed the trees dumping leaves on individual fey so I led them on a wild chase, causing them to bunch up. And allowed the surrounding forest to attempt to bury them, all at once."

"That was . . . good," I said, amazed he'd been able to noticed anything in the midst of all that.

"Good enough for a respite; not good enough to finish this," he said grimly.

"One of the riders who pursued us got away," Pritkin added.

"Then they'll be on the hunt again soon. And all our weapons are back there." He nodded at the way we'd come.

"What weapons?" I asked.

"The tree with the illusion—the one showing all of us?"

And, okay, that cleared up one thing, at least.

I nodded.

"It's rigged with everything the dark fey could spare. We intended to make Aeslinn's people believe that they'd blown us up along with one of the enemy arsenals."

"His fey have been pursuing us relentlessly," Pritkin added. "Ever since he lost you. Going to ground isn't going to work if he thinks we're still alive."

"And you can't shift out," I said, getting a bad feeling suddenly.

"No. I assumed the potion was active on you. How the devil—"

I held up a hand. I was working through something, and clinging to a guy whose body was surging up and down to the beat of those great wings wasn't helping my concentration. But then, I didn't really need it.

Son of a *bitch*.

"I don't think that's going to work anyway," I told him.

"What isn't?"

"Shifting. Or hiding. Or going to ground—"

"What are you talking about?"

"I'm talking about *Faerie*. I thought she let me in here because I pressured her—"

"You can talk to her?" Mircea cut in.

"Not . . . exactly. But I think she understands me. And I think I finally understand her."

"Cassie—" Pritkin began, through gritted teeth.

"She doesn't want us to run," I said bluntly. "She wants us to fight. She wants warriors, remember? And she's tagged us."

"That was only a theory—"

"It's more than a theory. She brought me here to throw a wrench into your plan—she must have thought it had a chance and she didn't want that. But dump me in the way, like right in the way, of those fey, and all of a sudden—"

"Chaos," Mircea murmured.

I nodded. "Not to mention that I can use the powers that allow me to fight here just fine, but not the ones that let me run—or take you out of here. It's her world and she's shutting me down. I was shifting all over the place back home, and you should be, too. You should have been out of here hours ago, but she doesn't want you out—"

"That . . . would make a lot of sense," Mircea said.

"It makes no sense!" Pritkin snarled. "What the hell does she expect? For us to take on an army?"

"You already did, and took a rather sizeable bite out of it," Mircea reminded him. "It appears that she wants another."

"How? What in the hell—"

"Can't you do what you did last time?" the goat suddenly asked, in perfectly accented English.

"No," Pritkin snarled.

"That requires a conduit, which we do not currently have," Mircea added.

"You can talk?" I said, staring at the little thing.

Those weird, rectangular pupils focused on me. "Of course, I can talk."

"Then why haven't you? You haven't said anything for days!"

"I didn't have anything to say to you. I do now——"

"And what's that?"

"Duck!"

And, shit.

The fey had already found us, probably courtesy of the one that got away. And demonstrated by the hundred or so fireballs suddenly speeding this way. Pritkin took off, but I was facing the other way, and had an excellent view of the wave of fire hurtling into the sky, strangely beautiful against the night. And highlighting a multitude of riders, just behind it, their sliver hair whipping in the wind as their bodies rose out of the treetops like black specters.

They looked like an army of grim reapers, being dressed to match their rides and with their capes flowing out behind them. And then flowing after us as we skimmed over the treetops, going insanely fast to outrun their spells, with no more obstacles in our path to slow us down. Only, this time, we were going the other way.

"What are you doing?" I yelled, to be heard over the cold wind that was slapping me in the face. The breeze tore my words away almost before they were out of my throat, but Pritkin must have picked up something mentally.

Faerie wants us to fight; we're going to fight, he said, and even his mental voice was savage.

You're thinking of the tree, Mircea said, coming up alongside.

You have a better idea?

Frankly, no.

Then stay tight. This is going to be close.

Mircea didn't respond, but I could feel his tension radiating through the bond we shared. And then practically screaming through it, as we plunged down through the trees, an army of fey on our tail, and they were moving faster, too. They swamped us just as we hit the platform, coming in for a hell of a landing that left us juddering and then rolling toward a hole in the trunk covered by more of that black felt. And then—

"Augggghhhh!" I yelled, as we plunged down, down, down through the middle of the huge, hollow trunk, completely in the dark except for the tiny bit of gray spearing down from above. Pritkin wasn't even attempting to break our fall, with those great wings folded tightly against his back. Leaving the only sounds the whistling wind, my screams, and Mircea yelling *"Now! Now! Now!"*

Before I even had time to wonder what he meant, we were bouncing on a huge net of vines, hard enough to send us flying several stories back upward, just about the time that all hell broke loose above.

I kept on bouncing while staring at a boiling orange and black firestorm. At fey bodies briefly darkening pieces of it here and there before they flew apart. At the rotting wood of the old tree engulfed in flame before starting to fall down at us in pieces bigger than a family car.

And then my brain surrendered and I passed the hell out.

Chapter Twenty-Eight

I awoke to the sight of a huge woman bending over me. Not that she was fat; muscle bulged out everywhere, from the sides of her thick neck to the bodybuilder-and-then-some sized forearms. No, she was just big, with a face so wide that it was all I could see until she pulled back a bit.

And thrust something out at me.

I scrambled back until I hit my head on what would have been a headboard if I was in a bed rather than on a pallet on the floor. Fortunately, the wall behind me was soft, like straw; unfortunately, it dislodged a shivering of dust that sifted down onto my head as me and the ridiculously large woman regarded each other. And then she thrust something at me again.

"Sop," she said.

It was a deep, gravelly voice, which would have freaked me out even more if I hadn't just noticed: she had little braids in her hair. They were woven with bits of colored string and ribbon and a few wilted flowers, like a girl made up for a spring festival. And her fingers were stained with different colors, not just the nails, but up to the knuckles, in a rainbow of earthen shades: burnt umber, dusty yellow, lavender, red ochre, and indigo. They were strangely festive, too, which was why it took me a moment to notice what she was holding out.

"Sop," she said again.

I stared from her to the bowl she clasped. It was earthenware, as big as a sink, and had a ladle's handle sticking out of it. And smelled smokey and rich and—

"Soup?" I asked, perking up, and tried to peer inside.

But I was in a half recline and she was something like eight feet tall, so that didn't work. I sat up and tried again. And, sure enough, it looked like soup, some kind of vegetable variety that smelled . . . kind of great, actually.

"Sup?" she asked, the great face turning inquisitive.

Her eyes were tiny, and appeared to be a little myopic, but they were a pretty pansy color. I met them, and suddenly, the hulking figure didn't seem so intimidating anymore. I nodded.

"Soup."

"Sup."

"Sooouuuup."

"Sooo-up?"

I nodded again and pronounced it a few more times. That seemed to be the right move, because her face broke out into a huge smile showing bright white teeth, with not one chipped or missing. She was young, I realized. Possibly younger than me.

I smiled at her. "Soup."

"Soup! Soup!" she was obviously delighted. "Soup! Soup!"

Somebody called her, and she glanced over her shoulder, then got up and lumbered out, happily muttering her new word. I tried the soup and made a face. It looked and smelled heavenly, but it tasted like nothing. Just nothing at all.

I frowned and started to get up, and found myself so dizzy that I stumbled. And when I put out a hand to catch myself, for a second, I thought I felt carpet under my fingers instead of rough old boards. It was disorienting, like the impressions that suddenly crowded me hard and fast: Mircea and Pritkin arguing about something, their voices loud in my ears; Pritkin holding me tight, pulling me back against the length of his body, warming my little pallet and calming my fears; various others coming in to check on us, huge, hulking shapes with shadows that ate the room, and then tiptoed quietly away again, amazingly light footed for such massive creatures.

I put a hand to my head and waited it out, but there were no more impressions. Just a faint dizziness that passed after a moment. I gave it another one, then tried standing up—more carefully, this time.

The room remained steady. And empty, with no one in sight, no furniture, and only a single lantern on the floor providing any light. I grabbed it and moved to the door, but there was no one there, either. Including my friendly neighborhood soup lady.

There was something else, though.

I had been about to call out, to see where everyone was. But I'd stepped into the corridor first and held up the light, and the words died on my lips. Not because it was dark, with only my own fire flickering on the walls. Or because it was kind of small, considering the size of the creatures who used it.

But because it was beautiful.

Here was a patch of woven straw, like a field of wheat curving over a hillside; there were a bunch of bug shells, arrayed in a winding line, with the low light making them glimmer like a rushing river; here was some green moss, standing in for a forest; there were tufts of dirty white wool clumped together amid dried rushes, like sheep on winter fields.

I lifted the lantern higher, and discovered that it wasn't the just the area around my door that had been decorated. The whole stretch down either side of the hall looked less like walls and more like giant tapestries. Ones that formed an abstract representation of a countryside as my eyes scanned across it.

The homeland the trolls had been forced out of, maybe?

I didn't know, but the more I looked, the more I saw: deep ochre cliffs, carved out of patches of clay; soaring mountains formed by striations in the bits of tree that poked through the wall; gushing waterfalls that followed the sweeping lines of bunched vines; a meadow covered in dried flowers. It was abstract, and more visible at a distance than up close, to the point that I couldn't tell whether the vista had been deliberate, or whether the maker's hands had just naturally formed the images in their minds as they worked. But I could see it all as I passed down the hall, brought to wonderful life by flickering lamplight.

I put out a hand, just brushing over a tiny sheep's woolly back, and wondered how they could bear to look at it every day, and remember.

Or maybe that was the point, Cassie!

The hall ended in a door that also looked too small for its users, with a balcony beyond that was somewhat sheltered from the wind by a knot in the great trunk. Or maybe a curving walkway would be a more accurate description, as it disappeared around the side of the beehive-shaped hut that I'd just emerged from. I twisted around and looked up, and saw a sizeable heap of other huts, like a small village, all wonkily woven together and piled up stories high, as if they were mushrooms growing out of the great tree. Yet they were holding steady despite their precarious perch.

They deserved a closer look, but didn't get one. I'd turned around, my attention caught by a flicker of light in the darkness. And saw something that stopped me in my tracks.

"I thought it was the soup," I said blankly.

Mircea turned from a spot a little way down the path, looking startled; I guessed he hadn't heard me. That was not a normal thing for a vamp, much less a master. But I could absolutely understand why.

Because the smoke I'd been smelling hadn't come from dinner.

Instead, the entire forest appeared to be burning, silhouetting his body against an inferno. The huge sentinel trees stood in ghostly splendor, their shade forming a vague, blue-black darkness as they faded away into the distance. But the highway system, what was left of it, now wove through the trees like a fiery ribbon. And several camps like the one behind us burned high on the side of silvery behemoths, some just blackened cinders now, while others continued to scorch the wood in huge scars above them.

Mircea grabbed my arm and I realized that I'd moved too close to the drop off. The walkway had no railing, and it was a ridiculously long way down. But I didn't step back.

The view from here was even more startling.

Many of the smaller trees in the secondary canopy had fled, leaving a large open space in front of us, and only bare, churned up earth below. Others writhed in place, like witches on a stake, as fire consumed them. Or stood stone still, their blackened corpses a testament to past anguish.

And present hate.

"Zeus was not pleased to lose more of his army," Mircea confirmed softly.

"Then why isn't he attacking us?" My own voice was harsh.

"Glamourie. The dark fey are particularly skilled. They deserted some encampments, leaving them for the light fey to find and burn, but I have been assured that they will not find this one."

That should have been a comfort, but it wasn't; I didn't know what would be right now.

I turned to look at him. His shoulder-length dark hair was blowing in the wind, backlit by the same random sparks that were reflected in his eyes. They were dark tonight, too, with no glow from rising power. I doubted that he had any left, with all the healing he'd had to do.

And, suddenly, I saw him again, back in that camp, where I'd first found him and Pritkin. The great Mircea Basarab, second in command to the North American Consul, leading light in the vampire world and one of the most powerful creatures I knew . . . staked and bleeding out and helpless. And I felt dizzy all over again.

"I can't do this," I told him, my lips numb. "It's too big. I just . . . I *can't*—"

"It's too big for all of us," he said, putting an arm around my shoulders and drawing me close.

I was shaking again, as I had been in bed at Gertie's, where the reality of what we were facing had finally hit home, undermining all of the lies I'd been telling myself. I was the queen of denial; an ace at compartmentalization. I always had been; it was what had gotten me through childhood at Tony's, carefully tracing the curlicues on piano legs while a head bounced down the hall.

But I couldn't seem to compartmentalize this. Couldn't shove it back into a little box and forget about it. Couldn't lock it up and throw away the key and tell myself that I'd think about it tomorrow.

Couldn't do anything, except stand there and shake.

Mircea held me for a long moment, before leading me over to a bench beside the hut. I sat, too abruptly. I was losing it; I could feel it happening. As if I was tearing away from whatever bedrock had grounded me and falling into an abyss, and I didn't know what to do about it.

To his credit, Mircea didn't tell me that everything was going to be all right. He didn't talk at all. He just sat there, one of my hands gripped in his, and watched the forest burn alongside me.

After a while, a huge male troll with a grizzled beard came out onto the walkway, which I was surprised could hold his weight. They really were huge, with muscles on top of muscles, massive heads and strange, patchwork clothes that reminded me of the hallway inside. The garments appeared to have been made out of whatever was handy, and then repaired with the same, over and over, across what must have been years. The end result was surprisingly beautiful pieces that were a mishmash of different types of cloth, leather, old suede, fur, and small ornaments picked up over a lifetime's travels.

His clothes probably told his whole story, had I known how to read them. Or had the language skills to ask. I didn't, so I just sat there, vaguely admiring, while something in the back of my head started screaming.

He offered us a couple of brown, lumpy things halfway between a cigar and a cigarette, which I declined and Mircea accepted. He accepted a light, too, conjured up between the creature's massive thumb and forefinger. The grizzled fey lit a pipe, another red flare in the night, then spat over the edge of the platform, a clear commentary on the light fey that needed no translation.

He moved silently down the path to greet a friend at the far end, and the two didn't speak, either.

It wasn't that kind of a night.

Mircea preserved the quiet, just sitting there and smoking for a while. And looking up at the stars, a few of which could be seen through gaps in the upper tree line. While the wind blew sparks through the air and a few fingers of moonlight pushed down through the canopy, their light battling with the glow from below.

It was a strangely peaceful scene, like having a break in hell's antechamber.

I pulled my legs up into a hug. And closed my eyes for a moment, enjoying the smell of Mircea's smoke, whatever it was. It didn't smell like Marco's cigars. It didn't smell like anything I'd ever known. Just another, small sign that we were sitting in an alien world.

"I discovered the truth about my wife tonight."

The words were quiet, so much so that they didn't immediately register. Just brought me out of a half trance, and caused me to turn my head toward him. I opened my eyes to see him letting out a sigh full of smoke that painted abstract pictures on the air. It was a bit surreal, watching the suave, elegant, and usually so-refined master smoking what looked like a badly rolled reefer, while wearing a hippy's tunic—a mottled green thing with leggings—and leaning against a hut. But nothing was normal anymore.

And then his words hit home.

"What?"

He took another draw, let it out, too, and stared at the stars some more. "The small creature we've been chasing was a friend of hers, a fellow sufferer, you might say. He told me, if not everything, a great deal. It . . . wasn't what I expected."

"What . . . did you expect?"

He actually took time to think about it, which was also unusual. The consul's chief diplomat always had an answer ready—or two, or three. But he seemed to be processing this, as if he'd learned about it only shortly before I showed up.

"I'm not sure," he finally said. "I spent so many years focused on finding her, that I think she became a prize more than anything else, a goal to work toward instead of the living, breathing woman that she was. Of course, I spent much of that time thinking that she was dead, but even after I discovered otherwise . . . I never really thought about her.

"I was too busy thinking about me."

I frowned. "You?"

He nodded, causing the line of smoke he was letting out to bobble, too. "I thought I was the knight in shining armor, rushing to her defense. The one rescuing her from a terrible fate. The hero."

"And you weren't?"

He laughed, and it sounded genuine. Not bitter or harsh, as I'd have expected, but just a laugh. Under the circumstances, it was jarring.

But he didn't seem to notice my reaction this time, nor did he answer the question. He just sat there, smoking some more, while the forest burned and the trees fled and I wondered what I'd do if a party of Aeslinn's men flew by, on their strange, savage rides. Run back inside in fear, or fling myself over the balcony and attack them?

And then I wondered what was wrong with me.

"It is strange," Mircea murmured. "To go for years—centuries in my case—thinking that you know yourself, only to find out that you never did."

I didn't say anything, but when he offered me his smoke, I took it. Because that had sounded a little too close to what I'd been thinking. I didn't know myself anymore; didn't know who I was or who I was becoming. Didn't know anything.

Except that the smoke was rich and heady, and made me even dizzier.

I handed it back after a couple of puffs, before I fell off the bench.

"For years, I told myself that I was doing this for her," Mircea continued, his eyes distant. "To undo a terrible wrong; to prevent a senseless death. Or, after I discovered that she did not in fact die, that I was rescuing her and punishing the brute who had taken her.

That I was doing it to reunify the family, to allow my daughter to know her mother, to—"

He broke off. "A thousand things. I told myself a thousand things, and all of them were wrong.

"All of them were lies."

"Mircea—"

"I was doing this for *me*," he said, his voice suddenly insistent. "And not out of some great love for her; in truth, I realize now that I never really knew her. But out of pride, anger, arrogance. Someone had done this to my wife; someone had dared to take her from me; someone had hurt her and therefore had hurt me, and I was going to make them pay.

"I imprisoned my brother for centuries, to force him to show me where she'd died, so that I might find a way back through time to save her. I pursued Pythias, every one, to persuade them to do me this service, and take me back there. I plotted and planned and schemed—

"And all of it, every single bit of it, was for me.

"And yet, I couldn't see that. Until now."

I frowned some more. Vamps usually weren't all that concerned about motivations. A human court might take into account that you hadn't meant to kill someone, for example, that it had been an accident. A vamp court wouldn't care.

But this wasn't a court of law, and Mircea looked like the reason behind his actions mattered greatly to him.

"No," he said, and there was bitterness in his voice now, a tang in every word. "I didn't understand. I never thought about how much I was hurting those around me, neglecting my family, alienating my daughter, destroying my relationship with you. I was blind to all of it—and then I discovered what my wife has been doing all this time, while I pursued my selfish quest."

"What has she been doing?" I asked, having no idea how to respond to that.

He leaned forward, his forearms on his knees, the half-smoked cigar dangling from between his fingers. The pose was casual, even relaxed, but his face was fervent. "Far more than I have. Or that I could have imagined.

"She was one of a group of experiments the gods were doing while they were here, attempting to make . . . I suppose you would call them super soldiers, for their constant wars with each other. Vampires were another early experiment, as were weres. As were many of the types of dark fey who exist today."

I blinked a little, trying to take that in. It would have been harder, except that the Senate had already been informed of some of it by Dorina, Mircea's daughter. She had become a senator recently, to replace one of those lost in the war, and that decision—controversial though it had been, considering that she was a dhampir—had been paying dividends.

She had worked prior to her elevation as a freelance operative, sometimes taking on Senate commissions for her father, and other times hunting down revenants for nervous masters who had accidentally sired a monster and wanted to cover it up before anyone found out. In the course of that, she'd met a lot of people, and seemed to have a gift for getting information out of them that no one else could.

She'd continued to use that talent on behalf of the Senate, and the stories she'd been bringing back had certainly livened up some meetings, although I hadn't been sure how much of them I believed. But I guessed they must be true. And they did explain something.

"That's why Aeslinn sent a whole squad after her," I said, remembering.

Mircea and I had gone back in time to rescue his wife from a terrible death at his brother's hands, who had been an unstable, mad dog killer who thought that she'd insulted him. But, on arrival, we'd discovered that she'd already rescued herself, only to be promptly kidnapped by a bunch of fey. We'd followed them into Faerie, but lost them before we'd gone very far.

"Aeslinn knew who he was dealing with," Mircea confirmed. "Even if we did not. And yet, she escaped from his people, shortly after they took her from Earth. I do not know what he wanted from her, but it probably had to do with the god-blood in her veins. The gods used their own power to experiment with, and the king appears to be obsessed with it. But she denied him his prize, and ran."

"And she did not come back to me."

"Where did she go?" I asked, not sure that I wanted to know. Mircea's jaw had just tightened, and the hand holding his smoke had clenched.

But I didn't think he'd heard me.

"No," he said, staring out at the burning forest. "She didn't come back. She wasn't as self-interested as I was. She understood that this isn't about us, what we want, what we need. What selfish desires we have.

"It's about more than that." He turned to me abruptly, the dark eyes intense. "Which is why we need you to talk to Faerie."

Chapter Twenty-Nine

W hat?" The sudden change of topic threw me.

"Or try, at least," Mircea amended. "I have attempted it, multiple times, since we realized that we might have a new ally. But I have had little success. It—she—does not communicate as we do—"

"Mircea—"

"—but more like . . . like a ransom note. Only instead of words being cut out of a newspaper to make a new message, she sends bits of memory. I believe she is trying to connect the dots for us, but I cannot understand her. I cannot even see what she is sending as clearly as you do."

"Yes, but—"

"When we were following you through the Common, everything was crystal clear, as if we were actually there. But when I attempt it—" he shook his head. "It is dim, distant, almost unrecognizable. Voices distorted; images skewed. I do not know what kind of communication this is, but I do not think it is wholly mental. I think it is some kind of soul bond, but I do not have a fey soul—"

"Neither do I!" I said, finally able to get a word in edgeways. And worried that he seemed to be serious.

And then he confirmed it. "No, but you have one that is part god. Part of a creature from the universe that Faerie was born into, and still inhabits, even if she is cut off from it now."

"Then borrow my ability, if it's that important to you!"

"As I said, I have tried. But this is not an ability Cassie, it is what you are. The spell that links us allows us borrow many things, but there appears to be limits. You cannot drink blood and gain sustenance from it, and I cannot do this. At least, not well enough."

I abruptly got up and walked to the edge of the platform, to see the fires below still burning. Several trees had gathered around one of the fiery ones, using their roots to kick up dust to try to put out the flames. They succeeded, but too late.

I saw them stop and wait for a moment, with almost human anticipation for their friend to move, to respond, to show in some way that life endured. Only to slowly move away, when this did not happen. Leaving it behind to join the blacked forest of the dead, scattered across the scarred landscape below.

Their own world, I thought bitterly. If the fey would do this to Faerie, what would they do to us? What would *he*?

"Cassie?"

"Where did your wife go?" I asked roughly.

"To find us allies in this war. The king has a god on his side. We need all the help we can summon against him if we are to have any chance of victory."

We need Faerie, floated in the air between us, but Mircea didn't say it. If he had, I'd have turned him down flat. Not because he was wrong—we did need help, all that we could find. But because I doubted that she would give us any.

But he didn't ask.

And it didn't matter anyway.

"I can't talk to her," I said.

"From what you told us earlier, you already have."

"No," I spun around. "*I* talked. She used me, the way the gods always use us. The way she just did when she almost got us all killed. She didn't *talk* to me!"

I don't know what was on my face, but whatever it was seemed to surprise him. The great Mircea Basarab actually blinked. But he'd spent a lifetime negotiating with creatures far scarier than me, and it didn't last.

"But she did attempt to communicate. She has been focused on you—"

"We're fighting the same enemy. She must have seen the three of us when we attacked Aeslinn's capitol, and decided that we could be useful. But she isn't treating us as allies. She's treating us as cannon fodder, who can be thrown at her problems until we're used up and she finds some new patsies! She could have killed us all tonight, and for what? To deprive Zeus of a few more soldiers he doesn't care about anyway?"

"But that is the point," Mircea said. "We don't know what she wanted—or more vitally, what she *knows*. She seems to see everything here; she must have some inkling of what the king is planning. And she is willing to negotiate—"

"We don't know that—"

"She gave you what you wanted tonight—"

"She gave me what *she* wanted!"

"And are they mutually exclusive?" He looked at me steadily, the beautiful eyes sober and dark. "Can we not find common ground?"

I gazed back at him, impressed in spite of myself. I might have rattled him slightly, and the news about his wife had clearly done far worse. Yet he remained cool, calm, logical. He could think.

That made one of us.

All I could think about was putting my fist through Zeus's face.

"Cassie?"

I didn't answer for a moment. My emotions were all over the place, maybe because I'd just gotten up. Or because I'd just almost died for the fifth time in as many days, along with the two men who meant the most to me in the world.

Whatever the reason, I kept veering between terrified and furious, with no idea which one I'd settle on. Or whether it even mattered. What the hell could Cassie Palmer's fury do?

Mircea gave me another moment, probably sensing the boiling emotions I was just barely keeping in check. But I knew him, and I could feel his tension. And unlike me, he had a plan; I knew he did.

I just hoped it was a good one.

"What do you want me to do?"

* * *

The room he took me to was large and round and looked out onto another side of the complex. The view wasn't any better, but it was almost as expansive, with an oblong opening cut into one wall as big as a picture window. Or maybe an oversized T.V. would be more accurate, since it sputtered and fritzed as if with bad reception. For an instant, I thought I saw another scene inside of it.

But if so, it was gone too fast for me to make anything out, and I wasn't too interested anyway. Because Pritkin was sitting in front of it, on some rugs and pillows which made up the room's only furniture, with his back to us. Until I made a sound, and he turned his head.

And then he was on his feet like lightning.

And while Mircea made the feys' camouflage look good, Pritkin made it look . . . normal. I blinked for a moment, taking in a patchwork tunic and leggings in a variety of greens and browns, which he wore with the ease of old habit; the blond hair, which in the absence of anything to torture it with, was freshly washed and lying more or less like a normal person's; and the face, freshly shaved and sporting several new bruises. He looked like a fey, I thought.

I wondered if he knew?

"Cassie." He stared at me like he'd just seen a ghost, and then a second later, he was across the room and I was being enveloped in a hug so hard that I thought I might break. But I didn't mind.

I wouldn't have minded if he'd kissed me, too, but we had an audience. Including the small goat-like creature, sitting on a pillow and sipping something out of a cup half as large as he was, an old troll woman with more giant cups on a tray, and something shaggy in a corner. The shaggy thing was hunched over, and was presumably sentient since it was wearing a hat. But was otherwise just a pile of gray rags, gray hair, gray everything.

I opened my mouth to ask about it, but then Pritkin did kiss me, and I forgot everything else. And when we finally broke apart, the troll woman had gone and the shaggy thing was right there, by my elbow. Causing me to jump slightly, as it faded from a mountain man with rough, weather-beaten skin, a massive beard, and disheveled gray dreadlocks, to—

"*Arsen?*"

"Shhh!" he told me desperately, golden eyes peering out from underneath the tattered brim of the hat. "I'm Feilan now."

"Feilan?"

"One of a race of half fey, half humans who prowl the wastelands, serving as scouts, spies, errand runners—" he fluttered a hand. It was a graceful gesture, which looked completely out of place given the way he was dressed. I wondered what had happened to all that shiny armor.

And then I wondered what the dark fey would do to a Svarestri nobleman, and understood.

"You're in disguise."

"Of course, I'm in disguise. I'm surrounded by enemies!"

"They're not the enemy," Pritkin said.

"Tell them that!"

"I will, should they discover you. Although, if you'll stop fiddling with the glamourie, they won't."

The shaggy abruptly returned, and Arsen scowled at us through the huge beard. "The dark fey excel at glamouries. You can't know that this thing will hold!"

"They excel at fey glamouries. That one is demonic."

That did not appear to reassure Arsen much. He looked like he'd like to rip off the clothes and the spell enchanting them, and run screaming into the night. But apparently, he was made of sterner stuff. He just sat down instead, on some of the floor pillows, and eyed Pritkin malevolently. Who did not appear to notice or care.

His eyes were only on me.

"I talked to Cassie," Mircea informed him, and okay, that got a reaction.

"About what?"

"You know what—"

"I said no!" Pritkin snapped. "She's been through enough, and we can't trust that bloody "goddess" to do a damned thing—"

"Except to help us. Considering that we face a common enemy."

"You don't know that! For all you know, that bitch wants to pit us against each other—"

"Why? Humans are no threat to her—"

"—and watch while we kill each other off!"

"—and we've coexisted for millennia. It's the gods—"

"She tried to have Cassie killed!"

And, okay, that had been a roar, and was accompanied by a swirl of magic so strong that it peppered the air. I breathed it in and it stung my lungs. I tasted it on my tongue like acid. I felt it on my skin like tiny sparks from a bonfire, the same one that I saw burning in Pritkin's eyes.

Suddenly, he didn't look like a fey anymore. He looked like what he was—a demon lord. And one who was clearly over this conversation.

He took me by the arm and we ended up down a hall and in another room, almost before I understood what was happening. It was much smaller than the previous one, and judging by the pallet on the floor, was another bedroom. It looked like mine, except that it had a window, if a cutout in the straw qualified. Which I guessed it did, as it left shadows from the flames outside flickering over the small space.

There was no other light, not even a lantern, so things were pretty dim. But I could see those eyes, burning like green candles in the night. And I suddenly wondered if I knew this man at all.

Then he kissed me again, and my doubts fell away.

Yes, it was Pritkin, the man I knew, the man I loved. Different, with how tentative the hands were that roamed over me, as if he'd never touched me before. Which I guessed he hadn't, not as a whole person. Not since Wales, when he was little more than a boy, and not yet the man I knew at all.

But he was making up for it now, his hands suddenly turning hungry, famished even, and desperate, as if he couldn't believe I was there. And while I had a thousand things I would have liked to talk about, I liked this better. A lot better, I thought, stripping the t-shirt over my head.

But that seemed to bring him back to himself, and he paused. And, this close, the eyes really were startling, a vivid, unearthly green, boiling with power. And with anguish, the same that stilled the hands on my body.

"I thought I'd lost you."

Words stuck in my throat. Not just because of what was on his face, the knowledge of how close we'd come. But because I was suddenly back there, remembering—

I buried my face in his chest and his arms gripped me, so tight. "I thought I'd lost you," he said again, and his voice broke.

My own arms went around him, my nails biting into the skin of his back. "No."

"I almost did—"

"No!" I looked up at him, and in the tug of war between fear and anger, anger won. "He doesn't get to do that. He doesn't get to put that look on your face."

"On *my* face?"

He stared at me for a moment, and then abruptly pulled away, walking over to the other side of the room. A hand went to the back of his neck, and he shook his head as if to clear it. "On my face," he repeated.

I wrapped my arms around myself, suddenly cold without him, despite occasional gusts of heat from the fire outdoors. The night was actually pretty chilly, although I hadn't noticed before. Kind of like this room, suddenly.

"Is something wrong?" I asked.

He looked up, and the eyes were tortured. "How can you ask me that?

"Because I'd like to know? Did I do something—"

"Did *you*?" he repeated, looking stunned.

I frowned. I wished he'd stop doing that, stop parroting me. And just talk to me!

I said as much, which won me a glare. And that oddly made me feel better. The vulnerable man of a moment ago was a stranger to me; this man I knew.

Especially when he came back over and grabbed my upper arms.

"You almost *died*. What those bastards did to you—"

"Don't."

"They hurt you. I let them hurt you—"

"You saved me."

"Not soon enough." He crushed me to him again, and this time, there was an air of desperation in it. "I couldn't reach you. I couldn't do anything—"

"You killed them. All of them!"

"Not fast enough. Not before—"

"Stop it!" This time, I was the one to pull away, and there was genuine anger in my voice. "I don't want to think about that!"

"Neither do I. But we have to—"

"Why? It's over!"

"It isn't over. This war isn't over! Faerie is using you, like Zeus is using Aeslinn—we're just pawns in their stupid games. She's the one who brought you here—"

"I know."

"—there is no way you could have done that on your—" he stopped. "What do you mean, you know?"

I crossed my arms and looked at him. It probably wasn't very intimidating in just a bra, but I was past caring. "I figured that out a while ago. She jerked us all in here, me, Rhea, Guinn—"

"And tonight, she did it again! You barely survived last time, and I can't—" he stopped again, his jaw tightening. But then he came out with it, bluntly, because he was Pritkin. And I'd never met a more straightforward man in my life. "I can't protect you here."

"You did—"

He shook his head. "That was a one in a million shot that paid off. I had no time and wasn't even sure what I was doing. You could have died in that camp. You *should* have died!"

I stepped forward again and brushed his uncharacteristically floppy bangs off his forehead. And then let my hand move down to cup his cheek. He'd bathed at some point since I saw him last, but hadn't bothered to shave, and his bristles were approaching a beard. But it felt good. He felt good.

He closed his eyes.

"I couldn't get to you," he said. "None of us could. The dark fey wouldn't even attempt it. There was an army between you and me and *I couldn't reach you.* Tell me you understand."

"I understand that you saved me," I told him quietly. "That I would have died without you. But . . ."

I hesitated. I didn't want to admit it, but someone else had helped, too. And Mircea had been right: we needed her. As much as I'd have liked to consign her and Zeus and every other god I could find to some particularly nasty corner of hell, we were outmatched.

We couldn't do this alone.

But she'd brought me in here, and put me into danger, and I doubted Pritkin could see past that right now. So, I was left pleading the case of a creature I didn't trust any than he did. It figured.

"But?" The blond head tilted.

"But Faerie helped, too," I said, trying to keep the bitterness out of my voice. "She conjured up all kinds of beings out of legend, scaring the hell out of the fey. I never would have made it across that camp otherwise. And then, at the end, she was the reason I got through the portal. She sent an army of demons—the memories of them anyway—to buy me a few extra seconds. It worked."

"It barely worked." Pritkin's voice was raw.

"Barely still counts."

His forehead touched mine, and his voice was a whisper. But it told me everything I needed to know about what he'd been through in those long, fraught minutes. "I can't do barely. Not again."

I didn't know what he wanted me to say. I didn't think there was anything that wouldn't be a lie. So, I didn't try.

I kissed him instead, putting all my feelings into it, everything I couldn't say. How scared I'd been, how unbelievably scared, and then how hopeful, when I realized what was happening, what he was doing to give me a chance. I'd paid a price to get out of that camp, but so had he, and he was still paying it, would be paying it, since I didn't think that this new, unified form was reversable.

Yet he'd done it immediately, without thought, without hesitation. He'd done it for me. I'd never had anyone care about me like that.

Or like this, I thought, when his hand caught mine, halfway under his tunic.

"We don't have to do that," he said roughly. "This isn't . . . we don't have to do anything."

"I want to—"

"How can you? After what they did?" The green eyes blazed into mine, and if ever a face said that he wished they were alive, just so he could kill them again, that was it.

"Because Zeus doesn't get to decide that, either," I said steadily. "Not what I do, how I feel, how I think. Not anything. Not him or his creatures."

Pritkin stared at me for a moment, as if in amazement. His hand trailed down my cheek, to my lips, to my chin, to my shoulder. And there was wonder in his touch, too.

"I don't know why I'm surprised," he said softly.

But I didn't get to ask about what. His lips caught mine, but it was different this time. Like the hands that slowly undressed me, as if he wanted to burn this into his memory. And so did I.

I'd been so sure that I'd never see him again, that I'd never hold him, that I'd never—

Something ignited in me, a hunger that had nothing to do with food and everything to do with the fact that we were both here and alive. It seemed like a miracle. And, suddenly, slow wasn't good enough.

I pulled his tunic over his head, fighting a little with it, eager and hungry, so hungry. I devoured his mouth, pulling his head down to mine, and met fire with fire. We half fell, half tumbled onto the flat little bed, ripping the rest of each other's clothes off—more or less.

I was wearing my bra and Pritkin had a legging halfway up one thigh when he entered me, and it was so good, so perfect, so wanted, that I didn't know whether to laugh or cry. He seemed to think the same, the look on his face a mirror of what I was experiencing, the unaccustomed clumsiness of his actions a litany of everything I felt. I arched up and he gasped; he growled and I laughed. But I wasn't laughing for long.

I was panting and choking and writhing and biting my lip on a scream. But it was one of the good kind; how long had it been since I'd had one of the good kind? Probably the last time we did this, I thought.

But we'd never done this, because I'd never been with this man. He was the same but different, in ways I couldn't quite define, because I couldn't think properly. But, yes, he'd changed.

I didn't know what that meant for our future, but I knew what it meant for right now, as a supernova burst over me, through me, almost before he'd started properly. I buried my face in a blanket to keep from yelling the house down, and bringing a bunch of concerned, massive creatures to peer in at us, an image that had me laughing and coming and laughing and coming, and then giggling hysterically as Pritkin looked down in consternation.

"Are you alright?"

"No. But I think . . . I will be," I told him, putting a hand behind his neck and pulling his head down to me. "I think I will be."

Chapter Thirty

I rolled over on top of Pritkin sometime later with his body still inside mine. It felt good, having him so close, so much so that I didn't want to let him go. My hair framed his face as I looked down, and let a finger trace one of his eyebrows.

They'd blended with his skin tone when I first met him, almost making it seem like he didn't have any. They were more obvious now, as he'd darkened a few shades in the Vegas sun. But the unshaven jaw was the same, and the eyes . . .

Even when I'd been bitching about Pritkin's looks, grasping at any flaws to persuade myself that I didn't find him as attractive as I did, I'd loved his eyes. There was simply nothing to fault there. Or anywhere else, since all I saw now was the man I loved.

Okay, and muscles. Lots and lots of muscles. Covered by a pelt on his chest that was considerably less bear-like than Marco's, but fuzzy enough that I could rub my face in its softness.

Something that I was really appreciating right now.

He smiled slightly. "It's going to be difficult to walk this way."

"We'll make it work."

I kissed him, then let my lips trail across his cheek to his jaw and then his earlobe. He arched up as I caught the small bit of flesh between my teeth, and shifted position inside me, making me groan. And then squirm a little, which had him closing his eyes, even as his body hardened. It felt so damned good that I did it again, and again, and again, until he rolled me onto my back and punished me properly.

And I still didn't let him go.

He collapsed on top of me afterward, breathing a little hard, and my hands started smoothing up and down his back. Only to stop at his shoulder blades, where the wings had been. I found the claw marks on one side, where a demon lord had taken a chunk out of him once, leaving deep furrows in the flesh. But his natural healing abilities had washed away all signs of his other fights.

And of his transformations.

"Faded," Pritkin said, before I could ask. "The wings are physical manifestations of the spirit, like the bodies Faerie grants to souls who stumble in here. Solid enough, but they disappear when no longer needed."

"I thought they were a one off," I said, remembering the first time I'd seen them.

He'd absorbed the towering white appendages from a creature who'd had them naturally, after it was harvested by a demon purveyor of souls. Exotic spirits were used like books or movies in the hells, to permit the purchasers to experience another life for a time. Pritkin's father was said to have a whole library of them, allowing him to explore worlds lost to time, or swim through long dried-up seas, or fly . . .

But Rosier's "book dealer" had joined forces with an Ancient Horror—one of the creatures imprisoned by the demon high council ages ago for their incredibly destructive ways—and almost murdered everyone in the hell region known as the Shadowland. Only Pritkin's ability to absorb more than just memories from the harvested soul had saved it. But the great wings had soon disappeared, and I'd assumed that they were a limited-time thing.

I guessed not.

"They're supposed to be," he said. "That is why especially rare souls retail for so much. They can be used up, and once they're gone, they often cannot be replaced."

"But it doesn't work that way for you?"

"No."

It was terse, and I realized that this might not be a topic he relished, since the ability came from his demon half. That was also where Mircea had acquired his wings, by borrowing them from Pritkin through our bond. Only his had left ridges on his shoulder blades, wrinkled lines of flesh like long healed wounds where they'd attached.

But try as I might, I couldn't find any here.

"Vampire bodies and souls are fused," Pritkin said, as if reading my mind. "That is one reason they're so powerful. But it also means that a change to the spirit causes a change in the body. Demon bodies, even half demon ones, are more . . . malleable."

There'd been an edge to that last word that I didn't like.

"Are you alright?" I realized that he'd asked me that, but I hadn't done him the same courtesy.

"I don't know." He rolled off and we turned to face each other, but I couldn't see his eyes. The firelight flickered over lowered lashes, shading them.

"Meaning?"

He ran a hand up and down my side, following the curve of my body, but it wasn't a sensual gesture this time. More as if he simply wanted to reassure himself that I was really there. And, like Mircea earlier, he took his time replying.

"I spent years telling myself that my other side was a monster who killed my wife," he finally said. "When it seems that the monster was the one I married. But I pushed all of my guilt, my horror, my shame, onto my incubus, so that I wouldn't have to face what I'd done. And now . . . I don't know who I am anymore."

"There's a lot of that going around."

He looked up then, but his face was in shadow, and his eyes appeared black. Almost like his counterpart's had, before the reintegration. I found that they didn't disturb me so much anymore.

"What?" he asked.

"Mircea has been dealing with the same thing. He's waking up from his obsession, which is good, but now he's realizing all that he lost to it, and it's shaken him."

"That's why he wants you to talk to Faerie," Pritkin said grimly. "To make all this mean something."

"This doesn't mean anything."

A blond eyebrow quirked. "Says the Pythia? I thought hidden meanings and prophecy were your stock in trade."

"Prophecy says that we all die in the end," I told him, my fingers playing along his ribcage. "That we kill the gods and they kill us, until there's nobody left. Except for maybe an Adam and Eve type who start the whole thing all over again."

"And where did you hear that?"

"The legend of Ragnarök, or one of them. Jonas keeps sending them to me. There are many versions, and none are particularly pleasant. But the older ones are the scariest. They say that we all die, that it's the end of everything, with no one left alive afterward—"

"Prophecy is bullshit! We make what's meant to be!"

I smiled slightly at his certainty. I wished I shared it. "Like I said."

He frowned. "Where did this come from?"

"This what?"

"This . . ." he couldn't seem to find the right word, and looked even more troubled as a result. "It doesn't sound like you," he finally said. "You're usually the perpetual optimist."

I smiled more genuinely that time, because that was not how Pritkin would have described me six months ago. 'Snarky whiner' maybe, or 'dangerous ignoramus,' and he wouldn't have been wrong. Perpetual optimist sounded better, although it wasn't remotely true these days.

"As you said, we're all adrift. You and Mircea don't know who you are anymore, being in the middle of change, and I . . . wish I was."

"You've changed," his voice was rough. "A great deal."

"Perhaps." I let my fingers trace patterns in the fur on his chest. "But the things that have changed for me don't have an upside. They don't give me more power, or help me think more clearly. If I was truly my mother's daughter, I wouldn't have needed rescuing yesterday. If I had half her power, a third, a *tenth*—"

"Power isn't all there is—"

"In battle? Yes, it is!"

I started to get up, but he stopped me with a hand on my arm. "In battle, Napoleon regularly won with smaller numbers. He concentrated his armies on one vulnerable point in his opponent's line, and overwhelmed them where they were least expecting it. Tactics, audacity, knowledge about your enemy—there's a thousand things that can turn the tide of war."

"I'd still rather have the big guns," I said harshly, and sat up.

I wasn't sure where I was going. Just that the walls seemed to be closing in and I needed to move. The flickering firelight wasn't helping, reminding me of that damned tent, and of the bastards who had terrorized me. And even though they were dead, and I knew they were dead, I could still feel them, their hands moving over me, their weight bearing me down—

Some goddess I was!

But Pritkin grasped my hand, halting my movement.

"Yet you saved yourself without them. With nothing on your side but intellect, resolve and amazing courage—"

I frowned at that, because that was a lie, and we didn't do this. We didn't lie to each other. "You were on my side. You got me out, you and Faerie—"

"We opened a door; you walked through," Pritkin said stubbornly. "You made it all the way across that terrible camp, with a thousand fey warriors looking for you, with no Pythian power, no magic, not even a weapon in your hand. Yet despite the best they could do, you slipped through Zeus's fingers once again."

"I didn't—"

"You *did*. And you *have* changed. You're not the same woman I met, six months ago, no matter what you may think. She was smart and stubborn and talented and spirited, but she wasn't the leader you've become. She had promise; you have fulfilled it."

"I've fulfilled nothing! I've barely kept myself *alive*—"

"But you did do that. With a senior god—*the* senior god—and an entire army of fey against you. And you're still here."

I stared at him, wondering why Pritkin, who usually saw everything, couldn't see this. "I wouldn't be here without you. And Mircea. And my court—"

"The hero going it alone is for the movies, Cassie. In real life, that gets you killed. Successful generals have armies around them, attract loyal followers, and make powerful alliances. That is how you succeed. That is how you win."

Win. I almost laughed again, but choked it back. Even continued survival seemed like a long shot right now, yet he was talking about winning. But it was good to hear, good to know that he hadn't given up, that he had some hope left. The day that Pritkin threw in the towel . . . I honestly didn't know what I'd do.

I felt my body relax as his hand smoothed up and down my arm. Felt warmth flow through me, along with something more important. Until the firelight was just light again.

And light couldn't hurt me.

"You've already changed," he told me. "You simply need to see it."

I shook my head, but didn't reply. I didn't want to argue, especially now. I felt warm and safe and happy, and desperately wanted to hold onto that feeling. Life had shown me how precious, how fleeting it could be.

But it didn't feel that way right now. Lying here with him, I found some of that lost optimism. It was crazy; I was in a dark fey treehouse, somewhere on an alien world, being hunted by a monster. But Pritkin was here so it felt like home.

It felt perfect.

"I'm just sorry that you had to sacrifice so much to get me out of there," I told him.

"I didn't sacrifice anything."

I had been tracing the patterns of light and shadow on his hipbone, following the fascinating topography of the muscles there and on his thigh. They felt tense, as if he was carrying too much tension in his body, too. But at that I stopped.

"Then what would you call this?"

"Overdue," he said, and it was mild. Petting the lion seemed to have tamed his usual fiery temper. But there was nonetheless an edge to the words. "Mircea isn't the only one who has been ignoring reality. I was so caught up in my own delusion that I risked not only my life, but yours as well."

I frowned. "I was put in that camp by Faerie and bad luck, not by you."

"Yes, by me." He met my eyes and his were fully visible now, hard and bright and strangely shiny. "That was the only thing going through my mind, as you threaded your way across that hellscape. I couldn't see you half the time; the projection began skewing wildly once the fey who started it was dead. Sometimes I could see things from your perspective, and the rest—" his jaw clenched, to the point that it looked painful. "I was seeing you through the eyes of those bastards, just before they dusted away. And you looked—"

He stopped again, and his hand tightened on my arm.

"I looked terrified," I finished for him, because it was true. There'd been no fearless heroine there. It had been white, bloody knuckles all the way, and a heart about to pound out of my chest and a bruised body clinging to a thin blanket—

"You were magnificent," Pritkin said, taking my face between his hands. "You could not have done better. It was *my fault*. You ended up in that damned camp rescuing *me*—"

"There was no alternative—"

"There was every goddamned alternative!" He got up suddenly, and strode around the small room, looking like a vengeful fire god, the leaping shadows panting his naked body with dangerous patterns. "As soon as I reunified the two halves of myself, I broke through the feys' potion with ease. I could have done that all along. I could have saved us—me and Mircea—and you would never have been needed. Faerie could have kept her damned hands off you and we would have been fine!"

I sat up. "You couldn't have known what would happen."

"I could have." He glared, and it was impressive, even in this lighting. "When I took on the responsibility for your safety, when I promised Lady Phemonoe to help you, that should have been it. I should have immediately done what was needed to recapture my power and maximize our chances. Yet I held on—to my anger, my resentment, my fear—and every day that passed I put you in danger. And when I saw you there, in that tent, when I saw your face—"

He broke off and knelt in front of me again, and his own face was terrible. "My fault. My mistake. One that will never happen again."

I didn't belittle his apology by brushing it aside. It didn't matter what I thought, which was that we'd all made mistakes. None of us was perfect, least of all me. I had no room for throwing stones.

Not to mention that he'd had plenty of reasons to fear his demon nature. How did he know that reunifying wouldn't end up putting me in danger, instead of the opposite? He'd made a choice—

"I made a *mistake*," Pritkin repeated, as if he'd heard me. "I've been afraid of power my whole life, ran from it, tried my best to evade and deny it. I saw what it did to people, the monsters it made out of them, and swore it wouldn't do the same to me.

"But the night that Ruth made her gamble, when I lay there, clutching her desiccated body . . . I learned the wrong lesson. My power had gotten out of control, to the point of taking a life, so I doubled down, cut myself off from it, tried to amputate it. Ripped my psyche in half to leave it nowhere to go, and nothing to work with—"

"That was understandable," I said, trying to comfort him. But all I received in return was burning eyes.

"It was *stupid*. What I should have learned is that power is a tool, one that must be mastered or it will master you. All my efforts to deny my nature only hobbled me. If I had known what I should have—what any other incubus *would* have—I could have shut down Ruth's spell before it began. I could have saved her—and saved myself the agony of having killed her.

"I could have saved you."

"You *did* save me—"

"Not from the trauma, nor the pain, nor the fear. Not from the sheer bloody horror of that place. You paid the price for my stubbornness, and I—" He suddenly hugged me tight. "I will never forgive myself. Or forget the lesson."

I couldn't breathe, but I didn't object, because I was suddenly remembering my mother's words to me. She'd said that it would be better if Pritkin learned about his power among his own people—had this been why? Had she seen a glimpse of what was coming, and wanted to spare me?

"Your mother was right. This should never have involved you."

"It was my choice," I said, and then realized that I hadn't spoken that thought aloud. "Are you reading my mind?"

He pulled back. "Our bond is strong at the moment. Some things leak through."

"How much?" I asked, suddenly worried. There was one thing we still had to talk about, one very important thing, but I wasn't ready. I didn't know when I *would* be ready, and I felt myself start to panic a little. I hadn't planned on this, or rather, I hadn't planned on it now—

"What is it?" he asked, frowning.

"I—" I tried to stop the images that flashed across my mind, but it didn't work. He and me and Mircea, coming together to fight off Zeus, although not in the normal way. Bodies entwined, hands slipped over sweat-slick skin, breath coming faster, while above us, a storm of magic churned away, attempting to push back the lightning trying to devour me.

It had worked, combining all our energies into one, magnifying them through Pritkin's power, and forcing back a godly attack. But it had been close. And afterward, I'd had to accept that the repercussions weren't likely to be confined just to my peace of mind.

They might destroy my relationship, too.

I looked up, and as I'd feared, found Pritkin scowling at me. The low light gave his face hollows and angles it didn't usually have, and for a moment, made him look like a stranger. A stranger who was low-key furious.

And then I stopped trying to fight the memories, just wanting this over with, wanting a clean slate between us. Even if it destroyed us, I couldn't do this; I couldn't lie to him. And the scowl abruptly got worse.

"Is that what you think of me?"

"Is . . . what?" I asked, not sure that I understood the question.

"Is that what you think of me?" he repeated. "That I would prefer for you to die than to share you? When it was my damned incubus who came up with the idea? Is that really what you think?"

"No?" I said, because that was obviously the right answer, yet he didn't look any happier.

"I want you to *live*. That is my only priority—and it should be yours!"

I started to agree with him, because he was right. I absolutely would have died had we acted differently and Pritkin would have been drained. Zeus might have his power right now, and it would be our fault. And, honestly, everything that had happened since had made me more sympathetic to Pritkin's incubus, who had been lying on the floor while I explained my fears, with an arm flung over his eyes, because we'd just fought off a god and all I was worried about my relationship.

It was absurd.

But then something in me rebelled, as it had then. Because that was wrong; it wasn't absurd. I wasn't a robot, somebody who went through all this . . . this utter bullshit . . . and was fine the next day. I needed him, I needed *this*, I thought, as he took my hand and brought it up to his cheek. And just that, a simple touch after everything we'd been through, was enough to reduce me to tears.

"You are my priority," I told him shakily.

"I can't be. You know that—"

"Well, you are anyway!" I said, suddenly angry. "How is it okay for you to freak out over me being in danger, but not okay for me to do the same? How is it all right for you to risk yourself, over and over for me, but I can't do it for you?"

Pritkin regarded me steadily. "I'm not Pythia."

"And I can't be Pythia without you! I *can't do this*—"

"You can. You're—"

"If you tell me that I'm the strongest person you know, one more time," I said, my voice low and dangerous.

And yet, it didn't intimidate him, because nothing intimidated him. I found myself clasped close instead, his hand on the back of my head, my face buried in his shoulder. And this was it, I thought dizzily.

This was all I wanted.

"As long as I live, I'm yours," he said hoarsely. "Know that, if nothing else."

"As long as you live," I repeated. That wasn't the reassurance I craved.

But Pritkin didn't say anything else. He couldn't, not without lying to me. And we didn't do that.

Instead, I got a pull back after a moment, and a finger under my chin. And a pair of suddenly mischievous green eyes looking into mine. I stared back, not understanding what was wrong with him.

This was serious!

But he wasn't, and for the first time, I saw him again—that young man I'd known briefly in sixth century Wales, with the wicked smile and the playful ways and the bright green eyes that promised all sorts of devilry.

This is who he is, I thought. Who he really is. All I'd known was the tortured half of him, the piece that was functional, if only just, moving through life as a penance more than anything else, punishing himself for what had happened to that bitch of a wife.

But that wasn't who he was supposed to be, and I suddenly, passionately wanted to get to know *this* man.

He smiled at whatever was on my face, and leaned in. And whispered something in my ear that had my eyes widening. And me remembering a little catalogue of delights that he'd conjured up once, on a Welsh riverside.

I'd been shocked by the illusion, which had been prompted by my lack of the local lingo and his of modern English. So, he'd propositioned me in a new way, by crafting images of us in a variety of unlikely poses. Very unlikely, in a few cases.

At the time, it had freaked me out.

But now . . .

I was tired of war and death and pain and fear. I wanted to feel something that was as unrelated to any of them as possible. I made a selection.

And once again, Pritkin seemed to understand, and I saw his eyes soften. "Are you sure? The others will be waiting for us."

"Let them wait."

Chapter Thirty-One

That took a very long time," the goat complained, when Pritkin and I reentered the large, main room. "My people are more efficient."

"Be silent," Arsen snapped.

The goat scowled at him. "I will do as I like. You don't control me anymore—"

"I have never controlled you. I don't even know what sort of misbegotten creature you are!"

"One that your people made, just to drain the life out of. But I got away, and I don't answer to you—"

"Then shut up for the sake of decency!"

"Why decent?" the goat looked confused. "I merely pointed out that they could have been faster. We have important issues to discuss, and there they are, taking more than an hour to—"

Arsen threw a pillow at him.

"If it takes longer than a few seconds, you're doing it wrong," drifted out from underneath it.

I looked around, but didn't see our fourth—or fifth, if you counted the goat. "What happened to Mircea?"

"With the trolls," Arsen said briefly. "They wanted to borrow his eyes."

"For what?"

"To find out how much time we have," Mircea said, striding back in. "The answer is not enough."

"I thought you said Aeslinn's people couldn't find us here!" I said, as he passed me, went to the window and looked out.

"Under normal circumstances, no," he agreed. "But the trolls have an observation platform higher up, and I spotted the rest of the king's forces on the way here. They would likely have been here already, but he'd sent many of them away."

"So, they portalled back, regrouped, and are coming after us."

"That would appear to be the case. And our recent explosive event showed them the general area in which to look."

"With so many searchers, no glamourie will hold," Arsen said, standing up. "We must leave."

"Can we get out through the tunnels?" Pritkin asked.

Mircea shook his head, continuing to look at something below the window ledge. "They are currently clogged with the captives the trolls rescued from the camp, and some of those are injured. They can only go so fast."

"You can't use tunnels anyway," I protested. "Aeslinn is lord of earth—"

"The tunnels through the tree roots," Mircea clarified. "The forest has become . . . sympathetic . . . to our cause. And the king cannot read through them."

"He can with an army to spread out over the entire forest!" Arsen said. "You underestimate him—"

"Not at all. That's why we're going to lead him away, so that the evacuation can continue."

"Lead him away?" I repeated. "But . . . we're the ones he wants, especially Pritkin—"

"Which is why he will follow us."

"—which is why, if he catches us, nothing else matters!"

Mircea gave me a flash of dark eyes. "We aren't going far, just to another root tunnel well away from here. Then we'll use an illusion on our rides, and set them free, so that they can lead him even farther afield."

"Rides? What rides?"

He leaned out the window and then pulled back abruptly—

"No. *No!*" I said, because two more of those black, snake-like dragons had just risen into view. One was carrying a small troll, which had to be an adolescent since he was only around six feet tall. But he must have been as strong as his larger counterparts, since he had the second dragon by the reins and was calmly ignoring its thrashing.

Up close, the strange mounts were even more terrifying than I remembered. They almost looked like voids; black paper cut outs that absorbed all light around them. Until they turned just right, and the optical illusion failed for a second—

The Chinese artists had gotten it wrong, I thought, my skin ruffling as I stared into slitted, golden eyes.

They'd gotten it way wrong.

Mircea must have noticed my expression. "We have a good head start, Cassie. They won't catch us—"

"With each of them carrying two?" I furiously gestured at the beasts. "We'll be weighted down—"

"Not each of them," Arsen said. "I can blend in with the army when it gets close enough. I must get back to warn the nobles about what the king is planning."

"We don't know what he's planning," I pointed out, as one of the horrible things screamed.

"I thought that was your job."

"Each of them will be carrying one," Mircea agreed, before I could give Arsen the answer that deserved. "Unless you count our small companion who does not weigh much."

"And what about me?" I asked. "What am I going to ride?"

"Nothing. You aren't really here."

"What?"

Pritkin drew me to one side. "Mircea told me that he cannot hear a heartbeat from you, or feel the blood rushing through your veins. We think Faerie didn't want to risk you again, and so used a mental projection instead."

"The way you first visited us in those tunnels," Mircea added helpfully, while the young troll clambered off his ride and into the room, and handed Mircea the reins.

"I am not a projection!" I said, staring from one man to the other. "I threw things at the fey—"

"With Faerie's help," Mircea said, mounting up. "She makes rather better projections than I do."

"This is insane!"

"Cassie, we have to go. And you have to go back," Pritkin told me.

I stared at him. "I'm not leaving you!"

"Not yet," Mircea agreed. "You have to See for us first."

Pritkin shot him a you're-not-helping-look, and pulled me even further away. "I don't like this any better than you do. But you can't hold this form forever—"

"Then have Faerie pull me in! Bodily, like last time—"

"No!"

"Pritkin! That wasn't a request! I'm not going—"

"You have to! I can't do what I must with you here. I have to know that you're safe—"

"Safe?" I stared at him some more, in utter disbelief. "There's no 'safe' anymore, not for any of us—"

"But there is better than here," his face was savage.

"You just finished telling me how strong I was," I pointed out, matching his fury.

"And you are." He licked his lips, and behind the fury I saw something I'd never expected form Pritkin: fear. Not for himself, but for me. And then he confirmed it. "But I am not. I can't see you go through what you did in that camp again, not and stay sane, do you understand?"

"Then . . . then come out with me. Fuck Faerie. Get to a portal and—"

"And what? There's no running from this, Cassie. The only way out is through."

"And what am I supposed to do while you're going through? Sit at home and—"

"You're supposed to *live.*"

"And help us do so," Mircea added. "We need whatever aid you can provide, *dulceáţă*, and we need it now."

"You said Faerie helped you in that camp," Pritkin reminded me.

"I—yes, but—" one of the damned dragons screamed again, and it felt like a knife through the brain.

"Then perhaps I was wrong, and she is on our side. And if she has information that we need . . ."

He let it trail off, let me decide, but it wasn't much of a choice. They needed to get out of here—now—and the longer I dithered around, the shorter lead they'd have. I wondered if Faerie had planned it that way.

I wouldn't put it past the bitch.

All right, I told her vengefully. Alright! If you have something to say, now would be the goddamned—

The world cut out.

I fell into a crowd of people, so thick that I couldn't see anything else. I was crouched down, but when I stood back up, nothing changed. Everyone in the damned place was taller than me, by a lot.

They also had delicately curved ears, the kind that made my heart seize. But these weren't Svarestri. I knew that because of the hair color—mostly dark brown—and the eye colors—varied—and the skin tones—even more varied. The latter was the most striking, since along with the usual black, brown and beige, there were rainbow hues not found on Earth, unless you were checking out a demon enclave.

Only these were more pastel tones—lavender, pink, yellow and a soft green—instead of the more vivid hues of the demon world. They looked like flowers, I thought, watching a woman pass by in a floaty lilac tunic and trousers, with matching boots and dangly amethyst earrings. And hair that Saffy would have envied, a true, cotton-candy pink with no discernable roots. It went well with her saffron-colored skin—

"Alorestri," Pritkin's voice said, as if he could see her, too. "Or, rather, one of the mixed children who form an underclass there."

"Yes, but what is happening?" Mircea said. "Can you get higher?"

I realized that he was talking to me, and looked around. And finally spotted a circular bench around a small tree, not far off. I climbed up—

And saw a towering pile of blue-black rocks with a huge waterfall spilling over them in the distance. And a man calling out something from a raised platform in front of the falls, which I couldn't understand. Although that might have been because of the sound of all that water crashing in my ears.

But Pritkin didn't seem to have that problem.

"The Summoning has been called," he said, repeating the fey's words. "Great Nimue is dead, and a successor will be chosen. The Summoning has been called; let the heirs return—"

The scene abruptly changed, enough that I almost fell. And when I looked back up, I found myself in a great ice chasm, where a black and inky pool churned away far below, in the midst of a forest of stalagmites. It might have been a portal; it might have been anything. All I knew was that it scared me, with vapors rising from its surface like grasping hands, trying to draw me in.

A woman was there as well, high on a rocky promontory, above the pool. It took me a moment to recognize her: Elena, Mircea's wife. A dark-haired beauty dressed like a fey in a simple tunic and trousers, and backing up. Before reversing course, running full out and diving—

Straight into the pool.

"As I said," the goat's voice floated over the scene. "She departed for Jotunheim, to enlist the frost giants in our cause. But she has not returned, and I despair for her."

"She isn't dead," Mircea's voice said roughly.

"How do you know?"

"Faerie wouldn't be showing me this if she was."

"Ah. Good point."

The scene changed again, and this time, I finally knew where we were. The great domes and towers of Aeslinn's original capitol, set among the mountain fastnesses of his realm, burst into view along with the sunrise. My breath caught once more at its beauty, pale marble shot through with veins of gold, and now caressed by orange fingers of light. And perched on a mountaintop so high that it seemed to float among the clouds.

It was the closest thing to Olympus I'd ever seen.

And then I was gasping again, for a different reason, when the view rocketed forward, sending us racing across the skies and then into the city, along parapets and down staircases, and finally into what appeared to be the bowels of the mountain itself. And into a small, cramped, dark room, lit only by a few wavering candles. Where a small group of fey sat around a table.

"—telling you it can't be done!" A middle-aged male said.

"He'll feed us and our houses to those monsters of his, and we'll all end up fodder. And for what?" Another agreed.

"Better fodder than slaves to a madman!" A fist hit the table.

I recognized the last speaker, a tall, fat fey with a beard that I'd seen talking to Arsen in a previous vision. He'd reminded me of a fey Santa Claus at the time. Not so much now.

"Arsen was right," he said. "All you do is talk. I've heard each of you complain about the king's descent into madness, yet none of you will lift a finger to stop it!"

"Arsen," a fourth fey said bitterly. "Yes, let's take advice from a boy whose father's blood stains these stones. Lord Áskell opposed the king, and look where it got him—"

"So, you admit you're a coward—"

"If it keeps my head on my shoulders, yes. Dying for nothing isn't bravery, you old fool. It's madness."

A fifth fey intervened, before the argument turned to blows. He was older than the rest, with genuine bags under his eyes and lines etched deeply around his mouth. "Lord Oril is correct. Moving without more allies does nothing except to ensure our deaths. If you want our agreement, you must show us something more than words. A great deal more."

And then, just as fast as they'd come, the visions cut out. Leaving me, Mircea and Pritkin staring at each other, and Arsen flailing, because it didn't look like he was as used to visions as the rest of us. He hit the floor, in the midst of a fluttering of tattered robes, and Pritkin looked at me.

"Thank you. That was . . . informative."

"Three of us," Mircea agreed, from atop his strange ride. "And three tasks to be performed."

"What tasks?" I asked, right before a fourth vision hit.

A familiar, run-down castle sat on a spit of land above a river in Romania. Half frozen water churned away below, gray and laced with shards of ice, while above, a great black dragon gave a shriek of challenge that echoed off the mountains and came back at me, over and over, a never-ending clatter in my brain. Aeslinn, I thought, staring up at him, and not just him. The setting sun reflected off his great black hide, causing the scales to glint like shards of obsidian as he banked, but it wasn't the sun in his eyes.

It can't be, I thought, gazing upward. They're not there anymore. That was in the past—

The great screech came again, loud enough to threaten to shudder my flesh off my bones, and then the huge wings hugged the body close and the massive creature dove, maw agape and claws extended—

Straight at me.

"—Summoning," Pritkin was saying, as I snapped back to reality with a jolt. "The first vision was in the central plaza in Avalon, where Nimue's proclamations were read to her people."

"The Summoning is ancient," Arsen protested. "It hasn't been used since—"

"Before the gods?"

He frowned.

"Are you alright?" Mircea asked, watching me.

I nodded, and tried not to look as off-kilter as I felt. "It . . . hits me that way sometimes," I said, and saw his eyes narrow.

But if he suspected that I'd seen a fourth vision not visible to the rest, he didn't say so. The dark gaze met mine, but there was no mental voice, either, which might have been overheard. There was nothing but a slight tilt of the head, so insignificant that no one else noticed.

He *has* changed, I thought, and looked away.

"Nimue is dead," I said, remembering something that I'd overheard Aeslinn telling Zeus.

"That's the point," Pritkin agreed. "Great Nimue is dead, and a replacement is sought. The Summoning has commenced, calling all prospective heirs home."

"And what does that have to do with us?" Arsen demanded. "None of those green bastards will lift a finger to help us, no matter who wins. Use the chance to steal lands from us, perhaps—"

"Steal them back, you mean?" Mircea asked, with a raised brow.

Arsen snarled at him.

"But the Green Fey hate Aeslinn," I pointed out. "They've fought him for centuries. Surely, they'd want him destroyed—"

"And are happy to sit back and let Caedmon attempt it," Arsen snapped, talking about the third great fey ruler. "They won't risk it themselves!"

"One might," Mircea said, looking at Pritkin steadily.

"What?" I said. I knew that look. Mircea thought he'd just won an argument, which worried me because I hadn't known we'd been in one.

"Perhaps," Pritkin said, and then said no more.

"What does that mean?" I asked, looking from man to man. It seemed that they'd found time for conversations that didn't include me.

"Mage Pritkin is Nimue's great-grandson," Mircea reminded me. "That gives him, if I understand correctly, the right to contest for the throne."

"What?" Arsen stared at Pritkin as if he'd never seen him before.

"Contest?" I said. "What do you mean contest?"

"If I win, I can command the Green Fey armies," Pritkin said. "Which are currently—"

"No! No, you *can't*—"

Pritkin caught my arms and continued speaking even as I fought him, making me hear this. "They are the only intact army left in Faerie. The dark fey are scattered and divided. Some have been useful as auxiliaries, but many prefer to stay neutral. And they have no single leader to unite them now that their king has been taken by those loyal to Aeslinn. But the Green are battle hardened, disciplined troops. They could turn the tide."

Yeah, they'd been talking, I thought, furious. "If you survive, and if they'll even accept you! You're half demon!"

"They'll likely assassinate you even if you win," Arsen agreed, still looking stunned.

"Will it be enough?" Mircea asked him, as if this was already a done deal. "Could you convince the nobles to fall into line, if they knew that they had the Green Fey as well as Caedmon's army on their side?"

"I . . . possibly." Arsen frowned. "They're cowards—not by nature, but as a tactic to stay alive. But with another army—"

"Two," Mircea said succinctly. "I will find my wife, and the help she sought. I will bring them back to you."

Arsen just looked at him, and the expression on his face made me like him for the first time. He looked the way I felt, as if he was confronted by madmen who talked of taking thrones and recruiting giants as if it was nothing. His eyes moved to me, as if wondering what insanity I was planning.

Which would be none, because the old fey had been right—this was madness!

Pritkin pulled me aside. "We don't have much time—"

"We never do! Is this what you want? To let the damned fey finally kill you?"

He'd been about to say something, but at that, he paused. "What I want?" he asked, with a strange look on his face. "What I want is to go back to the suite, lock and ward the door to your rooms, and drink a marguerita on the balcony together whilst we watch the sunset. Then take a leisurely bath in that huge tub of yours before going to bed, where we will stay for a week—"

"But you aren't going to do that," I said tightly. "Are you?"

I knew the answer before he spoke. There was no safety here, but there was none anywhere else, either, if we didn't end this. Zeus would just keep coming and coming, and eventually, he would beat us. Because we cared about our people, mourned every death, agonized over those we sent out that never came back. And he . . . didn't.

You can't reason with madness, with evil, with hate. You can't persuade it, can't compromise with it, can't evade it. You can only fight it.

I knew that as well as Pritkin did, I just . . .

I felt my face crumple.

He took it in between his hands, and kissed me. "When this is over, we'll have that week," he whispered. "Not at court, but somewhere beautiful, where no one can find us."

"A year," I countered brokenly. "Somewhere back in time. I know the place . . ."

"A year and I won't want to come back."

"That's the idea."

He kissed me again, and I felt tears on my cheeks, and didn't know whose they were, his or mine. And I didn't find out. Because when I opened my eyes again . . .

I was back in my closet.

He was gone.

Chapter Thirty-Two

I could see them, if I concentrated: Pritkin standing there as my body dissolved like mist, until he was clutching only air; Mircea yelling something—I couldn't hear the words, but I could see his mouth move; Arsen letting loose what looked like a curse and jumping to his feet; and the little goat staring about wildly.

But the small creature wasn't looking at me, or even where I'd been. He was staring at something past me. He must have had some kind of extra senses that warned him of what was about to happen, because he hit the floor right before a fireball tore through the room.

I had a split second to see the giant ball of flame splashing the walls with color, the firelight reflecting in Mircea's widening eyes, and Arsen throwing himself backward, clearing it just in time. And then Pritkin cast a ward in front of the window, which the burning plasma hit and bounced off before coming back this way. Causing me to try to deflect it—

And have the entire wall of my closet burst into flames instead.

For a second, I thought the spell had gotten me, my confused brain forgetting which world I was in. But then I put a hand up to shield myself, and realized that the fire had come from me. I had manifested a golden whip to try to catch the spell, which was instead dragging a burnt-edged gash through my wallpaper. And the plaster behind it. And the concrete—

I reabsorbed the whip, but it was too late. A row of Augustine's couture went up in flames, just as the suite's wards kicked in. They attempted to extinguish the fire with some kind of white foam, but it didn't want to go out. That set up a battle royale that quickly had me drowning in oxygen-sucking whiteness, while boiling clouds of smoke cut off the light.

I stumbled back, looking for the door, but the only illumination were bright flashes from Augustine's burning gowns, twisting and writhing like those dying trees in Faerie. They jumped out at me as I thrashed about, in vivid spires of emerald, ruby, amethyst and pearl. And then disappeared just as fast, when the clouds closed up behind me.

All of a sudden, I couldn't breathe, couldn't hear anything but the roar of the fire, and couldn't see. I was about to say the hell with it and shift out, when I remembered: I was Pythia. I didn't have to put up with this shit!

Something I demonstrated when I grabbed hold of time, causing the boiling clouds to move slower and slower, and finally to stop.

That would have surprised me—I didn't get two time stoppages in one day—but I was kind of busy suffocating to death. Stopping time didn't sweep the ashes out of the air, or stop me from sucking in burning sparks with every breath, or grant me any bonus oxygen. But this might, I thought, rotating my wrist as if turning a great dial.

And then sweating and straining and heaving, because this dial was rusty and didn't want to budge.

But it did. It took a lot more effort than usual, but I felt the gears of time slowly move inside my grasp. And then, reluctantly, begin to reverse.

I forced them backward, feeling like I was pushing a freaking freight train . . . loaded with iron . . . attached to Gibraltar! But I pushed anyway, putting my all into it, and, finally, it worked. Whole dresses popped out of charred remains, their colors bright and bold and beautiful once more. They sprang back onto padded hangers, which themselves were clean and new again. While drifts of foam retreated, the blackened walls flooded over with subtle patterns, and burnt carpet bloomed fresh under my feet.

And I fell back against the soft line of clothes, panting and staring and wondering what the hell.

I stayed there for a long moment, hugging the wall and trying to breathe. My lungs were convinced that they couldn't risk it and wouldn't be told otherwise, leaving me in danger of suffocating in a closet full of fresh air. And when they finally got the message, I turned dizzy from gulping in too *much* oxygen.

But I still didn't move.

I was actually afraid to.

And then I was afraid of something else.

"No!" I yelled, and jerked upright, feeling the room spin around me. But not because I was seeing two places at once, as I should have been. I tried and tried, but all I saw was the inside of my closet, or of my eyelids when I tightly closed them and concentrated. *"Pritkin!"*

But he couldn't hear me. He wouldn't have been able to, even assuming he'd survived the attack, because he'd done more than protect Mircea just then. He'd protected me, too.

He'd severed Lover's Knot.

I could actually feel it: an aching emptiness under my breastbone where our connection had been, as if something with roots inside my flesh had been abruptly ripped out. He must have had it on a password, I thought, gripping my sternum. He wouldn't have had time for anything else. And had somehow remembered to speak it in the midst of all that, because he was in terrible danger but he wouldn't risk me.

He wouldn't risk me.

And, suddenly, I was furious, throwing shoes, purses, frilly couture—whatever I could get my hands on. I didn't want the gorgeous stuff; I wanted *him*. Scared out of my mind in Faerie was better than being here, alone and not knowing what was happening, not able to help him or even see what was—

I stopped abruptly, staring at myself in a mirror. My hair was everywhere, dried drool was crusted at the corner of my mouth, and a bottle of nail polish had come open and splattered me with red, like a sword slash across my body. I looked crazed.

It was nothing to how I felt.

"Let me see them," I told Faerie unsteadily.

No response.

"Damn it, *let me see them!*"

The silence continued. Maybe she couldn't show me anything. Without the conduit of Lover's Knot, she might have no way to form a bridge between us.

Or maybe she just didn't want to.

Because then I might find a way back there. Might figure out how to pull myself in as she had once done. And she wanted me here, where the fourth task was waiting.

The fourth impossible task.

It hit me then, to the point that I staggered over to a bench and sat down, with too much to take in all at once. It felt like my brain was bursting, but one thing was clear. One thing was freaking crystal.

She was *insane*.

She'd just sent Arsen into the lion's den to preach treason to a bunch of frightened old fey who'd likely kill him as a sacrifice to their god-king before he'd been there five minutes. She'd sent Pritkin, a *half demon*, to take the throne of the Green Fey, who Arsen himself had admitted would gut him before they allowed that. She'd tasked Mircea with recruiting some mythological giants on another world. And me . . .

With fighting a god three hundred years back in time, along with his damned army.

She *is* insane, I thought, chills creeping over me. And here we were, listening to the madwoman, or mad goddess, or mad *planet*, because I didn't even know for sure what she was. Had we gone mad, too?

It certainly looked like it.

And now, maybe most of us were dead.

I bent over, holding my head in my hands and rocking back and forth a little because there was no one to see me. You know them, I told myself. You know what they can do. And that was before Pritkin's shields were reinforced with the power of a couple hundred fey! They're *fine*.

And they probably were.

But they wouldn't stay that way.

"I can't do what you want," I whispered, after a minute. "And neither can they. You're sending them to their deaths."

Nothing.

"Damn it, listen to me! He's here: Zeus, Aeslinn, whatever you want to call him. Right here, right now! So, whatever he did at that castle, it's *done*. It's a part of history, and if I change it, I could *change time*. I could end up trashing the world, might even succeed in wiping us all out, and then who are you going to use? *Who are you going to sacrifice then?*"

More nothing. But it was a pregnant nothing, as if a certain mad goddess was actually listening. Which was too damned bad because I didn't have anything else to say.

I got up and started straightening the little room, slamming things around, and ignoring the way my hands were shaking. And probably making a bad matter worse since I had no idea where anything went anymore. Elspeth, one of my new acolytes, had rearranged everything recently, and now I couldn't find shit.

"And don't tell me that Zeus can time-travel, because he can't, all right?" I added viciously. "He said so—and yes, I know the gods lie! That's all they do, lie and use people. But he isn't lying this time, because I know how he got back there!"

I suddenly paused, my hands stilling on a bunch of wadded up hosiery. I'd told the truth just then, but hadn't recognized it until the words left my mouth. It was as if my subconscious had been putting together clues while I was busy freaking out, and had finally presented me with the answer to one of the biggest questions I'd had: how did Zeus get an army back in time?

And, of course, that was how he did it.

Of course, it was.

I slowly sat down again.

Mircea had taken part in the interrogation of Jonathan, Aeslinn's pet necromancer, because no one else could get anything out of that messed up brain of his. But getting inside someone's head risked them getting inside yours, and Jonathan had learned something. Specifically, that Mircea was desperately looking for a strange little fey who had information about his missing wife.

Since said creature had been imprisoned in Aeslinn's dungeons, it had been an easy thing to let it loose—in eighteenth century Romania—after planting the idea that it could be found there in Mircea's mind. The idea had been to tempt him to use my abilities to shift back in time and find it. And, in turn, to prompt Pritkin and I to go looking for him and fall into a trap.

It hadn't happened quite like that, but close enough. We'd all ended up back in the eighteenth century, where we were promptly captured so that we couldn't interfere in the battle for Issengeir that was about to commence. Jonathan had known that we were sharing gifts—he'd done something similar with Jo—and had figured out that we could pool our abilities and jury-rig a god.

That could result in his master losing the battle, so he'd needed to get us out of the way before it began. But that wasn't good enough for a man who had suffered at our hands. He planned to kill us, but he'd wanted to gloat first.

And that was where I'd made my mistake, I realized, and it hadn't been a small one.

Jonathan had created a portal, a huge thing in the sky beyond the craggy cliffside where we'd all been sitting. It had linked us to the battlefield, and had almost looked like I was watching the latest action movie on the big screen. But it hadn't been fiction, and what I'd witnessed had been traumatic enough that I hadn't thought to ask: how the hell had Jonathan created a freaking time portal?

Because that was unquestionably what it was. We'd passed through it ourselves not long afterward, and had ended up in modern day Faerie. And that . . .

Was impossible.

Especially considering that Jonathan was only borrowing the abilities of a Pythian acolyte, and not a Pythia. Not that even Gertie could have made a portal like that. She'd demonstrated as much by barely sustaining a much smaller one for a couple of minutes while we were trying to spy on Aeslinn.

Yet Jonathan had done it? With only an acolyte's access and little knowledge of the Pythian power? He'd outdone *Gertie*?

No way in hell.

But maybe there was one in heaven.

I blinked, looking at this new idea from all angles, but not finding a flaw. At least, not one that I couldn't answer. I'd wondered why Zeus hadn't just absorbed Jo's abilities for himself, which would have allowed him to time travel without needing any bothersome humans. But maybe Jonathan had gotten to her first, and grafts like that didn't work twice. Or maybe the Pythian power required a human to channel it, because that had been the conditions under which it was first granted.

Of course, my mother hadn't had any problem utilizing it, but then, she'd been admitted to the Pythian Court. She'd been granted access that Zeus didn't have and couldn't get, except from someone who already had it. So, he had used Jonathan and his slaughtered bit of soul to start the portal, and then his own power to expand it.

And he'd expanded it a lot. You could have flown a small jet through that thing. Or marched through an army, because that was what he'd done.

He, Aeslinn, and a large group of fey had used the portal to take up residence in old Romania ahead of the battle, just in case it went wrong. They had lost the first time, before Jonathan went back and messed with time, and they weren't going to risk it again. And when history repeated itself . . . what did they do then?

I didn't know, and I was having trouble concentrating on it. Because I wasn't seeing Zeus or Aeslinn or their damned castle anymore. I was seeing Billy.

He'd been amazing that day. I could see him evading dozens of fey warriors, who might have been well trained but had no experience dealing with ghosts. Much less one who was constantly switching forms.

The metaphysical wind from Faerie streaming through the portal had hit him in bursts, giving him a body one second and taking it away the next, in unpredictable flickers. But he'd used the advantage that gave him, making his way through a gauntlet of fey by attacking them in bodily form and then evading them in spirit. All while waiting for just the right moment—

To strike.

He'd rushed Jonathan, grabbed him out of literally nowhere, and taken him over the cliff. And that was where my thoughts cut out in remembered horror. It had happened so fast, that I hadn't understood what was taking place until it was over.

And hadn't realized I'd lost him until he was already gone.

"Knock 'em dead, kid," had been his last words to me, right before he went over the edge, and I—

I'd fucked it up!

I'd been so emotionally compromised following his death that I hadn't been able to think straight. Not for days, and then, when I could, my thoughts had scattered whenever they even approached that moment. I'd found myself physically running away, surprising Pritkin with extra-long jogs, pushing myself to exhaustion so that I didn't have to think.

And I hadn't.

I'd used every trick in the book to help me grieve by not grieving. It was why I hadn't yet taken his empty necklace off; I couldn't accept that he was gone. But that had had consequences, hadn't it?

Yes, we'd killed the fey that Jonathan had with him. And checked the area for more, sending war mages scattering across the Romanian countryside. But they'd been using human magic, not fey, and they could have missed something.

Just as I had.

Because who said that Zeus had shut the portal down, once they all went through?

The Pythian power guarded the time line and started shrieking if anything threatened it. So, I had assumed that whatever Zeus had done, it had been in Faerie, and that he'd just been hiding out on

Earth before going back there.　　　But what if, instead, he just hadn't finished?

What if he'd kept the portal open, if only as a pinprick to lessen the power loss? But one that he could expand whenever needed? That would allow him to keep working on his plan while also ensuring that Aeslinn showed up in modern-day Faerie before anyone got suspicious.

"They're going back and forth, aren't they?" I whispered.

No one answered, but it didn't matter. The pieces were finally falling into place. Zeus hadn't done something; he was *trying* to do something, and was going back and forth in time to accomplish it.

When he'd told me that he couldn't time travel, it had been both the truth and a lie. He couldn't go just anywhere he wanted. But he could travel between the present and that windswept hillside in eighteenth century Romania, courtesy of a dead man's spell that he himself was fueling.

He *had* made plans, as Gertie had said, ones that didn't involve Pritkin. But they'd been interrupted by our trip back in time to that damned castle, during which he'd remembered a man who he'd been made to forget. One who held the key to almost unlimited power.

So, he'd dropped everything and gone after us. First trying to drain Pritkin through me, and when that didn't work, by kidnapping him and Mircea. But that last had been a fluke, hadn't it? Zeus had gotten lucky when my guys followed a goat through a portal that neither of them should have been able to see, and neither he nor Aeslinn had been in camp when it happened.

And the fey who had been there were clueless.

Aeslinn's people didn't know much about Earth, and hadn't realized that they'd just captured one of the leaders in the war against them, along with the man their king wanted above all others. They'd only reported it once they finished cleaning up, causing Zeus and his puppet to have to travel all the way back to Faerie from somewhere else. Or somewhen.

It would explain the delay in his arrival at camp. The message about the two captives had almost certainly gone to Dolgrveginn, the city in the clouds that I'd seen in my vision, but Aeslinn was no longer there. He had been there, yelling at Arsen, just prior to my shifting his general halfway across Faerie. I had assumed that he'd remained in place, striding about his throne room and acting crazed, but what if he hadn't?

He had Caedmon threatening invasion, a bunch of mysterious "pets" that needed food he was fast running out of, and a bunch of disloyal nobles that he worried about almost as much as they worried about him. I didn't know everything he was facing, but I knew one thing: he wanted this war over every bit as much as I did. So, would it be surprising that he left shortly after Arsen, to try to make that happen?

He'd almost certainly gone back to Romania to finish the job that he had started, only to get called away yet again, when word finally reached him about Pritkin and Mircea. And to find, once he made it back to Faerie, that I had rescued his god's prize before he could get there!

He had therefore grabbed me instead, and when I escaped . . .

What had he done then?

I stared at the carpet, frowning. He'd sent the army after us, hoping that they might get lucky, sure. But he'd also probably gone back to his first plan, the one that he'd been working on before we kept rudely interrupting him.

If he couldn't win one way, he'd win another.

The only thing I didn't understand was why his dragon form had been so huge when I saw it in Faerie, compared to what it had looked like on Earth. But maybe the location was the reason. He wasn't on Earth then, or right next to a portal to it, which sapped his power; he was in his own realm where he was stronger.

So, instead of three hundred years passing and bulking him up, it had simply been the difference between seeing him in his element and seeing him on an alien world. Like the wound where his missing hand had once been, which had looked centuries old, but which could be put down to ramped-up healing abilities from carrying around a god. I'd already seen what they could do on the Thames.

I just sat there, feeling stunned for a moment. Because my crazy theory explained everything: why Aeslinn was so foul tempered—he had victory in his grasp, but Zeus was obsessed with his prize and kept pulling him off target. Why it had taken him so long to arrive at camp when he had a portal right to it. And why Faerie had jerked me into her realm so abruptly. She might not want to work with me any more than I did her, but she had realized what was happening and was desperate.

Kind of like I was now.

Because I might have figured out what was going on, but how did it help?

"I'm going to need more than that," I told her. "Pritkin, Mircea and I—not to mention Mircea's entire family—barely beat a small part of Zeus's power, just whatever was leftover in my veins from that battle on the Thames. What am I supposed to do against the real thing? When I don't even know what his plan is?"

Faerie did not seem to have an opinion on that, and it infuriated me.

"You throw these crazy ideas at us, do this, do that, hop to it! Risk your lives for me, your friends, your lovers, everything. But don't expect me to risk anything for you, or even to tell you how to accomplish any of it. And you think that is somehow going to *work*?

I'm telling you; *I need more than that!* Or you can find yourself another—"

And just that fast, something grabbed me.

Chapter Thirty-Three

How do I keep it on?" Cassie asked.

Mircea turned from the wardrobe to see her frowning at the oval of black velvet in her hands. The mask was a moretta, designed to cover the entire face, except for two almond-shaped openings for the eyes. There were, of course, no straps.

"Open your mouth."

She looked up at him, blue eyes startled. "Why?"

"Trust me."

She shot him the look that deserved, the same that one of his own kind might have returned for a similar suggestion. Cassie wasn't vampire, but she'd grown up among them, and had absorbed a healthy dose of their cynicism. Requests for blind faith always raised her hackles.

"Why?" she asked again, more suspiciously.

Mircea took the mask and turned it over, displaying the small knob that jutted out from behind the mouth. "You're meant to bite it."

She stared at it for a moment, then turned a pleasing shade of pink. "I . . . that's . . . oooh."

"The Moretta was quite popular in eighteenth century Venice."

"I'll bet it was! God forbid that a woman think she has something to say!"

"It originated as a mask worn by women on their way to convents to confess," he told her, amused. "It was designed to keep them silent, and thus anonymous, ensuring that penance was assigned without respect to their social standing."

"So, if they couldn't talk, how did they confess?"

Mircea paused, having pulled one of those shapeless T-shirt abominations halfway over her curly head. "Do you know, I have told this story many times, yet no one else has ever asked me that?"

"Well, maybe they should. And I can undress myself!"

Something she demonstrated by pulling the shirt the rest of the way off, and then standing there with her arms crossed over her chest, despite the fact that she was still wearing a scrap of satin far more attractive than the garment that had concealed it.

"If you prefer." He stretched out on the bed and propped his head on his hand, preparing to enjoy the view.

"That wasn't . . . you're not . . . I didn't mean . . ." she stopped, probably sensing how much he was enjoying this. It had been some time since he'd been with a woman who recalled how to blush. It was refreshing—to a point, he decided, as she turned her back in order to strip off her jeans.

He would never understand modern fashion. These days, women wore satin and lace next to their skin, and clothes no self-respecting peasant would have once deemed acceptable on the outside. Jeans. He regarded them with disapproval. Heavy, thick, ugly things, serviceable for the miners and cattle ranchers for whom they had been originally intended, perhaps, but much less appealing on the rounded contours of a woman's body. Such softness was made for *finer things, for silks and satins, laces and jewels, for silken stockings with seams up the back, conveniently pointing the way to—*

"Do you have to watch me?" Blue eyes regarded him over a pale shoulder.

"It is a small room."

"You could look away."

Mircea considered that. He supposed he ought to tell her that the dark canal outside had turned the room's window into a tolerable substitute for a mirror. But he hardly saw why that mattered when he had seen the lovely curves on display more than once. And more than seen, he thought, smiling, as Cassie's eyes narrowed.

"It would be an interesting exercise in self-control," he agreed. "But then, I am exercising enough as it is."

She didn't ask what he meant. She merely made one of her little huffing noises, and tossed the jeans over a chair. And went back to what she'd been doing.

The panties, he was glad to note, matched the bra. He thought that they might have been among the sets he had gifted her, but wasn't sure. However, it was gratifying to see that modern society was slowly circling back to the bare look of his day—from pantalettes and bloomers, to briefs and bikinis, and now to thongs. He much preferred the latter, particularly when they ended, as this one did, with a small curl of ribbon over the sweet, firm mounds below, like a bow on the nicest of packages.

Then again, there was something to be said for the older fashions. And for all those layers that women had once believed it necessary to wear. A man really felt like he'd accomplished something by the time he finally managed to—

He belatedly noticed Cassie frowning at him again, as she bent to pick up the heavy folds of samite that made up her evening's attire. "Are you listening?"

"Absolutely."

"Then answer the question!"

"And what question would that be, dulceáță?" he asked distractedly. She had figured out what he'd known all along, that the gown would not accommodate her bra. The low, square cut necklines of current Venetian fashion were infamous throughout Europe, even leading to a fad in rouged nipples since they were so often on display.

This dress wasn't that extreme, but modern undergarments were not going to work. Which was why the bra quickly joined the heap of discarded clothing. Leaving her wearing only the thong and a pair of eighteenth-century silk stockings that she pulled on, and tied with embroidered garters over the knee.

"About the mask!" Cassie said impatiently, looking up from her work.

"Oh, yes." He closed his eyes to better concentrate. "They became popular outside the convents as they concealed a woman's voice as well as her face. Renaissance Venice was a small town by today's standards. Everyone knew everyone—at least, everyone in the nobility did. Your voice could give you away at inopportune moments, at a gambling establishment, a theater, when visiting a lower-class lover . . ."

"That doesn't explain why I have to wear one," she said, her own voice strained. Mircea opened his eyes to find her struggling with the heavy folds of the dress.

Being a gentleman, of course he went to help.

"If you're wearing a moretta, no one will expect you to speak," he explained, moving behind her. "And while your Italian is perfectly acceptable for modern conversation, anyone of the period would doubtless find it . . . odd."

"And we can't afford to attract attention," she said reluctantly.

Mircea didn't answer. The dress was on her shoulders, but that left it open in front, as all the supplementary elements required by a fashionable woman's toilette had been ignored. His hands slid around the rich, gold shot silk to the equally smooth skin that it was doing a very poor job of concealing.

"Mircea," she said, and it was difficult to tell whether his name was meant as a warning or encouragement. He decided to assume the latter until more evidence presented itself, and ran his hands up to the soft, warm mounds spilling out of the bodice.

There was nothing else like the feel of a woman's body, he thought, pulling her back against him. Nothing else in nature had the supple, yielding strength of it, the warm, satiny feel, the rich, intoxicating scent. He'd spent five hundred years exploring them and never had enough of the little sounds they made, the ways they moved, the enticing feel of their skin under his lips, the surge of pride that came from making them—

"W—we're going to be late," Cassie protested.

"Something that would be a concern if I was not with a time traveler," he murmured, kissing her neck, while his hands went to work further down. Maybe he'd get some rouge, after all, but not for other's eyes. Just his own.

She shivered delightfully against him. "That's against the rules."

"You are Pythia," he reminded her. "You make the rules."

That was apparently the wrong thing to say, judging by how quickly she turned in his arms. "I don't! And I shouldn't even be here. We shouldn't be here!"

"You know why we are," he said, his eyes serious for once. "This is important. We need Gabriella's vote."

It was an understatement. For the first time, the six senates that ruled the vampire world were considering an alliance under a single ruler. It was something that none of them wanted, but they were at war, and a concerted effort was needed if they weren't to face destruction. But the ingrained habits, and hatreds, of centuries were not so easily put aside, and getting the number of nods he required had proven to be the greatest challenge of his career. He had enticed, bribed, flattered, begged and threatened his way to a larger margin than anyone would have believed possible just a few short months ago.

But it wouldn't be enough.

Not without Gabriella.

"And you think you're going to get it how?" Cassie asked.

Mircea had neglected to give her the full details of their mission, not wanting to put her off. But now that they were here, he supposed he should come clean. That or get packed off back to Vegas, considering that she was giving him a stare worthy of her predecessor.

"This is an era of change," he said. "The dual consulship that governed the European Senate for three hundred years is coming to an end. Our consul is preparing to leave for North America to establish a sixth great senate. Her co-consul is staying behind, ruling alone for the first time. There was bound to be trouble."

"Trouble?"

"People see the change of regime as an opportunity, and Anthony as weak without his Cleopatra."

"You mean they're going to kill him?"

"If they can." Mircea went to fetch the rest of her ensemble. "They hope at least to drive him out. Some masters have been chafing under the consuls' iron fists for some time, and believe this to be their best chance to regain autonomy. Others see an opportunity to vie for the top seat."

"They could vie for it now," she pointed out.

Mircea shook his head. "Anthony was known to be practically indestructible in duels, even before acquiring Louis-Cesare as a *champion. Which happened shortly after the would-be rebellion, come to think of it. I often wondered why he thought he needed the extra help . . ."*

"But he doesn't have him now, right?"

"No, but dueling Anthony was a fool's bet. He'd run you around the ring, letting you hack away at him while he healed virtually instantaneously. I saw him heal once while a sword remained inside of his body. It was messier coming out than going in."

Cassie winced.

"His go-to method was to wait until an opponent started to tire, then dart in for the kill. But in battle . . . well. It doesn't have to be one-on-one, does it? And even great Anthony has his limits."

"So, why didn't it work? This rebellion of theirs?"

"The usual reason. Some bright soul realized that he could be a minor level master in the new regime or a hero to the old, after selling the revolutionaries out. He chose the latter."

"Then . . . nothing happened?"

Mircea nodded, bringing over the large armful of accoutrements—chemise, corset, panniers, and petticoats—that he'd assembled. As well as the elaborate triangular stomacher, meant to fill in the bodice of the dress, and heavily embroidered in gold thread and seed pearls. They weren't going to fit Cassie perfectly; this house belonged to a woman of his acquaintance who was currently out of town. But it would be close enough.

Cassie frowned, watching him. "I need all that?"

"You'll be glad of it soon," he assured her. "It's chilly tonight."

"But it's all so . . . much."

Mircea wasn't sure if she meant the three-foot train, the scads of handmade lace around the ballgown's three-quarter length sleeves, or the twenty-five yards of silk in the dress. It was beautiful fabric, which could manage to look gold at one angle and ruby red at another, but it wasn't lightweight, especially in quantity. The whole mountain of finery was almost bigger than she was.

"That was the idea," he said, laying it all on the bed. "Go big or go home is not a new concept."

She appeared unconvinced. But fortunately, her mind was more on the mission than her wardrobe, and she quickly returned to the point. "Then how are you going to blackmail Gabriella? 'Cause I assume that's where this is going?"

Mircea nodded. "Our information was that there was a wide scale rebellion planned, and Gabriella was a ring leader, passing orders from the far-flung conspirators to the coordinating council in Venice. However, while others were executed, we could never prove anything against her."

"But you think you can now?"

"Let us hope so. In our time, she is the leader of a powerful coalition on the European Senate, and as such, her vote carries others. To be precise, her vote carries five, which would get me almost to my goal."

"How convenient."

Mircea decided to ignore the obvious sarcasm. "Isn't it, though?"

Cassie gasped in reply, probably because he'd pulled off the dress, dropped the chemise over her head, and was now lacing her into the corset. Mircea loosened it as much as he could and have her fit into the dress. It did not seem to improve her mood.

"You're the Senate's chief negotiator. You can't think of a better way to gain her support than blackmail?"

"Blackmail is an excellent negotiating tactic."

"Like seduction?" she asked tightly. And Mircea began to understand why she was being so prickly this evening.

"I realize that it may be hard to imagine," he said, letting his hands rest momentarily on her shoulders. "But not everyone finds *me as charming as you do. Getting the evidence will require a bit more finesse."*

"Who said I find you charming?" she asked, playing with a lock of his hair.

Mircea smirked.

She noticed, and snatched her hand away. "I can think of a few other words," she said, crossing her arms and planting her feet.

As far as intimidation went, that look left a lot to be desired, but he bit back the comment. But apparently not the twinkle in his eyes. Cassie's frown tipped over into a scowl.

"Are you going to explain why the taxi service needs to get dressed up like . . . like this?" she demanded as he tied on the panniers. They weren't the ridiculous things of the French court, which could be three feet wide on either side, making the women wearing them look like they were carrying a sizeable table underneath their skirts. But they also weren't the simple bum roll used by the lower classes.

Cassie looked down at herself, and then up at him, and clearly had no idea how lovely she looked, with her curls shining in the candlelight and her figure exaggerated by the over-the-top fashion of the times. It might have made her look silly to modern eyes, with ribbons and embroidery on even the petticoats and lace everywhere. Just an adorable little doll-like creature . . .

But Mircea didn't have modern eyes. And some of the most dangerous women he'd ever known had once dressed like this. Although none of them had held a fraction of her power.

Yet she didn't see it. Even now she didn't, despite the fact that they had recently discovered who her mother was. Cassie had been surprised by that, astounded even, yet it hadn't seemed to change her at all.

If anything, Mircea thought it had made her more apprehensive, more conscious of the burden of her blood, more aware of the power that prickled at her fingertips. And more afraid of misusing it as the gods had done, to their own and their followers' destruction. It never ceased to amaze him that that was what kept her up at night: the fear that her power might be used to hurt, instead of to heal.

He didn't know what to make of her sometimes. He comforted himself with the fact that the Senate never did. From their perspective, everyone was on the take; everyone had a price. And the longer it took for her to name hers, the more worried they became that they could not meet it.

Was she going to try to take it all? To attempt to rule, and rule alone, as the gods had once done? Was she not negotiating, not demanding, not conveying her desires because she desired everything?

They worried and schemed, and some even moved against her—and were blocked as soon as they did so, and quietly dealt with. So quietly that no one seemed to be sure whether he had protected her, or she had done it herself. That was good. That uncertainty about just what she could do stayed hands and quieted whispers.

There would come a day when she would no longer need his protection, and he was sorry for it. But he was excited too, to see what she might become, this tiny goddess. Who was looking at him impatiently, because he had yet to answer her.

"My mental abilities are extensive," he said mildly. "But even I might have a problem convincing people that I am a five foot two, beautiful brunette."

"Brunette?"

"Don't worry; that's why we brought the wig."

"What wig?" Her eyes went to the box on the bed. The rather large box. And widened. "Is that . . .?"

Mircea just smiled and turned her around again. And began pinning her into the complicated, multipart dress. Cassie watched him in the mirror, biting her lip.

He finally finished the toilette, including the wig. It was ridiculously large, but went well with the dress, which required balancing out. The last touch were some rubies set in gold at her ears and neck. "There," he told her. "Now you look like a rebellious countess."

"Which is necessary why?"

"The conspirators are using humans as messengers, to avoid magical eavesdroppers, and because nobody pays attention to them. Particularly not in a city that has tourism as its lifeblood."

"And we're going to intercept the messenger."

Mircea nodded. "He will deliver his letter straight into your lovely hands. I will tell you where to be, and distract the countess long enough to make her late for the rendezvous. All you have to do is palm the note."

"So, I do all the work while you 'distract' a 'beautiful brunette?'" Her hands smoothed up the front of his shirt, in a manner that should have been seductive. Only there was enough nail involved to make Mircea think of a cat, temptingly showing its furry underbelly—right before the claws came out.

"I can assure you, seduction is not on the menu tonight."

"Not even of me?"

"I don't need to seduce you," he said, helping her on with a pair of gold slippers. And running a light hand up the back of her calf, to tickle behind her left knee. It jerked slightly, as it always did, despite her claiming not to be ticklish.

"And why is that?"

He let his eyes go big and round and guileless, a spot-on imitation of the look she always gave him when pretending to innocence. "We're already here."

Blue eyes flashed. "And we're about to be late!"

She flounced out of the room, leaving him alone and grinning. Their errand shouldn't take long, and the night was young. Which was good; he had plans for it.

Chapter Thirty-Four

"Cassie?" the resonant voice came from my bedroom, breaking me out of my trance. "You about done in there?"

Marco.

Shit.

"Uh, uh . . . just a minute!" That probably would have been more convincing if I hadn't had a panicked squeak in my voice.

But it must have worked, since he didn't immediately come in, probably afraid of catching me half dressed. Marco was like most vamps—not to mention most gladiators, who had frequently practiced in the nude. He didn't have a lot of bodily modesty.

Except where I was concerned. Only it wasn't modesty in my case; it was respect. I was his boss now, no matter how rarely we acted like it, and vamps took that kind of thing seriously. Which meant that I probably had a minute to get my shit together.

And I needed it, because I had just been attacked by a rogue brassiere.

It was pale blue satin, cool and almost buttery to the touch, part of a set that Mircea had gifted me back when we were together. I thought I'd gotten rid of them all, bundling them up and tossing them out after we broke up, since it hurt too much to wear them. To feel the luxe lace and soft satin, and remember other things . . .

But I guessed not, because it suddenly flew up at my face.

"How do I keep it on?" Cassie asked.

Mircea turned from the wardrobe to see her frowning at the oval of black velvet in her hands. The mask was a moretta, designed to cover the entire face, except for two almond-shaped openings for the eyes. There were, of course, no straps.

"Open your mouth."

"Cassie?" Marco's voice came again, wrenching me back to the present. "Is something wrong?"

Yes, I thought, panting, and ripped the damned bra off my head, where it had been clinging like a face-hugger out of *Alien*. And scrambled away from it, because it wasn't a vision trying to have its way with me this time. It was an imprint.

A very weird one.

That was the bra I'd been wearing that night in Venice, which meant—technically—it could have picked up some of what had happened. But while the world was being etched by imprints all the time, soft surfaces rarely held onto them well. Maybe some old tapestries, hanging dusty and ignored in a great hall, but nothing that regularly went through the laundry!

And then there was the fact that it was trying to eat my face.

The bra flew at me like a demented blue bat and I stumbled back, ducking behind the shoe island. And toppled a pile of clothes onto the damned thing when it started to follow. And then Marco's voice came again, causing my head to jerk up. The echoing quality of his voice made it clear that he was now in my tile-covered bathroom.

"Cassie?"

"Almost done!"

I had no idea how much time had passed while I was mentally away, because Earth and Faerie had different time streams. But since he wasn't freaking out, I guessed that it hadn't been the half day or so that it felt like to me. However, he was sounding worried, and Marco didn't do worried for long.

So . . . yeah.

Find some freaking clothes, already!

"Cassie? Damn it—"

"On my way!"

And I would have been, except for a pale, blue satin bra strap, peeking around a corner.

Shit!

The crazed piece of underwear lunged for me again and I threw a dress at it, which happened to be Big Bird. But despite the fact that, between the feathers and the embroidery, Augustine's creation weighed a ton, the bra didn't collapse onto the floor. Instead, it rose higher into the air, carting the dress along with it like some kind of feathered specter.

And that was bad.

That was very bad.

Ghosts might mess with you, but they rarely attacked. They lost more power than they gained going after a living human, and normally backed off after scaring the crap out of you. But imprints were mindless; they didn't make calculations like that. And while they did lose power over time, as they were slowly overwritten by other things, in the meantime they could really mess you up.

People had been known to get lost in especially strong ones, which could put your brain into a death spiral where it lived the imprinted event over and over, unable to break free. Some victims had ended up in insane asylums, on feeding tubes, with doctors unable to explain what had happened to them. And while this one didn't contain one of the usual nightmares, it was as strong as shit and I didn't want to die in there!

"Cassie," Marco warned. "If you don't come out, right now—"

"No! Just . . . just give me a minute. One more minute!"

I didn't want Marco to be grabbed by the damned thing, either. Or have to explain what was going on when I didn't know myself. I had enough problems; I didn't need my guys thinking I was crazy, too.

And then the dress dove, backing me into a corner.

There was nothing over here but mirrors, so I snatched off my stained T-shirt and wrapped it around my hand, to keep the feathered monstrosity from touching my skin. And I succeeded—sort of. I managed to grab the dress around the waist and hold it back, so that the imprint couldn't drag me back under.

But it was struggling and fighting and—

Goddamnit! I was not getting beaten up by a freaking bra!

Only I kind of was.

I thought about aging it to powder, but the spell died on my lips. My power had been going crazy ever since I soaked up the remnants of the goat guy's energy and I didn't want to risk it. So, I snatched up a belt off the floor, intending to tie the demented thing down long enough to escape.

Only to be treated to the sight of the bra strap slowly emerging from the neck of the dress, like something out of a horror movie. Or like a cobra ready to strike, and the next second, it lunged, I screamed, and it was abruptly snatched out of the air. But not by me.

"Marco!" I yelled, to be heard over the sound of half a dozen .44 Magnum slugs slamming into the once fine fabric, nailing it to the floor. And then two more to be sure, because Marco used an eight-round magazine.

He ejected the clip, slammed another one home, and looked at me.

"Sorry. Thought we got 'em all." At least, that's what it looked like he said. I was momentarily deaf and couldn't be sure.

"*What?*"

He said something else, but my ears were ringing so loudly that I couldn't hear. And now my eyes were stinging from the gun smoke, so I couldn't see much, either. Which was why I flinched when a huge hand cupped my face and the clamor in my head abruptly calmed down, so fast that the lack of sound staggered me.

"There, that's better, isn't it?" he asked.

I honestly wasn't sure.

And then he cursed. "The *fuck*?"

I looked around, my heart in my throat, expecting another attack since that was all I freaking got anymore. But I couldn't spot one. Unfortunately, that wasn't true for Marco.

He grabbed me by the arms and looked me over, horror dawning on his face. I didn't understand for a second, until I caught a glimpse of myself in a mirror and winced. My long-sleeved T-shirt had covered a multitude of sins, but I'd stripped that off.

And what was underneath wasn't pretty.

My body might have been resting in front of Gertie's fireplace for most of yesterday, but it had been in a fight for its life the day before, and it showed. Mircea had tried to heal me after our battle with Zeus, and had somewhat succeeded. But while I was alive and functional, I was as scarred up as an old piece of furniture.

The bulbs in here were less forgiving than the lamplight at Gertie's, the last place I'd seen my true reflection. And they were busily showing off all the burns and bruises, the healing wounds with puckered skin, even the bone-deep line that a god's wrath had carved into my forearm. I thought that some of the smaller scars might be a bit more blurred around the edges than before, but that could be my stinging eyes fuzzing my vision.

"Going to have trouble wearing strapless, from now on," I said, trying to lighten the mood, only to stop at Marco's expression.

He very definitely did not get the joke. For a moment, I saw the face that others had glimpsed through the years, mostly ones who were no longer alive to talk about it. The complete lack of expression on the strong features, the eyes equally dead except for pinpricks of fire deep inside the pupils, the fangs out and fully extended . . .

He was terrifying.

And, for a moment, I was duly terrified. Until I noticed: the hands holding me were firm, but so gentle that they didn't even hurt my bruises. He was furious, but not with me.

He turned me around, still silent, and traced some large wound I couldn't see that ran halfway down my back. It must have been a deep one; I could feel his finger following the channel it had carved, like tracing the course of a river. It made me shiver, but not because the skin there was especially sensitive. If anything, the opposite was true, with the scar tissue robbing me of sensation.

But while I couldn't feel much physically, I could feel plenty mentally, a tangled snarl of emotions—shock, pain, shame, and regret—hitting me hard. I didn't have Mircea's abilities, so Marco had to be projecting his feelings, something a master with his experience just didn't do. Only I guessed I was wrong there, since the initial barrage was followed by their more forceful counterparts: disbelief, agony, humiliation and guilt.

Especially the latter, with even the spillover like a great wave swamping us, because he hadn't been there; he hadn't protected me.

"You couldn't have—" I began, but the words were drowned out by another crashing wave of sentiment. And if the last had been a high tide, this one was a tsunami. An ocean-liner-wrecking, coastline-savaging monster that washed all other feelings away and left only one in their place.

Rage.

"Who did this to you?" Even the voice was different, I thought, suppressing a shudder. Only not well enough, apparently, since he cursed again. "*Who?*"

"It's . . . complicated," I said, stalling for time. Which I couldn't use, as I honestly didn't know what to say here.

This needed a hell of a lie, and I'd never had much luck lying to Marco.

"I thought you'd had a bad day," he rasped, his hands tightening. "Got thrown around the training salle at Gertie's. But no acolyte did this!"

"No."

"Then who did?"

I didn't say anything that time. Not because I didn't trust Marco—although, in fact, I *didn't* trust Marco at the moment, who I could see in the mirror, and who looked perfectly capable of taking on Zeus himself right now. But because he was a vamp.

And they were the closest thing to a true hive mind on Earth.

He would never willingly break a confidence, but that didn't mean that some stray thought might not get out, or that some master with mental abilities might not go snooping. Mircea's guys were less susceptible to that sort of thing than most, since they borrowed some of their master's talents. But less susceptible isn't immune, and we were parked on top of a hotel stuffed with high-level vamps.

And plenty of them were curious.

Marco also had been adopted into the family, not made a vamp by Mircea, so his mental abilities weren't as strong to begin with. And he was emancipated now, weakening them even further. That had been done for me, so that he could head up my bodyguards while allowing me to attempt to look impartial. So, I couldn't complain, but I also couldn't risk this getting out.

Having people who were reeling from the cost of the invasion of Faerie find out that our next challenger was the king of the gods would be . . . not good. Especially when I hadn't figured out what to do about it. If there was anything that could inspire a general panic, that would be it.

And I really didn't want to see what the Senate did when they were panicked.

"You're going to start talking," Marco said, in that freaky voice. "Right now—"

"I can't—" I began, only to feel mental fingers poking into my mind before I'd even finished the sentence.

I gasped out loud, because Marco didn't do that. Not to family; not to me. It was a violation of privacy, an assault, the kind of thing that you saved for enemies—

"Then tell me who the enemy is, and I'll do it to him!" Marco snarled.

"I told you; I *can't*—"

"Goddamnit! A name, a face, I can't protect you if I don't—"

And just that fast, he got it. Maybe he was better at this mental stuff than I'd thought. Or maybe I was just too tired to properly resist, having had too many shocks, too close together, for too many days now.

But it was like a flood gate had opened, and he got everything: the fight on the Thames, the chat with a god in Gertie's garden, the second fight in my bedroom at her court, with silver fire literally eating its way across my body. And then my terror in that tent in Faerie, and the mad scramble across an enemy camp, heart pounding, vision blurring, death nipping at my heels. I saw when he realized how close it had all been, when he understood exactly who we were fighting.

Even worse, I saw when the shock opened his mind, when the information spread outward like another flood, spilling over the guys in the suite and then spreading outward into the family at large—

"No!" I yelled, grabbing the mental threads Marco was showing me, and jerking back. I was just trying to slow down the spread of information before it was too late, but I ended up doing more than that.

A lot more.

I ripped the godly name, the face, everything, out of his mind, and not only his. It felt like the information was on strings, and when I pulled back, they came with me. I drew it out, all of it, every last bit of knowledge from every last mind, like winding a skein of wool around my hand, even though I couldn't even do that to a low-level vamp, much less to a two-thousand-year-old master.

But I did it anyway. And saw in my mind's eye hundreds of astonished faces abruptly go blank; saw a vamp who had just dropped a platter in shock stare at it in confusion, not remembering why he'd been so clumsy; saw heads turn to look around them in bewilderment, as if they'd been about to say something, but had forgotten the thread of their thoughts. Because I had it, wrapped around my mental hand, even though I didn't know what to do with it.

I didn't even know how to feel, standing there, holding a thousand minds in my grip. If I let go, would it damage them? Would it leave them forever as dead eyed as Marco currently was, like a computer set on idle? Had I destroyed half of the family, including every vamp at my court, with my carelessness?

You knew your magic was going crazy! I thought, furiously. You knew not to use it! What have you *done*?

I didn't know, and once again, I didn't have anybody to ask. Mircea would know what to do, but he wasn't here and I couldn't contact him. I had to figure this out on my own, but I didn't know anything about the mind. That was his realm, like magic was Pritkin's. I didn't do this!

I wasn't even supposed to be *able* to do this. I stood there, panicking, which was starting to become my default, because I didn't understand what was happening to me lately. Not any of it!

Pritkin and I had magnified my power on a couple of occasions, giving me extra energy, but it had never been like this. It had been a great river pouring through us, like when we'd battled Zeus for my life. It had been so powerful that it burned . . .

Because Pritkin, Mircea and I had been channeling *Pythian* power, I realized, growing *Pythian* energy, hurling *Pythian* might into a single spell or at a single enemy. It had hurt because I was a human trying to channel the power of a god, and just getting some help bearing the burden. But this wasn't like that. This . . .

Was mine.

The energy the goat creature had been shedding had been absorbed by me. Not by the Pythian power, a well that I borrowed from, just like I borrowed abilities from Mircea and Pritkin. But *me*. Cassie Palmer, the little nobody with a goddess for a mother . . .

Who was finally acting like it.

I stood there for a moment longer, clutching a thousand minds in my fist, and then opened my mental grasp and let them go. I watched them evaporate into nothing, all those strings, all that knowledge. The same nothing that was on Marco's face—for a second.

And then it was like his brain rebooted, and an expression crossed his features.

It was gentle amusement.

"There, that's better, isn't it?" he asked, and patted my cheek. And then his eyes widened.

"Don't see me," I said harshly. "You don't . . . you don't notice anything unusual about me."

The dark brown eyes, which a second ago had looked so shocked, abruptly flipped back to normal. And smiled. "What were we talking about?"

The fact that I'm going *insane*?

"You . . . you were saying something about . . . about getting them all?" I said shakily.

But Marco didn't seem to notice.

"All the stuff that got a dose of whatever was floating around in here," he said. "The wild magic and all that."

I nodded silently.

"Although we thought it missed the bedrooms, but I guess we were wrong," he added, clapping a hand onto my shoulder. "Relax for a minute. I'll go get the girls."

"What girls?" I asked, but my reaction was slow from shock, and he was already gone.

Chapter Thirty-Five

I stared after him.

Relax.

Sure.

But I was a little wobbly on my feet, so I took his advice and sat back down on the bench. And then just stayed there, wondering how to feel. It wasn't every day that you discovered you were a goddess.

Of course, I wasn't. I was a demi-goddess with delusions of grandeur who was going to get bitch slapped back to reality real freaking fast once the power surging through my veins was used up. But for the moment . . .

I raised a hand and could almost see tiny sparks of golden light follow the movement, and whirl around my palm. It was probably my imagination, because I was too out of it to restrain my brain, which felt like it was just doing its own thing up there. But while the visuals might be suspect, the idea behind them was sound.

That goat guy had been shedding godly energy like it was going out of style, and I'd absorbed a whopping amount of it straight into my very human veins. No wonder my power had been going haywire! I'd always been the brakes on this train, me and my complete lack of stamina. That was why Pritkin ran me all over the hotel, trying his best to whip me into shape.

How strong I was physically had a very big impact on how much power I could wield.

Until now.

I stared at the pretty sparks, and watched them chase each other through my fingers, over my palm, and across the back of my hand. They looked like the jewelry Devi sometimes wore, tiny golden chains that connected finger rings to a bracelet, and glinted under the lights whenever she moved. Only there was an extra animation to these, almost like they were alive.

They reminded me of playing children, chasing each other around and around a back yard. Or newborn lambs, gamboling across a field. Or a bunch of excited puppies—

A wave of stark terror slammed into me out of nowhere. It washed gooseflesh over my skin, had my heart threatening to pound out of my chest, and made me dizzy enough to go down on one knee. A panic attack; I recognized it immediately, having had enough of them through the years.

I just didn't know why.

But this one was bad enough to threaten to knock me out.

Fury saved me, as red hot and all-encompassing as Marco's had been. It hit like a fist, without warning, just as the fear had. And for a moment, the conflicting emotions wrestled inside my skin, like two rival armies clashing.

Once again, fury won.

I was tired of being scared. I was tired of jumping at my own shadow, of second guessing everything I did, of living with my spine so tense that it ached when I got out of bed in the morning. I was tired of it all!

So, get off your damned knees already!

I got off my knees, grabbed a pair of Keds and shoved my feet into them. I didn't bother with socks, since I didn't know where they were. And because I didn't care.

Gertie had always said that, if someone wanted to see her in her Pythian finery, they shouldn't show up without warning, should they? She'd said that waiting was good for them, that it reminded them that getting an audience was a privilege, not a right. She'd said—

She'd said that some years went by and nothing happened, and then decades passed in a couple of days. I felt like that today, as if there'd been this major shift, some seismic change that I didn't understand or want. I wanted her, suddenly and fiercely, because she'd know what to do.

But, instead, I was Pythia now.

I got up, found another long-sleeved Tee, and started to pull it over my head. Only to realize that my bra was stained as well. It was splattered with the same blood-colored nail polish that had decorated my shirt, causing me to start searching for a replacement.

And to pause again, when I caught sight of the crazed one on the floor.

The now burnt and tattered brassiere was writhing menacingly against the carpet, as if it was trying to pry itself off the slugs to come at me again. I stared at it for a moment and wondered about my life. And then I wondered about other things, like the fact that I'd just been to a second vampire ball inside of a week.

I jerked my mind away from that thought pretty quickly. I'd done my quota of thinking for a while, and my brain felt bruised. Only to remember a blustery day in early fall, when Gertie had dragged me through not one, not two, but three different puzzles in the same afternoon, several of which had had an arduous physical component to them. We'd finally ended up back in the pretty garden behind her court, for an afternoon tea that I was too tired to eat, sprawling instead on an uncomfortable wrought iron chair while she deliberately buttered a scone at me.

"Did you think a Pythia only gets one challenge per day?" she'd asked, noticing my expression, and eaten her snack.

I scowled at the memory, and went back to hunting for support garments. I finally found a sports bra in an accessory bin, poked at it cautiously, and then jerked it on when it failed to drag me into a nightmare. I followed it up with the T-shirt and finally!

I was dressed.

Would wonders never cease?

I grabbed a brush and my makeup bag, and sat cross-legged on the floor in front of one of the closet's many mirrors, to make myself look as normal as possible. The light was considerably better in here than in my dressing room, where I needed better bulbs. I hadn't asked about them since vamps, especially master level vamps, were shit at knowing about normal stuff, and the hotel's maintenance division was already run off their feet dealing with a bunch of prima donna freeloaders in the form of the Senate.

I hated to bother them about something as stupid as slightly too weak lightbulbs. But it wasn't like I could just shift down to the local hardware store and get them for myself. Being Pythia gave you all kinds of little problems, as well as the big ones.

Like Venice, I thought, and almost poked a mascara wand in my eye.

I sighed and gave in.

The night shown in the imprint had ended up being kind of fun, despite the fact that I'd been dragging around fifty pounds of samite. Because Gabriella had preferred to do her business at parties, and she threw a good one. The ballroom had been expansive, maybe a third of the size of a football field, with high ceilings painted with murals of cupids and nymphs and Zeus enthroned in glory, which was kind of disturbing now.

It had needed the room. There must have been several thousand people there, with servants having to hold trays over their heads to get appetizers to people and dancers making balletic movements to get around the forest of panniers. Not surprisingly, the party had spilled out all over the house and into the gardens, and was still a crush.

That was by design, allowing Gabriella to talk to any number of people in an evening, all of whom had a perfectly good reason for being there, and who were hard to identify thanks to their masks. Venetians wore them for half the year, stretching the concept of Mardi Gras to the breaking point and then some, by linking it to every saint's day and festival they could think of. And with the conspirators using humans as messengers, there were no tell-tale auras to identify them as would have been the case for vamps.

It also helped that the city had been a major hub of the vampire world for hundreds of years, dating back to when it was one of the few open ports where any vamp could go without tripping over somebody's territory and getting their throat ripped out. It had declined in prominence by the eighteenth century, with most political activity transferring to the new vamp capitol in Paris, but plenty of important types still had houses there—and thus perfectly good reasons to go. Mircea had said that more conspiracy happened in ballrooms than in senate chambers, and he should know.

So, was it just a coincidence that he, Pritkin and I had gotten into trouble at another vampire ball, this one in Romania, happening at around the same time?

Or that I'd just been forcibly reminded of it, in the most unlikely of ways?

I glanced around the closet, a tingle running up my spine. The bra twisted and writhed, but nothing else was acting weird. Well, weirder than it was supposed to.

The only other magic in here was Augustine's, and even it wasn't doing much. The gowns usually went into hibernation when not being handled, to preserve the "charge" built into them, which didn't last forever. And if anything else had been radicalized by some free-floating power, it wasn't obvious.

Magic called to magic, I'd always heard, especially if it was the same kind. And Augustine employed a lot of fey magic in his designs, to confound other designers who couldn't do it, and because he was part fey himself. It seemed like the kind of thing that might have attracted the attention of a certain nosy goddess.

Of course, that didn't explain why Faerie would be using my underwear as a way to talk to me. She'd been dumping visions straight into my brain for two days; why change now? Unless she didn't have a choice. After all, she'd never sent me anything until I was actually in her world, had she?

So, maybe she couldn't do it here, and had had to find some other way.

I had a sudden image of an alien goddess rifling through my underwear drawer, a frown on her face, while she hunted for something that might help. And came up with a vague imprint that she'd heightened, brightened, and turned from a few shifting shadows into a cinematic tour de force worthy of the Common. And had then sicced it on me, because she was not subtle.

Or maybe she'd decided that I wasn't that bright.

Either way, it seemed deliberate. Like that imprint was supposed to tell me something, only I wasn't sure what. I watched the mad little brassiere squirm against the carpet some more, but it reminded me of exactly nothing, because nothing had happened on that trip.

I'd eaten hors d'oeuvres, admired everybody's outfits, and waited for the right time. And then stood beside the canal behind Gabriella's brightly lit palazzo, and tried to look like somebody expecting an assignation. My imagination had run a little wild—it had been that kind of night—to the point that I'd been picturing a luxurious gondola, gliding up to carry me off to an evening of sin and debauchery. Or a mysterious man in a cloak and tricornered hat, and one of those weird volto masks like the phantom of the opera wore, pearl white and glowing in the moonlight.

In the end, there *had* been a gondola, with a huge, gilt lantern out front and red velvet curtains hiding the shiny black cabin. And a masked man, his blank face splashed with light from the house as he peered out at me. But there was no assignation, or even a conversation. He'd leaned from the cabin, handed me a note, and then sailed on down the canal without even stopping.

I'd been left looking after him, and wondering if that was it. I'd finally decided that I guessed so, and went back to Mircea. He'd read the note, scribbled out a copy, and paid a boy to deliver it to the countess. Who by then was outside, loitering where I'd just been.

Then we simply . . . left.

It had been pretty anticlimactic, but it had provided a useful building block to the coalition. A number of people had suddenly become much warmer to the idea of cooperation, helping Mircea to get his needed nods. With everything that had happened since, I'd all but forgotten about it, but maybe I should have paid more attention.

I finished putting on my makeup and took a break, sitting with my back to the bench and my head on the cushiony top behind me. My brain felt fried, with too little information about some things and too much about others, and both sides were duking it out for computing power I didn't have anyway. But this couldn't wait.

If a goddess was desperate enough to go on a panty raid, things were probably pretty dire. So, I thought about that party full of perfumed conspirators in Venice, whirling through the night secure behind their masks. And then about all those carriages of vamps we'd seen headed into Aeslinn's little bolt hole in Romania. And got a sinking feeling in my stomach.

This wasn't the first time I'd heard about traitors.

Mircea had expected Caedmon to help him find his wife, which the king of the so-called Blue Fey had offered to do—just as soon as he dealt with Aeslinn. Since the war was disrupting Faerie and causing chaos, and Mircea had no way of knowing how that chaos might impact Elena, that hadn't been good enough. But alienating an ally wasn't smart, so Mircea had turned to Plan B.

Plan B, of course, was the goat, who knew more than Caedmon probably did, but which had gone missing while we were fighting at Issengeir. It had remained in the eighteenth century, so that was where we'd gone looking for it. And as a result, had started this whole mess.

Because finding it again had proven to be a bitch.

I'd gotten us back to the right time and approximately the right place, but had then lost the scent. I realized now that the creature had been taken into that damned castle of Aeslinn's, which was parked just on the other side of a portal into Faerie where my power didn't work. So, it could only detect him during times when the castle's portcullis was open, providing a link between worlds.

But I hadn't known that then, so we'd been left searching around, slowly zeroing in on the location whenever I got a clue.

Mircea had gotten more and more agitated as we did so, not that he'd looked like it. Someone who didn't know him well wouldn't have noticed anything, but I saw that aristocratic jawline getting tighter and tighter, and finally asked him about it. And was informed that every inn we'd stopped at had been crawling with traitors.

That was the word he'd used: traitors. People who had long been recognized as the consuls' enemies, but who the Senate didn't have enough evidence to act against. He hadn't been too concerned at first, since many were locals. Romania, or Wallachia as that part of the country had been known then, had been a hotbed of animosity against the consuls for centuries, and was the center of the rebellion that had greeted their accession.

But after a while, he'd started to notice more and more out-of-towners, people who had no earthly reason to be roaming the wilds of his old homeland. Not any of them, and certainly not all at the same time. Which was why we'd hired a coach, stolen some clothes, and crashed a party.

Well, that and the fact that goat guy was at the same castle where all the vamps seemed to be going. And where Aeslinn and his godly handler were hanging out with an army of fey. And were planning to join up with the conspirators to make sure that they won this time, because that was the only thing that made any sense.

And the fact that I'd gotten this information from a bra did not change that.

I gave up pretending to be normal, stretched out on my closet floor, and stared up at the ceiling.

There was no way to know what kind of ripples might result from a change that big. Hell, Aeslinn might even succeed in screwing himself over, because I didn't think that our consul was just going to take that. If rebels killed her consort, she'd have to avenge him—her pride and position in the vamp world would demand it—setting up a major supernatural war. And she'd need allies, thus possibly making the coalition happen a lot sooner in order to rip Aeslinn a new one.

And potentially do the same thing to our world in the process.

Because our alliance wasn't as sturdy as it looked. In fact, one of our main worries had been that something would happen to overturn the delicate balance between groups and send us spiraling into conflict with each other, during or right after the war with Faerie. It was a real threat, since there were plenty of cracks in the supernatural community.

The senates didn't like each other, considered weres to be fit only for servants, and loathed the Circle, their main rival for power. For its part, the Circle dealt with the vamps through gritted teeth, was highly suspicious of weres, and hated the covens, who hated them right back. The covens didn't really trust anybody except for a few fey, and they kept a close eye on them. And while the weres occasionally worked for the vamps, they only did so for profit, and looked down on them as much as they did everyone who wasn't clan. Not that that stopped them from also fighting among themselves!

It was hard enough to keep everybody in line and focused on the prize as it was. How much worse would it be if conflict broke out hundreds of years ago? In a time when there was no common enemy to unite us?

We might rip ourselves apart, with no godly help needed.

So, no, I didn't know what changing that one event might do, and neither did Aeslinn. But he might be crazy enough, or desperate enough, to take the chance. Great time to bail on me, Gertie, I thought viciously, as Marco stuck his head back in the door.

Chapter Thirty-Six

Marco looked relieved to find me dressed, if a bit taken aback at the scowl on my face. "I have three little girls who need to get ready, too," he said, as I sat up. "But their rooms are off limits. Think you can help them out?"

"What girls?" I asked again, right before I spied them, peering out from behind Marco's tree trunk legs.

There were three small heads—one black, with a giant afro escaping out of the hood of a pink bunny suit, which could in no way handle the fluff; one bright orange-red, which was usually a 'fro to rival the bunny's, but which had been tamed by someone into long, Victorian style, sausage curls; and one brunette, with a silky fall of pin straight hair that, as usual, had several plastic barrettes clinging for their lives to the ends of the strands.

For a moment, I just looked at them. I didn't know what Marco was thinking. The girls didn't store excess clothes up here. Not to mention that they weren't supposed to be here at all, with the apartment going crazy.

"It's all right. I shifted them, Lady," a voice came from behind Marco, as if reading my mind.

I looked up to see Rhea standing in the door to the bathroom, wearing her lacy Edwardian finery, and looking a little tense. I blinked at her. "I thought you'd be a while yet."

"My place is with my Pythia."

"Rhea—"

Her jaw set and her chin tilted upward, and it was amazing how much that simple gesture changed her whole demeanor. The soft brown hair was the same, with a few wispy curls falling out of a loose chignon, as was the sweet face and ladylike attire, which a moment ago could have come straight out of a Gibson Girl cartoon. She still looked era appropriate, only now it was more like a Suffragette kneeing a cop in the tender regions as he carted her off to jail.

In other words, she looked *exactly* like Agnes. I usually gave up when the jaw made an appearance, but this was important. This was her last chance to spend time with her mother before Gertie's spell took effect.

"Nothing is happening here," I pointed out, as she and Marco came inside. "You should go back; take your day—"

"Nothing?" Rhea looked at me as if I was crazy.

"Nothing now," I amended.

"No, nothing now." It was bitter. "I missed it. They drugged me and I slept in—"

"Which was fine—"

"It was not fine! Just yesterday—" she broke off, spotting the writhing bra, and the frown between her eyes grew noticeably deeper. "What is that?"

"Shit," Marco said, and drew his gun again.

"No!" Rhea and I said together, because one of her charges had just decided to brave the bear in her den and toddled past me.

I threw a heavy coat over the brassiere, while Rhea chased the runaway. "Imprint," I explained. "It grabbed me earlier."

Rhea looked alarmed. "Are you alright?"

"Yeah, it was one of the good ones."

"I didn't know there were good ones," she said, rescuing the girl and tucking the barrettes neatly into her sweater pocket. Melia immediately looked happier, and went off to destroy some couture.

"Sometimes," I said, not wanting to get into it.

But Marco did. "You're telling me this thing isn't just animated?"

"Well, yes, but—"

"This gonna be a problem? To you or the court?"

I shook my head. "Not every psychic can pick up on imprints. It's . . . kind of a specialty."

Marco scowled. "And nobody else around here has that specialty?"

"Most of them are too young to know, or to read an imprint, even if they did encounter one."

"How about if one hunts them down? This place just got turbocharged with magic. On top of everything else, now I gotta look out for imprints stalking the halls?"

I almost said that I was pretty sure this was a one-off, meant as a clue for me. But I didn't want to get onto the topic of Faerie right now. Marco looked tense enough without being told that a possibly crazy, ancient fey goddess might have breached his security.

"Most imprints are too muddled for anyone to pick up on," I said. "Even an adept. And much of the rest are weak and indistinct. Like watching a clip from an old movie late at night, on a bad T.V., while you're drunk."

Rhea laughed.

"No, seriously. The world has lousy playback. Plus, the little snippets you get are usually really short."

"Like the Haunted Gallery at Hampton Court," she said.

I nodded. "That's one of the most famous."

Marco looked confused.

"It has an imprint of Catherine Howard," I explained. "One of Henry VIII's wives, who he beheaded for infidelity. It's said that, when the guards came to arrest her, she ran down the hall toward the chapel, where she thought the king was, to beg for her life. The imprint is of the moment she realized what was happening and broke free, fleeing for maybe ten seconds until the guards caught her."

"How do you know that's not a ghost?" Marco asked skeptically.

"It's billed that way on the tours, but they're likely wrong. A ghost is a disembodied spirit—it can think. Meaning that it does different things at different times, just as you do. An imprint doesn't. It's like a movie on repeat, sometimes playing continually, sometimes just at certain hours of the day or night. But it's always the same."

"Huh." He looked thoughtful. "We had an arena that nobody liked training in, back when I was a gladiator. Everybody thought it was haunted."

"Maybe it was."

"Naw. Nobody wanted to hang around that place for eternity. But I heard stories."

"Like what?" I asked, curious. Marco didn't talk about his past very often.

The huge shoulders shrugged. "One was about an older man, sitting on a stool and sharpening a gladius—a type of short sword— in one of the buildings just off the arena. I never saw him, but a guy I knew came out of the back one day, white as a ghost. Said he saw a new fighter and asked him his name, but the man never acknowledged him or even looked up. And when he went to grab his shoulder—"

"There was no one there."

He nodded.

"Sounds like an imprint," I agreed. "A ghost would have had a reaction. They don't like people invading their space."

Marco frowned. "Yeah, but I don't see why that would have created an impression. Not with some of the stuff that went on just outside!"

"Imprints aren't about big splashy spectacles, though," I said, as Tamsin of the amazing sausage curls came over and plopped down onto my lap. She was one of the coven girls, the little initiates who had been sent, for the first time in ages, to the Pythian Court as a gesture of goodwill.

It was quite a gesture, since the covens didn't trust anybody, and to send their children here . . . well, no one had ever thought they'd see it. But the girls had adjusted remarkably well, except for finding human stuff endlessly fascinating. The other two tiny terrors had headed straight for Augustine's magical mayhem, only to be headed off by Rhea. But what was Tamsin playing with?

An eyelash curler out of my makeup bag.

She laughed and waved it at me, as if she'd captured a magical sword, only to be immediately distracted by a glittery eyeshadow palette.

I gave it to her, rescued my eyelash curler, and sat her in front of the mirror to paint her face. She seemed delighted to do so. Warpaint appeared to be a concept that the covens understood.

"Imprints aren't like a Hollywood movie," I added to Marco. "Think more of an independent film—"

"Is that why they're all so crappy?"

I shot him a look. Marco's idea of a good flick was big budget, action packed, and light on plot. Or a historical that he could make fun of, because everybody was too clean and had all their teeth.

"And meaty," he added, when I pointed that out. "And not missing any limbs or eyes. And tall, with shiny hair and no scars. Every peasant looks like a lord—"

"Yes, so you've said," I reminded him. "My point was that imprints are about feelings. That's what forms them, a storm of raw emotion all at once, like in a murder. Or else many happy days spent in one spot, like a favorite old tire swing that generations of children have enjoyed, that carves an emotional rut over time."

Marco frowned. "I seem to recall the people in the arena having plenty of emotions."

"Yes, but so did the people around them, which could overwrite and muddy the imprint. But an old fighter, no longer as strong and healthy as he once was, going to out to face an opponent that he knows he can't beat? That would be the kind of thing that makes an impression—literally."

Marco suddenly looked uncomfortable. "Yeah, I can see that."

"So, there *are* good ones?" Rhea asked, while I wished that I'd chosen a different example. "Like that tire swing?"

"You've never encountered one?"

She shook her head. "Not my gift."

Lucky her.

"If you've ever walked into a room and immediately felt either happier or more apprehensive for no apparent reason, that might be an imprint," I told her. "Mild ones don't really grab you; they just color your mood."

"And this one put you in a good one?"

I eyed the coat, which was moving ominously, thanks to the persistent little thing underneath. "No, but that wasn't the content's fault. But I need to get rid of it. Could you possibly?"

She looked puzzled, probably wondering why I didn't just deal with it myself. Which I would have, if I wasn't afraid of taking out the whole floor along with it. Right now, it would be like trying to swat a fly with a bazooka.

But she didn't ask. I pulled the coat off, and a moment later there was a little pile of powder and some tarnished slugs. And she'd apparently been paying attention at Gertie's, because the carpet underneath was pristine.

Well, except for a bunch of burnt edged holes.

I sighed.

"That never gets old," Marco said. There's nothing a vamp likes more than a display of power.

I nodded in agreement, but frowned at the remains. Faerie might have sent it to hunt me down, but it could have been my own heightened abilities that had supercharged it. Which meant that any other imprints I encountered might have the same effect.

"I should probably get some gloves on," I said, and the frown between Rhea's eyes returned. "You wouldn't happen to know where they are?"

She glanced around, somewhat helplessly. "I did. But that was before—"

"Hurricane Elspeth?"

"She means well."

Yeah, that was the mantra we'd all been using, and it was true. Our magical grandmas absolutely meant well. Which did nothing for my chances of avoiding another booby trap.

The hunt turned into an odyssey. Elspeth had rearranged things in a way that might have made sense to her, but to no other human being. Why were belts and bobby pins in the same drawer? Or jodhpurs and jeans? Or scarves, slippers and pantyhose . . .

"Not pantyhose," Rhea said, her eyes widening. "Elspeth is almost one hundred and eighty years old. Back when she was a girl—"

"Oh, my God," I said, as light dawned.

"—they were called *stockings* . . ."

"She *alphabetized* them?" I stared at all the little drawers in all the built-ins. There were so many.

"That should make it easier, though, right?" Marco asked. "Just look for 'G'"

"Or 'H' for hand," Rhea said. "Or 'M' for mitten—"

"Or 'C' for cold weather," I added, scowling. "Or 'O' for outerwear!"

"Whelp, I should be going. Call me when you ladies want an escort downstairs," he said, and headed out the door.

"Not a chance. You take "G".

He sighed.

Marco and I started a search for where a hundred-and-eighty-year-old might have stashed my gloves, and Rhea tried to keep the kids from destroying my closet. And bit her lip, while giving me odd glances whenever she thought I wasn't looking. I finally took the bait, after searching through 'L' for leather and 'K' for knitted with no luck.

"Is something wrong?"

She had the grace to blush, but then the chin came up again, and she answered me. Because Rhea wasn't the timid little thing she'd been when she first came to court. I didn't know how I'd ever bought that act, considering that she was the product of the shrewdest mage I'd ever known outside of Pritkin, and Agnes freaking Weatherby.

Probably a good thing I'd gotten her young, or she'd be running this place by now.

"I was just wondering . . . why do you need gloves?" she asked. "You never have before."

"I'm not usually sensitive enough to have to worry about it."

"But you are today?"

"Today has been . . . different."

"How different?"

"You know, I'm not entirely sure."

"She got juiced up from whatever that goat thing was shedding," Marco said, elbows deep in one of the larger drawers. "Remember, I told you."

I scowled.

Apparently, everyone had understood what was happening except for me.

For her part, Rhea looked like she remembered. She also looked seriously spooked, which . . . yeah. Even by court standards, today had been weird.

But before she could say anything, Mira of the pink bunny suit pulled a sequined ballgown off of its hanger. It was another Augustine creation, which morphed depending on the wearer's needs. His latest line was all personalized to the buyer, making every piece unique.

It had looked like a plain, off white, sequined dress when I'd first seen it, in his workroom some days ago. Leaving me wondering what the catch was—until I slipped it on, and it transformed into a gold and silver sunburst pattern that was not only uniquely beautiful, but utterly different from anything I'd ever seen. The fluttering sleeves had shifted to liquid silver, as had much of the long skirt. But covering the entire middle and radiating outward in glimmering lines that covered most of the gown was a stylized sun, picked out in every shade of yellow and orange sequins and beads.

It was gorgeous and over the top and I had yet to find anywhere to wear it. Which was why it was a little concerning to see the dress shimmer and flicker—and change. Into a vision in bubble gum pink, with sequined party balloons that floated about all over it in a multitude of happy shades.

"Oh, no!" Rhea said, looking horrified, and grabbed it.

And had it morph again, into a dark red, slinky number with a capelet of black lace that cascaded down from the shoulders. It was velvet now, with the sequins retreating to merely highlight the tone-on-tone quilted roses that bloomed all over the luxurious fabric, and took the romantic vibe to ridiculous heights. All it needed was a fan and a mantilla.

Rhea looked surprised, Mira laughed and clapped her hands, and Marco sighed. "Maybe this wasn't my best idea."

"It's fine," I said, and took the dress, but it didn't change back. Or, rather, it did, squirming under my fingers in a slightly disturbing way. But it didn't return to its original form. Instead, it cascaded down to the ground in a wave of pure silver, but this time, there were no sequins in sight.

Large, scale-like platelets covered the slimmed down skirt, and the pretty top, which a second ago had been a deep vee, and was now a silver breastplate with a high-necked gorget. And the sleeves, which on Rhea's version had been absent entirely, were now full length, fitted and silver bright, with overlapping sections that almost looked like—

"Armor?" Marco cocked an eyebrow at me. "You planning on attacking somebody?"

"No. I don't know what's wrong with it." I shook it, but it steadfastly refused to morph again.

It looked a lot like a set of fey armor that I'd bought from a shop in a coven enclave a while ago. Augustine had purloined that one, to serve as a template for my acolytes' new attire, which could also change under pressure. The chiffon draperies of its usual state could quickly shift into something far more appropriate for a court at war.

The downside was that I'd never gotten my outfit back—until now. Maybe Augustine had used it as a template for his new collection, too? I didn't know, but my pretty new ballgown was now ready for battle.

And someone was even less pleased about that than I was.

"I knew it," Rhea said roughly. "I *knew* it!"

I looked up and found her staring at the gown with the blush fading off her cheeks—all the way off. Leaving them dead white and kind of scary, especially when paired with her expression. "Knew what?" I said blankly.

"Can we have a moment?" she asked Marco, through what sounded like gritted teeth.

"Yep," my stalwart defender suddenly found somewhere else to be.

"Marco," I called after him. "I don't know what you want me to do with the girls—"

"Fred said to dress 'em up like elves. He's planning a thing."

"A thing for the thing?" I said, but didn't get a reply. Except from Rhea, who snatched the dress out of my hands.

Chapter Thirty-Seven

The dress didn't switch back, but stayed silver bright. That remained true even when she shook it under my nose. "*This is why I'm back,*" she told me. "I know what you're planning!"

"Do you?" I wished she tell me.

Or maybe not, I thought, as she backed me into a corner. "You're going after him, aren't you?"

"After who?"

"Don't lie! You think I don't know you? I *know* you! You almost died yesterday—and the day before! I saw your flesh ready to *slide off your bones*. And yet here you are, about to go back and take on the king of the gods!"

"What?" I stared at her. "No, I'm—"

"*Don't lie!* As soon as I got up and realized you were gone, that you hadn't waited—I knew. I told Gertie she was a fool! What did she think you were going to do? Come back here and have a tea party?"

"Well, actually, we did have—"

"Did you listen to what Annabelle said? Did you hear? Or don't you care?"

"Care about what?" I asked, confused. "You don't believe—"

"*Of course, I believe her! Why the hell wouldn't I believe her?*"

"I'm not—I wouldn't—you're not ready—"

"You're damned right I'm not ready!" she grabbed my shoulders, and there was nothing left of the demure acolyte now. "Not to be Pythia, not to face the kind of dangers you do, not to *lose you!* Think about *that* before you run off and—"

She suddenly let me go, grabbed the dress with both hands, and began trying to shred it, only it didn't shred. So, she tried to age it, sending a swirl of the Pythian power through the room, but it didn't age, either. Or, if it did, it wasn't noticeable.

"Damn Augustine!" she snarled, and ran off to grab a pair of scissors out of my dressing table.

And, okay, no. I followed her, rescued the dress and pushed her into a chair. She tried to get up, and the look on her face said that that wouldn't bode well for my wardrobe. So, I strapped her to the chair using bonds of the Pythian energy, which caused her to curse inventively—she'd been hanging out with the boys too much, it seemed—and to thrash around, almost enough to overturn the chair.

I just stared at her for a moment; I'd never seen her like this.

I grabbed the kids, who were ignoring us in favor of plundering my closet, and put them in front of my weird accessory bin. It was the place where I kept all of the stuff that came with Augustine's finery, but that I would never wear in a million years. They set about happily pawing through it, and I turned my attention to my furious heir.

Who had stopped rocking, but who was now glaring daggers at me.

"We've never dueled," I reminded her. "I'd prefer that this wasn't the first time."

"Would you care to hear what I would prefer?" It was biting enough to make me blink.

"You already told me. The question is, did you tell anybody else?"

"What?" She looked confused.

"Did you say anything about this to anyone?"

"Such as?"

"The acolytes? Hilde? Marco? Anyone?"

"Gertie—"

"Anyone *here*?"

"No. I just returned—"

"Good." I leaned back against the wall in relief.

God, that had been close.

"Why? Afraid they'd stop you?" she challenged.

"No, I'm afraid they'd go without me. And get into serious trouble—"

"And you won't? You really think you can take him? That . . . that *thing*?"

"No."

"Then what is the point?" Rhea glared at me, her face now flushed and her hair everywhere. "Getting yourself killed isn't going to accomplish anything! It's only going to weaken us—"

"I agree."

"—terribly just when we need to be at our strongest! If we're going to win this—" She stopped. "What do you mean, you agree?"

I sat down on the pouf in front of her, because it was the only other seat in my dark hole of a dressing room. It put me below her eye level, which, according to all the advice on intimidation I'd received after becoming Pythia, was a bad idea. It was why the

Pythian throne was on a dais, and with the chair built so high that I needed a damned footstool not to look like a child dangling her feet.

But I didn't care. I wasn't trying to intimidate Rhea. "I need your help," I said. "Can you help me?"

She blinked, but it was a suspicious little blink, like she was sure I was trying to put something over on her.

I frowned. "When did you decide that you can't trust me?"

"Never! I do trust you—"

"Then what is this about?"

She struggled some more, but finally gave up, panting. "You! You're not—you don't—this isn't what a Pythia *does*! Fighting gods and running off to war—you were in combat, and not only this week, but at the attack on Aeslinn's court. And before that, you battled Ares! Do you have any idea—what if you had been killed? What on Earth were we supposed to do then? But you keep on doing it, you keep fighting—"

"As opposed to?"

"There are others to do that! Pythias *plan*; they *think*; they See glimpses of possible futures and help the Circle determine the best way forward. They don't lead the battle themselves!"

I slumped back against the wall and looked at her. "That's the problem, though, isn't it?"

"What is?"

"I suck at planning." It was stark, but I wasn't in the mood to lie. "I suck at most of it, actually. Except, ironically, the fighting bits."

"Why ironically?" she asked, looking taken aback. But at least she listening, although I wasn't sure that I wanted her to.

Who wants to have to admit that they don't know what they're doing? That they're in over their head, and that having others thinking about how great they are isn't so wonderful when it isn't true? When you know you're floundering ninety percent of the time, and just hoping that somebody else screws up worse than you do.

And then they do, or a Hail Mary pass completes and you don't die, and you desperately try to learn some more, so that maybe you won't the next time, either. So, you kind of know what the odds are there, and just try not to think about it. Until somebody like Zeus comes along and makes you think about it.

Only he probably kills you, too, so that doesn't really help, does it?

But at least it allowed me not to give a damn about Annabelle's creepy vision. I'd already had the night sweats and the panic attacks and the sobbing fits and the whole I'm-going-to-die-any-day-now hysterics. I'd had them for *months*.

Because I'd told Pritkin the truth: this didn't end well.

In all that stuff that Jonas had sent me, the books and notes and scholarly articles, there was one bit that we'd never discussed. That we'd never even edged around, because what was the point? But if he was right and we really were facing Ragnarok, well, there was one small issue that had kind of caught my eye.

We lost.

The legends differed on a lot of things, but on that they were pretty consistent. The gods died in the war, but so did everyone else, including all of the descendants of Loki. Which sucked for me as one of said descendants.

Loki seemed to be a stand-in for chaos in the storyline, rather than an actual person. Jonas had linked him with Prometheus, the Greek god of fire, since both of them were fire gods. And since both were imprisoned and tortured for striving against the autocratic control that the pantheon had exercised over everybody else. Prometheus gave fire to mankind—had Loki also lit a fire under us, to want freedom?

If not, his daughter Hel, known as Artemis to the Greeks, certainly had, although whether she'd meant it for our freedom or hers was debatable. But she'd created the great snake Jormugandr, also known as the ouroboros spell that protected the Earth, to guard it after she kicked the other gods out. And, right on cue, that spell had killed Thor, AKA Apollo, when he tried to re-enter this realm, or had weakened him enough that Pritkin and I had been able to finish him off.

One god down.

Then had come Tyr, known as Ares to the Greeks. That story was slightly less straightforward, but with hindsight, it was possible to see how it fit together. Hel's dog, Garm, her constant companion and protector—otherwise known as my father, Roger—was supposed to be killed by Tyr/Ares during Ragnarok. And that had pretty much come true. A bunch of Spartoi, the sons of Ares, had killed both my parents by pursuing them until they'd had to commit suicide to get away.

That wasn't as crazy as it sounds. Mother had bound her soul to the ouroboros spell, which was why the gods couldn't get past it. But that also meant that, if her soul left this realm, the spell would break. So, she couldn't be killed by the Spartoi, or this universe would once more fall into the hands of the gods.

She could, however, bind her soul to my father's, a human necromancer who specialized in ghosts—including his own, apparently. And both of them could enter a talisman after death that he had created, which functioned like Billy's necklace. It fed them enough energy to remain on this side of the spell and to anchor it.

The legends also said that Tyr fell dead shortly after battle from the wounds that Garm had inflicted, and even that was sort of true. Because my mother hadn't planned to stay in that talisman forever. She knew that Tyr/Ares would be back someday, and she'd intended to emerge and fight him, drawing off his energy to replenish her own.

That was possible since the gods didn't die as humans did; they just ran out of juice. Replace that juice, and they were back, good as new. She'd even worked to give me a demon army to use to distract Ares while she fed.

But while that hadn't worked out like she'd planned, since Tony had turned the talisman into a paperweight and carted it off to Faerie—no, really, that was how my life worked—the prophecy still came true. The plan that she and dad had come up with was exactly what I'd used to defeat Ares. I'd turned a distraction in the form of the ravenous ghost of Apollo loose to fight him for power while our side deflected one of Ares' own spells back at him.

Two gods down.

And two legends come true, from a certain point of view.

And while that was great for battle planning, it wasn't so great for me. Which was why I'd been doing what I always did with stuff I couldn't handle, and ignoring the shit out of it. I'd thrown Annabelle's prophecy on the heap with all the rest, because if it was right, I was toast, and if it wasn't, then what the hell good was it? Either way, I had stuff to do.

Like figuring out what to say to Rhea, who was starting to look seriously concerned.

"Take now, for instance," I said. "I have Aeslinn, Zeus and maybe a couple hundred fey displaced in time, and no idea what to do about it. Even Gertie didn't know, so how am I supposed to fix this?"

Rhea looked at me blankly for a moment, her former passion replaced by shock. I didn't usually discuss the war with her. Until recently, she had been having enough trouble just learning how to shift, making up for a lifetime of being denied any training.

"But they're not . . . they can't . . . how is that *possible*?"

I explained how that was possible, but the news didn't get the reaction I'd expected. Rhea still looked shocked, but there was element of outrage to it as well, as there had been with Tillie when I'd mentioned a time traveling god. That broke the rules as we had come to know them, and I guess carting an army through time did as well. Pythias usually chased a single, or maybe a couple of rogue time jumpers, not however many Zeus had with him.

And Rhea was pissed about it.

I'd expected her to be terrified, but instead the blush was back in her cheeks and staining up as high as her forehead, and there was a furious glint in her eye that very much reminded me of someone else. And I'd probably just screwed up, hadn't I?

Because I didn't want her involved in this.

"What?" she said, seeing my expression.

"It's just . . . you need to promise me that you're not going to go off and do something stupid—"

"*Me?*" The outrage grew exponentially, and yes, those eyes were definitely flashing now. "*I* need to promise *you?*"

"Yes. If I fall in this war, you're the only one standing between us and—"

"If you fall in this war, we're all fucked!" Rhea snapped, causing me to rear back slightly, because that was not remotely like her.

"That isn't true—"

"That is *completely* true and everybody knows it but you! You go about taking on gods, getting injured, hurting yourself . . ." And just as fast as the anger had come, it left, to be replaced by tears. "You can't keep hurting yourself. You can't keep doing this!"

I knelt beside her chair; she looked seriously upset. Her breath was hitching, and her eyes were flooded, and I immediately felt bad. She was nineteen; she was too young to have all this dumped on her. It wasn't fair.

"You're twenty-four," she whispered. I guessed I'd spoken aloud.

"But I'm Pythia," I said, and watched her face crumble.

I held her for a while as she sobbed, awkward though it was with the bonds restraining her. But I didn't want to let her up, not yet. I wanted that promise first.

"And I want one from you. But I'm not going to get it, am I?" she challenged, when I asked again, her face wet and red and angry and tragic all at the same time.

I didn't answer. I had no idea what I was going to do. If this was a test at Gertie's, I'd have failed for sure.

"There was an uprising against the European Senate," I said instead. "At the end of the eighteenth century. It was discovered and the leaders were executed, so no big deal. Most people have probably never even heard of it—"

"The fey are going to join the conspirators, aren't they?" Rhea said. "They're going to make sure they win."

It looked like she was as quick as her mother, too.

"And with fey forces plus prior knowledge of what happens, they might be able to," I agreed. "The question is, what to do about it. I thought Gertie would know, but I think she was as confounded by everything as we are. And Mircea and Pritkin are missing, and I have no idea when they'll be back. And going to the Senate or Circle . . . let's just say that I can't see that helping."

That was an understatement. The two big powerhouses in the supernatural community were more than capable of dealing with day-to-day problems and even some next level ones. They could fight dark mages, fey, even demons, when required. But gods?

That was a little out of their league.

Not that they hadn't been scheming anyway, as that was what the Senate did best. But lately, they'd been shooting me more and more side glances in council sessions, like they expected me to suddenly come up with some grand scheme to get us out of this. Like I wasn't floundering as much as they were. And without hundreds of years of experience to draw from!

So, no, I didn't think help was what I'd get if I told them that Zeus was back.

"Then . . . what are we going to do?" Rhea asked, looking bewildered.

"I was hoping you'd have an idea."

She stared at me some more. I imagined that I must have looked similar when talking to Gertie. Expecting to be given instructions on how to solve this when how would she know? But it was so easy to fall into the habit of looking to others, of following orders instead of leading, of learning instead of teaching.

But this was my fight, and the Pythian Court's fight, because this was what we were here for. The audiences in my impressive new reception hall, the diplomacy to try to mend fences in the supernatural community, the parties in my pretty new couture, were all useful in their own ways. But they weren't the point.

This was the point.

"You—you—"

I waited patiently.

"You could call on the other Pythias," Rhea finally said, a little desperately. "Like the ones who helped to battle Ares!"

"I could try. But then, we got lucky that time, didn't we? None of them died. If a single one had, it could have destroyed the time line, every bit as much as any god could do. There is a reason Pythias don't normally team up. Not to mention that it took everything they had just to slow Ares down.

"If we hadn't come up with something else, he would have won."

Rhea didn't say anything, but I could almost see the cogs reversing course in her head. Going from protect-the-Pythia mode to something else, something scarier. Because we couldn't just ride this one out.

But if she came up with any epiphanies, she didn't say.

"You could do one thing for me," I told her, after a moment.

"Anything; you know that."

"Ask Françoise if I've had any unusual mail lately." Françoise was my appointment secretary, and handled my mail—bushels of it.

"Unusual . . . how?"

"I don't know. Just something Zeus said when we talked."

Rhea didn't seem to know how to respond to that.

I released her bonds, and then noticed that the kids had managed to outfit themselves. I wasn't sure that huge feather boas, sequined belts and a towering fur hat counted as "elf", but it would have to do. "And can you take the girls back to Fred?"

She nodded, probably glad to have something straightforward to do. But she didn't move, other than to get back to her feet. And then she just stood there, biting her lip.

Before, once again, surprising me.

"I loved my mother, and I hated her," she blurted out. "Growing up, that is. I thought that being back there, at Lady Herophile's court, might change that, might give me some clue as to why she sent me away, why she brought me back, and why she kept me at arm's length, never letting me in, never letting me help."

"Did it?"

"No. If anything, it reinforced what I already felt."

"I'm sorry. Maybe I shouldn't have—"

"No." She shook her head. "It was a good thing. I understand her better now, not everything—I'll likely never know everything. But about who she was, what drove her. She was ambitious; she wanted the position—so badly! She craved power, but she was afraid of it, too. Afraid that she wouldn't be good enough, that she couldn't handle it. I never knew that; never thought she could feel . . . less than. But she did.

"Yet she did the job anyway. And she was brilliant at it!"

On that, there was no argument. "Yes, she was."

"It showed me—she showed me—that you don't have to be perfect, or even enough. No one ever is, not for this. She knew that, every day, she might be facing something she couldn't handle. But she faced it anyway. She found a way."

She took my hands suddenly, her face earnest and trusting and fervent and all the things I didn't deserve, because I wasn't the woman she thought me to be. "And so will you," she said, frowning, as if she knew what I was thinking. "*So will you*! You remind me of her, so much."

I smiled, a little tremulously. "I'm not sure if that's the nicest thing you've ever said to me, or the scariest."

Rhea laughed, a little wildly, but it was good to hear. "Neither am I."

Chapter Thirty-Eight

I finally located some gloves—under "t" for some reason—and emerged into the bedroom to find Marco patiently waiting. He'd escorted the girls downstairs because shifting into a deserted bedroom is easier than shifting into a crowded apartment. And because he seemed to think that the suite contained some kind of threat.

But I didn't see why he'd come back for me.

Until we reached the dim jungle that the hub had become, and found the boys still hacking at the foliage, trying to drive it back with knives, axes and what looked like a machete. I almost asked them where they'd come up with the latter, but decided against it. Those kinds of conversations rarely went well.

But, despite their efforts, the greenery was growing almost faster than they could rip it up. They'd managed to clear a space around the door to the living room, however, and Marco and I picked our way across the leafy carnage in that direction. Only to find that things weren't much brighter next door.

Night had fallen beyond the expansive terrace, with only a few electric smears breaking the darkness. The other side of the hotel, where my audience chamber was situated, had a view of the Strip, which splashed the hardwood floor with neon colors even after sundown. But here, only a little dim city light filtered in, along with the haze from the blood red Dante's sign on the roof, recently reignited, that gave everything a slightly ominous air.

Like the small puddle around a lamp, which was wandering around on its own and muttering darkly.

I stared at it, caught off guard in spite of everything. It was a floor lamp with a large, fringed shade that usually stood over an armchair in case anyone wanted to read. But now it was on the move, prowling around on its ornate iron "feet"—which were causing the muttering sound, as the metal creaked and strained.

It had plenty of room to maneuver, since the entire living room and, from what I could see, the terrace beyond, had been stripped bare. There weren't even any curtains at the broad sweep of windows or paintings on the walls. There was just the lamp, hunched over and shaking its "head" slowly back and forth, while the trailing cord gave off occasional sparks.

There was also one other thing.

I tilted my head, wondering what, exactly, I was seeing. I couldn't get a good look at it, as it wasn't solid. It looked like a breaking wave had invaded my suite, filling the air with almost transparent water vapor, only that obviously wasn't right. I moved forward a few feet and realized that a mirror had shattered on the far wall, and the million little pieces had exploded outward into the room.

They hadn't fallen to the floor, however, but instead stayed suspended and coiled in on themselves, hence the breaking wave effect. And unlike the lamp, they weren't moving, although individual pieces were turning gently here or there in gusts of wind from the open doors to the terrace. Now that my eyes had adjusted, I could see that they sent pale light shadows to spot the darkness, like the strobes in a very subdued nightclub.

The whole thing was strangely beautiful, like a weird kinetic sculpture or a rainbow of diamonds spread across the empty room, sparkling whenever a stray beam of light hit it.

Marco pulled me gently back. "I wouldn't get too close, if I were you."

"Why not?"

"All those little particles can become a whirlwind if they spot anything they don't like. Almost flayed a couple of the guys while we were clearing out the living room."

I winced.

"And the lamp isn't much better."

"The lamp?"

"Bastard already electrocuted three of us. We're waiting until it runs down before tackling either of them again."

I looked back over my shoulder as he pulled me up the stairs. "Electrocute? But . . . it's not plugged in."

"Yeah. But it doesn't run on electricity anymore, does it?"

Good question, I thought, as we passed through the white and gold doors into the foyer. And I got another surprise. At least I know what happened to the furniture, I thought, looking around the marble octagon.

It had always reminded me of a bird cage with its white walls painted with golden lines, and its domed and ribbed ceiling. Except for today, when it resembled a junk shop. A very odd one.

"What the hell?" I said, and Marco sighed.

"We've cleared out the worst of it, but you had a lot of furniture."

"Had?"

He nodded. "Unless you like 'em this way."

I glanced around again at what was left of my decor. I did not like it this way. And neither did a jade green pouf I'd rescued from a magical thrift shop some time ago, which usually could be found running about underfoot like an overly excited puppy.

The mage who had enchanted it had given it the ability to follow basic orders, and the girls had taught it to fetch. As a result, the little footstool could frequently be seen galloping about, delivering forgotten books to classrooms, or trotting obediently behind a small child, transporting her dolly in regal splendor. It had caused some problems at first, tripping people up in its enthusiasm or scaring the crap out of Annabelle's overfed cats. But we'd finally found a happy medium, which was why I wasn't pleased to see it backed into a corner, being menaced by a fake fern.

Unlike the plants in the hub, this one hadn't overrun the small room, thanks to plastic stems and silken fronds. But it *had* crawled out of its pot and off its stand, and was spidering across the floor like some kind of alien monster. The pouf was trembling and trying to dodge, but there were obstacles in the way, and some of them were scary, too. The fern finally lunged, getting a tendril around one of the pouf's small, round feet, and all four tassels jumped into the air in alarm.

I tried to pry the tendril off, but it was stubborn and wouldn't let go. "Marco?"

He grabbed the fern with an expression of disgust, and had it lunge for him instead. Which resulted in a lot of green confetti showering the floor a moment later, because Marco had had enough of this shit. I picked up the pouf, only to have it cower into my armpit in fear.

"What the hell?" I said again, with more feeling.

"Sorry," he grimaced. "I thought we'd removed most of the dangerous ones."

"They're all dangerous! And that fight was days ago! Why are they like this?"

He shrugged. "Don't ask me. All I know is, you're gonna have to redecorate."

Yeah.

I guessed so.

We stood there for a moment, surveying the wreckage, while a couple of vamps attempted to wrestle a coat rack onto the elevator. That would have been easier, only the rack didn't want to go. I winced in sympathy as it caught one of the vamps upside the chin with a vicious right hook.

The guy in question was Yvain, one of the vamps that Mircea had made when he first became a senator and lived in Paris, and he had quite a temper. That was always surprising, since he was a light blond with almost colorless blue eyes, and looked like he would have been as cold as ice. But he could go from zero to a hundred in a second flat, and you always knew it. His fair skin concealed exactly nothing.

Like right now.

He had just flushed cherry red, probably at the indignity of being punched by an inanimate object. It wasn't the first time, judging by a patch of redness on his cheekbone and another on his forehead, which he hadn't had time to heal. And by the fact that his hair, usually scraped back into a discreet clip at the base of his neck, had come loose and was sticking to his face.

And then the rack did it again, and the colorless eyes flashed gold.

Well, crap.

But surprisingly, since Yvain was a master, calling up his power didn't seem to help. The coat rack had grown hefty wooden arms and a thick, almost human appearing chest, making it look like a seamstress's dummy crossed with a prize fighter. A good one.

The fight suddenly ramped up, with the vamp's powerful blows sending wood flying. But the rack healed the damage almost immediately, with new fibers flowing like water as they recoated the fist-shattered spots and bulked them up even more. Meanwhile, Yvain was taking pile-driver-like damage to the face and torso, which would have turned a human into a bleeding sack of mush.

He was faring better, but not by as much as you'd expect. Something that seemed to surprise him, given the expression on what was left of his face. Considering his age, he'd probably been in a lot of fights, some even desperate.

But this was new.

Join the club, I thought, as he staggered back from a blow that would have dented iron, and finally noticed me. He snarled again, showing off a missing fang, and then jumped back into the fray, since the last thing a vamp wants is to be beaten up while the boss looks on. It didn't go any better this time, resulting in him cursing at his partner, who had only managed to trap one of the beefy arms.

That might have been because said partner, a Latin lover type named Jose, was having his own problems courtesy of a pair of custom drapes. They had wrapped up his head and cut off his vision, while the cord did its best to decapitate him. Yet Marco did nothing about any of this.

Unless you counted crossing his arms and narrowing his eyes. Maybe because his boys were embarrassing him right now. Or maybe because of the opposite: it would have been humiliating for a couple of master vamps to need saving from a battle with a coat rack.

Even one that they were clearly losing.

I heard Yvain's patrician nose crunch, and hugged the footstool even harder. But I didn't interfere. Marco handled the guys. We had a strict division of labor, and he didn't like it when I stepped on his territory—any more than I did when he messed with mine.

But somebody else wasn't in the hierarchy, and she'd had a bad day.

"Stars and symbols!" Saffy said, causing me to jump because I hadn't seen her come in. "Stop playing around!"

Yvain said something I didn't understand, because the beating he was taking was currently so fast and so unrelenting that it looked like his head was a speed bag at a gym.

"What?" Saffy said.

He grabbed the huge, wooden club of a fist in both hands, which didn't stop the beating, but did muffle the effects somewhat. "Y-y-you think y-y-you can d-d-do better?" he demanded, only it sounded more like a request.

She rolled her eyes. And muttered an incantation which had the coat rack shuddering all over and losing its rhythm, and the drapes falling away to squirm about the floor. Finally released, Jose screamed in frustrated rage, and kicked and pummeled and tried to shred the rack, only to end up spitting teeth. Yvain pulled him off, and the two vamps finally managed to grab an arm each and wrestle the wretched thing onto the elevator.

The three of us just stood there and looked after them for a moment, silently.

"Do I want to know why they're not taking the stairs?" I asked Saffy, as the stairwell door rattled ominously.

"No."

Okay, then.

That left me stuck until the elevator got back, with a bunch of once expensive furniture that had morphed considerably from its original design. Some of it seemed relatively benign, including a grandfather clock, which now looked more like the tree its wood had come from. Bark had spilled over half of the shiny wooden body, and thick, twisted limbs had sprouted from the top.

But that was less disturbing than the coils of rich, brocaded fabric that covered a third of the floor, and which I finally recognized as a small sofa pillow that used to sit on the couch. I didn't see the couch itself, but that may have been because the pillow had eaten it. It was now huge, and sprawling in an array of sluggishly moving tentacles that it had definitely not had before. One of which had just snagged the edge of the curtains that had been menacing Jose.

And began slowly dragging them closer.

The attack was silent, except for the wild thrashings of the curtains, the edges of which kept grabbing hold of things to try to save themselves. But it was all for nothing. The one-time pillow ruthlessly hauled them in and under.

And, after a moment, flopped out another fat, brocaded tentacle.

"I'm shifting us downstairs," I told Marco. "Hang on."

"You're doing no such thing. We don't have a landing pad set up yet—"

"I don't need one. I learned a new thing." Assuming I could manage it with my head spinning this hard.

"—and the elevator will be back in a minute." He eyed me cautiously. "You want a soda or something?"

"I don't want a soda!"

"As long as you don't pass out on me."

"I'm fine, I just—"

And then an armchair reared up on its hind legs and sprang at Saffy.

I cursed, Marco shouted, and Saffy blasted it with another spell, causing it to fall back onto all fours. She also sent a lasso spell to wrap around its legs for good measure, giving it trouble when it started ahead again. It nonetheless kept coming, lumbering our way with a menacing waddle as another vamp—a stud named Rico— came in from the suite.

As usual, he was dressed in jeans—black today—and a plain white t-shirt, one of the arms of which had been rolled up to hold a pack of cigarettes, or possibly to show off his tats. He looked vaguely like the Fonze on a day off, only better looking and with slightly less hair gel. He had a gun at his back, because he always had a gun, but he didn't draw it. He just looked at the chair, which was slowly coming to murder us, with a raised eyebrow.

"You owe me fifty," he told Saffy.

"Not now!"

"Is that one of the Louis XVs?" I asked, as realization dawned.

"It's a reproduction," Fred said, coming in with a plate of cookies.

"We paid five grand for that!"

"Still a reproduction." He looked at Saffy. "There's a problem in the kitchen."

"I know."

"No, you really don't." She cursed and ran back out again. "I think they're mostly dead," Fred added.

I looked up, startled. "What?"

He proffered the plate.

And it took me a heart clenching moment to realize that he was talking about the cookies.

"Damn it!" I said, and shoved the gruesome things away.

"You're missing out," Fred said, munching happily. I thought about reminding him that one of them had chased him across the kitchen not so long ago, but was too busy staring at the cookies. Which were no longer moving, but were not remotely back to normal.

Unless they'd been baked with hateful little faces and slitted eyes, and hands clutching makeshift weapons. Even worse, some had cannibalized their brothers, sticking the purloined arms onto their bodies with icing or melted gummy glue, in order to hold even more weapons. A few had half a dozen extra limbs sprouting from various body parts, and one had two heads.

"It's okay," Fred said again, seeing my face. "These were in the oven when everything went down. They don't have any glass in them."

I stared at him.

"Fifty?" Marco asked Rico.

"Saffy thought everything would have run out of juice by now," Rico said, helping himself to a cookie. And then pausing when he got a good look at it.

"Then why hasn't it?" I asked.

He shrugged. He typically did not have an opinion on magic, except that he didn't trust it. Which was ironic considering that he was trying to date my heir, a powerful witch.

I guessed love was blind.

"They should have," Fred complained, while he dug out a wallet. "Some mages used this kind of thing as home security, back in the day, but it's expensive, magically speaking. Saffy said they wouldn't last longer than a couple hours, tops."

"Home security?"

"You know, like those suits of armor they have downstairs."

He was talking about some of Dante's stranger decorations, the kind that could come alive to pummel belligerent drunks, if needed. But those were part of the overall ward system of the hotel, and operated on clearly defined rules. These didn't.

And magic without rules was . . . not good.

"Only most people don't have armor hanging out in the living room anymore," Fred continued. "But they do have—"

"Coat racks and drapes," I said.

He nodded. "Anybody gets past the wards you got on the front door, well, you just sic the fridge on 'em. At worst, it oughtta slow them down long enough for you to get away, and at best—"

"I get it," I said.

I did not want to know what the best was.

"Why don't they simply buy a gun?" Rico asked, eyeing his six-armed cookie. And then shrugging and eating it anyway.

"It's old magic," Marco said. "From before they had guns. Didn't you ever see any?"

Rico arched an eyebrow at him. "Yes, I so often frequented great houses."

"It wasn't just the rich," Fred protested. "I knew a mage who lived in a hut back in Germany who enchanted a whip to guard the place at night. It slithered about like a snake; almost gave me a heart attack once."

"You're a vampire," Marco pointed out. Fred's cheerful lack of vampiric pride stuck in his craw.

"Sure, but that was before."

"Before you lost your dignity?"

"Before I became a vamp. And dignity can go hang if the alternative is getting eaten. The damned thing was twelve feet long!"

"I never had much use for mages," Rico said, munching thoughtfully.

"Smart man," Marco agreed.

"Until recently. The young one is all right, though."

"The young one is an exception. Most aren't like Reggie."

"No," Rico agreed. "They are not. Shall we go and throw them out?"

Marco scowled and tilted his head, listening. Apparently, the Circle's men were the cause of the latest commotion in the kitchen. He looked at me.

"I'm fine," I assured him.

"Take her downstairs," he told Fred, who handed Rico a folded bill. It looked like he'd gotten in on the action—and lost, because the apartment was still going crazy three days later.

"What's going on in the kitchen?" I asked Fred, who was putting his wallet away in some khakis he'd dug up to cover the reindeer boxers.

He shrugged. "What you'd expect. The Circle guys want to interview you about what happened in there."

"Ah."

"I take it you don't wanna talk about it?"

"I want to talk about this."

He joined me in regarding the cookie plate. "Then you should ask one of the witches. All I know is that anything'll do, as long as it's not sentient enough to throw off a command. But almost nobody uses this kind of thing anymore. Saffy said it fell out of fashion when wards became cheaper."

Yeah, but she'd also said that the magic would run out quickly. That seemed to be true of the cookies, which did not appear to have absorbed a great deal of power. A few were twitching, as if trying to get up enough energy to stab their bits of cane into Fred's fingers. But most were just lying there, glaring impotently.

Unlike the furniture, which was battling on, and for far longer than it should have done.

"Demigod," I said.

"What?" Fred asked, as the elevator dinged.

"The goat guy." He'd enchanted the apartment as he fled, turning everything in sight into his allies, and shedding a reserve of power into the air to keep them fighting even after he'd left. Which they still were, four days later, because his spells had been fueled by god blood, the same stuff that had charged me up.

And what else sheds god blood than a god?

"Demigod?" Fred repeated, frowning. "You sure?"

I watched the tied-up chair slowly waddle past, determinedly stalking Saffy. "Pretty sure."

Chapter Thirty-Nine

We finally made it down to what had become the bodyguards' floor, and back into my old suite, which had the biggest common space around. The guys had turned it into a rec room, which meant that the bullet holes in the walls had been covered by a dart board, the sofas had been shoved up against the wall to make room for a massive billiard table, and the gaming set up of the gods was over by the wall, with a T.V. the size of a movie screen mounted above it. There were also a couple of card tables scattered about, and a much-enlarged bar.

It looked like a frat house, if an upscale one, but there were some noticeable changes today. The T.V. was showing what I guessed was supposed to be a cheerful fireplace, with crackling logs, a red brick surround, and a wreath above the mantle. But when the fire covers half a wall, it goes from cheerful to slightly ominous pretty fast, spreading a hellish light over the scene.

But nobody else seemed to notice, so I kept my thoughts to myself.

There were other, more successful signs of the season, which I strongly suspected had to do with Tami, who was basically responsible for everything around here. If it wasn't security, which was Marco's job, or teaching the initiates, which the acolytes had taken on, it was Tami's domain—and she ran a tight ship. Or, at least, she usually did.

But it looked like even she was having trouble combating the guys' happy chaos, maybe because she hadn't had a lot of time. I imagined that finding the girls enough beds, rescuing some clothes, and soothing their fears had taken up much of the last few days. But she was determined to restore some sense of normalcy, which was why the card tables were groaning with food and a large Christmas tree was currently being decorated in a corner.

I put down the pouf on the way over and it galloped madly off to join the fun. And to add to the bedlam, by excitedly running around the stepstool Tami was balancing on, despite its training. I didn't blame it; it was probably just thrilled to be someplace safe.

"What the—" Tami paused, ornament in hand, to look down at the excited little thing, and then up at me.

She was looking cute, in a bright red, cold shoulder sweater with "Sassy Elf" written on it in spangly gold letters. She had matching gold beads on the end of her braids, giving her an ancient Egyptian vibe, and sparkly gold eye shadow, which looked great against her dark skin. I suddenly wished I'd dressed up more.

She grinned. "I knew it was too quiet around here."

"Chaos has arrived," I agreed.

"Too late," she said, glancing at the party, which was in full swing.

It looked like some friends of the court had been invited. I spotted a handful of high-level vamps clustered in a corner, clutching cocktail glasses and probably wondering when they could leave. A scattering of very loud coven witches were also in attendance, playing a raucous game of billiards, while another witch, in a Santa hat with a sprig of mistletoe in the brim, was following a handsome vamp around, looking hopeful and very drunk. There was even some of the hotel's usually overworked room service staff hanging out, probably after delivering the food.

It looked like they'd stayed to enjoy some of their contributions, and to dance to "Jingle Bell Rock," which was blaring out of a towering sound system. I smiled at them, and waved at the guy with the lizard tail who regularly brought up pizza. And then felt my expression fade when I spied a trio of guests over by the punchbowl.

Well, shit.

"How long have they been here?" I asked Tami.

She looked up. "Who?"

"The Graeae."

That was the formal name for the three old crones with the scrunched up, apple doll faces and long, trailing gray locks. Or, at least, that was how they usually looked. Tonight was a little different, because it seemed that the initiates had gotten hold of them, specifically their hair.

I had assumed that the little girls who made up much of my court would be afraid of the threesome, and they probably would have been had they seen them morphed into their alter egos. But the ancient warriors I knew had never been on display around here. Instead, their occasional visits had been marked with gentle caresses on tiny heads and murmured words in a language that nobody spoke, but that somehow everybody understood.

The Graeae liked kids; who knew?

And it seemed that the kids liked them back, or maybe they just viewed them as life-sized hair styling dolls. They'd no sooner seen the floor-length, tangled gray masses on their heads, than the brushes, combs and ribbons had come out. Even stranger, the old ladies had settled down on the floor in the living room, apparently content to be primped, adorned and fussed over by a bevy of little girls.

Which is why it wasn't all that odd to see them looking stylish tonight. Instead of the somewhat scary trash that used to fill the knotted mess they called hair—because they'd been known to stick half-eaten food up there for later—it was brushed and shining. And elaborately braided and studded with silk poinsettia flowers. It didn't help their looks much, which was hampered by them sharing only one eye and one tooth between them, but they were definitely festive.

"Must just have got here," Tami said, looking unconcerned.

"*Just* got here?"

"Yeah, why? Is there a problem?"

That was what I'd like to know.

The Graeae usually only showed up when trouble was brewing. They were drawn to it like moths to a flame, and when they didn't find any, they made some. Although the only thing they were doing right now was to cluster around the punch bowl, which the one who currently had the eye was peering at suspiciously.

It contained Tami's go-to party punch of ginger ale, orange sherbet and fruit juice, but they did not seem to approve. What I didn't approve of was the idea that they'd showed up at all. Not that I minded the company, but the chaos de jour was over, so what were they doing here?

Maybe looking to have some fun, Cassie, like everyone else!

I shook my head at myself, but grabbed a passing vamp and sent him over to keep an eye on them anyway. 'Cause if paranoid was a religion, I'd be the high priestess. And I'd had about all the trouble I could handle.

Having done what I could, I turned my attention back to Tami. And to the tiny initiate at her feet who'd become hopelessly wrapped up in tinsel. I squatted to free the little girl, only to have to duck even lower to avoid several older ones who were swinging a string of

Christmas lights around, trying to untangle it. Ominously enough, all of the lights were blood red.

I understood why when I finally stood back up, and got a good look at the tree they were working on, which could have come straight out of *The Nightmare before Christmas*. Not the tree itself, thankfully, which was vibrant and green, unlike the ratty black things they had downstairs in the lobby. But in spirit.

Which wasn't too surprising, since spooky Christmas was the theme for the newly reopened casino.

Casanova, the hotel's manager, had planned to tone down Dante's over-the-top theming, which had been designed to hide the hard-to-explain stuff that frequently went on around here. But that had been before a "gas leak" in the form of a dark mage attack forced him to close the place entirely. The hotel had remained occupied—by the Senate, who had needed a bolt hole after their HQ in the desert was destroyed—but since one of their members owned the place, they didn't bother paying the bills.

That fact had eaten away at Casanova's very soul, which I honestly thought might be made out of money. When he finally couldn't stand it anymore, he had come up with a plan to reopen. Not the drag with all the shops, which had been scoured bare in the attack, or the spa, or the bars or restaurants, the latter of which was occupied by feeding the Senate's functionaries, many of whom had both a pulse and an appetite.

No, just the casino.

It had been a hard sell, but the idea of zero revenue, for months, had lit a fire under Casanova's shapely backside such as no one had ever seen. He had pleaded, he had cajoled, he had charmed and flattered and may have even squeezed out a tear. He had also noted that it was going to look odd, with so many people coming and going all the time, and yet no official activity taking place. This wasn't the middle of the desert; this was the Vegas Strip. People would talk.

The Senate had bought it, although whether that was due to his explanation or as a bid to shut him up, I wasn't sure. But as a result, there were finally guests below again, and the big red sign was glowing on the side of the building once more, casting its fiendish light on all and sundry. It made me proud to see. Like the rest of us, Dante's was bruised, battered, and bearing scars, yet still standing.

And was now festooned for the holidays, in true underworld style.

So was our tree, which had Christmas balls in the form of skulls wearing Santa hats, a garland of bats, and scattered grim reapers, complete with tiny scythes. There were silvery cobwebs presided over by red-eyed spiders. There were caldrons with presents sticking out of the top. There were pert-looking witches in their sparkly best, riding broomsticks and pulling signs extorting everyone to have a "Wickedly Good Time."

It was strangely jolly.

"Don't look at me like that," Tami said, holding a blood-smeared scarecrow.

"Like what?"

"We have real decorations. But they're upstairs—assuming that they're in their box and not stalking the hallways. I couldn't risk having them down here, so I had to improvise from the hotel's stock."

"It's very nice," I told her.

"Liar." She climbed down off the step stool to survey her work. "Do you think the tarantula for a star was too much?"

I looked up, and then abruptly stepped back a pace, because it was huge. And hairy. And somehow fit the tree perfectly.

"I think it's . . . appropriate."

She sighed. "That's what I was afraid of."

"You're asking the wrong person," Roy said, coming by with a tray of pretty pink drinks.

"What?" Tami asked.

"Cassie doesn't know about Christmas stuff. Although we're here to educate her." He proffered the tray with a flourish.

My redheaded, checkered-suit-loving, Southern bodyguard had outdone himself today, in a sequined plaid number in red and green. It came with a tie featuring Betty Boop as a scandalous Mrs. Claus, showing off her garters as she bent over to shake a package. I assumed that she was the reason he had escaped the terrible sweater fate that had caught most of the other guys.

There was no sweater that could top that.

As well as being the dandy of the bunch, Roy was our resident mixologist, regularly coming up with new concoctions to tempt jaded palates. And when you live with people who have been around for centuries and drunk everything under the sun, that wasn't easy. But he usually managed, and tonight was no exception. The tray of drinks contained wide, shallow coup glasses full of something very pink, with flakes of what looked like edible gold that were catching the light.

"Take one," he told me. "They're named after you."

"After me?"

He nodded solemnly. "I give you The Cassie Palmer."

I took one. "What's in it?"

"Pink grapefruit juice, tart lemon soda, a few dashes of Peychaud's bitters, white rum, velvet falernum, simple syrup, a couple drops of maraschino cherry liquid for color, and edible gold flakes. It's sweet, tart and unexpectedly strong. Perfect."

I took a sip. My eyes opened wide. "It is perfect."

"Told you. I whipped up a drink for Mircea, too, and the mage—"

"What drinks?"

He looked around, then waved someone over. It turned out to be Paolo, who appeared to have recovered—including his temper. He was wearing a sweater with a couple of brown satin reindeer on the front with their backs to us, doing something that I couldn't immediately identify. Until I checked out the red sequined letters near the neckline: Santa's Twerkshop.

He also had a tray of drinks, and they looked pretty good, too.

"The Crusty Mage," Roy said. "An espresso martini—double shot—made with London dry gin, coffee liquor, and simple syrup. And in honor of the season, crushed coffee beans, chocolate shards and candy cane bits around the rim."

I felt my mouth start to salivate.

"And Mircea's?"

He looked over the crowd again. "I don't see that one—"

"And you won't," Tami told him. "That thing is lethal."

"It's delicious—"

"It's *lethal*. And I won't have one of you leaving a half-drunk glass around for the children to find."

Roy looked insulted. "We would never—"

"I know you'll never. Because if you want it, you'll drink it in the kitchen."

He sighed.

"What's it called?" I asked.

"The Boss. It has tomato juice, horseradish, Worcestershire sauce, lime juice, celery salt, garlic, black pepper—"

"That's a Bloody Mary."

"Don't you mean a bloody vamp?" Tami said archly.

Roy ignored her. "No, it's *the* Bloody Mary—"

"Meaning what?" I asked.

"Meaning that I used tequila instead of vodka, Carolina Reaper hot sauce instead of tabasco, chili liqueur, and pickle juice."

"Pickle juice?"

"You heard me. It's divine."

I decided to take his word for it.

"Here's your sweater," Tami said, sorting through a pile of presents under the tree and handing me a package. "Everyone's gotta have one. They're the only properly festive thing around here."

I took the box gingerly, hoping for the best but not really expecting it. Fred had arrived with me, yet he'd already been mugged by the sweater fairy. I could see him across the room, sporting a bright green oversized monstrosity with a reclining nude Santa on the front, who was holding a strategically placed gift box. Sparkly gold letters underneath spelled out "Wait 'til you see the package I have for *you*."

Fearing the worst, I opened my present. And discovered that it wasn't too bad. A silver sweater lay inside, bedecked with faux Christmas lights that nonetheless lit up when Tami pressed a switch. It was gaudy, but it was fun.

I put it on.

And then I noticed that it had a slogan, too: Get Lit.

I decided that that was good advice, and drank my drink.

It should have been a wonderful party, especially after I found a chair, somebody brought me a plate of food, and I finished noshing on a pile of sandwiches, potato salad and baked beans. And one of the cannibalized gingerbread men, who had a missing leg and a lolling tongue, but tasted good enough. I nibbled on it while watching some witches play a drinking game with a vamp who'd gotten a sweater with a bull's eye and some Velcro covered balls on it.

"You miss, you drink," it declared, and they were busy missing. The balls stuck in the vamp's hair, on every part of his anatomy except the target, and even in his open mouth when he tried to complain. And it wasn't likely to get any better. The more the women drank, the worse their aim, and it hadn't been good to begin with.

But they were nonetheless laughing uproariously, clearly enjoying themselves.

Elspeth came by, looking furtive for some reason, and didn't have time to talk. But at least I found out that "t" stood for "trappings". Of course.

How silly of me.

I even spotted Rhea, who I guessed had decided carpe diem, and joined the party. But not before changing out of the fussy Edwardian stuff she'd been wearing and into a red plush, swishy miniskirt and matching jacket, with "Santa's Bae" written on the back. She looked good, especially with the oversized red hat with white fur and pompom she'd topped it with. She was talking to Rico, who had somehow managed to dodge the sweater brigade.

But he didn't dodge the hat, which Rhea took off and stood on tiptoe to put on his perfectly coiffured head. I even thought he might have leaned down slightly, to help her reach him. He'd accepted that she was focusing on her career lately, and on helping me hold things together during the war, but he clearly hadn't lost sight of the prize.

Glad someone's having fun, I thought, and then scowled at myself.

I noticed that Tami had been keeping the kids away, to give me a chance to eat before I was mobbed, and to deal with whatever my issue was this time. But I wasn't dealing with it. Because what do you do when your problem is a god?

You die, and so does everyone that you love.

I found a place for my empty plate and went out onto the balcony.

Chapter Forty

The balcony here was a much smaller affair than the terrace upstairs. There was barely enough space for a chaise lounge and a small table, the latter of which had been used as a depository for empty beer bottles. But the place held oversized memories.

Like Pritkin telling me, long before we became a couple, that he believed in me. That I could do this. That I could figure it out.

I was almost glad that he wasn't here to see me now.

"Hey."

That was Tami, probably come to find out why I was being such a party pooper.

I didn't turn around. I didn't want to be talked to or lectured at or even comforted right now. I wanted a step, a move, something to give us an edge, and I didn't have it.

I didn't have it.

"You okay?" Her voice came again, like nails on a chalkboard, which wasn't remotely fair.

"Yeah."

"Uh huh." Something appeared on the rail beside me, glinting with flecks of gold. "I thought you could use a refill."

I took it. Somebody had chilled the glass, leaving it slippery even with the gloves. I held on with both hands, not wanting to drop it off the side of the building.

"Thanks."

Tami had her own glass, a highball, but inside was something blood red. And sticking out of the top was a crispy piece of bacon, a skewer with a line of baby pickles, and a stalk of celery. She crunched the latter at me with a sly grin.

"I thought you said everybody had to drink those in the kitchen," I pointed out.

A black eyebrow went up. "I said they did. I don't leave drinks around, especially not this one."

"Can I?" I asked, wondering if this was a good idea.

She laughed and gave me a sip—and a sip was enough.

"My god, that's hot!"

The grin grew. "Well, it was named after Mircea."

I almost choked, although for which reason, I wasn't sure. "I didn't think you noticed."

"Oh, I noticed. He's an ass, but he's a hot ass." She thought about it. "Or has a hot ass. Or both."

I took a swallow out of my own glass, to try to stop my tongue from burning off, which wasn't the best idea. Rum and tequila mixed in my mouth, and it was not a taste sensation. I took another drink and it was better, but still.

"How long does this burn?" I asked her.

"Well, I had my first an hour ago, and got tired of having all pain and no pleasure, so I poured myself another."

"An *hour*?"

"Well, you only had a sip. Maybe you'll do better."

I stuck my tongue to the side of my glass, and prayed for mercy.

It was not forthcoming.

"Would you like some ice?" she asked, after a moment.

"Shut up."

She grinned.

We drank in silence while my tongue slowly recovered. Or maybe that layer of skin had just sloughed off. I wasn't sure.

"What did he mean in there?" Tami asked, after she somehow finished her drink, and was munching her way through the pickles.

"What did who mean?"

"Roy. He said something about you being the wrong person to ask about the tree?"

I shrugged. "Tony."

"Ah." Tami knew all about the fat bastard who'd raised me, if you could call it that. "No Christmas trees for you, I take it."

"They're a Victorian thing. Brought over from Germany by Prince Albert, when he married the queen. They didn't have them in medieval Italy, when Tony was born."

"And the things they did have?"

I grimaced. "We didn't have those, either. Although there was a tree this one time, when I was about seven."

"Tony grew a conscience?" Tami looked skeptical.

"Hardly." I turned to look at her and leaned my elbow on the railing. "You mean I never told you this story?"

She shook her head. We knew a lot about each other, but I guessed I'd skipped this. I shrugged.

"The tree was out in the garage. It was a separate building from the house, and Tony never went out there. The guys used it to escape from him to 'work on cars.' Which usually translated to drinking and playing cards."

"What a shock." She glanced back at the room behind us, where, sure enough, a bunch of the guys were gathered around one of the now denuded buffet tables, playing poker and drinking beer.

"But that year, they'd also made a 'tree' out of a bunch of gradated sizes of tires. Little scooter ones were on top, and from there it spread out all the way down to the big truck type on the bottom. They'd even decorated it with things they'd found in the cars when they cleaned them out. Bullet casings, old shoes, a dead rat . . ."

"You're kidding."

"Perfectly serious."

"And what did you think about your first tree?"

"What did I think?"

"Yeah, did you like it, or run screaming out the door? 'Cause I know which one I'd have picked."

I blinked at her, wondering how to explain that it didn't work like that. You didn't have the right to 'like' or 'dislike' things at Tony's. They simply were and you accepted them. Passivity was a useful form of self-defense.

And then I wondered—was that my problem? Could a life-time of conditioning, of reacting to things instead of acting, of following instead of leading, really be undone by a few months' training? Even from someone like Gertie?

I knew how to react to a crisis in the moment; it was the main reason I was alive. But when I wasn't in immediate danger, then what? Did I return to that passive girl I'd been, hiding behind piano legs, hoping nobody saw me? Or did I find a new way to be?

I could fight, but could I do the rest of this job?

Gertie had seemed to think so.

But Gertie had also run scared from Zeus, as I'd like to do right now, only I didn't have that luxury.

I felt Tami looking at me. "Cassie. You know I'm here if you need anything, right?"

"I know. I'm just . . . a little distracted tonight."

"I get it. Just remember."

"Remember what?" I asked. That last word had had a strange emphasis.

"That you don't have to go through this, whatever this is, alone. You have people—a lot of us—who want to help. Okay?"

I nodded, just as one of the older initiates stuck her head out of the sliding glass doors. "We're ready."

"Finally! I'll be right there," Tami patted my shoulder and then bustled back inside. And a moment later, the Christmas tree lit up to great applause from the crowd. Nobody had enchanted any of the ornaments, probably afraid to after the mess upstairs, so the bats didn't flutter and the Santas didn't do . . . whatever skeletonized Santas did. But it was pretty.

The lighting of the tree seemed to signal the beginning of the evening's entertainment. I sipped Roy's concoction and watched Fred launch into a karaoke session featuring "Santa Baby." He'd cleared a space in front of the "fireplace" and recruited the initiates that I'd helped to dress up to assist him. He'd even taught them a few basic dance moves. It was adorable, and should have brought a smile to my lips if anything could.

It didn't, because I knew I had people—good people—willing to help me. The problem wasn't with them. The problem was me.

Gertie had spent a lot of time teaching me things, but she'd spent just as much not teaching me. Sitting by her fire, sipping tea, or waiting on a blustery park bench, not tapping her foot but looking like she might start at any moment. And forcing me to puzzle something out for myself.

Pythias didn't get instruction books, and the hardest part of the job was often figuring out what the job was.

I stared at the floor, waiting for inspiration, but every scenario I came up with ended the same way.

I could go back in time and try to enlist the help of the eighteenth-century Pythia, the fearsome Lydia, who had trained Gertie. All this was happening on her turf. And even though it was my problem, since the trouble came from my era, she might be willing to help . . .

Except that that wasn't how this whole thing worked. Pythias did not team up, for the reasons I'd given Rhea, and Gertie had erased my counterparts' memories after the battle in Wales to preserve the timeline. So, Lydia wouldn't know who I was, and if she was anything like Gertie when we'd first met, she wouldn't even give me time to explain. She might even kill me outright as some rogue threatening her turf.

Not to mention that three Pythias, or as good as in Agnes's case, had already taken on Zeus and almost died for it. Lydia was a bitch, but I didn't think she was that big of a bitch. I sighed and rubbed my eyes.

I could spy on that damned castle, using the method Gertie had taught me, and try to figure out some kind of strategy. But Zeus had power in the byways and was probably expecting that. I'd likely be attacked as soon as I tried it.

Okay, so I could . . . I could use my new little storehouse of power to attempt to take an army back in time, just as he had. But even assuming I could manage it, we were up against a god. And a shapeshifting fey king. Right in front of a gate into Faerie.

They could just retreat to an area where our magic didn't work, and close the gate up after them. But we didn't have that advantage. Not to mention that a move like that would likely exhaust me, leaving me with little to fight with afterwards, and result in my army being a sitting duck.

Damn it, Cassie, think!

I could go back on my own, thus preserving my store of power. To the moment when the bastards were thrown back to their starting point in Romania, after Aeslinn peaced out of the fight on the Thames. He'd be vulnerable then—furious, and not thinking too clearly—as well as wounded.

I thought I could take him.

Only I couldn't. That would deny us a couple of much needed allies in Arsen and Faerie, who had been recruited after that point. Not to mention that defeating Aeslinn would leave me facing off with Zeus. Could he operate independently of a body? He was possessing the king somehow, but could he survive without him, like a ghost? And finish the fight as he almost had in London?

I didn't know, but it seemed at least possible, and then there was his army to worry about . . .

So, come up with something else! I thought furiously. This was exactly like the problems Gertie had set me, deliberately making them seem impossible—from one point of view. But turn them, twist them, look at them through a different lens, and there was always an answer. There had to be!

Okay.

Okay.

What if I went back multiple times, to the same moment? If I did it right, I could have many Cassies at that damned castle, all at the same time. In other words, I could use time travel to make an army out of *me*!

Normally, that wouldn't work, since we'd all be drawing from the same well of energy—the Pythian power. And judging by its reaction when Pritkin and Mircea were trying to save me, it clearly didn't think that it was enough to take on the king of the gods. But right now, I had my own bit of power, didn't I?

I could feel it boiling under my skin, ready for use, practically aching for it. It had been causing me problems all day, because I wasn't used to being this juiced up. But maybe it was also the solution I'd been looking for.

For a moment, I felt my heart start to thud; I thought I had it.

But there was a problem there, too. Multiple Cassies meant multiple chances for Zeus to kill me, and he only needed to do it once. Because they weren't different people; they were all me just from slightly different times.

So, kill one and the whole line collapsed, whenever their moment ran out.

Damn it! I felt like beating my head against something, only there wasn't anything handy. Except for the railing, and that would probably put me in the freaking hospital.

What about Chimera, the Pythian spell to allow me to make duplicates of myself? Those weren't me; they were copies of me, with each containing part of my soul. So, when one died, that bit of soul just bounced back to the original instead of killing me. I'd used that spell plenty of times in training, to avoid a hideous fate at the hands of Ermengarde, the linebacker of Gertie's court. Maybe—

But Chimera also halved my strength every time I made a duplicate. Because half a soul doesn't channel as much power. And half measures wouldn't work against Zeus.

No matter how I looked at it, there was no scenario that didn't end in disaster. No wonder Gertie hadn't given me an answer, I thought. Maybe, this time, there wasn't one.

"Uneasy lies the head who wears the crown."

I realized that I'd dropped my head into my hands at some point. I looked up and found myself facing Adra, the leader of the demon high council, in his blond, wispy-haired, round cheeked human guise. And even he had not escaped the sweater fairy.

He was wearing a red, oversized Christmas sweater that said Ho, Ho, Hold My Beer. It had a couple of tipsy reindeer, and twin beer holders clutched in the fists of an inebriated-looking Santa. One of the holders gripped a sweating can.

The other can was in Adra's hand, although he wasn't drinking it. I wasn't entirely sure that he could, considering that the real guy didn't look at all like his meat suit. But maybe he wanted to fit in.

Considering that all of the guests in the vicinity of the balcony had just found somewhere else to be, I didn't think that was working so well.

"I don't have a crown," I told him, and scooched over, to leave him a place to sit if he liked.

He took it.

"Even worse, then. All of the trouble, and none of the rewards. I'm surprised they find anyone to take this job."

"As opposed to leading the demon high council?"

"Ah, but that has its perks." He drank beer, proving me wrong, and leaned back against the balcony railing. "Although, I doubt any of them could be compensation enough for what you are currently facing."

I regarded him steadily. "Are you spying on me, Adra?"

"Of course not." The face was in its creepy, I-can't-be-bothered-to-have-an-expression mode, but the voice sounded offended. "I have people for that."

"And they came to you screaming about Zeus being back." I didn't make it a question, since we both knew why he was here.

"It is the sort of news that captures one's attention," he agreed.

I didn't say anything. I could have filled him in, but if he'd gotten a report on my and Rhea's conversation, he already knew most of it. And frankly, I didn't feel like rehashing it all again.

So, I watched the party instead, giving my brain a break, and Adra watched it with me. It felt surreal, knowing that all this could be erased, any minute now. That Zeus could do something, hundreds of years back in time, and then—blip. A totally new world.

It made the whole party appear ephemeral, not solid like time should. The people seemed to have vague halos around them, that disappeared when I blinked my eyes, and even the music warbled in and out, as if it wasn't sure that it should be here. Or maybe that was me.

I drank my drink.

"What is the phrase?" Adra asked. "A penny for your thoughts?"

"You'd be over paying."

"A beer then?" he waggled his leftover can enticingly.

I held up my glass.

"Good choice," he approved. "This is truly terrible."

"They have better beer in hell?"

"No, but we do have a rather nice substitute. Sadly, it would likely kill you."

"Guess I'll stick with this, then," I said, and drained Roy's concoction.

Maybe two drinks inside an hour had made me loose lipped; I didn't know. But I found myself telling Adra what I was thinking, anyway. Not that it was all that interesting.

"There was this vamp at Tony's when I was growing up named Alphonse. He liked old gangster flicks, including ones that were so bad they didn't even get played on late night T.V. So, he got himself an antique projector and some big spools of film, and screened his own. Attendance was mandatory, but there was popcorn, so I didn't mind too much."

"It was polite of him to include you," Adra said.

"It was nothing of the kind. I wasn't invited for the pleasure of my company. I was there on fire suppression duty. That old nitrate film was highly flammable and the projector was crap and sparked sometimes."

"A bad combination."

"Yeah. More than one screening ended with the film catching fire, and getting these weird, burnt-edged holes that spread across it, eating people's faces, eating everything. Until it finally broke, right before the whole reel went up."

"This reminds me of that. Of the instant when everything still looks fine, but you smell the smoke. And know you're already screwed."

"That is . . . disturbing."

"Yeah."

I saw Tami holding up a tiny initiate, to allow her to see the Christmas tree better, and watched the colorful lights spangle the little girl's face. There was nothing magical about the tree; it was just tinsel, plastic and some gaudy colored lights. It had none of the power that was prowling around upstairs.

But there was magic, nonetheless, on the little girl's face and in her delighted smile.

I was proud to have given her that. Proud to have played a small role in providing some of the awe and joy that I had never known as a child. But it wasn't enough.

A Pythia had to do more than that, had to be more than that. I was on fire suppression duty again, and if I failed it wouldn't be film going up in flames this time. Zeus had shown me what it would be.

And while my mind might have trouble comprehending ruined landscapes and cities full of corpses, the smaller things, the more human things, I got just fine.

I spotted Rhea across the room, talking to Françoise, who was shaking her head. Didn't look like Zeus had sent me any letters. But maybe somebody else had.

I stood up. "Stay here," I told Adra. "I'll be back in a minute."

He shot me a sly look. "You have an idea."

"Maybe."

"Is it something I can help with?"

"I'll let you know."

Chapter Forty-One

I hate this place," I said fervently. And that was all I said, because Rhea clapped a hand over my mouth a second later. Then she froze, going rigid against me, probably for the same reason that I just had: we weren't alone.

We'd shifted onto a basement staircase, in darkness, since neither of us had remembered to bring a flashlight. Which was stupid; I knew how dim this place could be. But it wasn't quite dim enough.

The old, rough, vaguely golden stones under my feet were splashed with faint fingers of light, as if someone was holding a lantern, far away. And hushed voices could be heard in the distance, echoing up the stairs we were standing on. They weren't loud enough for me to make anything out, but they did cause me to hug the wall and wonder what to do now.

We were back at the old Pythian Court in London, but not Gertie's version. Her successor, Agnes, had held court in that same building, as had her predecessor, Lydia. But it hadn't been an option for me, after the place was attacked by a combo of dark mages and rogue acolytes some months ago.

That had not only destroyed the building I fondly remembered, but had also blown something else all to hell—the Pythian library. My acolytes had been bugging me to go back and rescue it for weeks, although how I was supposed to do that, I didn't know. I also didn't care, since I didn't want the creepy place anywhere near me.

Or its librarian.

She and I had a somewhat . . . fraught . . . relationship, not to mention that her library had almost caused me to have a seizure. Unlike Mircea's little imprint, this place contained hundreds, maybe thousands, of ancient donations to the court, and most of them seemed to have a story to tell. I'd been attacked the last time I was here by a swarm of the things, and had barely survived. And drowning in memory wasn't the way I wanted to go.

But then, neither was death-by-god, so I was kind of in a bind here.

I bit my lip, wondering who, exactly, was down there, because the librarian was a ghost and they didn't need lanterns. Considering that this was the night that everything went up in flames, I didn't like my options. Especially when the dim light started moving across the stones, blushing first one part and then the other.

But not like someone was walking around. More like someone was swinging it while jogging this way, which was not good. But was better than when it abruptly went out, leaving me staring at utter darkness—

Until it reappeared a second later, right in our faces.

"Whatcha doing?"

"Auggghhh!"

I came off the wall, hand up, a spell boiling in my palm. And paused it just in time, since I knew the sweet old face being lit up by a small lantern. Damn it!

"It's all right," Annabelle called over her shoulder, as I fought not to scream. "It's just Cassie and Rhea."

"Oh, my God," the latter half of that equation said, slumping against the wall. "Oh, my God."

Somebody cursed from downstairs, but I didn't care. My spell throbbed in my hand, spangling Annabelle's face with watery light. She had on a nightgown, a frilly thing with lots of lace, peeking out of the top of a flowered robe. The flowers in question were cabbage roses, which went better with the fuzzy pink slippers than her Pythian finery had, but were so incongruous in this setting that I just stood there for a moment, staring at her.

"There are dark mages upstairs, setting charges," I finally said. "They're about to blow this place to kingdom come."

"Yes, isn't it exciting?" Her cheeks were as pink as her shoes. "I never got to do anything like this until I met you."

I stared at her some more before slowly closing my fingers, cancelling the spell. I needed another drink. And then I noticed the one she was holding.

"What is that?"

She looked down at the large, white, stoneware mug she was gripping in the fist that didn't have a lantern in it. "Oh, just some tea, dear."

"That's . . . not tea." The mug had contained tea a second ago; now, a lone teabag, dry and unused, sat at the bottom. And nothing else.

Until it abruptly changed back into a properly milky mug of English breakfast.

Annabelle took a sip. "It's rather nice. I don't need a refill this way," she confided.

"What's wrong with it?" I demanded, a little louder than necessary, but my nerves were shot.

She tried to take another sip, but the dry tea bag bumped her nose. She frowned, cross eyed, at it. "Nothing. It'll be all right in a minute. It's caught in your spell."

I looked down, but my hand was just a hand. I looked back up. "I didn't cast a spell."

"Not that one. The one from before. When you sent the top three floors of Dante's back time."

"What?"

She nodded. "The vampires had to find temporary rooms for us all, you see, while they sorted things out upstairs and mine is on the floor below the bodyguards' level, with some of the Senate's officials on it. They've made themselves quite a nice breakroom down there, I must say. They said that room service took forever and they became tired of waiting, sometimes for hours, for tea, coffee, what have you. So, they repurposed a bedroom—"

"Annabelle."

"Yes, dear?"

"What *happened*?"

"That's what I'm trying to explain. I was in the breakroom, making myself a cup of tea before bedtime, as I wasn't planning to go to the party. Seeing gives me a headache and I was—oh," her hand came up to cover her mouth, causing the teabag to bump her nose again. "I'm sorry! I wanted to apologize, if whatever I said earlier was upsetting. I can't control it, you know, and often can't remember what I said afterwards—"

"You said she is going to die," Rhea rasped, coming off the wall.

I guessed she hadn't recovered yet, either.

"Yes, well, death doesn't always mean actual death," Annabelle said earnestly. "It can, of course, but it's rather like the Death card in the Tarot. It can also—"

"Annabelle!" I snapped. My patience was gone, just freaking gone. "What happened to the *tea*?"

She looked at me blankly. "What tea?"

"That tea!" I pointed at her cup.

"Oh, didn't I say? The functionaries wanted a room with some snacks—"

"No! *That* tea! Right *there*! Why is it doing that?"

She looked down again. "You mean, aging back and forth?"

"Yes!"

"Oh, well, when you turned back time, I had just cast a spell to do the opposite. It takes so long for the water to heat up—they don't have proper electric kettles in the break room yet, and—" she saw my expression. "Anyway, I've gotten into the habit of helping the process along. So, the two spells are fighting at present. But they'll sort themselves out eventually—where are you going?"

I didn't answer. I just pushed past her and went downstairs to talk to Hilde. Who I knew—I *knew*—was waiting for me somewhere below. And sure enough, she was at the bottom of the flight of stairs, tapping her foot with all the patience of her sister, which meant none at all.

For once, I was too annoyed to care. Or to take in the vast, cavernous room behind her, with its sprawling stone floor and ancient pillars and fantastic number of late Victorian display cabinets holding a few millennia's worth of trouble. Right now, I had enough of my own.

"I turned back time in my *closet*," I told her. "To keep from burning down the hotel. Not for three floors!"

"That may have been what you meant, but I assure you, it was not what you did," Hilde said placidly.

"But I *can't*—"

"Normally not, perhaps, but today seems to be about breaking rules, does it not?"

That was brazen, considering what she was currently doing. I looked behind her, to where a gaggle of her closest conspirators had the grace to look a little shame faced, at least. Unlike Hilde.

"Well, you turning up should solve one of the problems we've been having, at least," she informed me.

I crossed my arms. "You're stealing the library!"

"We're retrieving the court's property—"

"Now? There's a hit squad upstairs!"

"Yes, which is why it must be now. Any sooner, and someone might notice. Tonight, we know where everyone is, and what they're up to."

Which was exactly why I'd chosen this moment to come back, although I wasn't going to admit that. "Must be nice," I said instead, looking at her pointedly.

She looked back, unphased. "We discussed this, if you recall."

"Yes, and I said I'd think about it—"

"You've had weeks now—"

"—and I'm still thinking!"

"Nonsense." Hilde swept it away. "You're here, aren't you? To ask the librarian for help with the unprecedented situation we are facing?"

"No."

"No?"

"No!" I turned away.

And had Annabelle pop into being almost on top of me. "It's so good to have you," she said, as I stumbled back. "We're having a problem with the incantation, you see, and—"

Rhea caught me before I fell, while the relentlessly cheerful doomsayer babbled on. I was left looking up at a large, freestanding arch, which promptly shocked the hell out of me as soon as I put out a hand to steady myself. Son of a bitch!

I jerked back, feeling like I'd just had a run in with an industrial strength Taser. "What the hell?"

"From the original temple at Delphi," Rhea said quietly, while helping to steady me. "It was part of the Pythia's inner sanctum along with the omphalos, the navel of the world."

"The what?"

She made an elegant gesture at something sitting near the arch. It was maybe four feet tall, made out of yellowish marble, and shaped vaguely like a beehive. There were also some carved . . . things . . . on the surface, although if they were supposed to be bees, Delphi had needed a better artist.

"That's the navel of the world?" I asked, nursing my hand.

Rhea nodded. "One of them. There's another in Jerusalem, modelled after this one, but ours was first. There's a copy of it in the Delphi Museum."

"Uh huh." I didn't want to hurt her feelings, but the world's navel was an outie and not a good-looking one.

"The legend says that Zeus released two eagles on opposite sides of the planet, and the navel is where they came together. It was considered to be the center of the world, and was the stone over which the ancient Pythias gave their prophesies—"

I decided that my hard ass throne wasn't looking so bad, suddenly.

"—while the arch was the gateway through which Apollo was said to have visited his priestesses."

"Visited?" I looked back at the hulking thing, paying more attention this time. It was tall—like far more than the two stories of space it supposedly had—with the top disappearing into darkness and the bottom splashed with lamplight. It was made of the same yellowish stone as everything else down here, although it looked older. There were cracks spidering across the surface, blocks that didn't fit together quite right, and noticeable chips around the edges.

In other words, it was the crumbly, low-rent kind of ancient rather than the awe-inspiring type, but Rhea was looking at it with pride, nonetheless.

"You mean . . . they used that thing to come to Earth?" I asked, for clarification.

She nodded. "According to legend. That was before your mother's spell, when the gods regularly went back and forth. I suppose it must have been some sort of portal—"

Yeah, that's what I was afraid of.

"—but, of course, it doesn't work anymore. The ouroboros spell cut it off."

"Then why keep it?" I asked harshly. Here we were, fighting a war against the gods, and the damned Pythian Court had a doorway to their dimension sitting in the basement? The fuck?

Rhea seemed a little taken aback.

"It's . . . tradition. All of this," she gestured around at the huge room. "It's part of our heritage—"

"A heritage from when we were slaves to Apollo. It's sick!"

"It's history." She frowned, probably because Rhea was a big history buff. "Our history, the good and the bad—"

"And currently blown to bits!" I never thought I'd be happy that the Pythian Court had gone up like a massive firework, but here we were. For once, it seemed that we'd actually gotten a break.

"Can we get back to the point?" Hilde inquired.

"Good idea!" I strode off, despite having no idea where I was going.

"This way, Lady," Rhea said, catching up. And steered me toward a door on the other side of the room that was shaped roughly like a pyramid with the top cut off. It was wider at the bottom and narrower at the top, and totally black inside. Fun.

"Just a moment." Hilde's voice wasn't raised, but it was commanding. I felt my footsteps falter, maybe because she sounded so much like her sister. And then got mad at myself for it; I had bigger things to worry about than a damned library!

Annabelle popped into being in front of me again, leaving me looking directly into a huge pair of blue eyes. "It's the spell, you see," she said breathlessly. "No one's used it since Lydia was a girl, and none of us were alive then—"

"So, go ask Lydia!" I pushed past her. Only to stumble when she suddenly reappeared in front of me again, so close that we both almost went down. "Stop doing that!"

"Then stop running away from your responsibilities," Hilde said, coming up behind us.

"I'm fulfilling my responsibilities!" I snarled, turning on her. "I'm trying to deal with a god, and you're worried about a library!"

"Which may yield clues as to how to fight said god—"

"Then research! Read! Do whatever the hell you want! Just leave me—"

"We can't leave you alone," the voice was a bit sharper this time. "We need to move the library out of here, to the new court in Las Vegas, where we don't have to worry about evil forces trying to destroy it—"

"So, move it!" If I was lucky, it would keep them busy for a few months. I spun back around, took a couple of strides—

And had an acolyte in fuzzy pink slippers reappear in my face. "We've been trying," Annabelle said, as I stumbled back. "But none of us has ever used the spell, and the omphalos won't work without it. The librarian is the only one who knows it—"

"Then ask her!"

"They have," a voice intoned from behind me, freezing me in place. "But I may only release it to the Pythia."

I slowly turned around and there she was, a deceptively demure looking woman that reminded me of Melanie Wilkes in *Gone with the Wind*. Her hair was dark and looped up in braids beside her head, her eyes were blue—as far as I could tell, since she was semi-transparent—and she was wearing a high-necked, old fashioned, demure blue dress. You'd never guess that her whole head could open up, like something out of *Beetlejuice*, with the entire skull rimmed in teeth.

But it could.

I saw it my dreams sometimes, and I didn't want to see it again. Or whatever other tricks she might have. I also didn't want to waste more time. "Then do it! Give them whatever they want, just leave me out—"

"The Pythia's touch is a necessary component," the librarian said mildly, consulting a book that was floating in the air over her almost transparent hand. Then she looked up, with an identical expression to the one that Hilde was currently wearing. It was eerily familiar, since it was also the one Eugenie had pulled out whenever I wasn't sufficiently docile.

And I did not have time for that kind of hell.

I turned around, marched back over, and slapped my hand down on top of the ugly beehive. "Do it."

The librarian and Hilde exchanged a glance, and then everyone hurried over, as if something momentous was about to happen. The librarian consulted the book again, adjusted her spectacles, and intoned some words in a language I didn't know and didn't care about. Especially after exactly nothing changed.

I stood there. The girls stood there. The librarian's semi-transparent body bobbed slowly up and down.

"Is . . . is it supposed to light up or something?" Annabelle asked, in a loud whisper.

I felt my blood pressure tick up a couple more notches.

"Was there something else?" Hilde demanded.

The librarian consulted her book again. A small frown appeared between her eyes. The spectacles were adjusted once more. "No. That was the complete ritual."

"Maybe it's broken?" Devi asked, bending over to take a look at one of the navel's many hairline cracks.

"It's always looked like that," Chloris said, smacking it with her stringy old lady arm. "It's solid enough."

"Well, maybe the incantation was pronounced wrong. Does anyone know ancient Greek?"

"I do," the librarian said, looking annoyed.

"Yes, but I meant anyone else."

"Are you sure you don't remember the last ritual?" Cecily asked Tillie, who was looking more like a Christmas tree than ever with the lamplight shining on her golden updo.

Tillie scowled. "The last time it was used was 1781!"

"Yes, and?"

"I wasn't born then!"

I turned around and strode off.

"Where do you think you're going?" Hilde asked. "We have to figure this out."

This time, I didn't even slow down. "You figure it out. I have work to do!"

"Lady Cassandra—"

"Don't Lady Cassandra me! And don't follow me! Any of you!"

"Why are Pythias always so testy?" I heard someone whisper.

Rhea caught up with me, looking a little chagrined. "If you say they mean well," I warned her. "I swear to God—"

"I was not going to say that," she assured me. "This way."

Chapter Forty-Two

The place was atmospheric; you had to give it that.

We threaded a path in between cases glittering with gold and silver plate, chests of jewels, and piles of antique weapons. Pieces of the latter seemed to vibrate slightly as we passed, chiming with a music too faint to hear, although I could feel it in my bones. There were also reliquary-style containers, a few just simple wooden boxes, but most encrusted with jewels and hanging from ropes of pearls as big as my thumb, with glass or crystal side panels showing off the shriveled contents.

Some of which appeared to be moving.

Stop it, I told myself firmly, and didn't look too closely. But I could have. Because the room wasn't so dim anymore.

Candelabras flared to life beside the walls, near the pillars that formed a circular colonnade around the periphery of the big open area. They didn't light all at once, but tracked us across the space. Meanwhile, the pillars threw shadows ahead of themselves, long gray fingers that broke up the golden light into something that resembled reaching hands, clutching for us.

It gave a weird, spotlight-type effect to the remaining light, which sparkled off the contents of the cases and moved across our faces. It striped the room, first from one direction and then another, as different light sources flared or went out. You'd think the Pythian Court could afford a few extra candles, I thought, to avoid giving people the creeps!

But I guessed not.

The experience did answer a question, however. I'd always wondered how Agnes had amassed the large number of anti-poison devices that she'd owned. I'd assumed she must have traveled the world, slowly picking them up from gnarled old mages or dusty shops. That, basically, the collection had been the work of a lifetime.

When, in reality, she'd just had to go downstairs.

We finally reached the oddly shaped door. Inside, I could make out nothing besides more dark, stretching to apparent infinity. I wondered how we were supposed to find anything in there.

Then a long line of sconces flared to life, pair by pair on either side of the corridor walls, stretching for what looked like a city block. They flooded the place with light as if in invitation, only it wasn't one I wanted. I repressed a strong urge to turn around, to go back to the party, to get drunk and forget the whole thing.

But Rhea was looking at me, obviously expecting better things.

Act like a Pythia, I told myself, and stepped inside.

Age and history seemed to fold around me as I did so. I could almost feel the weight of it, to the point that I looked up, wondering if the ceiling was about to fall down. Like the corridor, it was made from old, hand-chiseled stone that had been cut into huge slabs, some with worrying cracks in them. Laura Croft would have felt right at home.

I was less enthusiastic, and that was before I looked back down.

And noticed something . . . odd . . . about the rooms we were passing.

Fat, square doorways opened off of the corridor at irregular intervals on either side. They matched everything else down here, with heavy, crudely cut lintels, no actual doors, and chipped stone sides. They would have looked perfectly appropriate in a pharaoh's tomb.

But the interiors . . . were something else entirely.

There was a French country drawing room, like something Marie Antoinette might have used, with pale pink walls, pink and gray striped settees and a gorgeous gray-veined marble fireplace. Next door was a Moroccan-looking space with pierced wooden screens, beautiful carpets and brass lanterns, and colorful pillows scattered around low-rise tables. Then came a garden with a lion's head fountain and a mass of autumn roses draped over an old stone wall with a door set into it, which led to a cozy sitting room. And, finally, there was a rock-cut chamber with a wooden lattice of cubbyholes on the walls, filled with what appeared to be thousands of scrolls.

Even stranger, all of the rooms were alive.

The French sitting room had a large window with a tree outside, showing blue skies through the branches where little birds were hopping about, chirping at each other. The Moroccan-looking room had a brass tea service on the low table, with a thin thread of steam escaping from the delicate spout. The garden had water trickling from the lion's mouth, and fallen leaves dusting the stones or blowing through the air. And the rock-cut room had a bald man who was returning a scroll to one of the cubbyholes.

I stopped dead.

"Who—" I lowered my voice. "Who is that?" There was no way he was a servant of the house. I knew that without even asking. And not just because the court's servants went home at night, and didn't live in. But because he looked . . . *antique.*

I don't mean old; he appeared to be in his early forties, with the little ring of hair around his otherwise bald head still mostly brown. But he wore an unbleached woolen tunic and a rough leather belt and sandals, all of which appeared to have been made by hand. And he had crooked, yellow teeth that I glimpsed when he yawned, which looked like they'd never been near a dentist.

He didn't look old, he looked *old*, like from another time.

One that was apparently alive and well inside that room.

I felt a soft hand on my shoulder. "I should have warned you," Rhea said. "The library is a bit . . . unusual."

"*Unusual?*" I tried to look at her, but my fascinated gaze refused to budge. It was taking in the ancient oil lamp swinging from a chain overhead, which the bald man had bumped with his shoulder when he passed. It threw wildly leaping shadows onto the cave-like interior, and sloshed a small puddle of oil onto the floor. The oil stayed there, reflecting the light, and glimmering wetly against the somewhat dusty stones—

For an instant.

Then it was gone and the lamp extinguished, plunging the room back into darkness. Like the man, who disappeared as he approached the door, while I was trying to pull Rhea back out of the way. But there was no need; there was no one there anymore. Even the scent of the wick and the faint trace of olive oil on the air was gone.

Suddenly, all I could smell was dust.

"Each Pythia puts the records of her era into a room of her own design," Rhea explained. "They're called Legacy Rooms because they contain her complete story: the times she averted disaster, the discoveries she made, the treaties and agreements she concluded, everything."

"Fascinating," I breathed.

"But, of course, records deteriorate over time," she added. "Even parchment doesn't last forever, and it would be fantastically expensive to charm thousands of books and scrolls against decay over millennia."

"So, they do . . . what?" I asked, wondering why I didn't even see any dust motes turning in the air. The room looked like it hadn't been disturbed in ages.

"That," she said, as a man appeared out of nowhere and lit the lamp with a word. Dim golden light spilled out in a circle, brightening the gloom. And highlighting his body: middle aged, yellow teeth, wearing an unbleached tunic with a few ink smears on the fabric . . .

It was the same man. The one who had just left with a scroll in his hand. The same scroll that was somehow back in its cubby hole, the wooden roller on the end gleaming like the top of his bald head.

At least, it was until he took it down again and left, bumping the lamp on his way out. Once more, the room was plunged into darkness. Once more, the place smelled of nothing but dust.

"There was some sort of mistake with this one," Rhea said. "Each room is on a time loop of varying lengths, most of an hour or two. It gives a reader time to get in, find the information they need, and get back out again. Then time resets, starting over as if nothing has ever happened."

I suddenly realized why all the books on the shelves inside the French drawing room had looked so fresh, with well-oiled spines and sharp lettering, as if they hadn't aged a day since they were put in place.

Because they hadn't.

"But this is one of the older rooms," Rhea continued. "From an early Pythia, and something went wrong with the charm. Instead of an hour, it loops every—"

"Couple of minutes," I said, as here came Baldy again.

She nodded, watching the man with a small frown. "It makes it very challenging to get in there and peruse anything. The loop also makes it impossible to take anything out—that's true of all of them—as time resets on schedule, regardless of where an item is, causing a book to vanish from your hands. It ensures that nothing can be lost, as nothing is ever really removed. But it can be quite annoying!"

"I'm sure."

"And the fact that the servant keeps coming and going makes it hard to read anything even in the short time you have. I know; I used to try to get in there as a girl."

I bet she had. Rhea had a scholar's mind and an inquisitive attitude, what might have been called nosy on a less likeable person. The badly timed reset had probably driven her crazy.

"I tried using a cloaking spell," she added, "to sneak in without the servant seeing me. It seemed to work. But I'd no sooner taken down a scroll and begun reading—"

"You read ancient Greek?"

"Koine and some Doric. Although the scrolls in there are more like Homeric Greek, with many even older. They were hard to decipher, and every time I tried, the scroll disappeared before I could do much of anything."

"Because time had reset."

She nodded in remembered frustration.

I wondered what some ancient Pythia hadn't wanted anybody to read.

But, right then, that wasn't my problem.

"So, Gertie has a library down here, too?" I asked. That was why we'd come. We were on a quest for Gertie's private papers, because I had a hunch—one I really needed to be right.

She nodded. "Yes, this way."

We'd have made better time, but I kept stopping to peer into different rooms—there seemed to be an unending line of them—and different eras. I didn't see any more people, although there was a songbird in a large golden cage in a medieval-looking space, with sunlight streaming through the windows. And a couple of squirrels chasing each other around a tree outside of a Renaissance-era, multipaned window, through which I could see a huge, beautifully illuminated book lying open on a pedestal. There was also what looked like an ancient dining room, with murals on the walls and Roman-era couches clustered around a low table piled with gorgeous looking food. And a dog, who had just dragged a whole roast chicken onto the floor, and was happily gnawing on it.

I guessed if you ate anything in there, you really were hungry again in an hour.

There was also a large cat a few doors down, curled up in a chair in a more modern-looking room, with a fire burning in a red brick fireplace, and a nice, squashy armchair pulled up alongside.

A very familiar armchair.

"Mr. Tubbins," Rhea said. "You're not supposed to be down here!"

She bent and scooped the cat up into her arms. He was a handsome, gray, fluffy boy with bright blue eyes, and did not seem to appreciate his nap being disturbed. Rhea ignored the ruffled neck fur and the slightly bristled tail, however, and carted him out of the room.

"I thought you couldn't do that," I said.

She looked up from stroking his unhappy little face. "Do what?"

"Take something out of one of the rooms."

"Well, you can, it just disappears when the time is—oh. You're talking about—no." She shook her head. "This is one of the Pythian Court cats. This court. They sometimes sneak down here and sleep in front of the fire."

"Then . . . we can go in?" I looked back at the room again.

"Of course. These are the Pythian libraries. There's a large, conventional one for general knowledge, with a collection that gets cycled out from time to time. But you said you wanted Lady Herophile's private papers—"

"Yes."

"—and they won't be in there." She glanced back inside the room, cuddling the cat. "This was my favorite reading nook, when I was younger. This library has a longer loop than anywhere else, almost four hours. It was a nice place to relax."

"There must have been nice places upstairs, too."

She nodded, absently stroking the cat. "But there were people there. There were none in here."

I assumed that she was talking about Agnes's acolytes, who hadn't exactly seemed fond of her. I'd had a few bolt holes at Tony's, where I could curl up well away from short-tempered vamps and their mercurial master. Some of those might have seemed pretty strange to other people, too.

"But it's odd, seeing it again, after experiencing the original," she said. "It feels like Gertie should be here, as if she might step out of nothing . . ."

Yeah. It did. Especially when I crossed the threshold, and found myself back in another time.

My breath had been fogging the air in front of me from the moment I came down here; the Pythian Court didn't waste heat. But it suddenly stopped, and not just because of the warmth emanating from the fireplace. But because I knew this room.

I knew everything in it.

Gertie's private study looked exactly the same as always. There was the card table with the worn edges, the drapes with the ridiculously long fringe, and the cheerfully crackling fire. Even the pince-nez were the same, as if she'd just stepped outside for a moment and would be right back to claim them.

But something was different.

The line of mementos was even there, scattered along the mantlepiece, but now there was one more. A small, triangular, glass bottle, thick and slightly bubbled. I picked it up before I thought—

And saw myself.

It was just a flash, maybe three seconds long, showing me laughing with Agnes. That had been a rare event, but Gertie had set us a challenge that day, a ridiculously difficult game of tag. We'd had to find and send home all the other acolytes capable of shifting, who were hiding from us somewhere in a ten-year span of time, before she returned from her shopping.

They had scattered all over London, and they kept shifting away, whenever they spotted us. So, we'd had to work together to succeed, which would win us a weekend off. Fail, and we had to shine all the girl's boots by morning. And Agnes had warned me that they would deliberately get them extra muddy, just to be assholes. In fact, we'd found the last one doing exactly that, splashing up a storm down by the river, before we cornered her.

We'd arrived at court breathless and pink cheeked and covered in mud, after our captive ran us for half a mile. But we'd made it to the front door just before Gertie, with the twisting, yelling and cursing acolyte in between us. I'd thought I was going to have a heart attack, but instead, Gertie had laughed . . .

I felt my stomach constrict, as if someone had just punched me in it.

I put the bottle back.

There were a few more changes: additional bookcases lined the walls, to hold all of Gertie's papers, I guessed, and the door to the bedroom didn't open. I knew because I tried it, my heart racing a little, my suddenly sweaty palms slipping on the worn brass that stayed stubbornly closed.

Had I actually expected her to be in there? In her gaudy nightwear, sitting on her bed against a pile of pillows, and looking up at me over the top of a book. Displeased to be disturbed, but not enough to order me out. She didn't do that to her girls.

And, for all too brief of a time, I had been one of those.

"Are you alright?" Rhea asked, as I just stood there, facing the stubbornly closed door. One that would always be closed now. Like Billy's locket would always be silent.

I felt my hand come up, clenching on it, too, and there was nothing.

Just nothing at all.

"Cassie?"

"I'm fine." It was harsh, but that didn't matter. The fact that Rhea had used my actual name instead of the ever present 'Lady' meant that she already knew I was lying.

But I didn't turn around to reassure her, because I couldn't do that right now. I couldn't pretend. Which I guessed she realized.

"I . . . I'll be next door. There was something . . . I'll be next door."

I heard her leave, soft footsteps on an equally soft old rug, the colors a little faded where the sun shone through the window, and with a few threadbare spots. But it had never been replaced, since Gertie liked it that way. She'd liked a lot of broken things . . .

Stop this! I told myself savagely. Or you're going to have a lot more people to mourn, and pretty damned soon! Just shut up and find it!

I looked around the room, trying to see past the nostalgia, the memories, and the grief, and to view it as Gertie would have. As she must have after she'd figured out the puzzle. The one that wouldn't leave her alone, the one that had kept her up at night, the one that had stumped both of us.

But not the one she'd given up on, because Gertie didn't play that way.

If she had one defining character trait, it was stubbornness. She had tracked me across time like a bloodhound, never giving up, never giving in, until I'd thought I would scream. And then she'd tracked me some more, even after I left her dunked in icy rivers or flailing in a bog.

It hadn't mattered. She'd simply gotten out, dried off, and returned to the chase. Which is why I knew, I knew, she wouldn't have just given up on whatever those Tarot cards had been trying to tell her.

She would have chewed on it, poked at it, and lost more sleep over it, tossing and turning in her bed while those damned cards spun around and around in her mind. Even after I left; even after it didn't matter anymore. Because I mattered to her, and she'd wanted to help.

One last lesson, she'd said, but that lesson had never completed, had it?

She could have blanked her memory and forgotten all of this, forgotten Zeus, forgotten me. But I didn't think she had. Not until she'd solved it. Not until the day, maybe months later, maybe years, that she got it. I *knew* she had.

But then what? I was gone by then, and so was Rhea. How to get the information to us? How to tell me without telling anyone else, and thus endangering time?

The only thing I could think of was for her to have left it here, among her personal papers. But hidden, somewhere even Agnes would never find it. But somewhere, if I came looking, might catch my eye. Somewhere . . .

Like that, I thought, catching sight of a familiar pack of Tarot cards, on top of a bookshelf.

I went over, opened them up, and shook them out. They looked the same as before, the Marseilles' Tarot with its bright, candy-colored illustrations, like a coloring book some that kid had gotten hold of and gone to town. But there was nothing inside. No note, no clue, no anything.

Just the cards.

So maybe they weren't there for themselves, but as a marker. A "look here" kind of thing that only I would notice. But look at what? The bookshelf? Because it wasn't one of the new ones. It was the one I remembered, still in its usual place by the door.

And still holding Gertie's big mythology tome on the bottom shelf.

Like the cards, it was just as bright as ever, with its dark blue cover oiled and shiny and its gilt-edged pages gleaming. I pulled it off the shelf, my hands trembling slightly. If I was wrong, I was screwed. I needed help and I didn't know where else to look.

I knelt on the floor in front of the bookcase, feeling the weight of the heavy book on my lap. Please, I thought. Please, Gertie. There is no one else and I'm so alone. I have people all around me, but no one I can trust, not with this. I have to be the leader now, and I think you were wrong; I don't think I'm ready!

I *need* that lesson.

Please help me, one last time.

I opened the book, hardly daring to breathe . . .

And out fell a long, white envelope with my name on it, in a beautiful old copperplate script.

Chapter Forty-Three

I don't know how long I was in there. Time didn't start over, since the book didn't suddenly leap back onto the shelf, so it was less than four hours and probably much less. I do know that I was sitting by the bookcase, Gertie's letter held loosely in my hand, when I felt Rhea kneel beside me.

"Lady?" I looked up. "Are you alright?"

I didn't respond to that.

There were no words.

"Did you find what you were looking for?" she asked, her eyes growing concerned.

I came back to myself enough to shove the letter into my pocket. I would have burnt it, but it would just reset when the loop started over. Gertie had made sure that nothing could destroy her message.

I wasn't sure whether I was happy about that or not.

Rhea was looking at me, waiting for an answer. Because that was what normal people did. They answered back when spoken to, Cassie!

"No," I said, my voice cracking slightly. I cleared my throat, and tried again. "Gertie showed me this book the last time I was here and . . . I hoped it might help."

It was a bad lie, but Rhea accepted it. She nodded and stood up gracefully, somehow managing to appear elegant despite the Santa's helper outfit. She saw me looking at it, and grimaced. "I promised Tami I'd wear this tonight. She wanted something festive for the children—"

"You look good. All you need are matching booties."

She looked down at her sensible, low-heeled, black pumps. They coordinated with the wide black belt that cinched her tiny waist, but weren't particularly elf-like. "Red, with fur around the top?"

"Of course." I took the hand she offered, and levered myself back to my feet.

She smiled. "I'm afraid I didn't have any in the wardrobe."

"Should have asked Augustine. I bet he could have whipped something up."

She laughed. "And left snowy footprints wherever I walked? Or played 'Jingle Bells' on a loop until I went mad?"

"Or made you look like Saint Nick whenever you put them on." The other suggestions were a little tame for Augustine.

She shuddered. "Santa in a miniskirt?"

"Well, it would have livened up the party—"

"I think it was lively enough!"

I thought that Rhea hadn't been to many parties, especially of the vampire kind, but that wasn't the point I was trying to make.

"—but it would have disappointed Rico," I added. "He seems to like you just the way you are."

She blushed. "He's—we're not—that is, I explained that I can't—
"

"Have sex until the ritual?" I asked, to spare her from having to say it. I had been raised at a vampire's court, where sex was . . . just sex. A normal part of life and occasionally a useful tool in making alliances.

I'd played no part in the revelries at Tony's, since there was an outside chance that I might become Pythia someday. And the girl taking part in the symbolic marriage to the god had to be chaste. Until it was time for the changeover of power, that was, when the old Pythia lay dying.

Or was about to have fate catch up with her.

"But you're fond of Rico, right?" I asked, trying for casual.

Rhea's cheeks now almost matched her skirt. "I—"

"And he likes you. A lot, I think."

"I assure you; I would never do anything to jeopardize my position as—"

"You should keep him close. Just in case."

Rhea's eyes, confused and embarrassed a moment ago, sharpened. They reminded me a lot of her father's suddenly, and nobody had ever put anything over on Jonas Marsden. Or her mother, either, come to think of it.

And I guessed she'd bred true, judging by her expression. "Why?"

I shrugged. "We're at war. If things don't work out—"

"But they are. You're doing brilliantly—"

"Zeus is back. I almost died multiple times this week. Brilliant is not the term I'd use, Rhea." It was flat, but I needed her to understand this.

Only that didn't seem to be happening. Her eyes flashed, angry on my behalf. "But you didn't die! You *beat him*—"

"I beat Aeslinn," I said, more gently. "I escaped Zeus. Not the same thing—"

"Why are we talking about this?" she broke in, when Rhea never did. "You just said, back in the bedroom, that you know I'm not ready. That you'd never do anything to put me in danger—"

"I won't. But circumstances might."

"What circumstances?"

"I can't know that—"

"You couldn't know it then, either, but you said—"

"Yes, but that was before—"

"Before what? Before you read that letter?"

I had my mouth open, trying to get a word in, but at that I shut it. Abruptly. It only seemed to upset her further.

"That's it, isn't it?" she challenged. "What did Gertie tell you?"

I regarded her frankly for a moment. "You know, this job would be easier if I had an heir who wasn't quite so quick."

"And my job would be easier if I had a Pythia who told me the truth!" Her color was high, although for a different reason now. "If you honestly think the ritual might be in my near future, don't you owe me that? Don't I deserve to know what's going on?"

I didn't say anything for a moment; this was not a conversation I wanted to have. But she was right. She deserved the truth.

However, she wasn't going to get it, at least not now. My head came up, although not in an effort to stall. But because something was happening in the corridor outside.

The room with its cheerful fire and gleaming tassels and old-world paneling remained rock solid, caught in its little loop. Unlike the hallway, which had just shaken like an earthquake had hit it. Little siftings of dust were coming down like rain, and some smallish pebbles had broken free and were bouncing across the floor.

"The bombs," Rhea said, getting it before I did. "The Black Circle must be setting them off upstairs. We have to go!"

And we tried. But we couldn't shift from inside the room, probably something to do with the time loop. I also needed to make sure that my acolytes had gotten out before I left. We ran for the door, only to find the corridor bucking under our feet as soon as we crossed the threshold, sending us staggering against the wall.

I grabbed Rhea's hand and shifted us back to the main chamber, only to find the display cases dancing across the floor and a bunch of white robed grandmas clustered around the navel again. Or maybe still, as they didn't look like they'd moved since we left. Including Annabelle, who continued to clutch her strange cup of tea until a strong tremor hit and she dropped it.

It shattered into a hundred pieces on the hard stone floor, but reassembled a few seconds later only to shatter again when a display case fell on top of it. That was happening everywhere, with the taller and less sturdy cases toppling as the room came down around us. And as the acolytes clutched the more stable items near them one armed while beckoning to us frantically with the others.

"Over here!"

"What took you so long?"

"Hurry up! This whole place is about to go!"

"Then why are you still here?" I asked, starting that way.

Only to find myself abruptly shifted over to join them. I crashed into the navel, bounced off, and landed on my ass. Shifting without being prepared leaves you dizzy, especially when it's in between running footsteps.

But before I could say anything, I was jerked to my feet by Chloris and Hilde, and my hand slapped down onto the smooth top of the navel again.

"We were waiting for you," Annabelle said breathlessly. "We've figured it out—the spell, I mean. And—oh, who's the pretty boy, then?" she asked, catching sight of the cat that Rhea was holding.

"Annabelle," Hilde's voice snapped like a whip.

"Oh, yes. Yes, later. Well, as I was saying, we realized that the library follows the Pythia. We thought that you were a component of the spell, but that isn't it at all. Instead, you have to *activate* it and show it where to go—"

"Wait," I said, confused. "Are you trying to tell me . . . that this whole place . . . moves?"

"Well, of course it does!" That was Hilde, her white curls tinted gold with dust. "How else did you think we were going to transport it—book by book?"

I hadn't actually given it much thought, since I hadn't wanted the damned thing anyway.

"But . . . how is that possible?" I asked, staring around at the sheer size of the place. "You'd need a fantastic amount of power to even think about—"

"Yes! The Pythian power!" she growled. "Now can we please—"

"But I can't channel that much! I know—"

My thoughts were interrupted by one of the huge pillars falling, and smashing a dozen display cabinets to rubble just behind us.

"What do I do?" I asked quickly. The other columns weren't looking much steadier.

Hilde slapped her hand on top of mine. "Think about the library—think hard. Then shift—yourself—to where you want it to go."

"And that would be?"

"The basement at Dante's. It has already been prepared."

"Are you sure?" I looked up at the ceiling, which was at least two stories high and maybe more. It disappeared into darkness, so it was kind of hard to tell, but there was a feeling of space up there.

A lot of it.

Unlike in Dante's basement. Half of which wasn't finished and the other half had low, dropped ceilings. Not to mention that the guy who built it was a cheap bastard who had probably cut every corner he could.

"If it doesn't fit," I began.

"It will *make* itself fit—"

"But if it *doesn't*, it could bring the whole hotel down on our heads—"

"What do you think is about to happen *now*?" she yelled, as another pillar fell.

They were not carved out of a single piece of stone, but piled up in sections and then plastered over. I knew this because the round segments of this one hit at just the right angle to burst apart, and send wheels of stony death bouncing everywhere. Including one that came flying right over our heads.

"Shift, damn you!" Hilde yelled.

I shifted, while ducking down to avoid more tumbling stones and soaring donations, which were getting slung around as their display cases bit the dust, and glittering through the haze.

"Well?" Hilde demanded.

"Well, what?"

"Shift!"

"I *did*." At least, I thought I had. I'd felt the pull of the power, the disorientation of a shift, and the resulting energy drain, although not much of one. More like what it would take for me to shift a couple of months across time on my own. Not whatever would be required to take a massive library along with me.

Which was probably why we hadn't budged.

"Try again," Annabelle suggested urgently. She had somehow already acquired Rhea's cat, and was hugging him close while glancing up at the ceiling fearfully. Where large, dark cracks were now spidering down the walls like black lightning.

So, I tried again. But that time was even worse. That time, I didn't feel the Pythian power at all.

I tried again and again, grunting and straining—and went nowhere. It was like the power was ignoring me, or was telling me that I must be crazy, to think that I could shift a damned building! One that was fast coming down around our ears.

Another pillar toppled, almost on top of us, and an acolyte screamed. "Go!" I yelled, as dust billowed everywhere. "Get out of here!"

For once, I didn't get any arguments. They shifted out, all except for Hilde, who was yelling at the librarian, who had her nose deep in her book. And Rhea, who was looking around wildly before grabbing my arm. "Lady," she began. "I think perhaps—"

She cut off, choking, at a wild billow of dust. I couldn't tell if another pillar had fallen, because it was louder than a thunderstorm in here, with the sound of cracking stone and shattering glass. Not to mention that the dust was now so thick that I could barely see.

At this rate, I wasn't going to know that the ceiling had fallen until it squashed me.

We all needed to get gone!

"This should be working," the librarian was saying.

"Well, it isn't!" Hilde shouted. "Try something else!"

"There is nothing else—"

"Look, I'm obviously not strong enough," I said. "We have to—"

"No!" The librarian glared at me over her half-moon spectacles, her power so high that her eyes were a solid blue. "No! We are *not* leaving—"

"Then what do you suggest? If I can't shift it—"

"You don't have to shift it! The spell links the library directly to the Pythian power. It was set up that way by Apollo himself!"

"Who is *dead*! Like we're about to be—" I said, only to have a furious ghost grab me.

"It only needs the Pythia to tell it where to go. To take the reins of the buggy, so to speak, and steer—"

"I've taken them! Multiple times!" I yelled, as a massive crack echoed around the chamber, causing me to look up.

At where the entire ceiling had just split, halfway across.

And, okay, fuck this!

"Try again!" the librarian yelled.

"It doesn't *work*—"

"It did, though," Annabelle said, popping out of nowhere, right in my face.

That left her inside the startled librarian, who flailed around like a swimmer caught in a chubby sea. Annabelle ignored her and hugged a very unhappy Mr. Tubbins, who didn't look like he wanted to be here anymore than I did. His eyes were wide, and he was snarling and trying to bite. But Annabelle had him in a death grip, and a second later, the same was true of me.

"What the devil are you doing back here?" Hilde demanded, but for once, she didn't get an answer. Because the next moment—

"What is *that*?" the librarian shrieked, as I tried to process the fact that we were suddenly back at the party in my old suite at Dante's. Or what had been the party. It looked like a hellscape at the moment, as if someone had turned up the saturation on the T.V. to the maximum, until the whole room was bathed in orange light.

Even weirder, everybody was clustered in front of the balcony, staring out at something I couldn't see, and—

"Why is the floor shaking?" I asked, as it trembled under my feet, hard enough to make me stagger.

I would have thought that it was just me, but everyone else shook, too. And the Christmas tree took that moment to topple over, at the same time that a discarded tray of glasses danced off the edge of a table and crashed to the floor. For some reason, this room was almost as unsteady as the one we'd left behind.

"You brought us back successfully," Annabelle said, clutching my arm as Rhea and Hilde shifted in. "You didn't notice because this place is shaking, too—"

"Yes, but why?" I repeated, trying to see past the crush of bodies at whatever everyone was staring at.

It was something the ghost didn't seem to have a problem with, because she screeched again. *"What the hell is that?"*

"Not hell," Adra said, appearing at my side and waving an arm, causing the crowd to magically part in front of us. "It's much worse than that."

I didn't answer. I was too busy looking at the rippling cloud that was coming our way across the desert. I couldn't see what was inside it, but then, I didn't need to. Sand storms didn't topple buildings like dominoes, crack the earth like level ten earthquakes, or spread across the width of the horizon.

Or leave a changed world behind them.

What I could see through the distorting effect of the ripple looked like the vision that Zeus had sent me: a ruined world, a dead world, with nothing but a sky filled with orange sand that never settled, crumbled buildings and piles of sun-bleached bones. It was drawing inexorably closer, and everything it touched, it changed. As if there were two worlds, interposed over each other, with the old being rolled back to show the new.

I didn't repeat the librarian's question; I couldn't seem to speak at all. But Hilde answered it for me, anyway. "A Crucible," she said, her voice cracking.

"A Crucible? What do you mean a Crucible?" the librarian demanded.

"When a catastrophic change is made to the timeline, something that the Pythian power cannot compensate for, it causes a new reality to be born, one that forcibly grafts itself onto the old, creating something new . . ."

"I know what it is!" The ghost grabbed her by the shoulders. "Hilde—*what happens when it reaches us*?"

Hilde didn't reply, but I thought the answer was pretty obvious. I stood there, seeing time reform in front of my eyes, and didn't believe it. I'd been dreading something exactly like this, but now that it was here, I couldn't take it in.

Instead, I stared around—at Annabelle, crooning soothing words to the freaked-out cat; at Rhea, standing mutely at my side, her eyes reflecting Armageddon; at Hilde, having spent a lifetime in service to the Court, yet falling as silent as I was. At the children—my children—the initiates who had been placed into my safekeeping . . .

Along with the rest of the world.

And, finally, my paralysis broke.

"It appears that we are too late," Adra said, glancing at me.

"No. Not too late." I looked up at him. "But I'm going to need that help you offered."

Chapter Forty-Four

I appeared on the same bridge in old Romania where I'd first come in, four days ago, and immediately became very confused. Because it didn't look any different from the last time that I saw it. And I don't mean just the surrounding mountain peaks, turning pink and gold with the late afternoon light, or the rushing, icy river below, like a frazzled gray ribbon cutting across the landscape, or the spectacular light show that the sun was starting to put on.

But rather the traffic jam of vamps in a long line of carriages.

They were covering the bridge separating the castle and its small spit of land from the main road. Which was also stuffed with vamps, I realized as I looked behind me, for as far as I could see. It made me worry that I'd somehow shifted in too early.

I'd tried to thread the needle carefully, returning to the sweet spot between when I escaped from that forest camp in Faerie, leaving Aeslinn with no choice but to default to Plan A, and before he'd been here long enough to trash the timeline. So, days after I'd been here the first time.

Yet it sure looked like I'd never left.

Except that, last time, the carriages had been in disarray, in a snarl caused by everyone trying to leave at once, after a giant dragon screamed by overhead. Vamps had been attempting to rein in freaked out horses, fey had been fleeing from said dragon after it tore through the castle, and a drift of dust from the ruined structure had been hanging in the air. But none of that was the case now.

These buggies were in an orderly line, their horses were calm and unbothered, and the skies were clear. It *was* a different day, I realized. But it looked like the party had been rescheduled.

It also looked like someone remembered me. I hadn't been there ten seconds when a furious vamp launched himself in my direction from the top of a nearby carriage. And was immediately shifted off the bridge and into thin air, where he stayed for a moment, his legs working and his mouth open in shock.

He looked like a cartoon character who doesn't fall until he notices that he should be doing so. Or, in this case, until I released him. He plunged into the icy water far below, yelling his head off, and suddenly, I had the bridge's full attention.

A bunch of vamps rushed me, and I coiled a golden whip out onto the stones to make their decision easier. Half of them stopped—the smarter half, I assumed—but the rest kept coming. So, I snagged a carriage with the Pythian power and threw it at them, horses and all.

I didn't see if it landed, because the scene in front of me suddenly winked out, leaving me looking at something very different—and infinitely scarier.

"Yes, I know!" I told my power savagely. "I'm trying. I didn't expect them to be here!"

I didn't get a response back, except for the same thing that it had been showing me ever since that first glimpse of the Crucible. What flashed across my vision looked like one of the films in Alphonse's screenings, after the blaze started to eat it. Pieces of everyday life flickered in the background, with people going about their business without a clue that a fire was consuming the edges of their world—and quickly working its way in.

Only this fire . . . was being fought.

Parts of the picture went up in flames as I watched, and through the black-edged holes a new image emerged. A bleak landscape, a dead world, a miserable terrain where nothing grew and nothing lived—for an instant. Then the first world resurfaced, bright and full of life and back in place, as good as new.

It seemed that a Crucible wasn't something that happened in one time period and rippled down to all the rest. That was how minor changes to the timeline worked, the kind that I'd been dealing with since starting this job. But these weren't minor; this was the wholesale slaughter of the past in favor of a new reality, and that . . .

Happened very differently.

The new timeline that Zeus had made was attempting to graft itself onto our own all at once. It was changing the world in one fell swoop, from the precipitating event right down to my era. And would probably have already succeeded except for one thing: it was being opposed by another god.

Or by a god's power, at least. The Pythian power had thrown itself into the fight, using everything it had to resist the changes that were happening, not here and there, but everywhere, all at once. A titanic struggle was taking place as two opposing forces fought for the future.

And so far, we were losing.

I watched as the fire ate relentlessly onward, retaking ground that it had just lost. And the Pythian power retreated, unable to repair that much damage. I felt its panic through our connection; knew that it couldn't stop what was happening.

But it could slow it down, buying me a chance to do the rest. Only I had no idea how long I had. But given the fact that it kept screaming at me, not long.

The terrifying images winked out as abruptly as they'd come, leaving me looking at a bunch of vamps on the opposite side of the bridge, staring over the edge at the guy I'd just dunked. I doubted that I'd killed him, considering that the drop ended in water, but that didn't appear to have improved their tempers any. They spun and rushed me, fangs out, at least two dozen this time, and coming from more than one angle.

And I snagged another carriage, this time with the whip.

There were no horses attached to this one, with the harnesses lying cut and limp on the ground. Somebody had slashed through them with a sword and taken off with the animals, deciding on the better part of valor. Which explained why there were no people inside when the glowing golden strand I was holding coiled around the roof through the open windows, and starting slinging the heavy coach back and forth like a cudgel.

The carriage was wood, and immediately started to burn, sending shards everywhere. And as I'd noted in the kitchen earlier, flying, fiery stakes are a vamp's worst nightmare. My attackers scattered as my own vamps had done, right before the whip burnt through my hold and sent the carriage tumbling into the river.

So, I snagged another.

I started walking slowly forward, wrecking things as I went, because I needed to clear the bridge. And because vamps were all about showmanship, and the whip looked more impressive than a power they couldn't see. And it was impressive, sending light shadows dancing over the stones, sparkling off the surrounding ice, and turning the imposing carriages into so many piles of burning debris.

And, suddenly, a lot of the occupants weren't in battle mode anymore. Ladies in fine silks and ruffled satins, men in velvets and embroidered waistcoats, and servants of all varieties spilled out onto the bridge as I approached. Some untied horses and leapt onto their backs, flashing me wild eyes as they galloped past. Others ran away on foot, some vampire-quick, just blurs in front of my vision. More were human slow, but not wasting time.

And then a spooked coachman tried to turn too quickly and toppled over a carriage full of screaming women.

I assumed that they were human, since they kept calling for help instead of ripping the carriage to shreds to get out. Some vamp's harem, probably, or canapes for the evening who hadn't yet figured out their function. I sliced off the back end of the coach with the whip and they tumbled out, their heavily made-up faces staring around before they scrambled back to their feet.

They fluttered past me, panniers flapping, like a brightly colored flock of birds, and I kept pressing ahead. My efforts had two results. The remaining vamps scattered, with the ones who couldn't get past me jumping over the side of the bridge, as that was better than dealing with the fiery wood flying everywhere. And Aeslinn finally noticed that he had company.

I hadn't seen him, being too far away to get a good look into the castle's courtyard. Although it probably wouldn't have mattered, since it was surrounded by a wall with a short tunnel through it, so I only had an obstructed view. And Aeslinn, in a crowd of seven foot tall, fair haired fey, was hard to pick out.

Until now, I thought, when he suddenly erupted out of the crowd, returning to his giant form.

I stared upward, having forgotten how incredibly impressive that trick was, not having seen it since our fight on the Thames. He was easily nine stories tall, blocking out the late afternoon sun, which caused an incongruous halo around the great head. The body, meanwhile, threw a chilly shadow over me and half the bridge.

And over the fey, by the look of things. I still couldn't see them too well, but the ones right around Aeslinn didn't seem happy. Just as those in Faerie hadn't recognized their king in dragon form, these didn't seem to understand that the naked giant that had suddenly appeared out of nowhere, roaring my name, was on their side.

They'd probably figure it out, but I didn't think that rational thought was foremost in their minds just now. Especially the couple who'd had the misfortune to be occupying the space in front of a massive foot as Aeslinn started toward me. I could see them through the tunnel as they were ground into the pavement, their bodies reduced to unrecognizable smears of flesh, their blood running in rivulets between the flagstones, and their long, silver hair dyed bright red.

Their king didn't even appear to notice.

He crossed the courtyard in a couple of steps, reaching the gate that separated our worlds before abruptly slamming on the brakes, so hard that he stumbled. Not because he wouldn't have fit through, something he seemed to have forgotten in his desire to rip me to shreds. But because stopping hadn't been his idea.

I couldn't see the god hovering around him at the moment, but I didn't have to. The bellows of outrage and the twisting, flailing giant were more than enough. And then the portcullis rang down, providing a hard barrier between worlds.

Aeslinn might want to fight me, but Zeus seemed to have other plans.

"Nice dress," he said, with the sudden calmness of the huge face a stark contrast with the writhing body.

I glanced down at the shiny silver battle dress I was wearing, which would have looked completely over the top anywhere else.

Here, it just seemed to fit. I looked back up again. "Thanks. I didn't know if I'd get another chance to wear it."

"I am sorry to hear that," Zeus said, and actually sounded like it. "There were two possibilities: that you had read the letter and were here to discuss terms, or that you hadn't, and had come in a vain attempt to defeat me. I preferred the former."

"You're forgetting one. That I did read the letter, and that I'm still here—"

A vamp crawled back over the side of the bridge and threw a knife. The whip intercepted it before I consciously told it to and slung it back at him, which normally wouldn't have mattered. Any vamp, including a baby, could heal a wound from a steel-edged weapon in seconds. But this one was flung with inhuman force and struck him in the neck, half bisecting it and sending a spurt of blood arcing over the snow.

"—to defeat you."

"Ah, bravado." The great head inclined. "A common weakness of our kind—"

"I am not your kind."

"And yet, I see our power haloing you, as it did not before. Can I assume, then, that you have discovered a use for the creature you stole from me?"

"The demigod, you mean?"

The huge lips pursed. "Oh, nothing so lofty. Say rather experiment—"

"Designed to leak godly power? What have you been doing? Chasing down everyone with a scrap of god blood and breeding them to make yourself better donors?"

He looked faintly surprised. "That was quite a leap."

"Not really. I grew up around people who sucked the life force out of others in order to live. They call their donors blood pigs. Only you don't need blood, do you? You need this." I slapped my whip against the ground, leaving a black burn mark eating into the stones.

It was deliberately provocative, but he didn't take the bait. "As do you. But your borrowed power will run out considerably before mine."

"Except that the power you've been seeking lately isn't *for* you. If you needed that much, you'd have never lasted this long. Or you'd have gone after Nimue ages ago."

"As clever as your mother, I see."

"But you didn't go after her. You used your own version of blood pigs instead, for hundreds of years. Breeding them, making them stronger, hunting for more and more of those forgotten bloodlines, the ones your people left behind.

"Until recently. When that suddenly wasn't enough anymore. What changed?"

But, this time, I didn't get an answer. "Yes, your mother was always quite intelligent," he mused. "Although she used her gifts poorly, and your father—"

"What do you know about my father?"

I cursed myself for a fool as soon as the words left my lips. I wasn't supposed to let him get to me. *I* was supposed to bait *him*.

At least enough to get him to open that gate, and come out here. It was a good way to end up a smear on the pavement, but it was the only chance I had. But my emotions were all over the place right now and not always responding to good sense.

"More than you, it would seem," Zeus said, before I could get my equilibrium back. "Your father and I had plenty of time to talk, whilst in Faerie."

"He's in a *paperweight*—"

"Yes, giving me a captive audience."

I felt a surge of pure, blinding rage pour through me. "You're lying! He wouldn't have talked to you!"

The huge shoulders shrugged. "He didn't much. It surprised me; most ghosts tend to be rather loquacious. But his reactions told me a good deal. As for the rest . . . well, you didn't think you were the only Seer among us, surely?"

It took me back, although it shouldn't have. The bastard had a hundred gifts, most of them stolen. "Did you eat one of those, too?"

A great eyebrow rose. "No, I was born with that particular gift. Which was how I saw you opening the former Pythia's letter—"

"Unless you planted it in her mind! All of it—"

"Is that what you've been telling yourself?" he asked, sounding surprised. "Oh, no, no, that won't do. I Saw your eyes when you read it; Saw it resonate. I understand wanting to save face, to come back here and make a splash, but that won't do at all."

"And who are you to tell me that?"

"The only one who seems to care anything about you. Your people are happy to have you die for them, to use you up to postpone the inevitable a little longer. They have such short lives; perhaps they feel it will be enough. But I see the potential—"

A random vamp came running at me, screaming, from over the side of the bridge. I sent him back there, sans the leg that my whip had just burnt through. And had another blur come at me so fast from behind that I almost didn't see her.

In fact, I *didn't* see her. I saw the vamp look at something behind me, and turned in time to watch the clouds of smoke being disturbed in her wake. And then she was over the bridge as well, when my whip caught her, but not in the water. Vamps were already hauling their drenched bodies onto the frozen bank below, and I didn't want to have to fight her twice.

So, I threw out a hand, catching her halfway through her fall, and used the Pythian power to strap her to the base of a huge pine tree. And only then recognized Mircea's old acquaintance Gabriella, who was looking a little less countess-like at the moment, with her dark hair everywhere and her lovely face set on snarl.

But she couldn't break the bonds, something she realized after a moment. So, she used vampire strength to drag them through the heart of the tree and out the other side, where they promptly constricted and left her staggering into the water. Where, a moment later, the severed tree landed on her head.

Zeus sighed, an expression of disgust crossing his features.

"Hard to get good help," I said.

"Indeed." The large eyes turned back to me. "Which is why I would much prefer you. And you would much prefer me. I can do for you what your parents could not—"

"Leave them out of this!"

"Why?" Now it was his voice ringing with challenge. "They didn't leave you out, did they? They dropped you into the middle of it, then promptly abandoned you—"

"They *died*—"

"Yes, on purpose—"

"—to save the world!"

Now he looked impatient. "You know that wasn't the plan, Cassie. Your mother wanted to rule—not part, but all. She gambled and lost, but she couldn't accept that—"

"She exiled *you*."

"But depleted herself so much in the process that she had to go into hiding from the very demons she once preyed upon. She couldn't feed, and thus couldn't regain her strength, and the years weighed heavily. Eventually, she began to starve—"

"I know all this!"

I was trying, I really was, to control myself, but my mouth seemed to be on autopilot. I'd never felt the storm of emotions surging through me that I did then, never thought I *could* feel so much, all at the same time: knee-trembling fear, but enough fury to overwrite it, because I wanted him to *burn*; despair, because I knew how unlikely that was; longing, for friends and lovers I would probably never see again.

And then there were my parents . . .

I shied away from that topic, hard, but it didn't make a difference. There was a hurricane inside me, and had been ever since I read Gertie's letter. My self-restraint felt like a dam facing a tsunami; sooner or later, something was going to give.

But not now! I told myself.

Not yet!

"Eventually, she grew desperate enough to disguise herself, and go to the Pythian Court," Zeus continued, relentlessly. "To feed on the energy there—the only well deep enough to slake her thirst. But Apollo's power wasn't a demon lord, to be drained so easily. It kept her on a tight leash, and she was no longer powerful enough to overcome it, and take the whole of it for her own.

"But it allowed her to continue existing, and plotting, and while she was there, she met another plotter, didn't she? Your father. Freshly returned from a trip back in time to the Stuart age, where he had been apprehended by the Pythia of the day—Agnes, I believe her name was?"

I nodded, blindly. It was taking everything I could do to ride the waves of emotion and not be drowned by them. And it looked like he was finally feeling something, too. The huge face had become animated, the great eyes were shining and the towering body had dropped to one knee, to allow him to get closer to my level.

But I guessed it wasn't close enough. The next moment, he shrank back down to normal size, leaving him basketball-player-tall by human standards, but tiny compared to his alter ego. He walked forward, to the opposite side the gate, and I found my own footsteps mimicking him, until we were only maybe ten yards apart.

The king's body had ripped through his clothes during the transformation, and his hair was matted and tangled, as if he hadn't stopped to comb it in a while. He also looked tired and gaunt, as if carrying a god was becoming a burden beyond his capacities— especially this god. But the eyes were silver fire, and burned so brightly that I could barely look at them.

"You know the truth now," Zeus said, his voice a seductive whisper. "You felt it in your bones as soon as you read it—"

"No—"

"But you did. And it wasn't surprise I saw on your face. It was many other things— resignation, disappointment, pain—but not surprise. You already suspected it; how could you not? The secrecy, the lies, as if they had something to hide—"

"Stop it!"

"Why? Are you so afraid to face the truth? Come, come, Cassie, you're a time traveler; you met your father in a completely different era. Did it never occur to you that he could have come there from anywhere? Anywhere at all?

"Or anywhen."

I didn't respond that time. I couldn't seem to focus my thoughts. I'd known that Zeus would do this, would attempt to suborn the only person left with even a chance to stop him, and had thought I was prepared. But I'd been reeling ever since that letter, not only at the information it contained, but at the implication.

And it looked like I still was.

"Your father was human, yes," he continued mercilessly. "But not from the era in which you found him—or even from your own. He came from many years in the future, after my people returned to rule the Earth once more."

"He came back to stop me, and he died for it.

"The question is, will you?"

Chapter Forty-Five

I stared up at Zeus blindly, feeling a thousand things, none of which I could articulate. He looked back, and for a moment, I could actually see him. Not Aeslinn, but the guy who was really running this show, the man behind the curtain.

He had changed appearance once again. Instead of a close cropped, Edwardian haircut or long, flowing golden locks, this time he was sporting a head full of graying curls. And in place of a three-piece suit or blindingly bright suit of armor, he had on a simple draped garment in a deep purple that looked ancient Greek. But the eyes . . . the eyes were the same. So blue that they redefined the color, and so warm, so gentle, and so sincere, that I almost got lost in them for a moment.

And then I shook my head and the spell broke, if there had been one. I looked back up, and my own eyes were hard. "If I must."

He sighed in exasperation. "And what a waste that would be; a foolish waste. You've read the prophecies; you know how this ends." He suddenly grabbed the iron lattice separating us, rattling it and startling me. "But it doesn't have to."

"And this is where you tell me you can make it all better?" I rasped, barely recognizing my voice.

"No, this is when we argue some more, until you realize the truth of it yourself. I've dealt with humans before; I know how they think—"

"I'm not human, either!"

"No," he agreed. "You're not. Your parents left you betwixt and between, didn't they? Not truly one thing or the other. It's hard; I know—"

"You know nothing!"

"I know that you could rule with us; after all, we are your people, too. But instead, you're fighting on the wrong side and making everything infinitely more difficult than it needs to be. Accept it, Cassie: our return isn't a potential. Your very existence proves that. We aren't coming back; we already have. In the future, perhaps, but that doesn't make it less real—"

"The future can be changed!" I'd just seen the evidence of that with my own eyes. And the sight of a boiling storm of time reforming itself across the desert wasn't something I'd quickly forget.

"But not the outcome," Zeus said, his voice flat. "There are many roads to our final destination, but they all end in the same place. We return to rule the Earth once more—"

"To destroy it, you mean!"

"Not enough of it, it seems." The voice took on an edge. "We missed some in the magical community, missed *him*. We were looking for leaders and great powers, not garbage men—"

"My father . . . was a great necromancer," I gasped, struggling to breathe past my anger.

"He was a *garbage man*. He was *nothing*. And as such, he slipped past us, when more powerful mages failed. Slithered away into the desert with the other vermin. Where they pooled their magic, and used old, forbidden spells to send him back through time, to try to change history. To deny us what is rightfully ours—"

"None of this is rightfully yours!"

"On the contrary." The blue eyes were now as hard as twin sapphires. "You were savages when we found you; little more than beasts. All across the world they remember us, by different names, but they *remember*. Of course, they do—they would yet be scratching in the dirt but for us! And yet, what did we get for it? Praise? Gratitude? Worship?"

"You *enslaved* and *murdered* them—"

"They were enslaving and murdering each other long before we arrived! At least we gave them something for it! And what did they give us in return? Rebellion, defiance, treachery. Not least of which came from that bastard of a father of yours. But he and his little group, stewing in the desert—they didn't know what to change, did they? Didn't know what had gone wrong, or where. And their leaders were too dead to tell them."

I didn't reply, and not only because my head was reeling. But because some movement behind him had caught my eye. Only it wasn't the vampires this time.

It was the fey, still at a distance, but edging closer. They seemed to have conquered their fear, now that their king was back to his normal size, yet they were staring at him strangely. Maybe because they'd just seen him transform into something startling.

Or maybe because they could see someone else—not Aeslinn, but the creature that rode him.

I had assumed that Zeus was projecting his image just to me, or that I was picking up on flashes of his real self through my clairvoyance. But if so, the fey must be clairvoyant, too. And seeing the awe on their faces, the wonder, the *worship*, turned my stomach.

He's just a man! I felt like screaming. And not a good one. He has more power than you; that's all. That doesn't make him better!

But to them, it obviously did.

They were regarding him with reverence, while I was getting looks that clearly said that I was dead, just as soon as their god finished talking to me. Yet he was the one who would enslave them, while I was trying to set them free. It made no sense.

Or maybe it did.

"Chaos scares people," Pritkin told me once. We'd been fighting with those damned wooden practice swords of his, that were lighter than steel but stung like hell if they caught you unawares. He'd gotten past my defenses and spanked me on the ass, sending me stumbling, only to catch me before I hit the floor.

I'd swept his legs out from under him in return, which had earned me a raised eyebrow. I saw it up close and personal, having landed on top of a hard body that had rapidly gotten harder. I'd squirmed a little, making it clear that I noticed, and he'd flipped us with a knee between my thighs and a dangerous glint in his eyes.

"On the other hand, I like surprises."

"Do you?" I'd struggled for a minute, stupidly. He was so much stronger that it was ridiculous. The only way I had to beat him was using the Pythian power, which was considered cheating. And while it was tempting, the extra two miles he'd make me run wasn't worth it.

Besides, it wasn't an entirely uncomfortable situation to be in. I'd stretched sensually after a moment, and watched his eyes change. But he hadn't pressed his advantage, because he had a point to make.

"There are two kinds of people: those who enjoy change, who welcome it, who are excited by it—"

"How excited?" I'd breathed, and gotten a stern look in return.

"—and those who hate and fear it. The latter will do anything, suffer anything, to avoid it. They will make up excuses as to why they are doing this or that, ridiculous though some of them may be. But the truth is that they prefer familiar chains to the vast, terrifying unknown, and a future with no script for it already written."

We had been talking about certain groups in the magical community who were in denial over what we were facing. The fact that the battles we'd fought had largely taken place elsewhere in time, or on another world, had left many people angry over the constraints that the Circle had imposed, which they didn't think were necessary. But I thought that the same principle applied here.

The fey would follow Aeslinn and his master off a cliff, rather than risk a future that they couldn't predict. Even if it had the chance to be far, far better! Of course, it could be worse, too, but I didn't see how. Even if they ended up on top of the heap in Faerie, they had to know that it was completely at their god's sufferance. The rug could be pulled out from under them any time he felt like it, since he was the only one who held any power.

Yet they preferred their chains.

The god's hand jerked, hard enough to rattle the lattice again. He didn't seem to appreciate my attention wandering, even for a moment. I looked back at him, and suddenly wasn't sure who I was talking to anymore.

It was Zeus's face, but it was Aeslinn's hateful expression. Only the two were changeable, fluid, weaving in and out of each other as if trying to exist in the same space at the same time. Which I guessed they were, but it didn't make it any less disturbing.

"Do you know why you first met your father in that dank dungeon, under Parliament?" Zeus asked abruptly, focusing my attention back on him.

"No."

"He and his allies blamed the Circle for the fall of the world, since it supported your mother's treasonous spell. They thought it must have become too weak or too corrupt to do the job properly, and keep us out. Your father therefore went back to a time when the Circle was consolidating its power, to try to disrupt it. He and his fellow conspirators hoped that, by killing the king who was giving it support, they would cause it to splinter, and be forced to bring in more magical groups to help carry the load. Then, if one of them fell, the others might pick up the slack—"

"You aren't a time traveler," I interrupted. "You didn't See all this. You're guessing!"

Zeus didn't bother to deny it. "I Saw some, and your father's reactions confirmed the rest. I'm good with people, Cassie; I pay attention. Which is how I know how much you're hurting now."

"I'm not—"

"It was bad of your parents, wasn't it?" he asked, speaking over me. "Not teaming up, in order to defeat their mutual enemy—that was fair enough. But to have a *child*. One they doomed from the start."

"They didn't—"

"Oh, but they did. You won't win this war, but for the sake of argument, let's say you do. That everything somehow falls into place and you triumph. While your friends are celebrating, while the magical world erupts in cheers and rejoicing, what happens to you, hm? Don't you deserve a fairy tale ending, too?"

"And you're going to give it to me?"

"I could. It depends on whether we can reach an agreement. And before you ask how you can trust me, can I point out that I didn't send you here to die alone? Or use you as your mother did, to talk the demon high council into entering the war on your side. Only it wasn't your side, was it?"

"Stop it!"

"It was hers. I don't know if she planned your birth, to use you as a weapon against us, but she certainly took advantage of the opportunity, didn't she? To persuade the demons who despised her to help her daughter fight off the terrible gods." His voice was low-key mocking now, and I hated him for it. But what he was saying fit; I was horribly afraid that it did. "They were to be a distraction, allowing her to drain great Ares and thus return to full strength. Giving her a belated victory over us all, and never mind the cost to you—"

"She didn't!"

"We both know that she did." The voice was merciless now, pounding on me like hammer blows. "The demons would never have helped her, but they were the only force dangerous enough to capture Ares' attention, even for a moment. She needed that moment, and thus, she needed you."

"Stop."

"But in the end, Antonio took your parent's souls off to Faerie, disrupting her plans, and you defeated Ares on your own. But your parents couldn't have known that, could they?" His head tilted curiously. "Tell me, did they seem fond of you, when you visited them, back in time? Or were they a trifle guilty? Especially your father; human hearts are more easily bruised, after all. Did he seem ashamed of what they had done, for one final chance at victory?"

I didn't answer that time.

I couldn't have if I'd wanted to.

Because I *had* gone back to see them. I didn't know how Zeus knew that; maybe another guess. Or maybe that's what anyone would have done, filled with questions but no answers. And I hadn't gotten any from them. I didn't know what I'd expected, but the cold reception I'd received, especially from my mother, hadn't been it. And father . . . had been acting twitchy, off balance, and yes, ashamed. I hadn't seen it then, but looking back, it fit his actions perfectly.

And nothing else did.

"Think of it," Zeus said, his voice little more than a whisper now. "To have a child, a sweet baby girl, to nurse her at your breast and rock her to sleep every night, and all the while, you're planning to betray her." I flinched; I couldn't help it, and of course, he saw. "Oh, you don't like that word? Well, which would you prefer?"

"I wouldn't prefer any of this!" I realized that I'd sunk down onto my haunches at some point, with the golden whip spitting and sputtering against the ground at my feet. It was eating a furrow into the stones, but I didn't care. It was hard to care about anything, when every word felt like it twisted a knife in my gut.

"My apologies, but hard truths are necessary if we are to save you—and I would save you, Cassie. I don't have to; I can finish this on my own, and yet . . .

"You have done what few have ever managed, and impressed me. You waged a war, almost alone, and destroyed two senior gods. The last who dared attempt such a thing was Heracles, and I raised him to godhood. I could do the same for you, allow you to take your proper place at my side.

"Or, you can continue this foolish war, knowing that, even if you succeed, you will only seal your doom. If you prevent my return, your father will have no reason to risk his life with precarious spells, and slip the leash of time. He will never come back, never meet your mother, never sire a daughter. And you . . . dear Cassie . . . will never be born."

I made a sound not unlike a sob, and he smiled slightly. "It's a terrible conundrum, isn't it? Lose, and you'll be destroyed, just another demigod on the trash heap of history, with the others who forgot where their power came from. Win, and you eradicate yourself. Not dead, so that others might remember and mourn you, but *erased*, utterly and completely. Time will reform around you, and a new future will be born, but you will not be in it. Your friends will not know of your sacrifice; your lovers will not remember your embrace. It will be as if you never existed. Merely a blip on the timeline, a goddess' final joke . . ."

His voice trailed off, and I blinked away tears, only for others to immediately take their place. They were streaming down my face, probably had been for a while as they'd spotted the ground below me, melting the snow. But I couldn't seem to stop. I was basically kneeling at his feet, but I couldn't do anything about that, either; the pain was paralyzing.

I heard the gate go up, the rumble and screech of old, rusted metal, and a moment afterward felt him kneel in front of me, and warm arms encircle me.

"You don't deserve that fate," he said, his voice suddenly kind once more. "You cannot win this war, but you can *survive* it. I can elevate you, protect you from time's destructive embrace. I can even protect the humans you love so much from their well-deserved fate. We don't want them, after all; they were never the objective. And the demons we do want . . . they prey upon your people, do they not? Our campaign against them will ultimately help you, too, all of you.

"Fight me, and you know what I will do to this world.

"Help me, and you can save it—and yourself." I looked up, and the face was all Zeus, with nothing of Aeslinn visible anymore. "It is not wrong to want to live, Cassie," he said gently. "To live and love and be happy. How often have you been allowed that, in this impossible position you were left in? Not many, I think. But we can remake your fate, and the fate of this world. Together, we can do wonders. All you have to do is give me the slightest bit of trust. Can you do that? Can you trust me, just this once?"

I looked into those blue eyes, and for a second, I did trust him. There was nothing but genuineness there; nothing but love. That feeling I'd experienced in the first vision he'd ever sent me came flooding back, and it was all the joy and acceptance and peace I'd ever wanted in the world. For a moment, I just stayed there, kneeling in the snow, drunk on it.

And then I shoved him away.

"You ate your *wife*," I said, and shifted to the end of the bridge. "*Now!*"

Chapter Forty-Six

I'd barely moved back far enough, because suddenly, there was a massive library sitting on top of the bridge. I shifted again, to get out of the way of the gigantic billow of dust that accompanied it, which threatened to choke me. And then I just paused for a moment, staring.

I'd never seen the Pythian library from the outside before, but the huge, sand colored building would have fit in perfectly in its original home in Delphi. It was rectangular, like a classic Greek temple, only with a dome—over the rotunda where all those display cases had sat, I assumed. It also had a wide portico supported by six huge statues of what looked like ancient Pythias, their bodies draped in chitons and mantles, and their faces as serene as if this sort of thing happened every day.

But the graceful symmetry of the main building had been undone by a bunch of extra wings that headed off at crazy angles, like the legs on a spider. I assumed that they were a relic of the time after it ended up underground and no longer needed to worry about aesthetics. But they were in the open now, and left an enormous mess that scrawled across the surrounding hillsides, clogged the river and completely covered the bridge, where the central temple continued to sit in defiance of logic, high above everything else.

I shifted to the top of the portcullis for a better view, then almost fell off when gravity finally took hold of the library. The closest wings broke away with gigantic *craaaacks* that echoed across the mountains and came back at me with almost physical force, while the contents spilled into the river below. The cascade of rubble and fine statuary made a pale mountain out of the bridge, and also landed on the spit of land where the castle was.

And where a massive cascade was currently pouring through the portcullis, as if the library was vomiting into the fey world.

But the geyser wasn't made out of rubble. Or even out of water from the spilled fountains that were streaming down the new mountainside, carving cascades through the dust. Instead, the multicolored surge came from a mass of Adra's demons, who were hurtling through the portcullis and changing as they went.

You could see when Faerie's power caught them, transforming them from spirits into living flesh. There were no disembodied souls in the world of the fey, and although the demons had been told this, I don't think that some of them had understood until they hit the ground. And looked up in shock and wonder at the equally shocked fey.

They were beautiful, I thought, as some of them paused to examine newly solid limbs, wings and other appendages that I didn't have names for. Maybe half were encased in brightly colored scales that flowed over massively muscled bodies like armor. Others had brilliant plumage like birds, including one with a tail twice as long as it was, that ended in a froth of bright lavender feathers. A few also had fierce, bird-like faces, that stared about with burning, fire-lit eyes. And more were indescribable—creatures so different from anything on Earth that I couldn't process what I was seeing.

They broke the mind, and not just mine. The fey soldiers took one look at the invading horde suddenly jumping, slithering and flying at them off the stones. And ran.

But someone else didn't.

The demon horde took off in pursuit of their prey, and I heard another thunderous crack from behind me. I turned to see the huge dome of the library shatter as a giant forced his way out. Sand colored blocks exploded everywhere, another mountain of dust billowed into the air, and a huge, furious face stared around, looking for the cause of all this.

And found it, a second before an enormous stone came hurtling at my head.

I shifted onto the riverbank and sent a dozen random hunks of rock, none smaller than a large car, flying back at the furious fey king.

They hit the back of his head, causing him to stagger, and me to be forced to shift onto the debris mountain to avoid retaliation. A rain of rubble tore by overhead, and slammed into the river bank, hard enough to bury huge shards of a wall six feet deep into the ground and to mow the surrounding trees down to stumps. Zeus was no longer toying with me, and playing hide and seek wasn't going to work for long.

But I couldn't take both him and Aeslinn in a fair fight, so I needed an unfair one. Which I was supposed to have by now! *Come on*, I thought, staring up at the sky. *Come on.*

But there was nothing there, or maybe I just couldn't see it through the swirling clouds of dust. They were as thick as a dense fog this close to the epicenter, helping to hide me. But I was finding it hard to be grateful while choking on a lungful of dirt and practically blind.

And then I was grabbed from behind.

I shifted away before the grasping hand could do more than rake what sounded like claws down my armor. And landed farther up the mountainside, panting and confused, having not seen the attack coming. And I should have.

Because what staggered out of the dust below me . . . was hard to miss.

I'd ended up on a shelf of rock that jutted out over a relatively cleared space, and gave me as good of a view as possible under the circumstances. Yet, I doubted my eyes. Because that . . . was not a vampire.

It was easily three times the normal size and misshapen, with a body so bulging in muscle that it ripped out of the fine, watered silk topcoat it had been wearing as I watched. Like its misshapen feet burst through matching silk-covered shoes, sending the rhinestone buckles flying. I was left staring at what, a moment ago, had been one of the genteel looking party guests, indistinguishable from all the others, and now . . .

I didn't know what it was now. Just that it had slitted red eyes, a face caught halfway between human and something else, and a row of bony protrusions pushing out from its huge, hunched spine. Blood and bits of flesh clung to the spikes as they did to the elongated snout now thrusting out horribly from the creature's face.

It reminded me of a were, except that weres completed their transformations, becoming sleek, purpose-built predators within seconds. But this thing had stopped halfway, caught in a terrible, half transformed state, to sniff the air. Before bounding to its feet and leaping up the side of the cliff, all between one blink and the next.

And throwing me to the ground almost hard enough to knock me out.

There was a blast of hot, fetid breath in my face, and the sounds of fangs hitting metal, as the gorget I was wearing protected me when the creature went for my neck. As did the scales over my torso when it tried to disembowel me a second later. But the armor covering my right arm was less effective, or maybe it just felt that way when the crushing force of those jaws clamped shut.

I screamed and the creature began to whip me back and forth, trying to sever flesh and bone from my body. Until the Graeae known as Enyo came out of nowhere, leaping through the swirling dust like an avenging angel and screaming like a banshee. And while there were a few silk flowers in her long, gray hair, nothing else about her was the same.

The baked-apple-doll-faced old woman from my suite had disappeared, replaced by a frightening warrior covered in gore and with a full complement of teeth and eyes. The former were long and pointed, the latter were yellow and slitted, and both complimented the four-inch talons on the ends of her hands. I'd only seen that version of her a few times before, but all of them had been memorable.

This was no different, as she jumped on the back of my assailant, wrapped her muscular legs around his torso, and proceeded to bury her talons into his misshapen head.

Only to have the same thing happen to her.

A pointed tail I hadn't noticed snaked up behind her, and stabbed her half a dozen times before I could yell a warning. And then grabbed her around the neck, tearing her off the creature's back and throwing her savagely into the swirling dust. I heard her hit down, somewhere on the cleared space below us.

I did not hear her get up again.

Her attacker turned on me with a snarl, and then leapt, the massive body just a blur of savage claws and teeth and whipping, bloody tail. But Enyo had bought me a crucial moment to get my bearings. And I thrust my whip into his torso and watched him burst apart in a firestorm of hot ash.

The horns rattled to the ground, the remnants of his flesh flew into my gasping, open mouth, and a dozen more assailants leapt up the mountain at me from all sides. I shifted to the cleared space below, and found Enyo on the ground and one of her sisters, Pemphredo, standing over her. And attempting to fend off what looked like an army of mutated vamps.

Half of whom were buried under an avalanche a moment later, which dropped onto their heads courtesy of Pemphredo's ability to cause "accidents" to her enemies. It wasn't enough to save us, but it gave me a moment of distraction to shift us out, landing back on the riverbank amid the forest of shards. They were casting huge shadows in the fading light, and I helped Pemphredo to pull Enyo back into one.

Only to realize that one of our attackers had hitched a ride.

Pemphredo took the hit this time, dropping her sister and leaping in between us as it sprang at me, and I watched in horror as what looked like a single, great claw erupted from her torso.

"Pemphredo," I whispered, and then I manifested my whip again and cut the goddamned monster's head off.

And had to immediately bite my lip on a scream as my injured right arm exploded with pain. It had probably felt the same when I'd used it a moment ago, on my last assailant, but I'd been too terrified to notice. I noticed now.

But the pain was the least of my problems. Because the vamp wasn't dead, despite having just lost a head, and I didn't have a stake on me. The body lunged, spewing blood from the severed stump of a neck, and I scrambled back, my hands searching for wood, wood, any kind of wood on the frozen riverbank.

And found only a bit that the current had washed up on shore, old and gray and crumbling in my grip. Then the massive body was on me, its hands searching for my neck. And then falling limp and sliding off, with half of a forest sticking out of its back, because I'd shifted every loose piece of wood that I could find from the tree line.

I fought to get free of the beast's dead weight, pushing and shoving and cursing. And then lying in the snow, panting and blood covered and wracked with pain, and completely unable to process everything that had just happened since it had taken maybe fifteen seconds. And that was from the time Enyo saved me until now, since these things, whatever they were, were ungodly fast.

And disgusting, with the warm liquid leaking out of this one's headless body hitting the snow and causing a small eruption of steam.

Or maybe that was something else.

I froze, trying to tell myself that the movement taking place inside the headless corpse was random death throes, even though I knew I was lying. Something was attempting to escape the confines of the great body, and a moment later, it succeeded. I saw it stream out of the creature's bloody neck like a ghost, only visible for the dust particles it was disturbing, and for a pair of familiar, bright red eyes.

I'd just seen them glowing out of the monstrous vamp's skull, only vamps didn't leave ghosts, which meant—

Shit, I thought violently.

And then it was on me.

But the demon, which was definitely not one of ours, no longer had a body to protect it. This time, *I* grabbed *it,* and squeezed, hearing it scream, a metal-on-metal screech that echoed down the canyon and threatened to deafen me as it writhed inside my grip. It sank metaphysical teeth into me, right before I returned the favor, spearing spiritual claws into its insubstantial body and jerking *back*.

A flood of power spilled out into the air, some mine, some the demon's. I saw when it realized what was happening, when it scrabbled and twisted and attempted to flee. But I hung on and started to feed, reabsorbing my power while also taking in some of its. Because I didn't know what else to do.

And because it wasn't godly energy that was suddenly flowing into me, but it was energy, nonetheless.

It was hot and peppery, almost slimy, coating my senses with a strange, alien taste. I gagged, but kept sucking it in, and after a second, it did help to staunch the gaping wounds that had been torn into my spirit. I felt them heal and scab over, while the gush of lost power became a stream, then a trickle, and finally, nothing at all. I drained my attacker faster than it could do to me, and I drained it dry, throwing the blackened residue onto the ground when I was finished, where it squirmed for a second before winking out, leaving only an oily stain behind.

I got to my feet, alien energy buzzing in my veins and my head swimming wildly. But for once my power wasn't yelling at me for changing time. I guessed we were past that now.

I shook my head to clear it and hurried back to the girls. And dropped to the snow on my knees beside the two bloody bodies. The threesome had been my defenders when I first took this job, after I accidentally released them from imprisonment by the Circle. They were thousands of years old, another relic from the age of the gods, and supposedly all but invulnerable. But Pemphredo was gasping at the sky, her face pale, with blood spreading around her in a seeping pool, and Enyo—

Was already dead.

I stared at her in disbelief, feeling my body go cold. And then colder still when something glinted in the low light, and I reached over to pull a shard of glass out of her neck. The jagged piece was nothing compared to the gaping wounds in her torso, red mouthed and terrible.

Yet it frightened me infinitely more.

There was a bit of black residue inside what appeared to be a shattered vial, near the bottom, and I didn't need to wonder what it was. It was the same sludgy substance that I had stared at in a fey tent until it felt like it had been burned into my retinas. Enyo hadn't died because she'd underestimated her opponent; she'd died because her power had been stripped from her.

I heard a faint sound, and looked up, my heart in my throat and my whip in my hand. Only to see Deino, the third sister, standing at the edge of the forest.

For a long moment, she didn't move, staying as stationary as the tree trunks around her. But something about the way she paused made me think of the chorus in a Greek tragedy, as if she wanted to rend her clothes and wail and beat her breast in a furious lament. And her sisters deserved it; they deserved all of it.

But she didn't make a sound.

She knew we were being hunted.

She just hurried forward, after a brief hesitation, to kneel on the other side of Pemphredo.

"Can you help her?" I whispered. "Is she—can you do anything?"

She looked up at me and remained silent, but her face said that she wasn't sure.

"Take hold of them. Take hold of them both," I told her unsteadily. "I'll get you out."

But she shook her head and grabbed hold of my shoulder instead. The women didn't speak much English, or often speak at all. But her meaning was clear. She wanted me to go with them.

"I can't. You know I can't—"

She shook her head again, more violently this time, and began pulling and tugging on me.

Until I caught her hand in mine. "I have to touch the library to send it on its way. Nobody else can do it. This is *my* fight."

She stopped, and her face crumpled. And then a veined old hand reached up to stroke my cheek. I'd left her and the others guarding the little girls who made up my court, but something in her touch said that she'd come after her girl, and didn't want to leave without her.

The thought had my breath hitching in my chest, but all I could do was squeeze her hand. "I'm not a girl anymore," I whispered, and received back a tremulous smile.

She grabbed her sisters, and I shifted the three of them to the cave, miles distant, where my court was awaiting the outcome of the battle. And where my acolytes were holding back Rhea, who was furious at me for leaving her out of this. But right now, that was looking like the smartest decision I'd ever made.

I looked back over my shoulder, even though I couldn't see much through the dust, and tried to ignore the shiver running down my spine.

Even with the potion, what could tear through the *Graeae* like they were nothing?

Chapter Forty-Seven

I didn't get a direct answer, but my power suddenly started showing me flashes of transformations taking place on all sides. Some of the vamps weren't affected—the new arrivals, I assumed, who hadn't yet had time to get a rider—but they were in the minority. And as for the rest . . .

I saw shoulders bigger than those of oxen tearing out of delicate bodices, thighs the size of tree trunks ripping through fine silk pantaloons, and horns slicing fashionable bonnets to pieces.

The skin colors also changed, flooding boring beige, brown or black with bright green, red and purple, with some of the distorted faces wearing the remains of fine powder and rouge. And, in one surreal case, a beauty mark, high on a twisted cheekbone.

But there was no beauty, as there had been with Adra's group. Or with the hybrid vamp/demon army that we'd used to invade Faerie, which had never looked like this. They'd gotten additional powers, but they hadn't become monstrous. Perhaps because of the agreement negotiated between the Demon High Council and the Senate, which had defined exactly what was and was not permissible.

But there didn't seem to be any rules here.

And the vamps weren't even my biggest problem. But they'd kept me busy long enough for Zeus to find me again, and to send a massive piece of the library's roof spinning at my head. Thanks to the dust cloud, I didn't see it until it was almost too late, and there was no way to dodge.

I shifted out, perhaps a second before it hit, and landed further upstream in a wobbly crouch. I couldn't go any farther and be close enough to see the signal. Which still hadn't appeared, God damn it!

I scanned the skies, but Adra had said there would be no way to miss it. That as soon as our troops had cleared the building, he would light up the air, letting me know that it was showtime. I intended to use the library to send Zeus and his puppet on the ride of their lives, but I had to give our forces time to get out first.

So, what was the hold up?

"Marco!" I whispered, trying to contact my team, but only received back a crackle in my ear, loud enough to hurt. "Saffy, Vi, anybody!"

Still nothing.

A group of my strongest fighters were inside the library, protecting the group of fey hunters that the Circle had sent to my suite. They'd been stopped on their way out of the hotel and pressed into service because they could locate any fey who tried to use their magic to hide from Adra's forces. But while it should have taken them a few extra seconds to run out of the building instead of flying out like Adra's demons, they should be well clear by now.

Yet there was no signal.

Or maybe I just couldn't see it. The departing sun was streaking the sky with sherbet colors of orange, pink and yellow, and the dust cloud was reflecting all that light. It had created an orange dome over the area, making it impossible to see anything inside.

I was going to have to get closer.

But that proved easier said than done. I'd intended to shift in and then out again almost immediately, as I only needed time to get a look at the gate. But a creature out of a nightmare lunged at me the instant I rematerialized, forcing me to shift again on the fly. I misjudged the distance the second time around, popping back into real space maybe six feet above the earth before hitting down hard.

I also hit on my bad arm, almost causing me to pass out as I rolled and bumped down a sharp incline. And two more mutated vamps attacked before I'd even come to a stop. They rushed me from opposite directions, but I was jumpy as hell and didn't hesitate. I lashed out, cutting one off at the knees with my whip and then slashing upward, causing the other to have to regrow an arm.

Which it did, almost immediately.

I stared at it; even a master vamp couldn't do that. It stared back, grinning. It was a barrel chested red one, and looked like a stereotypical demon out of a children's book. Only a children's illustration wouldn't have been naked, or had six-inch claws dangling from the end of massively oversized arms, or been leering at me with quite that expression on its face.

Like it couldn't decide whether to eat me or fuck me, or possibly both at the same time.

I helped it out with that, slashing out again and bisecting it with the whip, while staggering back to my feet. A master vamp could heal a wound like that, but it would take time. And I assumed that it would take a lot more after I whipped the bottom half of the body the length of a football field away.

What was left snarled at me, and sent a ululating cry echoing over the battlefield, loud enough to rival an air raid siren. I wanted to clutch my head in pain, but couldn't. Every vamp within earshot was now surging up the rock pile, seeking to overwhelm me by attacking all at once.

I shifted out before they reached me, landing back at the place where Enyo had died, and where the body of the dead vamp was sluggishly leeching blood onto the snow. And immediately fell to my knees, biting my lip on a scream. My arm felt like it hadn't been broken so much as shattered, my head was dizzy from too many shifts practically back-to-back, and I was gasping for breath. Leaving clouds in the air in front of me as I stared around, looking for the next threat.

But there didn't appear to be one.

My scent was all over this place, as evidenced by the huge claw marks and oddly shaped footprints that had churned up the soil in the short time I'd been away. They'd left a muddy mess of half melted ice and dead grass behind, but had already moved on, chasing my wildly jumping trail. And I really hoped that my new scent would be indiscernible from the old, keeping them away.

At least for five seconds!

That seemed to be the case, because no one jumped me. And the huge piece of roof that had almost crushed me to death was now actually helping. It had slammed into the bank at a slant, obliterating the previous shards and leaving a drooping ledge over the area, which was helping to shield me from sight.

At least from above, where the god's movements were casting constantly shifting shadows onto the snow, water, and dust cloud alike. They left the surreal scene even more so, like the haunting sounds of his creature's cries, echoing over the battlefield. Their screeches reverberated off the mountains and came back at me from all sides.

This was not one of those surreal, too-calm-to-be-believed pauses that happen sometimes in battle. Instead, it looked like the world I knew had already changed into something else, something alien that I didn't recognize. It was seriously unnerving me and kept my pulse hammering in my chest, unable to calm back down.

Or maybe that was Hilde suddenly appearing in my face.

She almost got herself skewered, but I managed to throw the whip aside just in time, leaving it hissing into the snow instead of her body. I fell back against the half-frozen dirt, panting and staring at the incongruously neat white curls on her head, which looked like she'd just come from a salon. And felt my blood pressure tick up a dangerous few more notches.

"What the *hell*?" I whispered furiously, when I could speak.

"I'd like to ask you the same." It was grim. "What happened to—"

She abruptly cut off, her attention snagged by some of the gyrations of the massive god above us. For once, her strident eloquence failed her, and she just stayed that way, mouth slightly agape. I wondered briefly if that was how Gertie had looked on the Thames, when she'd caught her first glimpse of what we were facing, but didn't know.

I'd been a little busy at the time.

Kind of like now.

"That happened," I said, reabsorbing the whip and scrambling back to my feet. "What are you *doing* here?"

She shook herself, and those sharp brown eyes met mine again squarely. "What do you think? Trying to discover why the Graeae returned a bloody mess! And why the library is still here. I warned you—"

I cut her off with a look, and it must have been a good one, since it actually shut her up for a second. "And I warned you to stay out of this! If something goes wrong, you and the court are the only line of defense we have left!"

"Well, it appears that something has gone wrong," she pointed out. "And as your senior acolyte, I have a duty to—"

She broke off again, catching sight of the dead vamp's head leering out of the snowbank. I couldn't blame her. It was even more gruesome in death than it had been in life, and that was saying something.

"What is *that*?"

I started to reply, only to stop short. Not because the item in question was haloed in a splatter of red from the impact when it had landed, one that had traveled halfway up the snowbank. Or because the face was stuck in a very lifelike snarl, captured at the moment of death. But because of the eyes.

They'd already iced over, turning them into mirrors for the sunset painting the sky behind us. It boiled redly in the fixed irises, making him almost appear alive again. The color was impossibly vivid, like fire distilled, like lava trapped under a frozen lake, like—

Like the stone creature at the battle at Issengeir that I'd seen from the perspective of David, the war mage who I'd followed into his last fight. It had had lava, too, spewing from its neck with which it had tried to defend itself and its master. I could still see it, scattering in a vast plume across the pewter-colored sky, like someone tossing a handful of rubies . . .

And, suddenly, I understood.

My head twisted around, staring behind me. And remembering all the huge, lumbering, mountain-sized soldiers that the fey had created for their army. And the fact that most of them had *been* huge and lumbering, instead of liquid fast and agile as the Senate had been warned to expect.

Because Zeus and Aeslinn had made some friends during their time in the hells, namely things called Ancient Horrors—demons so powerful and so vicious that even the Demon High Council feared them, and had locked them away on distant worlds, under enchantments supposedly impossible to break.

But what was without factoring an elder god into the mix. Aeslinn had set them free—we hadn't understood how at the time—but we'd been warned that they'd been used to animate some of the elemental soldiers guarding the king's lands, to make them even faster and more deadly than they already were. It was why we'd been expecting a terrible fight.

And we'd gotten one—but not from them.

Most of the creatures we'd encountered at Issengeir had been old school earth magic, with no demon presence inside. Because the demons—Zeus's little pets, I assumed—were here, stuffed full of god blood and possessing some vamps. The same ones that he planned to send to join the rebellion, and wipe the floor with us in a different era.

"Cassie!"

I looked up, and found Hilde staring at me with concern, which was nothing to how I felt.

"An Ancient Horror," I said, my lips feeling numb just from the words.

Then I pushed past her and hurried over to the vamp's body, my freezing hands scrabbling around in his clothes.

"What are you doing?" she demanded, her sensible shoes crunching over the snow to join me. "And what the devil do you mean, Ancient Horrors? They were all killed—"

"No, we were meant to *think* they'd been killed," I said, turning out the bastard's pockets. "A few were scattered around the battlefield to give that impression, but most were here. Inhabiting Gabriella's vamps—"

"Why, in heaven's name?"

"Because an Ancient Horror can't go swanning into the Senate or the Circle's HQ without opposition! They look like their name implies, ensuring that they'd never get past the wards. But in vamp form, they can hide until everyone's in place, then attack all at once—"

"We'd wipe the floor with them," she said staunchly. "The Corps—"

"A single Ancient Horror was turned loose on the Senate recently, and it took twelve senators and the Pythian power to defeat it, and it was touch and go then!" I looked up, and saw my words register. "They can't take an army of them, Hilde. *That's* why we're here."

I had wondered why Aeslinn had been so willing to send one of them against us. He'd wanted to attack the army we were building on Earth before it reached his forces in Faerie, but in doing so, he'd tipped his hand. Yet, he hadn't seemed to care.

Because he wasn't planning on using them there, in the present, but here in the past.

Where no one would be expecting a damned thing.

"You expect us to fight those things, as well as Zeus?" Hilde demanded.

"No, I expect Adra to. But his boys are busy in Faerie and will be until our hunters can join them. I have to get to the gate, wait for the signal, and get Zeus out of here as scheduled. Once he's on the ride from hell, we mop up."

A surprisingly strong hand grabbed my wrist. "You have an angry god and an army of ancient demons between you and that gate—"

"I also don't have a choice—"

"—not to mention that something has gone wrong with the mages. They should have been out by now—"

"The library took damage when it landed. They may have gotten cut off—"

"Or they may be dead."

"They're *war mages*. They don't die from having a wall fall on them!"

"They also don't stay trapped by said wall for this long. Send the library now."

I looked up at her, sure I'd misunderstood. "What?"

"You heard me." The old lips were pressed into a grim line.

"It would kill them!"

"As you pointed out, they're war mages. They knew what they signed on for."

I just stared at her for a moment. "Saffy and Vi and half of my bodyguards are with them. You can't expect—"

"I can." It was implacable. "These are the decisions that a Pythia has to sometimes make. We have to look at the bigger picture—"

"The bigger picture is that Adra's demons can't find the fey without them!" I said, furious. "If even one of them gets away, he can warn the Aeslinn of this era about what's happening, and then we're right back where we started! They'll make different plans, and we're all—"

"Then I will go inside and find them," Hilde said, causing another pause while I stared at her some more. And then grabbed her arm even harder than she'd grabbed mine. "Like hell—"

"I just pointed out that we sometimes have to make sacrifices," she said, meeting my gaze unflinchingly. "You can't look for them and the signal at the same time. If they find their own way out whilst I am searching, you must send the library immediately, never mind if I am out or—"

"You're not going to be searching!" I interrupted furiously. "Zeus is in the middle of the goddamned rotunda!"

She looked at me implacably. "There is no other way."

"Find one." It was vicious and I didn't care. I wasn't losing anyone else today!

Hilde regarded me, not unkindly. "We all have a role to play," she pointed out. "I cannot do yours. Let me do mine."

"I will. And yours is to guard Rhea, and train her, and help her, if I fall. The others are acolytes; you were almost Pythia. She'll need you."

Her arms folded. "Then what would you suggest?"

I swallowed, and had to almost force the words out. But she was right. There was no other choice. "Pick one of the others—"

"Which one?"

"You choose. Whoever you think has the best chance . . ." of coming back, I didn't say, because this wasn't about that anymore. "Of success."

This seemed to be acceptable, and the old head inclined slightly. There was no talk about the fact that our odds had just gone from bad to terrifically bad, no mouthing of platitudes, no comforting words. Simply acknowledgement of the reality we were facing, and of what we had to do to salvage this.

If she hadn't been born in the era and body that she was, she'd have been a damned five-star general.

"Find an observation point," she said simply, and shifted out.

Chapter Forty-Eight

I stared after her for a moment, wondering how I ended up leading a bunch of women like that. As usual, I didn't have an answer. And I didn't have time to kneel in the snow, wondering about it!

I went back to the search.

Like everything today, it was harder than it should have been. The watered silk topcoat and breeches that the vampire had been wearing were in tatters, and not just because of the all the stakes that I'd slammed into his back. But because he'd already been a disaster, with his flesh completely unable to contain the rapid changes that the demon had forced onto him.

There was blood everywhere, gushing wetly from tears in his arms and legs, which had ripped open like his clothes. Stringy muscle and yellowed fat could be seen in some, pushing past the flesh like stuffing between frayed couch cushions. Or what they were—stretch marks that had stretched too far and become lesions.

Yet many had already healed in the short period he'd had before I killed him, leaving shiny pink scars behind. It made him look almost like he was wearing striped tights. And reminding me how quickly these things recovered.

I searched faster.

Finally, my hand closed over a leather pouch on a thong, which the creature's body was lying on. It had been slung around his neck before I took his head off, and was now stuck under five hundred pounds of muscle. But while I didn't have Mircea's strength anymore, I did have desperation and managed to tug it loose.

And had five little black vials spill out into my hand.

I just knelt there for a moment, remembering the terrifying struggle inside that tent in Faerie. Not the one with Aeslinn's guards, but the one with myself. I'd been too afraid to do what was necessary, and if Pritkin hadn't pulled the biggest rabbit out of the largest hat in history, my cowardice would have cost us everything.

Slowly, I turned to look at the battlefield again.

I could see it in patches, whenever the wind tore a hole in the dust cloud. I could also hear Aeslinn roaring orders at the vamps, which I wasn't sure they understood since they were in whatever language the fey spoke. I didn't understand them, either, not having Pritkin to translate for me anymore, but I didn't need to.

The rage in his voice was plenty good enough.

It sent chills through me that had nothing to do with the cold. They were the same ones that I'd felt in that tent, sapping my energy, strangling my breath, making me want to huddle into a little ball and pray that this would all just go away. But they didn't hit quite as hard.

Knowing that I was doomed no matter what didn't eliminate the fear, unfortunately. But it made it more manageable. I wasn't fighting for myself anymore; I was fighting for everyone that I loved.

And I wasn't going to fuck it up this time.

I shoved the vials into a pocket and shifted. And, immediately, things looked very different. I stayed where I was, while the chaos in front of me slowed way, way down. Until the churning clouds of dust were boiling at a snail's pace, and glittering in the fading light like veils of gold dust. Like Villi's body as it melted away, or like the hundreds of fey that Pritkin had drained as I raced across that camp to safety.

There was no safety here, but this was as close as I could get. I got to my feet and started walking forward, controlling my shift as Gertie had taught me, reducing its speed to let me to see what was happening before I stumbled into the middle of it. And to spot Zeus's pets before they spotted me.

And there were plenty of them.

Some were moving so fast that they looked like they were in real time. They emerged abruptly out of the dust every few seconds, flashing by in a blur or pausing to look about wildly. And without having to fight for my life every second, I had a chance to look back—and wished I didn't.

Because the changes they were undergoing . . . hadn't stopped.

The demons seemed to have realized that vamp flesh wasn't like human. It wasn't alive in the normal sense, and didn't need all the organs that had once kept it going. It also healed rapidly—especially when they were pouring massive amounts of life energy into it—and could therefore be manipulated in startling ways.

It was the same thing that the vamps themselves often discovered, when they became old enough and powerful enough to manipulate their own forms. But the powers they developed were never like this. They were often beautiful, or at the very least, helpful, since vamps would never deliberately desecrate their own bodies.

But the demons had no such compunction. And what they were making out of their new servants reminded me bizarrely of the cookies the girls had been baking back in the suite. Only they hadn't merely hijacked random limbs; instead, entire bodies had fused together, busily forming something new.

And something horrible.

One example slithered past me like an overfed snake, with four or five bodies merged together in a single line. Most of the limbs had already vanished into the pulsating central mass, but a few stuck out here or there, writhing uselessly in the air. A delicate diamond ring resided on one slender hand, glittering in the low light, before it was drawn inward, too, swallowed by an acre of flesh.

I froze as the creature glided past, becoming longer and thinner as it rearranged the new raw material to its liking. I couldn't seem to make my feet move, although I could have walked right through it like a ghost since I wasn't really there. I wasn't really anywhere during transition, being merely a potential until I landed, which I had no intention of doing!

I didn't need to land in this particular corner of hell; I just needed to see, without anyone else seeing me.

So, *move*!

I did, as soon as the creature disappeared into the dust, but so did something else. It lumbered out of the clouds before I'd gotten ten yards: huge, vaguely human-like, and dragging a shattered pine tree like a club. I dodged the latter, despite not needing to, and then stared upward into what my overloaded brain finally identified as dozens of pairs of eyes, which were spotting its body like warts.

The pair closest to me were blinking out of a massive shank, halfway between the ankle and knee. And unlike the dark brown set a little way up, they were a pale, blue-grey and fringed by blond lashes. They looked like they belonged on a friendly, freckled face, with maybe a wispy attempt at a mustache under the nose that it no longer had, because it no longer had anything. Just the eyes . . .

They made me wonder if the vamp was still in there somewhere, trapped in a body that was no longer his, and which would likely never be his again. Could he read the demon's mind after having fused with it? Did he realize that, instead of being empowered or whatever lies Gabriella had told him, he'd basically been sold for parts?

Or was he isolated, a mind trapped in a body that it no longer controlled, all alone and silently screaming . . .

Cut it out! I told myself angrily. And get moving! Now!

I stumbled ahead, although I kept looking over my shoulder. I remembered one of Eugenie's stories about a monster named Argus, who'd had a hundred eyes. The gods had been responsible for that little experiment, and I'd often wondered why they'd thought that more was somehow better.

Now, I knew. Each set worked independently, moving about and constantly shifting. Giving the demon a 360-degree view and me a new definition of horrified.

And then it got worse.

"Casssssssssssieeeeeeeee," Zeus's voice echoed across the battlefield, eerily drawn out and elongated by the time distortion. "Youuuuu cannnnn'ttttt hiiiiiiddddeeeee forrrrevvvverrrrrrr."

Wanna bet? I thought viciously, and started to climb.

I found a path that something had carved through the rubble. It was at maybe an eighty-degree angle, but I nonetheless began making better time, my hands digging for holds in the dirt, my feet scrabbling for purchase on tumbled rocks, and my breath coming quick and ragged in my throat. But not because of the physical exertion or even the burden of maintaining transition.

But because of that.

"Ssssssoooooo brrraaaavvveee, annnddddd yyyyeeetttt ssssssoooooo hooooopppeeeellllleeessssss. Come out and let's talk."

The abrupt switch from distorted to regular speech made me stumble, and look around as wildly as Aeslinn's creatures had been doing. Zeus was searching for me in both areas, I realized—regular time and transition. Only he couldn't be—he couldn't be!

He had power over the byways, as he called the moments during a shift, something he'd stolen from a little goddess whose energy he'd devoured. But that was only true after he was inside them, and he couldn't take himself into transition on his own. He'd had to catch the end of my spell to attack me on the Thames—

Just like he had on the bridge, I realized. *That* was why he'd wanted to get so close. Not attacking immediately as most would have done, but waiting until he'd grabbed onto a piece of my power, to make sure that he could follow if I shifted away.

And fuck!

Every time, every time, I thought I had an advantage, he pulled the rug out from under me. Just once, I'd like to surprise him for a change. Preferably with a knife through the brain!

But instead, my own brain conjured up an image of a huge face, pushing into the surreal landscape of the shift and peering around. And although it was just my imagination, that was likely exactly what he was doing. I felt panic grip my throat until it threatened to choke me.

But then he made a mistake.

"We can salvage this, my dear," Zeus said, his voice as loud as a foghorn he was so close. "But my patience is not infinite."

And neither was his reach, or I'd already be dead. He might have figured out a way to enter transition, but that didn't mean he could automatically find me. He was as lost as I was, and if I kept moving, he'd stay that way.

I went back to mountain climbing.

And tried my best to ignore the beast with three heads that pushed past me, going down the narrow trail as I went up; and the one with numerous limbs, like a Hindu god, that jumped down almost on top of me from a higher perch; and the one that loomed overhead suddenly, cutting off the light. But the last caused me to glance up and then to freeze, staring at eight, hideously distended legs dropping from a body that was trying to take on its final shape. But which was already beginning to look a lot like—

My eyes jerked away, not able to cope with the sight of a giant spider made out of cannibalized human parts. And had my concentration wobble, causing me to drop briefly out of transition. I recovered almost immediately, yet a second later, there was a bastard sniffing the air right in front of me, trying to pick up my scent.

I stumbled back, and found myself looking at a handsome, dark-haired man wearing snow white linen and embroidered velvet. I guessed all the vamps couldn't change if Aeslinn and his master wanted their plan to succeed. But although he might look human, he didn't act it, dropping to all fours and snuffling in the dirt, before bounding off in the direction of the scent puddle that I'd left on the riverbank.

I leaned back against a wall of rubble for a second, almost dizzy with relief. And that was all of the time I had before an earthquake hit, shuddering the mountain under my feet. The ground lurched, blocks as big as my body tumbled past, and I looked up through the billowing clouds of dust—

To see a great hand, swooping down at me.

I slowed time even more and dodged out of the way, and Zeus hit the stone beside me instead of my body. Yet it was enough to send me tumbling back into the normal world. And as soon as I did, five more of his creatures leapt for me. They fell onto the place I'd just been, ripping and tearing at the ground, and I crawled out through the middle of them, having pulled myself back into transition barely in time.

Only to have the great hand clap down again, almost crushing me against the stony ground.

I had to practically stop time to save myself that time, falling back against the dirt from the effort. I landed face up, and was therefore able to see the grime in the lines of the huge, but very human-looking palm as it came closer. It was one of the more surreal moments of my life, and was almost the last, as I barely slithered out the other side before it hit down.

It caused another, not-so-minor avalanche, but I clung to a half-buried column and stayed in place. And then looked up to see the setting sun glinting off the jagged teeth of the gate that I'd been working so hard to reach. The debris fall had cleared the path in front of me, showing me my goal in the distance, and for a second, I felt my heart leap in my chest.

Until I noticed: The signal wasn't there.

The light blushed the ugly, chipped stone of the gate's framework, turning it an incongruously pretty pink. But that was true all along the top of the wall, where pennants snapped in the breeze, their gold highlights glinting in the sun. But the gate remained just a gate, with the long, pitted, black iron teeth looking exactly as they always had.

Because of course it did! By using the byways, I'd managed to make it up here, but I'd also slowed things way down. Or sped them up from a real time perspective, since my shift was still a shift.

It was instantaneous, regardless of what speed I let it be in here. Meaning that Hilde had just left a couple of minutes ago. She probably hadn't even had time to send anyone into the library, or if she had, they'd only just arrived.

And, damn it! I couldn't stay here! I was lucky to have survived this long!

And right on cue, another earthquake hit, much harder than the last, throwing me off my feet. And this time, there was no doubt as to the cause. I looked up to see Aeslinn tearing out of the ruined dome, first the great chest and arms, and then the giant torso when I guessed he stood up.

For a second, I didn't understand what was happening.

And then I did, and my blood ran cold.

I kept eluding him, so he was moving to a better vantage point. He was leaving, and no, no, no—he couldn't! If he left the library the damned signal wouldn't matter anymore—nothing would!

My hand found the vials in my pocket and clenched.

And then I shifted, before I could talk myself out of it, not away but onto his great shoulder where I landed with a thud. Right by the thick neck with a pulsing vein, which I ripped open with my whip. The slender band of gold looked impossibly small next to the acres of flesh, being nothing like as big or as thick as it had been on the Thames when I'd been mainlining Zeus's power.

But it was good enough.

I slammed the vials inside, pushing against the fountain of blood that I'd just freed and which was gushing like a fire hydrant. I would have tried to take his head, too, but I didn't get a chance. A second later, I was ripped out of transition and sent speeding back toward the ground where I'd have splattered like a bug on a windshield, but I was caught before I could.

A giant-sized hand, ghostly pale and shimmering against the brilliantly colored sky, plucked me unerringly out of the air and brought me up through the clouds, bursting into clear air in front of a bloody face that appeared to be wrestling with itself.

Aeslinn looked apoplectic, with his physical hand pressed against the jugular, blood spurting from between his fingers. But Zeus seemed pleased, almost exultant. It gave the great face a split personality that was somehow a lot more frightening that plain old fury would have been.

The struggle was clear in the body, as well. The hand clutching the bloody neck reached for me, only to be struck away by the ghostly one. It was growing out of Aeslinn's stump, and looked as insubstantial as a cloud, but held me as firmly as iron. Leaving me panicked and breathing hard and waiting—

For nothing.

The huge head remained huge; the body continued to tower over everything; and worse, a sliver of Zeus's power bit into me, like a single fang. I tried to shift away, but nothing happened, his power curling around mine, riveting me in place. While the potion that should have severed Aeslinn's connection to his magic, and shrunk him down to size, did nothing.

I didn't understand! I'd stuck it in his goddamned jugular! The corks had been out of the vials, removed and flung aside. There was no way—no way—that it wasn't coursing through his bloodstream right now. And the fey had said that it didn't take much. Aeslinn might be huge, but he'd had five freaking vials!

But instead of rendering him helpless, it didn't seem to have done anything at all. The giant face bent down, and the genial features of the god won out, regarding me with faux concern. And then speaking in a whisper that, this close, blew my hair back.

"I'm sorry; were you not aware? That potion only works on *human* blood."

I stared up at him. "But . . . Mircea—"

"Was once one of you. It's why we often experimented on human stock—it is so much easier to control. The vampires, the Weres, even those sweet old lady "goddesses" of yours: all early experiments crossing human blood with some of our own. They would not have stayed on Earth otherwise, when your mother cast her nasty little spell, banishing us all."

"And Aeslinn . . . is pure fey," I said, cursing myself.

He'd also already healed, closing a wound that, on its own, should have been a death blow. He was covered in blood, but it hadn't been enough even to stagger him, and now a green shield spell cut me off from further attempts. Not that I was likely to have the chance to make any.

"As are his people," Zeus agreed. "It has made them quite useful allies. Although I am tempted, I truly am, to possess you instead. The king forgets his place at times, and controlling your body . . . well, it would be simpler. And would help me get close to that young man of yours, the half demon who has been so much trouble."

I stared up at him, my mind icing over, and he laughed, a booming sound that echoed over the mountains like thunder.

"You don't think we'd suit? Ah, well, perhaps not. And your human blood would make me too vulnerable. It would be a shame, would it not, to be taken down by my own potion? Not to mention that I don't think you're likely to be with us much longer."

The great head shook slowly.

"You gambled and you lost, just like your mother. And, like her, you've also made yourself into a nuisance. I believe I shall enjoy this," he said, as the fang bit deeper.

And as the shield spell around the giant body flickered . . . and went out.

It took me a second to realize what I'd just seen, and then my mind flashed to the guards back in that tent in Faerie. Not every fey was so dismissive of human charms, even among the Svarestri. And it looked like Aeslinn's perfect genealogy . . .

Wasn't so perfect after all.

"Surprise," I gasped, and shoved my whip into the giant torso, burning straight through to the heart.

I don't know if Zeus felt anything, but Aeslinn certainly did. And so did I, when the god's hold broke and the king sent me hurtling toward the earth, less deliberately this time than in the midst of massive a spasm. Only I didn't hit earth.

One moment, I was spinning helplessly through the air, and the next, I was plunging under freezing water.

Chapter Forty-Nine

The water cushioned the fall, but the impact plus the cold was almost enough to stop my heart. Which would have stumbled anyway when I looked up at the surface after a moment, and saw a ring of distorted faces staring down at me. I stared back, seeing them waver through the rushing current, and knew that I either shifted out or I was done.

Vamps could pull blood straight from their victim's veins through the air, even from a distance. Some liked feeding the old-fashioned way, for the visceral pleasure of it, but they didn't have to. And the more vamps, the faster the drain.

That many could suck me dry in seconds.

I'd barely had the thought when what felt like half of my blood was jerked out of my veins, clouding the river around me. I gasped in shock and almost drowned, and then tried again to shift. But that required concentration and I'd just lost mine.

Another pull hit before I got it back, hard on the heels of the first, like a hundred fists punching me at once. Followed by a terrible sucking sensation that caused me to choke and stop flailing. But not because I was no longer trying.

But because my body wasn't listening to my commands.

I felt my heart stutter in my chest, felt my lungs hitch, felt cold encircle me with a grip more severe than anything the frigid water could manage. It was like a bony hand clutching me, and I fought against it, because I knew what it meant. You have to get out of here, I told myself desperately; you have to!

I tried again to shift—anywhere, even just to the riverbank, where I could possibly get lost in the forest. It wasn't likely to work; a vamp is as good as a bloodhound, and that many could track me to hell and back. But I'd last longer than I would here!

Yet nothing happened.

Except for a third attack that I barely felt, except that it left me limp and strangely weightless. The sunlight, what there was left of it, had become a hazy smear across my vision. It went darker still as I sluggishly fought to make it back to the surface, for light and air and a chance, even as I felt that skeletal hand clench tight—

And abruptly jerk me down, down, down, into a vortex of flashing colors and rushing noise, and then inward, bursting through what felt like a wall of water and into—

I had no freaking idea.

I lay in a crumpled heap, more than half stunned, on a hard surface. A mass of sodden hair was in my eyes, and I couldn't see much at all. But I could feel, and that was air instead of water surrounding me, and stone underneath me. And there was light of some sort, dim but glimmering through the wet strands.

But before I could look for the source, I was coughing and choking and retching and puking. And then staying on my side and gasping desperately, like a beached fish. Because all of that had somehow cleared my airway.

I just lay there, sucking in lungful after lungful of strangely warm, slightly dusty air. It tasted like water in the desert, like ambrosia, like the best thing ever. For a moment, it encompassed my whole world. And it was a long moment, since I felt really weird— dizzy and floaty and lacking in pain, which was worrying in itself since my body should have been screaming at me.

But it wasn't, and I was too tired to figure out why.

So, I just lay there some more, with my cheek against the oddly warm stone, waiting for my senses to right themselves. And wondering where the hell I'd ended up. And how long it would take for the vamps to find me. And whether or not they could track me through a river.

And why everything was strangely pink.

I finally began to feel a little steadier, pushed my hair out of my eyes and started to sit up. Only to pause halfway. I'd had the vague thought that maybe I'd been sucked down by some weird current and pulled into a natural cave under the riverbank. One that had somehow trapped a lot of oxygen and was warmer than the outside air.

But I wasn't in a cave.

A crystalline matrix surrounded me, glinting like a prism. I reared back a little in surprise and it moved with me, in a kaleidoscope of different shades of pink. It was beautiful, containing every color from palest carnation to dusky mauve, with most hues hitting closer to the middle of the spectrum. A few of them were even edging into—

My brain stopped abruptly, and for a moment, I couldn't think at all. And when I could, it was to jerk away from the ideas swirling around in my head, both mentally and physically. Which resulted in me chasing myself around and around the small space as if I could outrun them if I tried hard enough.

It was panicked and stupid and didn't help at all, but I didn't know what else to do. And I wasn't going to figure it out, since a dead brain can't think! And that was undoubtedly what I was—dead.

And sitting inside Billy's ugly ruby necklace.

Acknowledging the idea, even just in my head, stopped me again. And for a moment, I froze, panting and freaking out and disbelieving. But try as hard as I could, I couldn't come up with another explanation.

Maybe because this place even smelled like him.

Ghosts can have a scent, something that often surprises people. Many spirits don't, unless it's a cold, vaguely chlorine odor, like a pool at midnight. But if it's relevant to their story or to whatever trauma is tying them to Earth, they absolutely can manifest all sorts of smells.

I'd encountered a number of them through the years, things like blood covered roses, from a spilled wedding bouquet, the kind of thing you'd expect. But also homemade bread, fresh out of an oven, from an old lady ghost who wasn't particularly bothered about anything, but was just hanging about to make sure that her grandchildren were all right. Or the scent of oranges, from a daughter whose father would always peel her one whenever they were in season, while sitting on their back porch. She was a bloody freaking horror with maggots eating her brain, but she still smelled like daddy's oranges.

Billy's scent was more subtle. It was a combination of tobacco, the whiskey he'd spilled on his shirt the night of his death, hair oil and Caswell No.6, an old cologne that he'd splashed on whenever he'd hoped that the evening would end in some feminine companionship. It had ended at the bottom of the Mississippi instead, where some cowboys had tossed him in a sack, but the scent lingered.

I could almost taste it on the air—or in the power, I guessed, since the talisman was solid. The smell was so pervasive that I actually looked around for a second, as if expecting him to be there. But only my own reflection stared back at me, out of a thousand tiny prisms.

This must have been what he saw, I thought blankly, on that fateful night a century and a half ago. He'd been cheating the cowboys at poker, gotten caught, and gone for a permanent swim. But since he'd previously done a better job of cheating a countess out of a truly hideous necklace, he hadn't died.

Or, rather, he had, it not being possible to breathe under a crap ton of water, but his soul had continued, fueled by the talisman at the center of the necklace.

The same one that had just caught mine.

"Yeah, it really sucked," the ghost said, lighting up a new cigarette from the smoldering ruin of the last one. "Took me forever to figure out what had happened, 'cause it's not like you get a manual, and there weren't a lot of other ghosts at the bottom of the river.

"Which was just as well, 'cause when I did meet 'em—hoo boy, those guys were assholes."

"Yeah, I've noticed," I started to walk away.

"Hey! Hey, come back!" He jumped off the garbage can that he'd been using as a perch and disappeared. Only to reappear right in front of me, halfway down the short alley. "You don't want to do that!"

"Don't I?" I crossed my arms and glared at him.

He'd been talking my ear off for the last five minutes, and seemed content to keep on doing so for as long as I was willing to put up with it. I'd met his kind before, and being nice got you nowhere. The trick was to outrun them, since all ghosts had a range—a limit on how far they could go from whatever they haunted, and still make it back before they ran out of juice.

Only that probably wouldn't work in his case, considering that I had the center point of his range clutched in my hand.

"It's an expensive necklace," he said, nodding at the small, plastic bag I held, which concealed a very old velvet case that was now missing most of its nap. It also had rust on its hinges, a missing front latch, and worrying marks on one side, like maybe a rat had been gnawing at it.

A big rat.

But the ghost was trying to sell it like it was the Hope Diamond.

"That center stone—that's a real ruby, you know? One of those pinky red ones, at that—they're really rare!"

"Yet it was on clearance at the pawn shop."

He frowned. "The setting is unfortunate, okay? But the advantages—"

"I'm not seeing a lot of advantages," I snapped. I'd just spent all of my carefully horded spending money on a gift for my governess, and now I was going have to come up with something else.

And despite the fact that Eugenie was a hard ass, she was surprisingly sentimental about birthdays, probably because her own mother had never cared for them. She'd left the little girl crying into her pillow every year, when yet another anniversary came and went unacknowledged. Eugenie therefore went all out whenever my birthday rolled around, not money wise maybe, but with well-thought-out gifts that she'd clearly sunk time and effort into.

So how was I supposed to come back to her with a hanky?

"It's an expensive piece," the ghost insisted. He had a weird accent for a cowboy, Midwestern meets Ireland, which probably spoke of an interesting backstory. One that he would no doubt enjoy telling me—at length—if I let him.

But that wasn't gonna happen, because I had stuff to do. But when I started for the street again, and the shop where I firmly intended to demand a refund, I found the ghost in the way. And he stayed in the way, no matter how hard I tried to dodge.

"Look!" I said, in exasperation. "I'm sure it's very nice, but it's not what I—"

"It's exactly what you need. You know why?" He did not wait for me to ask, not that I'd been planning on it. "It comes with me. I'm your gift with purchase!"

"That's what I'm afraid of."

"No, really." He dodged in front again when I made a sudden move, and ended up so close that I got caught in part of his body. I thrashed my way back out, spitting and spluttering, and feeling like I had ghost fragments clogging my throat. And eyes. And pores.

Damn it!

"Just listen, okay?"

"To what?" I spat again, my tongue feeling fuzzy. "I don't want a pet ghost!"

"Yes, you do. And I'm not just any ghost. I'm special."

I put my hands on my hips, because listening to the spiel was obviously the only way I was getting out of here. "You're special."

"You know it, sweet stuff—"

"Don't call me that."

"—and I got talents. For instance, did you know I can go up to fifty miles away from my little hacienda there? It's a talisman that gives me extra power that most ghosts don't have—"

"And this helps me how?"

"All kinds of ways! You like cards?" A pack appeared on his outstretched palm, which he shuffled one-handed. "'Cause I can make you a whiz at cards—"

"Didn't you just tell me that you were killed because—"

"A rare occurrence. And that was before I had my handy dandy disappearing trick to work with. I can make you rich—"

"I don't want to be rich."

"—but, of course, a girl like you wouldn't care about that. But I can do other stuff too. Like fetch things—"

"Do I look like I have a broken leg?"

"—and spy on people—"

"Why would I want you to do that?"

"I dunno." He flicked his cowboy hat back with a finger. "You tell me. But you need help, and don't lie and say you don't. A hundred and fifty years of people-watching teaches a man things. You got problems, girlie."

I didn't say anything that time, but I guessed my silence was enough to tell a poker player—even a shitty one—that he'd hit his mark. "Yeah," he said. "I get it. I got problems, too."

"What kind of problems?" I demanded. "You're a ghost. Your problems are over."

He rolled his eyes. "As if. Take that necklace. It gives me power, sure, and a bigger playground than most ghosts get. But it's also a vulnerability. I don't have a grave, or rather, I do, but it's at the bottom of the Mississippi—"

"That's unfortunate—"

"Yes, it is. 'Cause you don't get a lot of visitors down there, okay? Nobody to shed little drips and drops of life energy, like in a proper cemetery, to keep a fellow going. If I hadn't ended up in that ugly jewel there . . . well, I'd have faded a long time ago."

"But you did end up with it—"

"Yeah, and that's my point. It saved me, but it's also a weakness, ain't it? A lot of magic went into creating it. Lots of mages interested in disenchanting stuff like that, for whatever power they can get. And plenty of the poorer sort trawl places like that shop, looking for magical stuff that might bring 'em a windfall. It's only a matter of time before one of them finds me."

I stared up at him, and the soulful hazel eyes became even more so, almost to the point of parody. The rest of him looked kind of hard-bitten: a badly shaved jaw, probably an attempt to hide a baby face; a small scar on his nose, where he might have been punched by somebody wearing a ring; and a slick, gambler-esque outfit consisting of a red ruffled shirt and jeans that had never seen a prairie.

But the eyes were strangely compelling.

"And then, I'm dead—like dead-dead, you know?" he clarified, in case I'd missed the point. "I'll get sucked down to the depths, never to rise again. Never to do anything again, 'cept watch the water wash over my head, the fish pick my bones, and have no hope, no future, no anything. Until, eventually, I fade away, when the last of my power runs out, without ever accomplishing a damned thing.

"All that, when a sweet-faced girl could have saved me, if only she had a kind and loving heart to match her pretty, young, and if I may say so, pleasingly buxom—"

"Oh, my God!" I tried going around again, but once more, I had a ghost in the way.

And this time, he wasn't playing.

"Listen, sister. I don't know what the deal is with you, but we both got problems, all right? We're both losers at this game of life, and while I might be down a few more hands than you, you ain't doing so hot, either. The way I see it, we can team up and help each other, or we can keep on losin'. Now, which is it gonna be?"

I stared at him for a moment, and something about the blunt honesty got through when the flowery crap hadn't. Maybe because honesty was at a premium in my world, and always caught my attention whenever it showed up. Or maybe because he was right.

I was a loser, always had been, and things were not looking up lately. I could use some help, even if it was from a con-artist ghost. I looked at the semitransparent hand he was determinedly holding out, and slowly, tentatively, found myself taking it.

If anybody had glanced into the alley, they would have thought I was crazy, shaking hands with the air. But I felt something when his fingers enfolded mine, an odd warmth where most ghosts were cold. And a pressure, like a real hand there for a second, clasping my own.

"Good choice," he said. "I'm Billy, by the way."

"Cassie. Cassie Palmer."

"Well, it's nice to meet you, Cassie. I got a feelin' we're gonna be real good friends."

And we had been. We'd fought and fumed and yelled at each other, worse than any siblings. But Billy had been with me for years, had saved my life more times than I could count, and been a hell of a friend. And maybe, just maybe, he'd done me one last favor.

Thanks to his necklace, I was still here.

This wasn't over.

Chapter Fifty

My panicked scramble had left me closer to what I guessed was the surface of the jewel, where the fractals were less intrusive. It showed me back an image of my face, which was fuzzy and blurred, maybe because I was looking at a ghost. Or because the surface was scratched and cloudy, with all sorts of imperfections in the stone.

Or because it was less of a mirror than a window.

I crawled forward some more, and realized that I wasn't imagining things. Those were mountains in the distance, with snow-covered blankets of trees underneath. I could see out!

But it wasn't easy. The view was dim, like looking through thick, rose-colored glasses, ones with dirty lenses. But I finally found a relatively flat stretch with a clear bit of crystal, which gave me a glimpse—

Of a huge eyeball staring back at me.

I jumped slightly, and for a heart clenching moment, I thought it was Aeslinn. But then I realized that it was just some random vamp, holding the necklace up to get a better look at it. He and a bunch of the human-looking ones were stripping my body for souvenirs, something that I could see taking place on the bank behind him.

And if I hadn't figured out that I was dead before, I would have then.

I looked like a discarded puppet, I thought blankly. My skin was ashen, my right arm was turned at an impossible angle, and my slack face was being pounded repeatedly into the mud as a dozen hands fought to strip off my armor.

They finally succeeded, and dumped my nearly nude corpse back onto the bank, to lie limp and pale against the dark soil.

I tried to look away, but I couldn't seem to stop staring at it, even though it didn't look like me anymore. I'd always heard that dead people looked like they were sleeping, and maybe some of them did. But not ones who had died in combat, with their final struggles writ large on their features.

Suddenly, I was glad that I couldn't see most of my expression, which was currently buried in the mud. What I could see spoke of pain, terror and desperate longing left unfulfilled. Because I hadn't managed to shift out.

I'd been too confused, too afraid, too emotional. Pritkin had trained me to keep cool under pressure, but the lessons hadn't stuck when it mattered. And, God, what was he going to think when they told him?

My knees pulled up and I wrapped my arms around them, looking for comfort I didn't find, because I didn't know if he was alive to be told anything. There was no way to predict what the crucible might do to him, or to Mircea, or to anyone. But Zeus had said that the gods would go after the leaders . . .

Fuck!

I had to find a way to salvage this, but I was finding it hard to concentrate, or to think at all. And that wasn't helped by the scuffle outside, which had progressed to the point that all I could see was wet dirt, determined faces and wrestling limbs. It looked like more vamps had joined the party.

But then someone pulled the jewel out of the sand and slung it around his neck, giving me a better view past curls of dark chest hair. I could see my body in glimpses, in between thrashing limbs and flying fists, where some lesser vamps had gathered to try for mementos of their own. They were too low level to think that they had a chance at the necklace, which seemed to be the prize.

But it wasn't the only option on offer.

Through gaps in the fight, I saw vamps trying to tear my armor into pieces, although they were having a tough time as it was fey made. Others were stripping off my underwear, with one waving my bra around as if it was some huge trophy. One even snatched a lock of my hair, ripping it out with a piece of bloody scalp attached.

I flinched back, but then saw something worse. Much worse. A vamp grabbed my limp body, flipped it over, and tore open his trousers, because the desecration was apparently not going to stop with souvenirs.

And I suddenly discovered my breaking point.

I felt something rise in me, something that I hadn't even known was there. But it was big, it was powerful, and it let out a scream of unbridled fury that seemed to take on a life of its own, boiling around the interior of the jewel, but not like smoke. But as if a lightning storm had been unleashed within.

It must have been visible from the outside, since the vamp who'd just snatched the gem off of the last owner let out a yelp and dropped it in the water. Hands were soon scrabbling about under the waves, but I didn't see if they found it. I was surging outward, passing through the surface of the stone and going beyond, but not into the air.

Instead, I was suddenly looking up at the confused face of a demon. And then down to where he had one hand on my thigh, and the other on his engorged flesh. My own hand moved a second later, sliding sluggishly across the cold, gritty dirt, passing across my clammy skin, and then gripping the hot, slick flesh of the demon's pride and joy.

And ripped it off.

He screamed, and I screamed back, and discovered that dead vocal cords work just fine. And they *were* dead; I was dead, and already cold. It doesn't take long to extinguish a fire in conditions like these.

Or to rekindle it, when you're the daughter of a necromancer and the goddess of death.

I rose from the dirt, bloody, filthy and nude, and coiling a glowing whip out of either hand. They landed in the water, causing a vast amount of steam to boil skyward, which seemed to be cooking some of the vamps alive, judging by their shrieks. But I felt no pain.

Zombies don't, do they?

And that was unquestionably what I was. My spirit might have returned, but my heart refused to beat, my chest didn't rise and fall, and my blood, what little the monsters had left me, seeped sluggishly out of my many wounds. But that was because of gravity, not a sign of renewed life.

I was possessing my own body; I wasn't living. But the vamps didn't seem to understand that. Not the ones up close, who were fighting with their demons to get away before they roasted, and not the ones farther out, who tried calling forth the rest of my blood. As if they thought that I had somehow survived all of that.

There was more left than I'd have expected, since I'd looked utterly exsanguinated. My cheeks were alabaster, my lips ivory, even my nipples were marble pale. But little droplets of crimson were blooming all over my skin, nonetheless, before flying through the air to plunk against a crowd of outstretched palms.

Where most of them just dripped off, with the vamps too busy staring expectantly at me to bother absorbing them. And then at each other, when their latest effort had no effect. I decided not to wait until the shock wore off, and waded into the crowd, whips flying.

Most of the vamps didn't run. The wild eyes and twitchy movements of those closest to me seemed to indicate that they wanted to, but something was holding them in place. Probably the demons who had taken charge, as Zeus had of Aeslinn.

And they didn't care how many of their flunkies died.

Frankly, neither did I. The time line was already trashed, my supposed great plan was in ruins, and I was dead. Leaving me no reason not to go berserk on the whole bunch of them.

So, I did, flinging the whips around in a storm of flashing gold and flying flesh. Blood splattered down like warm rain; the tide turned purple in a steadily widening stain; and bloody froth washed up onto the beach. Even better, every rent, every tear, every missing limb gave me access to the spirits within.

I reabsorbed one whip to allow me to use that hand for pulling power from the flood of writhing corpses around me, sucking it in through nose and mouth and skin and eyes. It felt glorious, it tasted like wine and victory, and every pull brought power surging through lifeless veins. Enough of this and maybe I *could* take on Zeus.

Enough of this, and I could take on the world!

And someone else must have thought the same. Because massive boulders were suddenly raining down everywhere, splashing in the river, tearing furrows through the banks, and causing sand and water to fly upward in a confused storm. Aeslinn had survived.

Of course, he had. If he could heal a ripped open jugular, he could heal a heart wound. With Zeus pouring strength into him, he could probably heal almost anything. Probably . . .

I squinted at him through the fading light and flying sand, and decided to test that theory. Because the king of the fey looked different through dead eyes. Very different.

I was only able to catch glimpses of him as I fought on, but they were enough. I could see Zeus's aura haloing him now, as bright as a miniature sun, but it wasn't the only one in view. There were shadows there as well, other colors boiling across the surface of all that light, darkening it.

And forming pictures of other souls, specifically, those of all demigods Aeslinn had cannibalized and added to his arsenal over the years.

They looked like a multicolored cloak pulled tightly around him. Except that this cloak wasn't cloth; it was their butchered spirits and they called to me. It was a low-voiced chorus, a ripple of something so quiet on the air that it couldn't be called sound, and yet I heard it. Through the roar of battle and the rush of water, I heard it, and not just in my ears.

It vibrated in my bones, it sang in my soul, it pulsed with the energy that flowed through my own animated corpse. We were alike, they and I, with only one hope, one motivation, one longing left to us. All they needed to bring it to life was power.

So, I sent them some.

And I sent them a lot, using the same method that necromancers employ to raise zombies. Tiny bits of my soul went flitting across the space in between us, carrying shining banners of power that flowed out behind them. I watched them go as I continued lashing out with my whip, holding off a new barrage that had swum under water to evade my protection.

And saw the tide of battle change once again.

Aeslinn had just kicked out the side of the library, apparently intending to join the fight himself, but he never took a single step.

He didn't have time before a giant, ghostly arm peeled away from his body, but it didn't belong to Zeus this time. It belonged to a butchered boy, whose power and life had been stolen to allow his murderer to reach new heights.

And, for a second, I tasted it again: a burst of sweetness, the tang of strange, fey honey on my tongue, the kind that the boy had been eating when Zeus caught up with him, and which now suffused my senses once more.

Right before the great arm grabbed Aeslinn around the neck, and *jerked*.

The young giant dragged the king back into the building, and a second later, I saw other colors awake and swirl about him, like a rainbow-hued hurricane. They roared in challenge, in fury, in a hundred voices that spoke as one. And they fell on him, biting, slashing and tearing, all at once.

He screamed, an echoing sound of pure terror, and disappeared, shrinking out of sight as his stolen power was turned back on him. I didn't see what happened then, because his monsters had used the moment of distraction to jump me, what felt like all of them at once. We slammed back under water, a writhing mass of thrashing limbs and glinting fangs, with my view nothing but a tunnel of snarling faces leading up to the surface.

It reminding me of the moment before I died, only this time, I had the advantage. This time, I could shift away whenever I liked. But this time, I didn't want to.

I wanted them to *bleed*.

Chimera, I thought, casting the Pythian spell to create a duplicate body. It was usually used for training purposes, or for occupying two time periods at once, but needs must. And two of me would rain holy hell down on this river and everyone in it!

At least, we would, if the damned thing worked.

Chimera, I thought again, concentrating. And putting extra power behind it, not that I should have had to. It had been the hardest spell I'd ever mastered, but under Gertie's exacting training, I *had* mastered it.

Or maybe not, as nothing continued to happen.

Chimera! Chimera! I mentally screamed, as fangs sank into me from all sides. And then ripped back out, taking chunks of flesh along with them, and freeing me from their grip for a second. I used it to surge to the surface, to shout the word out loud, to hear it echo off all that tumbled stone—

But it didn't work.

The Pythian power . . . was gone.

Of course, it was, I thought, furiously. I was dead, and Pythias pass on the power when they die. And Rhea was miles away, assuming that it had even gone to her.

I was on my own.

So, I fixed that. I used the whip to burn a vamp's face off and sucked out the demon inside, a squirming, panicking, nasty tasting cloud. And then made myself some help.

Because the faceless vamp was still in there, but without his demon companion, he was irrelevant. And completely incapable of stopping me from sending another small piece of my soul to possess him, and use him as a battering ram against his fellow undead. And I guessed I'd chosen well, or maybe all vamps were tanks when they no longer had any self-preservation to worry about.

Or, at least not any that I was worried about, I thought, using his fists to punch through two other vamps' faces.

That would have worked better, but he ended up getting stuck inside their bodies, since the vamps in question were still fighting. It looked like Gabriella had chosen well, and recruited mostly high-level masters. Two of whom no longer had much in the way of brains, since they'd just been obliterated by my vamp's attack, yet they continued kicking, gouging, and clawing, grabbing his arms and trying to rip them off even as he lifted them out of the water and bashed what was left of their heads together.

That worked better, sending meaty chunks everywhere. It also released the vamps from his grip, who slid into the water considerably more tamed. And started to float about like so much flotsam until one of them was buried under another rocky barrage.

Because the big guns had just arrived. I looked up to see a mob of the hideous creatures I'd passed in the dust cloud, now even more horrible in the clear, open air. The sunlight was almost gone now, just splashing the horizon with an appropriate bloody line, but it gleamed off acres of scales, glinted on maws of teeth, reflected in terrible eyes.

I didn't know where they'd been; perhaps Zeus had been keeping them back to compensate for the shield that Aeslinn could no longer raise. But if so, he'd cut them loose now, and he'd cut all of them. Tit for tat, huh, I thought, as we all stared blankly at each other.

At least, my stare was blank, having no idea what to do against so many, or if there even were any options. It was like facing a smorgasbord of hell, only they'd be eating me for dinner, not the other way around. And probably picking their teeth with my bones.

This was it, I thought. This is where it ends. And I continued to think that as the beach was shredded by clawed feet and agitatedly whipping tails, as the water hissed and changed color under dripping fangs and drooling maws, and as bat-like wings were agitatedly flapped and screeching cries were sent echoing off the mountains.

And as the beasts completely failed to get any closer.

It took me a minute, but I glanced at the library, which was shaking and cracking under the strain of whatever battle was being fought in there. And then at the bodies floating in the water. Plenty had healed almost as fast as they were wounded, but others . . .

Pools of red spread about them, a mass of severed limbs bobbed on the tide, and the whole scene looked like the aftermath of some kind of apocalypse.

And in the middle of it, stood another monster, one with a golden whip and dead eyes, the daughter of their greatest foe, no longer breathing but still fighting and, to their eyes, possibly winning.

They were afraid, I realized.

They were afraid of *me*.

But they were afraid of Zeus, too, and didn't yet know which way the battle would go. So, a second later they hedged their bets, and sent a wave of vamps they didn't need and didn't care about to test me. While some of the larger horrors in back sent a barrage of stones flying at me, all at once, I assume under the assumption that, if one attack didn't take me out, the other would.

And it was a pretty good assumption.

A boulder the size of a beach ball missed me by maybe an inch, and decapitated a vamp standing not two yards off. I felt the breeze of its passing, was covered in the warm splatter of his blood, and was then blasted clean again by a giant wave from behind. It caused me to look around in time to see another boulder splash down, as big as a car this time. And to grab it with my whip, sling it around my head wildly, taking out the first rush of vamps, and then flinging it back at the bastard who'd thrown it.

Only to have to immediately dive to avoid a hail of smaller debris, which didn't help much. A bunch of jagged edged pieces tore by—and in several cases, through—me, including one that almost severed my good arm. That left me with two severely damaged limbs with which to defend myself from a horde of horrors, and that wasn't going to work.

So, I made some more champions, raising the two brain damaged vamps as well as three more whose demons I sucked out of the holes that the barrage had ripped into their hosts. I threw all five into the fray, trying to stop or at least slow down the attack. Although why I was, I didn't know.

I'd managed to keep Zeus in place, but a dead Pythia couldn't command the library to go anywhere. And I was about to be overwhelmed and probably torn to pieces and I didn't know how to stop it, or even what the point was anymore. I didn't know what the point was to any of this!

Until I looked down.

And realized that the jagged holes in my body . . . were healing.

Chapter Fifty-One

I watched a wound the size of my hand push out a dagger-like piece of stone, and then knit up cleanly behind it. At the same time, a protruding bone in my right arm popped back into place, the torn flesh smoothed out as if by . . . well, yeah. I guessed zombies could be healed by necromancers, if they had enough power, the same way that vamps healed their injuries.

And, suddenly, I had a stupid idea. So stupid that it made me feel dizzy, when I was in no way capable of that right now. Or ever would be again, unless . . .

If it's stupid and it works, Pritkin's voice echoed in my memory, *it's not stupid.*

I looked up at the charging horde, barely being held back by my thin line of defenders, and wondered what the hell I had to lose. Nothing, I thought. And extended my arms at the massive crowd and *pulled.*

There were wounds in almost all of them, and there was power behind those wounds, although it was fighting me. And it was fighting hard. Maybe because I'd gotten delusions of grandeur and tried to act like my mother and drain them all at once!

I quickly course corrected, concentrating on just the nearest two, who were about to break through my barrier. I sapped them badly enough that one broke and ran, with the demon and vamp apparently agreeing on something for once. While the other sank slowly below the waves, his eyes huge and terrified and disbelieving.

I could have turned him into another zombie, but I didn't. The draining of the first two had caused chaos in my attackers, including the monstrous ones, who were screaming something back and forth at each other in demonic shrieks. I barely noticed, too busy gripping my throat over the jugular, and waiting.

Come on, I thought. Come on! That was enough power to raise a dozen zombies. Heal me!

And the thing was, it had. I was staring down at my forearm, where a small gash had been a second ago. It closed up as I watched, and then even the scar went away, melting into the surrounding skin and leaving me whole and perfect.

In fact, all of the injuries I'd accumulated since taking this job were suddenly gone. Including the ridge of warped flesh down my forearm arm, where a god's lightning had eaten a trough in me. And the scar from a bullet wound that Agnes had given me, in that cellar where I'd first met my father. Mircea had healed it afterwards, but a dip in the skin of my ass had been with me ever since—

Until now. It smoothed out even as my fingers felt for it, dissolving away under my touch. And the moon shaped scar at the bottom of my spine, which I'd had since childhood, was gone when I searched for it.

And yet I was just as dead as before.

Maybe I've been gone for too long, I thought dully. Or maybe necromancer magic didn't work on anything but the dead, Cassie! You're trying to make death magic give life, and that is never going to happen.

The realization burned in my stomach like acid. Sure, I could use life magic to remain on my feet, could throw it at my enemies, could mold it in any number of ways, just like ghosts did. But no matter how long Billy remained tucked away in his talisman, and no matter how much power he absorbed, there was one thing he couldn't do.

He couldn't come back.

And staying dead meant no Pythian power, no wild ride for Zeus, no hope of victory. No anything. Except for an eternity in Billy's necklace, a trophy being shown off by some vamp to his—

Billy.

My thoughts skidded to a halt once again, hard enough for me to physically feel it. My hand was around my throat, but my eyes . . . were lifting. Not to the skies, where the last rays of the setting sun had slipped below the horizon, leaving stars blooming overhead and a deep, blue-black setting over the frozen landscape. But to the portcullis, which sparkled in my imagination, as if a flood of white light was spilling out of it and the freaking angels were singing.

Because Billy had finally transitioned, not as a ghost, but as a human. He'd gotten caught near a portal to Faerie, and had died before he could get away. Transformed, like all those demons Adra had sent chasing the fey.

Because in Faerie, there were no ghosts.

In Faerie, spirits were clothed . . . in flesh.

I didn't even hesitate. I took off for the bank, because one thing death does for you, is to focus the mind. That bridge was all I could see in the world, and yet I didn't even make it to shore. Grasping hands pulled me down as if trying to drown me, which wouldn't work.

But that would, I thought, as somebody almost ripped my foot off.

I stabbed whoever it was in the face with the jagged bone, flung my whip behind me, heard someone scream and felt the wound heal before I finished the action. All that life energy couldn't make me live again, but it could keep me going—for a while. But how long I didn't know, especially when I was having to constantly heal damage.

Stop thinking like a human, I told myself. You're not one anymore. And ghosts don't have the same limitations!

But they did have different ones. I surged up out of my body, intending to make a run for it in spirit form, and found my soul immediately attacked by a bunch of ravenous demons. I fell back into my corpse, desperate for the protection it provided, and then lashed out with the whip at the vamps, who were still clawing at me.

My lash severed three torsos in one go, and I saw them fall backwards into the water. And then, a moment later, witnessed their bodies rise again, perfectly healed. It looked like some of the big guns had decided to play, after all.

And then my odds got even worse, when an infuriated fey king burst through the half-destroyed library, screeching something at his men.

I didn't understand the words, but I didn't need to. He wanted me ripped to pieces, and he wanted it now. And he was likely to get it, because the remaining horrors finally took the field, all of them, coming from seemingly every direction at once, and nobody could stand against that, least of all me.

I went down almost immediately, desperately fighting but fully expecting never to see the surface again.

And I shouldn't have.

But something was happening.

I broke the through the waves a moment later, gasping for air I didn't need, when the assaulting horde abruptly released me. And saw a blur tear by, throwing water everywhere and ripping through the horde like a whirlwind. I blinked and looked again, thinking that some of Adra's demons must have realized what was happening and come to help me, because the fight was just that savage.

But no.

Because the huge tentacle that landed in the water beside me, clutching a terrified looking vamp . . .

Had a tasteful damask pattern.

I wiped some water out of my eyes and looked again, but the view didn't change. The pattern was a raised blue floral on a brown background, and had been selected by Tami because it matched the living room drapes. The living room of my suite back in Vegas, which was where the small, decorative throw pillow had resided until a demigod shed power all over it, and it ended up half a world away. In a river in Romania.

Eating a vamp.

I just floated there for a moment, unable to fully process what I was seeing.

It was huge, sprawling across the bank and a good portion of the river. But it didn't look like anything in nature, because nothing in nature had made it. It also had no head, no eyes, no anything but a mass of arms that squirmed and writhed and slammed one of the spare vamps a few times against a rock when he tried to escape.

Meanwhile, another tentacle was feeding.

The vamp providing the meal had ended up next to me, barely a body's length away. His eyes were huge and staring right into mine, as if pleading for help, even though he'd been trying to murder me a moment ago. But I wasn't sure that he was sane enough to remember that, or that I would have been in his place.

Because the end of the tentacle that had trapped him had just shoved its way down his throat, distending flesh and cracking bones, and was now moving horribly under the skin of his torso.

But it wasn't after flesh; this beast wanted power. The process appeared to involve sucking out whatever magic, AKA life force, the vamp had left. Which wasn't much, judging by the fact that his face had just turned gray and shriveled up.

And then things got weird.

"Flank 'em! To the left!"

I stared around as best I could in the deepening darkness, because I knew that voice. And then I saw him, standing on top of a mountain of rubble: Marco, with a thrashing vamp in one hand and a shotgun in another, the latter of which he used to shoot another vamp in the face. And then threw the remains of the strangled one at him, for good measure.

That wasn't so odd; Marco had hitched a ride on the library with the rest of my team. What was weird was what was behind him. And was now surging down the beach toward the group of vamps who had reached the shore.

And who did not appear to know what to do with a sight like that anymore than I did.

They hesitated for a moment, and that was all it took. But it wasn't Adra's army who attacked them. Instead, I watched my former coat rack come out swinging.

Behind it, a glittering cloud of glass shards tore across the sky, as if someone had thrown a net made out of diamonds. They glittered in the clean, pure mountain air, reflecting the surrounding snow, the stars overhead, and the confused faces of the vamps in a thousand little pieces. It was as otherworldly beautiful as it had been in my living room, and just as deadly.

My one-time mirror sliced and diced its way through a dozen vamps, sending them running, while a bunch of books from the schoolroom fluttered overhead like a flock of birds. They appeared utterly harmless, but having just seen what the mirror could do, the rest of the vamps weren't taking chances. They ran, and the tentacled thing beside me threw the desiccated vamp away, in order to grab a fresh one.

The body now looked like it was made out of crinkled paper, and acted like it, too. The water bore it away, as easily as if it had been a dried-up leaf, until I lost sight of it. And then Marco jumped into the river beside me, splashing a wave of icy water everywhere.

"Got her," he said, and I heard a crackle in the air between us.

"Well, get her under cover!" Saffy's voice replied. "I think asshole just realized he's got a problem!"

"Understood," Marco said, as another roar tore through the air, this time from the furious fey king.

It trembled the earth, but Marco ignored it, being too busy hauling me toward the bank. "What the hell happened to your armor?" he yelled.

"What happened to my comm?" I yelled back. "I couldn't reach you!"

I didn't get an immediate answer, because a bunch of what I guessed had been my dining room chairs took that moment to stampede down the beach, flowing past us after the remaining vamps.

They'd grown root-like appendages from their legs, allowing them to spider easily over sand and stone and debris. Spear-like protrusions had likewise erupted from their arms, which they were using to shish kebob any of Aeslinn's vamps that they could find. They reminded me of miniature knights, charging the battlefield with lances lowered.

Wooden lances.

"S'okay," Marco told me, when I clutched his shirt, to pull him back. He detached my hand and tugged off his latest massive polo—in eye-searing tangerine—and dragged it over my head instead. "They're on our side. We forgot we shoved all the weirdness into a room in the basement until the magic wore off. Seems that the library picked it up when it flashed in, and Saffy figured out how to enchant 'em—"

"And everyone else?" I fought with the acre of material I was now wearing, which was as big on me as a muumuu. "What the hell happened?"

"Those goddamned Pythian libraries happened. The individual ones, you know?"

I nodded.

"One broke on impact and caught us in a time loop. It left us stuck behind a collapsed doorway, on a cycle that lasted a handful of seconds. We couldn't contact you—or anybody else—to ask for help because it didn't give us a chance. And whenever we burst through the door, which we did about a hundred times—"

"It reset and left you trapped again."

"Yeah. We'd still be there if Annabelle hadn't found us."

"Annabelle?"

He nodded. "She said you sent her. She shifted us out and—"

He cut off when I grabbed him, and he seemed surprised by my strength. "Is she with you? Is she here?"

"No, she said she was going back to report to—shit!"

Shit, I agreed mentally, and not just because there went my best chance of getting a message to Hilde. But because a line of rubble had started peppering the beach, with pieces as big as train cars. Even just the sand being thrown up felt like being flayed alive, and completely blinded me as we took off, running parallel to the water.

We took shelter in the shadow of the mountain of rubble, which was the only option around, but was far too close to Aeslinn for comfort. But the mad dash had worked. He appeared to have lost sight of us, possibly thanks to the sandstorm he himself had caused, or to the darkness now flooding the landscape.

But whatever the case, the barrage was focused on our old location.

"Fuck!" Marco said, staring up at the attack as it flew overhead.

"If you're out . . . why hasn't Adra . . . sent the signal?" I gasped, despite the fact that I didn't need air. But it damned well felt like I did.

He shook himself and looked back down at me. "Once we got out of that wretched room, we weren't home free. It was confusing as hell in there—a maze of fallen stone and collapsed hallways. And there was some kind of next level battle going on in the atrium. We had to take an alternate route, through the tunnels, but even vamp eyesight couldn't make out much down there. We finally decided that two search parties would be better than one—"

"What happened?" I asked, trying not to sound as impatient as I felt.

"Nothing. We got out; the other group hit a dead end. We called them, to let them know what to do, but they're having to backtrack to follow our path. They should be here in—"

He abruptly cut off.

I had been trying to knot the side of the circus tent I was wearing, so as not to let it trip me up. It came almost down to my knees, and was wide enough to have fit three of me. Maybe four if we squeezed.

"In what?" I asked, glancing up—

And just like that, I was in another fight. But this time, it was with my chief bodyguard. And I had never before seen him look anything like that.

I stumbled back, Marco leapt for me with death on his face, and I barely managed to dodge. Because the undead have liquid speed, but so does a master vamp. One with glowing eyes and a snarl for a mouth and a clawed hand that came within a hairsbreadth of disemboweling me.

"Marco!" I yelled, which only seemed to enrage him more.

I grabbed a ledge of stone and pulled myself up as he tore by underneath, then rolled onto the top and ran. And I wasn't the only one choosing the better part of valor. It looked like even the demons thought that they hadn't signed on for this shit, and were heading for the trees.

They didn't make it.

Aeslinn turned them around, throwing enough sharp-edged debris in their way to threaten to turn them into vampire jelly. Faced with two unpalatable alternatives, they chose the one that didn't involve a vengeful god. The battle turned yet again, as an army of mutated vampires headed back our way.

Which left them in my only path to victory.

Not that I was going to make it anyway. Marco was right on my ass, and Zeus wasn't taking it easier just because his people were on the field. Or maybe he simply didn't care if he killed them, too. All I knew was that, suddenly, things had gone completely scorched earth, with lightning igniting the sky and striking down everywhere, and fiery rocks set aflame by said lightning bouncing down the rubble, as if we'd just been caught in a volcanic eruption.

Zeus started raining death on everyone indiscriminately, and Marco grabbed me by the ankle, ripped me off the cliff, and threw me against a broken wall. The force of that blow made me thankful that I was already dead, since my insides would have been liquified otherwise. I peeled myself off the stone and was immediately gifted with an up close and personal example of exactly how Marco had survived for two thousand years.

The following fight wasn't measured in minutes or even seconds. It was milliseconds at best, with him flowing through a dozen moves in the time it took me to blink. So, I mostly didn't, being too busy ducking and dodging, and then barely avoiding a haymaker that cut my cheek on his ring before splitting the stone where my head had just been.

The blow was hard enough to send a fissure running for a meter or more, cleaving the rock in two. And then a threesome of blows from ham-sized fists destroyed the rest of the wall, turning it into more rubble to join the rest that was tripping me underfoot. And before I could recover from that, a savage kick connected and sent me staggering, as I'd never had time to get my feet back under me properly.

Marco took the initiative and kept it, while I slipped on some rubble and landed on my ass. That turned out to be lucky since I missed having my head obliterated when his fist punched the side of a tree. The huge old pine went toppling over, and I yelped and cursed and backed the fuck up, hoping that the trunk landing between us would give me time to turn the hell around.

But no.

The tree split apart like a bomb had been dropped on it, and here he came. And I screamed and covered my head and went fetal, because that's what you do when you're about to be turned into mush. I was babbling something, in between shrieks, but I didn't know what, and it probably wasn't even coherent.

Until Marco jerked me off the ground by what remained of my hair, and pushed that savage countenance into mine, close enough that I could have felt his breath if he was bothering with things like that.

He wasn't, and even his coloring had gone vampire white. He shook me, hard enough that it might have killed me, all on its own, if I had to worry about that anymore. And then the hand that wasn't threatening to snatch me bald closed about my neck.

"Repeat that!"

"W-what?" I stared at him.

"Repeat what you just said!"

I stared at him, terrified; I had no fucking idea what I'd just said.

That was apparently not the right response, and he shook me again. And I started shrieking and crying, since there was no way I was getting out of this without roasting Marco, and I couldn't roast Marco. I'm so fucking dead, I thought, and then the hand was on my face, squeezing my cheeks together.

"What. Did. You. Say?"

"I don't know; I don't know!"

"You called me by name—what was it?"

I stared at him. "Marco?"

As before, that seemed to enrage him, but my mouth kept going anyway, a mile a minute. "Marco Carales! Y-You took the name from a little town in Italy, where you used to live. You h-had a house there, a farm, but then your wife and daughter died and—"

The huge hand squeezed, cutting off my voice. I hung there and stared at him mutely. "Anyone could know that! One chance. Your closet at Dante's. I told you a story—one no one else knows. What was it?"

I stared at him some more, knowing that I had seconds at best, and trying desperately to think. But I was roiling from shock, and was pissing-myself terrified, and that wasn't counting the demons trying to kill me and the vengeful god lighting up the sky. And the slow-moving nervous breakdown I'd been having since I first saw this freaking place!

Without warning, anger replaced the fear, and I jerked away.

Even more surprising, it worked. "How the hell should I know? In case you hadn't noticed, I'm *dead*!"

"*She's* dead! Cassie is dead! You killed her and stole her body, and I'm going to—"

"The *fuck*?"

"Don't bother to deny it! You're a demon!"

"No, *they're* demons!" I gestured at the army flooding up the stones toward us. It looked like we'd been made.

Probably the freaking tree, I thought, right before Marco grabbed me again.

"I'm a zombie!" I spat. "But I'm not going to be anything if—"

I broke off because Marco had just paused to kick a vamp back into several others, causing them to topple downhill. Like that was going to buy us more than a couple of seconds! I manifested a whip, slashed through a dozen more, and watched the body parts tumbled back down the rocks.

Maybe it would take them a minute to figure out whose stuff was whose.

And then Marco started for me again, ignoring the huge glowing coil in the way!

I snatched it back. "Careful! That'll burn right through you—"

He barely seemed to notice. "Who *are* you?"

"I'm Cassie, goddamnit!"

"Then tell me what I said!"

"About *what*?"

"The imprint! The one I saw once. I told you—"

"You mean the old gladiator?" I asked, and saw his eyes blow wide.

"The *fuck*?"

And then they were on us again.

But having Marco on my side was a big help, and once I got clear enough not to snag him with my whip, I discovered that there was a reason the old war stories always harped about the high ground. It gave a person a lot more options.

I took all of them, sending masses of stone crashing down onto the advancing horde, including whole lengths of walls, in between fiery lashes. Marco, meanwhile, waded into the fray, popping heads. Seriously, that was his go-to move. Not the crazy acrobatics he'd just shown me, but simply grabbing guys' heads, sometimes two at once, and—*pop*.

And ramped up healing or no, that hurts.

And then Zeus gave up on subtlety and nuked the hillside, apparently deciding to take all of us out, only zombies don't care about electrocution. But vamps do. And through the fiery rocks and the lightning bolts and the incinerating trees and the vamps puffing away like smoke on all sides, enough to send a swirl of fluttery bits like a storm across the mountainside, I lost track of Marco.

"Marco!" I screamed, and then kept on screaming it, loudly enough to have stripped my vocal cords if they weren't already dead. But nobody answered. Which caused me to curse and lash out at the remaining vamps repeatedly, watching them turn and run but deriving no pleasure in it, because Marco—

Was jerking me off my feet from above.

I thought it was someone else at first, and spun with the whip up and ready—

And saw the huge, familiar face, the wide dark eyes reflecting the whip's golden light, and the face stuck on disbelief.

And I almost lost my shit.

I grabbed him in a hug so tight that even he felt it, letting out an "oof." I didn't care. I was crying and shrieking and the whip was sizzling against the stones and—

"Let's . . . let's put that away, okay?" Marco asked, and I reabsorbed it.

Not that it mattered. The hillside was a complete hellscape, with fiery trees ringing the bottom like torches and burning rocks like meteors flying overhead and drifts of smoke scattered about like clouds. And Marco's face obliterating it all, as he cupped mine.

"You have a plan?"

I nodded.

"What do you need?"

"Get me there." I pointed at the gate above us.

"Okay."

Chapter Fifty-Two

Marco tucked me under his arm, like a linebacker headed for the winning touchdown, and sprinted up the mountain. And Zeus noticed, although how he spotted us through all that, I couldn't have said. Unless he'd already figured out where I was going, and been looking for me.

Yeah, that was probably it. He'd known what I had to do before I did. But doing something about it was harder than he must have expected, because Marco wasn't letting grass grow.

He was wind; he was a speeding bullet tearing across the landscape; he was so fast that the velocity would have been dangerous, except that we were both dead anyway.

And that was despite everything that Zeus was throwing at us. Sizzling flashes of lighting burst apart rocks on all sides, sending shards to bite our flesh and electric worms to crawl all over our skin. Boulders big enough to have flattened us in one go whizzed by our heads, hitting down everywhere, and half of them had been kissed by fire before they were launched, leaving molten rock literally spinning off the sides. Even one of the burning trees was hurled, a huge old thing that landed right in front of us, just as we were about to jump back onto the bridge.

It did more damage than all the rest, being too long to dodge and shedding fire as it spun through the air, causing Marco's already huge eyes to get even wider. He hit the dirt as it sliced overhead, rolled to put out the flames that threatened to consume him, then got back to his feet only to be knocked off them again by the bouncing trunk that was headed back our way. It chased us partly down the mountain before he managed to do a backflip over it, making my breath catch in my throat because I thought that was it.

And then I was sure it was, when I looked up, and saw a molten fireball the size of a dump truck boiling in Aeslinn's fist. Looked like he'd got his magic back, I thought dully. But then I noticed something else.

Aeslinn gave a roar of triumph that echoed down the river and back—one long line of vicious satisfaction—because he thought he'd won. But somebody else didn't like that. Somebody else was king of this walk, and brooked no challengers. Somebody else stopped eating vamps in the river below and paused, with all the waving tentacles suddenly motionless in the air.

Oh, shit, I thought, gripping Marco's shoulder.

Oh, God, oh, please, oh *God*—

And then a brocade leviathan launched itself at a rightfully surprised fey king.

Aeslinn just stared, because that's what you do when a huge, tastefully decorated, murderous throw pillow comes flying at your face. I watched it go for a second, and then we were on the move again, shooting back up the hill, jumping onto the bridge, and tearing down the stretch of pavement while dodging the maze of burnt-out carriages in our way—

And diving straight through the gate into Faerie.

I felt it immediately, like a dozen extra gravities falling on me all at once. I smacked face down onto the cobblestones of the courtyard, scraping my palms and barking my knees. And then stayed there, completely unable to get up.

I felt like a pancake being sat on by a bear, with couple more bears on his shoulders. I felt like a Zamboni had decided to take a leisurely trip over my spine. I felt like a building had landed on me, something that wasn't entirely untrue as Marco almost counted.

And it didn't get noticeably better when he rolled off.

My chest was as tight as if I'd had all the breath knocked out of me, maybe a couple of times, and I was somehow managing to be dizzy while just lying there. I tried to leave my abused body behind, and send my spirit crawling out through whatever wound I could find, and there were plenty of them thanks to that insane run. But it didn't work.

Nothing did.

I finally managed to raise my head, to look up at the ruined courtyard, to search for the new me, perfect and whole and shining like a proper goddess. Or at least, like a passable substitute. But instead, pain hit me in a hundred biting, clawing, ripping and tearing ways, and I sucked in a breath in shock—

And, oh, God—bad idea.

Bad idea!

My chest felt like somebody had stuck knives in it, hundreds of them, and my lungs—what the fuck was wrong with my lungs?

I didn't know, but they'd grabbed hold of the idea of oxygen now, and they were sucking it in despite the fact that every breath felt like fire. And was making me dizzier, because I was hyperventilating, as if years' worth of adrenaline had been released into my system at the same time. It made me shudder and flop about as if I was having a seizure, and maybe I was; fucked if I knew!

Marco grabbed me and flipped me over, and I made a sound in his face between a breathless gasp and a shriek, which was all my lungs could seem to manage. I didn't understand what was happening. Where was my new body? Why did everything suddenly hurt so goddamned much? And why was I scrabbling around in the mud and blood, and making those weird wheezing sounds instead of—

Blood?

I looked down at my hand, which was pressed tightly against my stomach, and saw red seeping through the fingers. I pulled it away, and there was blood in all of the lines of the palm as well, and staining the flesh as far as my wrist. The sliced-up polo had more blood blooming everywhere, in widening patches. For a moment, I just stared.

And then it hit me: Faerie hadn't given me a new body. She'd just fused my spirit with the old one. One that should have been healed after all the life energy I had been channeling, but wasn't, since that last run up the hill had injured me all over again.

In other words, I'd been returned to life just in time to die—again.

Fuck, I thought, and sagged heavily back into Marco's arms.

"Hold still," he said tightly.

I thought I was. But a look down showed that I was twitching and shuddering and writhing, the pain making it almost impossible to do anything else. I tried to stop; I really did. It didn't work.

"I can't—"

"Yes, you damned well can!" The voice wasn't the one Marco usually used with me, but the one I imagined he must have employed with those soldiers he'd once commanded, before a vamp got hold of him and gave him another profession. And Roman centurions didn't take a lot of crap.

I looked up into the big face above me, and saw the usual swarthy skin tone, half shaven jaw and bushy black eyebrows. They looked like caterpillars, since Marco couldn't be bothered to pluck them.

And they normally dominated any conversation being expressive enough to count as extra entities, all on their own.

But not today.

Today, they were lowered and furious, but concentrated, too. And those huge hands of his were moving over me with a familiar touch, staunching the bleeding, soothing the pain, and closing up the burnt and jagged flesh that our wild ride had left behind. It wasn't a perfect job; Marco wasn't Mircea, and he had never absorbed all of his master's healing abilities. But he'd apparently gotten enough.

I was left all scarred up again, looking like a rag doll that had been made by a less than talented six-year-old. Or a pair of jeans that had been patched one too many times. Or a lady Frankenstein's monster.

But I wasn't complaining.

I stared up at the sky and just breathed. It felt strange. I'd almost gotten used to not having to worry about being out of breath, or feeling exhausted, or wanting to simultaneously pass out and throw up, and having to try to reverse that, so that I didn't choke on my own vomit.

I'd also forgotten something else: the feeling of blood coursing through my veins, of my pulse beating a staccato rhythm in my neck, of the strange and wonderful sensation of *life* everywhere.

Even if it hurt like a bitch, I'd take it.

Light bloomed in the sky, throwing multicolored splashes onto Marco's worried face, and then onto his neck as he turned to look behind us. Not at the fey sky, where it was daylight, if trending toward late afternoon. But through the gate to the dark, night sky of the bridge and river, where stars were peeking out from behind the clouds overhead.

Or, at least, they had been a moment ago. It now looked like a hundred fireworks had just gone off, in every color of the rainbow. I could see Aeslinn's great head silhouetted by fire, dazzling.

For a moment, I didn't understand, and then I remembered: Adra's signal. He'd been right, I thought vaguely. It was impossible to miss.

And Aeslinn didn't. He might not have realized that our mages had just caught up to Adra's demons, and that the remains of his fey were now being hunted with a vengeance. But he knew this wasn't good and he wasn't waiting aorund to get surprised again.

He must have dealt with his challenger, since it was nowhere to be seen as he crashed through the side of the library, waded through the pile of rubble, jumped to the river and cleared the battlefield.

And screwed everything up in one fell swoop.

"No!" I screamed, sitting up and catching the attention of maybe a dozen of Aeslinn's vampires. They must have reached the bridge before Adra's signal, but the shadows had concealed them. Until the brilliant display lit them up, and I braced myself for yet another battle when I had nothing left. But then they glanced at the king, haul-assing it the hell out of there . . .

And jumped over the bridge after him, melting into the darkness.

I got up anyway and staggered for the portal. I was human again, and there was rubble from the library everywhere, scattered all over the bridge. All I should have had to do was reach out and grab a piece to send the once imposing structure on its way. But the power hadn't returned to me, and even if it had . . .

Aeslinn was already almost out of sight.

He'd emerged on the opposite side of the rock fall from where I'd fought my battle, which was drier than it should have been with the water flowing from the opposite direction. It had been dammed up by the mess we'd made and the diminished river provided a perfect highway out of there. And he was taking it.

No, I thought blankly. Not after all that. He couldn't just leave!

But the Pythian power ignored me again when I called for it, and when I tried to manifest a whip, having some crazy idea of using it as a lasso . . .

"Fuck!"

My whole body shook and I collapsed to my knees, agony shooting through me. My borrowed power, as well as whatever I'd had of my own, was gone. There was nothing left except what little was keeping me alive.

I couldn't do shit but kneel there and watch him go, tears of fury washing down my face that dwarfed the physical pain by a mile.

"I fucked it up," I rasped, feeling Marco come up behind me.

"You did everything you could—"

"I fucked it up!" I yelled, and cried, and beat my fists and forehead against the unforgiving stone, since it didn't matter anymore.

"Hey. Hey!" He grabbed me and I fought him, with no strength left and no reason, bowing my body upward and twisting from side to side. Not because I was trying to get away, but because I had to do something or I thought I would go mad. But I went nowhere, except back against Marco's solid bulk, and the strong, enveloping arms that couldn't comfort me now.

Nothing could.

Except that, I thought, because Aeslinn was suddenly back, landing on the bridge in a staggering motion so extreme that he almost fell off.

For a moment, we just stared at each other, both equally shocked. And then he was screaming and lunging for me, and Marco was dragging me back and I was cursing at the king, at Zeus, at both of them, being completely beyond reason at that point. I felt nothing but hate; if I died, I died, but I'd do it swearing in that bastard's face.

I didn't die.

But that had nothing to do with me. And everything to do with my court, who had just appeared on the rubble mountain below the temple, white draperies fluttering, old arms lifting, a god's power flowing through their practiced hands. And dragged another god backward, jerking him like a dog on a leash toward the ruined library, while he fought and snarled and tried his best to reach me.

And while Marco tried to pull me away.

"Wait," I said, grabbing his arm.

"Screw that!" he snarled. "You complete madwoman! You can't take him!"

"No," I agreed. "I can't. But *she* can."

"She who?" Marco had those great arms around me, but he'd stopped moving for a moment, which was how I felt his shock when he caught sight of another figure, farther down the slope, standing in the shadows but shining like a star.

Because the Pythian power didn't belong to me, did it? And it didn't die along with me. It left me when I passed, yes, as it did every Pythia. But it didn't just go away.

It went to the next in line.

It went to my successor.

But Zeus didn't see her. Zeus didn't even see the women dragging him backward. All his hate, all his focus, all his attention was on me, and the power he assumed I was wielding. I couldn't have won a fight with a two-year-old right then, but he didn't know that.

He didn't know that.

I stood up straight again, shrugging off Marco's hold, and the sight seemed to enrage the king even further. Possibly because Aeslinn's face was now withered and wrinkled and gray, with sunken eye sockets and the cords on his neck standing out in stark relief. Like maybe something had been snacking on his power, something huge, something that he likely assumed I had sent. The glorious fey king, once stunningly handsome and unageing in his vigor, looked like an old monster—

And another peered out from his face in glimpses.

The servant's great feet dug into the old stone of the bridge, cracking it around their shape; his arms tore at the air, trying to reach me; his great eyes narrowed in hate, with two minds looking out at me, but both now wore the same expression.

Guessed the avuncular grandpa act was toast, huh?

The girls nonetheless dragged them back another dozen yards, and Aeslinn started to look around, as if beginning to realize that I might have help. But when I walked forward, my hand raised, the great head jerked back to me. And if looks could kill . . . well, I'd have been dead again.

"The great Zeus," I said, my voice hoarse and scratchy and weaker than I'd have liked, but that only made it sound more contemptuous. As if I couldn't be bothered to increase it. "And a fey king of renown. Yet you can't beat one young demigod?"

"I will kill you slowly," Aeslinn promised, or maybe that was his master. Didn't know anymore; didn't care.

"You won't kill me at all. I thought you were just playing with me on the Thames the other day, but now?" I spread my arms at the carnage all around us, the scattered ruins, the burning rocks, the shrieks of his monsters, echoing off the mountains as they were chased through the night, and my voice strengthened with all the emotion I was feeling. "All this, yet I'm still standing. You know, I used to be impressed that mother beat you, all by herself. Now . . . I'm just surprised *it took her so long.*"

The sound that reverberated over the little valley then was not describable, since human vocal cords couldn't reach that high. I didn't know what kind of action would have accompanied it, but I'm fairly sure that it wouldn't have been survivable. But the girls timed their next pull beautifully, and I never found out.

Aeslinn flew back off his feet, and was dragged up the once lovely stairs of the Pythian library, fighting and clawing and finally finding purchase in the great doorway, which wasn't great enough for his bulk. The remaining giant hand and one foot scrabbled for a hold on the sides, and for a moment, I thought he would do it. That he would actually find the strength to pull off one last miracle.

But the court pulled again, in one mighty motion, giving it everything they had, and the Pythian power responded.

It didn't worry about the door that was already there; it just made a new one. Flinging Zeus's puppet back against the wall with enough force to crack it. The old stones had remained solid since he'd broken through on the sides, but now they gave way, the power punching a hole with his body and towing him back into the darkness even as he fought to hold on.

And Rhea didn't hesitate. As soon as he was inside, she sent the library on its designated course, one that I had already programmed in. The librarian had belatedly realized that the wording of the spell allowed the Pythia to tell the building where to go without actually going there herself. And I had just sent Zeus on the wildest ride in history.

I stood there, panting in exhaustion, as the building winked out of sight, taking its great burden with it. The outline, the only space free of dust and smoke, remained behind for a moment, like a temple-shaped cut out. And then the wind blew across it, taking dirt and little flurries of snow along with it, filling it in.

"That . . . was a hell of a thing," I told Marco.

And then I punched the ground with my face.

Chapter Fifty-Three

I knew I was still alive before I opened my eyes.

Death didn't hurt this much.

I groaned, squirming against clean smelling sheets, trying to find a comfortable spot. I failed. Everything was pain; everything ached. It was as if all my varied parts were yelling at me at the same time, responding to some roll call I hadn't asked for and didn't want, to let me know that they were present and accounted for.

And in shitty, shitty shape.

"You're not, though," someone said, and I cracked an eye to see Rhea, looking as lovely as ever, sitting by my bedside at Dante's.

She was wearing a demure blue gown, which should have looked matronly, especially with her hair in a sleek brown chignon, yet it somehow didn't. She also had a book and some tea, having gotten this bedside vigil stuff down to a science. She put the book on one of the night stands, which was more like a curved shelf protruding from the headboard, because my bed . . . was not exactly normal.

Let's be clear, it was an orgy bed. Round, vaguely futuristic, and huge, able to fit ten, maybe twelve in a pinch. Or possibly fourteen if some contorting was going on, which I supposed was the idea.

I wasn't sure who that said more about, me or the cobra loving queen of the Vampire Senate, who had lived here before me and had commissioned the damned thing. She'd intended for this to be my new court from the beginning, even while she was here. So, I wasn't sure which was worse: that she had planned to have massive, snake-y orgies in my bed, or that she'd thought I'd want to.

I shuddered. Okay, I did know. The former, the former by a mile.

I realized that Rhea was looking at me.

"Is there . . . whiskey?" I croaked. "Or tequila? I could really do . . . with some tequila—"

"No tequila." The brown bun shook decisively. "Or spirits of any kind. Doctor's orders."

"What doctor?" I said testily. "I haven't seen . . . a doctor—"

"Tami called for a healer, as soon as we brought you back," she informed me, moving to stick an extra pillow behind my back as I struggled to sit up. The fact that I found it difficult probably wasn't a good sign. "You have a perforated liver, among other injuries, but you should make a full recovery. She said—"

"Brought me back . . . from where?" I interrupted, because I have no manners. And because something had just struck me as odd. Very odd.

She paused. "Do you not remember?"

Yeah, I did. That was the problem. I grabbed her wrist. She felt solid, like the bed underneath me. But she couldn't be, right?

"Why am I here?"

She looked down at my hand in apparent surprise. But then the lovely eyes met mine, and she answered. "Marco patched you up, stabilized you until we could get you back—"

"That's not what I meant!" I looked around the room, but it appeared just as usual. A tan and blue color scheme that was a mix of high-end furniture, from the aforementioned orgy enthusiast, and kids' toys and drawings. Including the latest rendering of me, propped up on the bedside table behind Rhea's tea pot, which showed a stick figure with wildly curly hair and two different sized eyes.

And a couple of golden whips flying about her head.

Somebody had been telling stories, I thought, and looked at my heir again.

She looked placidly back. I guessed that, after facing down Zeus, I wasn't all that intimidating—especially now. I groaned, as another stabbing pain hit, letting me know that one of my ribs was still there and mad about it, and she pushed me gently back down.

"Even accelerated healing takes time," she informed me. "It will be a few more days."

"Why . . . am I alive . . . outside of Faerie?" I gasped, staying on topic. I needed to know that this wasn't some kind of fever dream. "The bodies made there . . . drop once you return . . . to Earth—"

"Here, drink this," she said, pouring me some tea.

I drank it, because I didn't have the strength to refuse. Then lay back against my now uber fluffy pillows and panted at her. "Goddamn . . . it—"

"Faerie didn't make you a body," she reminded me. "It merely fused your soul back with the one you already had."

"Then why didn't it . . . unfuse . . . when I left?"

Her forehead knitted. "I am not sure that is a word—"

"Rhea!"

"I will answer any questions you like," she assured me. "Of course, you would ask the hardest one first . . ."

"What's . . . hard about it?"

"The fact that you are not human—or fey. We know how both of their bodies react in Faerie, but your mother's blood complicates things. The best guess is that your outcome was the result of her lineage. The gods were energy beings who made themselves bodies when it suited them—"

"But I . . . can't do that."

"No, but it seems that you were able to hold on to what was made for you. Once Faerie reunited your soul and spirit, it . . . stuck . . . even once you left."

"It stuck? That's your explanation?"

She sighed. "I did say you started with the hardest one. But yes, that is the prevailing theory. No one really knows, as this is not a normal occurrence. You have something of a habit of doing things that are . . . unique."

"That's one way of putting it." Rhea was too polite to say 'fucked up', which I guessed I appreciated. But that still didn't answer my question.

"The battle killed . . . I don't even know. A lot of vamps," I pointed out. "And the demons morphed others out of all recognition. Shouldn't that have caused a Crucible, all on its own?"

She nodded. "Almost certainly, if they weren't from this era."

"What?"

"Adramelech came to see you yesterday, but you were asleep. He mentioned that he has been interrogating the demon prisoners they took in Romania, the ones they left alive, that is. And so far, the vampires they possessed are all from our time."

I frowned. "But . . . but they were recruiting *there*, in the past. I saw it."

"Yes, the idea seems to have been to infiltrate every major senate powerbase on Earth and then attack all at once. It would keep one senate from being able to help the others, as they'd be under assault at the same time. But that required hundreds of operatives, especially if they wanted to have troops left over to take on the Circle afterward. And they were afraid to keep recruiting in our time, as too many missing vampires might have been noticed."

"Yeah, so they moved their recruitment efforts to the past—"

"No, they tried to do so," Rhea said, sounding satisfied. "But your first trip back in time upset the initial attempt and the second time they managed to get everyone together—"

"I gatecrashed again."

"It's a bad habit," she grinned.

"Like you coming to my rescue?"

The grin abruptly faded.

"You saved the day, not to mention my ass," I told her honestly. "But there was a reason I ordered you to stay away from that battlefield. If Zeus had succeeded in killing both of us, there would have been no one to stand between him and victory. I can't be your priority, Rhea. Not when the stakes are that high."

"You weren't," she said, but this time, she didn't meet my eyes. "We shifted in with the initiates by a frozen waterfall, several miles away, as instructed. Where I stayed—"

Because the acolytes wouldn't let her leave.

"—until I received an enormous amount of power, and immediately knew what it meant—"

She stopped and swallowed, suddenly looking less like the confident young acolyte she'd been a moment ago, and more the frightened nineteen-year-old she was.

"I had to decide what to do, and they were all looking at me," she whispered. "And I . . . I decided I needed information, and went to take a look. And when I saw him . . . it just seemed that, if we were going to have to fight him eventually, it was better to do it when you'd already half killed him for us."

She still wouldn't meet my eyes, because she was lying and we both knew it. But it was hard to fault her, and not only because the gamble had paid off. But because, when the weight of the world had dropped onto her slender shoulders, she hadn't run.

Except in my direction.

"So, you decided to fuck Zeus up," I rasped.

She did look up then, her eyes big and startled, as they always were whenever I was less than genteel. Honestly, you'd think she'd be used to it by now. Then she laughed, an abrupt burst of sound that looked like it surprised her as much as it did me.

And then she did it some more, and some more. Before crawling onto the bed, since God knew there was plenty of room, rolling over onto her back and laughing until the tears streamed out of her eyes. It looked like maybe she'd needed that.

She finally hiccupped to a halt, and stared tearfully at the ceiling. The salacious mural that had once graced it and the wall behind the bed had been painted over with some nice ecru paint. But it had been done hastily, after I moved in and got a surprise, and probably could do with another coat.

"That's . . . rather terrible," she pointed out breathlessly.

"I dunno." I settled down beside her, and looked up at the vague shadows lurking behind the innocent surface. "Sometimes, late at night, I lay here and try to figure out—is that a faun, sitting on a log? Or a guy on a seesaw? Or a satyr with a really long—"

"You know," Rhea said, breaking in. "I have been wondering what it would be like, to have the Pythian power. I use it regularly, but I somehow believed that, as Pythia, it would be different. Better. Easier. I thought that part of what you can do was because of your office, and having the power fully.

"I was wrong."

She rolled her head over to look at me. "I didn't feel any differently when it came to me, not smarter or more confident or more capable. I was me, merely stronger. Meanwhile, you stared down an angry god with nothing, no power, no strength, barely even alive." She regarded me soberly. "I will never be the Pythia that you are."

I blinked at her. I'd been making a joke—that I wasn't entirely sure was a joke—about a satyr's giant peen, and now we'd gotten all serious. I wasn't in the mood for serious, probably thanks to the crap ton of drugs the aforementioned healer had me on. But Rhea was looking like she wanted some Pythian wisdom, so I searched around for some.

"You were bitchin'," I finally informed her.

She smiled slightly. "And you are high."

"Very true. But you were still bitchin'."

She laughed again briefly, and it sounded genuine. "I was. We all were. Including the acolytes." She sighed and threw an arm over her face. "They are going to be insufferable after this. They're downstairs now, drinking beer with the guards. I think they're planning to go after Zeus themselves—"

And, suddenly, I got a lot more sober.

"What?"

Rhea froze. I couldn't see her face due to the arm, but I didn't have to. She wasn't even breathing for a second. "I . . . wasn't going to tell you. Until later . . ."

"It's later."

The arm came away, and I saw a much more somber young woman, who was biting her lip and looking at me apprehensively.

"It's okay," I assured her. "Just tell me."

"The Pythian library was discovered in the desert outside of Las Vegas yesterday, in the approximate area of the old MAGIC complex. It was . . . not in good shape. The individual libraries were mostly left behind in Romania, where the great hallways broke off. We used a glamour to hide them until we can work out how to get them back to this century. But the main building—"

"I wasn't asking about the building," I said, but Rhea already knew that. And since she was talking around the subject, I could only assume that she had bad news.

"No one was there," she admitted. "Nor was there any sign of anyone—such as a body, for instance—"

And Aeslinn's would have been hard to miss, I thought dryly.

"—but the Circle sent in some mages—the fey hunters who helped us in Romania. They are experts at detecting fey magic, and . . . fey portals."

"He portaled out," I said flatly.

"There could be another explanation—"

"He portaled out."

Rhea didn't reply that time.

I looked at the ceiling some more. "I sent him on a tour of every disaster in the last three hundred years. He must have been incinerated a dozen times, including at the old Pythian Court, when all those bombs went off. The desert was to be the last stop, at the moment that Apollo ripped his way through a major ley line, causing all that energy to come crashing down into our world. It turned MAGIC into a glass slick, and almost killed a senior god. I thought there was a chance that it might do the same to Zeus."

"He may have escaped before the ley line disaster," she offered. "Perhaps . . . perhaps he didn't withstand it, he merely avoided it—"

"Then he fought off the Pythian power, while already seriously weakened. That doesn't help us."

This time, I was the one who threw my arm over my eyes. The last four or five days—I wasn't even sure anymore—had been the biggest challenge of my life. For a while there, a very short while, I'd thought that we had actually done it. That it was over. And now . . .

I had no idea what to do now.

"He ran," Rhea said suddenly.

I turned my head to look at her. And there was no lip biting in sight this time. Instead, there was a fire in those lovely eyes and a flush on her cheeks.

"He *ran*," she repeated. "Not once, not twice, but three times. From the Thames, from the library in Romania, and then from the desert—"

"Rhea—"

"The desert," she repeated savagely, and flung an arm in that direction. "Not fifty miles from here! But he didn't come after you. We had half the Circle here for the last two days, camped downstairs and patrolling the ley lines surrounding us, waiting for an assault that never came. *Because he ran*."

"Yeah." I didn't say any more; I didn't want to harsh her buzz. She'd earned it—they all had. But the plain fact was, I'd lost. We'd dug him out of the past, even prevented a Crucible. But victory meant dead, and he was still out there somewhere, waiting for a rematch.

And if the prophecies were true, I knew how that would go.

"We found his portal to the present, and destroyed it," Rhea informed me. "I think that was where he was going, when he fled from you in Romania. He cannot time travel again."

"That's good."

I continued to lay there.

"What?" she demanded, watching me. She was beginning to know me too well.

"Nothing. I'm just tired."

"You are not a good liar."

"I'm a great liar, just . . . not right now."

"Then tell me the truth. What is it? What's wrong?"

"I've already told you." I started looking around for my pillows, which I'd left at the head of the bed. I grabbed one. "There's no point in going over it again."

She was quiet for a moment. "You think we lose, in the end. Don't you?"

I lay back against a fat bolster, scrunching it under my neck for comfort I didn't find, and closed my eyes. Suddenly, I was tired. Bone weary and in pain, and I didn't want to do this now. I didn't want to do this ever.

But Rhea did. "What would you say," she asked slowly. "If I told you . . . that the prophecies are out of date?"

I cracked one eyelid. "Meaning?"

"Meaning that you've already won," she said, suddenly fervent. "You just don't know it yet!"

It was times like these that I wished I was able to cock an eyebrow at someone, in that elegant way that Mircea had, but mine didn't like to work independently. "You'd think I'd notice something like that."

She stood up abruptly, rolled off the bed and started to pace, which was a little odd for Rhea. I paced. She was usually more controlled.

But not today.

"I have a confession," she said. "When we went back to that infernal hillside, to do the glamour to hide the individual libraries, I stumbled across Gertie's old study. And . . . well . . ."

"You read the letter."

Rhea looked guilty when she spun back around, but defiant, too, and something else. Almost . . . triumphant? I didn't know what to make of that expression.

"I know I shouldn't have," she said. "That it was a terrible invasion of your privacy, but—"

"But you had a right to know. You're my heir; you're going to have to deal with whatever mess I leave behind. It's fair."

She shook her head. "It wasn't right. I should have waited for you to tell me."

I shrugged. It seemed like a minor point at this stage, and avoided an awkward conversation for me. "Well, now you know. If I lose, I die; if I win, I also die. Zeus even said as much. And that's not counting the old prophecies that say we all lose, in the end . . ."

"Not the prophecies that include you," Rhea said, sitting back on the edge of the bed.

"No prophecies include me."

"Yes, exactly!"

She put out a hand, but the bed was too big for her to reach me. So, she crawled back over. I watched her come while wondering what this was. She finally reached the center of the platform and took my hands.

"I've thought about it a good deal," she said, her eyes shining. "In truth, I've thought about nothing else for two days. And I think I understand why Gertie couldn't solve the riddle you presented. Why it took her so long to See the truth, when she was renowned for it. I think . . . she was looking into a future that no longer exists."

"Come again?"

"I don't think that Zeus was trying to change time. I think he was trying to change it *back*. I think there *was* a Crucible, but it wasn't the one we saw from the party, the one that forced us all to Romania. It was the one your parents caused twenty-four years ago. I think they were trying to change time, and that they succeeded—just not the way they planned."

I frowned at her some more. "Is this why there's no tequila?"

"What?"

"Did you drink it all? 'Cause you can tell me if—"

"No! *Listen to me*. I think the Crucible *already happened*. It occurred twenty-four years ago, at the birth of someone the gods did not expect. The old seers Saw true, but they didn't See you, for you didn't exist as time was originally written. You weren't a part of the story—until a determined mage from another time and a dying goddess had a child—"

"Bullshit!" I tried to pull away, but she held on, her face earnest and intent and determined.

"In the original story, your mother's spell was ultimately overcome. I do not know whether she starved, or whether the Spartoi caught up with her, or whether she fought the first two gods and then failed against Zeus, with her power exhausted. And it doesn't matter now. But as soon as she died, the gods returned, and exacted a heavy price on humanity for what they viewed as our treachery.

"But a handful of magic workers escaped, including a lowly garbage man whom the gods had deemed too insignificant to bother with. But he was stronger than they knew, and turned the tables on them, slipping back through time and returning to save us all.

"And he did.

"By fathering you."

"You're nuts," I told her, and finally pulled away, intending to get up and dressed. But she followed me and she wasn't wearing an acre of bandages that made her midriff all stiff, so she had the advantage.

"That is why Zeus is being cautious," she said, trapping me between the bed and the wall. "He doesn't know this new world that your birth created, and can no longer be sure that, if he fights, he'll win. Your existence changed time, rewrote history, and he can't be sure of anything anymore.

"That is why Gertie couldn't See you; she was in the old timeline, before the crucible of your birth changed everything. She wrote that she only Saw the truth when she concentrated on you, and stopped looking all around you. Because all around you . . . is in limbo."

"That's . . . disturbing," I said, not knowing what else to say. But Rhea nodded enthusiastically.

"Yes, but it's also a *chance*, the first one humanity has had in millennia! The old prophecies, the ones that say we lose, don't apply anymore. Your birth rewrote time, and left it chaotic. Unpredictable. With no clear outcome—"

"Which means that we could lose," I pointed out.

"Or that we could *win*. In a way, you already have, by depriving the gods of certain victory."

I stood there for a minute, feeling dizzy and confused and really unwell. My brain wasn't up to this today, or probably most days. That's why I left the hard stuff for Pritkin. But he wasn't here.

Although Rhea was giving a pretty good impression.

"And there's one more thing. The idea of a Crucible is that it changes time. Transposing itself over the timeline that was already there, reshaping it, like metal in a furnace's heat."

"Okay?"

"Cassie, don't you see? Your birth *started* the Crucible. You were here at the very beginning, the child who wasn't supposed to exist, the wild card, the spanner in the works—"

"Rhea, I swear to God—"

"So, Zeus *lied*. He told you that, if you win, you die. But how can you when you were the one that started this whole thing? In a Crucible, time begins anew. Everything starts from that moment, the one moment when everything changed. And that moment . . . was your birth. At which point you *were already here*."

I blinked at her.

"I can't promise that you'll survive what is coming," she said shakily. "Or that any of us will. But I can be fairly certain that winning isn't going to erase you. Nothing but another Crucible could do that, and we're going to make damned sure that he doesn't get one of those!"

I didn't say anything for a moment, and then my knees gave out and I sat back down on the bed, feeling like I'd just been hit by a ton of bricks. I thought I'd dealt with death, gone through it, come out the other side and accepted my fate. But clearly, I'd been wrong.

For the first time in a while, I felt the burden on my shoulders lift, and something else replace it. Something buoyant and light and stupidly joyous. Something that felt a lot like hope.

I pulled Rhea close and hugged her. Her hair had partly come down and it got in my mouth, and I didn't care. Or that my wounds were aching, and this hurt like a bitch. I told them to go fuck themselves, and squeezed her harder.

"You were right," I whispered. "You're not going to be the Pythia that I am. You're going to be better."

And I meant every word.

Epilogue

A day later, I still felt like hell. But I damned well didn't look like it. My shiny silver battledress had been rescued from a muddy riverbank, and with a little refurbishment from Augustine, it looked almost like new.

That was good. I wanted a certain someone to see it in all its glory. I wanted her to *remember* it.

I could have flashed into the Senate's impressive new chamber, at the orgy queen's house in upper New York State, but I didn't. Because, sometimes, you just gotta slam in through some doors. These were huge, solid wood, two-story and iron-banded, but a little push from the Pythian power and they made a very satisfying crash on the pretty marble walls.

Everybody inside the room jumped, and probably looked pissed, but I couldn't have said as I wasn't looking at them.

I was looking at *her*, a certain dark-haired countess in a plunging, blood red dress, who took one look at me and blanched under all her makeup.

She also made a run for it.

As if.

I shifted her back, slammed her down against the huge conference table, and manifested a golden whip from my right hand.

It wasn't as big or impressive as it had been in Romania, as I didn't have any borrowed power to help me out anymore. But it caused the nearest senators to rear back, and in one case to come out of his chair, possibly because the end was eating through the latest conference table right beside him.

Since I was responsible for the demise of the last stretch of mahogany, I really should be more careful, I thought, and looped it around Gabriella's neck instead.

She screamed, several people cursed, and the consul—designer of bedrooms and purchaser of replacement tables—raised a single eyebrow.

"Is there a problem?"

"No, just retrieving some property of mine." I looked back down at Gabriella, who was staring up at me as if I was the one with fangs. And, right then, I wouldn't have bet that she wasn't right. "I just came from the funeral of two friends," I hissed. "Ones that your treachery deprived me of. So, for your sake, I sincerely hope you have it."

An ugly ruby necklace quickly appeared on the shiny table top, which I carefully slung around my neck. It nestled back between my breasts where it belonged, and hummed lightly at me. For a second, I could swear I smelled Billy's cologne.

And then I cut her head off.

People screamed, weapons were drawn, and blood seeped all over the burnt wood of the tabletop. And I stuck my hand down the gaping hole of her throat and pulled out the writhing, black, smoke-like creature within. I didn't know what kind of demon it was, just that I'd promised Adra to bring it back for questioning as long as it played nice.

It did not play nice.

"Thank you," I said, slammed it against the table beside the countess, and ate it.

It writhed and twisted, screaming for help that it was never going to find, and I suddenly felt better than I had in days. I couldn't see my wounds, but I felt them closing up, smoothing away, and taking some of the pain along with them. I even felt a rib adjust slightly, one that the doctor had said was broken, but which clicked back into place with a little snick.

There was slight residue left behind on the wood when I was finished, but it would probably wash off. And Adra had other demons, ones his people had caught in Romania after they finished butchering a bunch of fey. I thought he'd be okay.

"What the devil—" Parendra, the South Asian consul, began. He was staring at me with his sword out.

"Not anymore." I tossed him the countesses' still-living head. "The full report is with the consul's chief secretary. Be careful who you let into your war conferences next time."

And I shifted.

Also by Karen Chance

The Cassie Palmer Series

Touch the Dark

Claimed by Shadow

Embrace the Night

Curse the Dawn

Hunt the Moon

Tempt the Stars

Reap the Wind

Ride the Storm

Brave the Tempest

Shatter the Earth

Ignite the Fire: Incendiary

The Midnight's Daughter Series

Midnight's Daughter

Death's Mistress

Fury's Kiss

Shadow's Bane

Queen's Gambit

Standalones

Masks

Siren's Song

Connect with Me:

Follow me on Twitter: https://twitter.com/CasPalmerSeries

Friend me on Facebook:
https://www.facebook.com/#!/KarenChanceBooks

Subscribe to my blog: News – Karen Chance

Sign up for my newsletter for notifications of new books, contests
and more: https://karenchance.com/signup